Do Not Disturb

Fiona Lindsay

CLOCHODERICK

Do Not Disturb was first published in 2019
By Clochoderick Press

Copyright © Fiona Lindsay 2019
Cover art by Rebecca Johnstone,
Fiona Lindsay and Catherine McAtier

Clochoderick Press
Flat 4
8 Townhead Terrace
Paisley
Renfrewshire
Scotland
PA1 2AX

A CIP catalogue for this book is available from the British Library

ISBN: 978-1-912345-13-7

Typeset by Andrew Forteath in Dante MT

Printed and bound by

Imprint Academic
Seychelles Farm, Upton Pyne,
Exeter, Devon, EX5 5HY

This book is dedicated to Vanessa and Wendy,

The Starbucks Girls

Prologue

Once upon a time, there were three little girls who lived at the top of a very big house in a Highland glen.

Amy was the tomboy, running wild across fields with the local lads, diving off rocks into the freezing cold sea, jumping out of hay lofts, searching for excitement.

Brooke was the brainy sister, the dreamer, the reader, her face always hidden behind a book, looking for drama and escape.

Jennifer, sharp as a tack, was the entrepreneur-to-be, selling her homemade tablet in the school playground at an 80% mark-up.

Now they're all grown up.

Chapter 1
Hotel Caledonia

'Five years I've worked for Joe Franchi, and this is how he rewards me. He's got no loyalty, no compassion, no –'

Amy was pacing up and down her small living room. She took a deep gulp of Chardonnay.

'You said yourself the takings were down,' Stuart said, glancing up from the page of quadratic equations he was marking. Not a particularly able student, judging by the slashes of red pen.

'You're as bad as he is. You've got no soul.'

Amy splashed more wine into her glass and drank back half of it at once. 'Would you like a drink?' she asked belatedly.

'Er, no, thanks. Not on a school night.'

Amy gave a strangled sound and drained her glass, refilling it immediately.

'Slow down, Ames. You're completely pished.'

'So would you be if you'd just lost your job and your home.'

Actually, this *was* Stuart's home. He'd moved in – what – about eighteen months ago? When Amy had first met him he'd been renting a grotty, ground floor flat in Gorgie. He'd begun spending more and more time at Amy's, sometimes four nights a week, and he'd suggested he move in. Not because he couldn't bear to spend a night apart from her, but because it was "such a waste of money paying rent on a flat when he was hardly ever there". Typical Stuart, Amy thought, depressed. Practical to the last, he was no Lewis Capaldi. If the earth had ever moved, it was only because of the building work on the tramlines outside. She threw herself down on the sofa.

Stuart gave up on his marking, obviously realising that he would get no more work done tonight. He sat down next to her, putting his arm round her and stroking her cheek.

'Amy, you're the best. You'll get another job in no time. Or you could start your own catering business.'

Amy nodded glumly – she couldn't think that she'd get another job that she would enjoy nearly as much as her present one.

'Actually, I've been thinking about the future –'

Even through her alcohol-sodden brain, Amy's senses were suddenly on red alert – surely he wasn't about to propose? Then she relaxed – Stuart wasn't what you would call impulsive. If he did decide to ask her to marry him, he'd be very traditional. He'd book a table at a posh restaurant – the Witchery, maybe, buy a diamond ring which was an exact fit and cost precisely a month's salary, and get down on one knee.

'I think we should buy a house. Paying rent's just money down the drain. I mean, this place was really handy for the restaurant, but we need to get on the property ladder.' Trust Stuart to refer to her beloved home as "handy".

'I'll need to think about it,' she said, knowing that she was being ungracious. 'I'm going to bed.'

'Wait there.'

Stuart went into the galley kitchen and returned a moment later with a pint glass of water. 'Drink this.'

'I don't want it.'

'Drink it. All of it.'

He sat down beside her and held the glass to her lips. 'Go on. It'll make you feel better, I promise.'

Sulkily, she complied.

'I did try to stop you opening the second bottle,' Stuart said, next morning, but gently. Amy glowered at his back as he moved quickly around the room, packing books, his iPhone and a Tupperware container of sandwiches into his backpack. She was still annoyed with him, although he'd probably saved her from alcoholic poisoning.

Later, she went downstairs and let herself into the restaurant. It was quiet, the traffic noises out on Broughton Street muffled. The windows had been boarded up and it was shadowy inside. Everything was scrubbed clean, the floor swept and the chairs piled up on top of the tables. She felt drained; there were many loyal customers whom she'd got to know and looked forward to seeing: the Wednesday night book group, a bunch of genteel New Town ladies who liked their chat – which was seldom actually about the book in question – to be oiled by tea and pastries. Then there was the studenty crowd who turned up late every Sunday morning without fail, always horizontal in the same corner. They'd often told her that she served the best hangover breakfast in all Edinburgh, a huge fry-up accompanied by thick, buttery toast, endless cups of coffee and several glasses of fresh orange juice with bits. There were the Christian students who came in for their Friday nights out, approving of the fact that she didn't have a licence to sell alcohol, the right-on Socialist crowd who approved of the fact that she served a wide range of vegan meals, the gay couples who came in for coffee and cakes. Then there was the retired lecturer from the university who came in most days to do the *Scotsman* crossword over a peppermint tea, but was always up for a chat. Amy suspected she was quite lonely – she would have to find a new bolthole now. On their last night, one of the student crowd had brought an acoustic guitar and they'd stayed open late, eating nachos, jamming and singing by candlelight. Pete, the sexy socialist, with his dark quiff, rail thin in his black skinny jeans, had leaned over the counter to hug her goodbye and she'd nearly broken down.

But it was all over now. She went out and headed straight for Valvona and Crolla, her idea of Heaven on earth, wandering around and breathing in the delicious aromas of roasted coffee, brie, fresh bread, mortadella, ham and spices: cardamom, chilli, paprika and saffron. Then, still trying to cheer herself up, she walked round to Harvey Nichols, where she tried out several exotic perfumes and browsed the shoes and gorgeous summer fashions before taking the escalator up to the Food Hall on the top floor. Now that she was unemployed, mind you, she wouldn't be able to afford the prices in here. She trudged down to Henderson's in Hanover Street, taking her herbal tea over to a table in a quiet corner. The room was blurry with tears. It was a couple of moments before she realised that her phone was vibrating inside her bag. 'Hey, Cal,' she said, feeling considerably better for hearing her oldest friend's voice.

'I've got a missed call from you from earlier. What's up?'

'Wild Mountain Thyme closed down. I'm out of a job.'

'I'm so sorry, Ames. I loved your wee café. It's a sad loss. Are you all right?'

Amy wiped her eyes with the back of her free hand. 'Apart from being single, unemployed and homeless, I'm fine.'

There was a pause; she could picture Callum's deep-set brown eyes, worried and thoughtful.

'You're really homeless?'

Amy sniffed, pushing a piece of chocolate brownie into her mouth. 'Soon will be. Joe's selling the flat along with the business.'

'What about Stuart?'

'He asked me to buy a house with him, but I couldn't go through with it. Taking out a mortgage over, like, 25 years. It seemed so...final. So he's moving back in with his mum and dad so he can save up for a deposit.'

'Are you sure about all this?'

'Yes. We weren't really going anywhere.' She ate her last chunk of brownie, savouring the rich, sweet taste. There was another pause, and she knew Callum was taking his time, thinking about what she'd been saying.

'Why don't you come home?' he said, at length. 'I know they're looking for a chef at the hotel. There was a huge row, and Fern's walked out. Didn't even work her notice.'

Nothing was secret in the small Highland village where she'd grown up.

'Marcel?' guessed Amy. The head chef had all the charm of a chemical toilet.

'Who else? Come on, Ames. It would be brilliant. We could hang out again – you, me, all the old gang. What do you say? It would save Jen having to advertise.'

'Would you want to work for Jen?' Amy asked. As beguiling as the thought of spending time with her old school friends was, she wasn't at all sure yet that she wanted to leave behind her life in Edinburgh and return to the village. She loved Broughton Street, for its myriad cafés and delis, its convenience for the city centre and the fabulous shops in George Street, including her personal favourite, the ludicrously expensive Anthopologie.

'Hell, no. But you know you want to. It'd be just like old times. The whole crowd: even Lewis is back –'

It was just as well Amy was sitting down, or she thought she would have collapsed. Callum was still talking but she could no longer hear. Her mouth was dry and her heart pumping painfully at hearing her ex-boyfriend's name. 'All right,' she told Callum, feeling much better, her hangover and misery forgotten. 'You've twisted my arm.'

It wasn't long before her phone rang again. 'Hey, Jen.'

'Amy, Callum says you want to come home and work for me.' Her sister always cut straight to the chase. 'Ames, please. I need you.'

That was a first – Jen pleading with her.

'Okay,' she agreed. 'I've had a few other offers, but you can have the benefit of my expertise.'

She bought another pot of tea and settled back in her seat, sipping it, her mind full of thoughts of Lewis. They'd fallen in love when she was just sixteen and he seventeen, later drifting apart. But she'd always felt as if it wasn't really over, that there was unfinished business between them. Whomever else she was seeing, Lewis had always been at the back of her mind.

And, in a few days' time, she would see him again.

'I'll miss you.' Brooke Grant stood on tip-toe to kiss James once again, oblivious to the queue of fed-up people waiting for the coach to Inverness. Buchanan Street Bus Station on a drizzly morning wasn't the most romantic of places – not very *Brief Encounter*. Central Station, with its vaulted glass roof, would have been better, but because she was a post-graduate student and permanently broke, she was having to travel to Kirklochy by coach. She wasn't wearing her glasses, however, which gave the scene a soft focus effect. It was a typical Glasgow summer's day – tropical, as in sweltering hot and raining at the same time.

'I'll miss you, too, but it's only for a few weeks.' Still holding her close, James stroked her hair.

'You will come and stay?'

'Yesss,' James said. 'Listen, sweet-pea, you'll have to go.'

'Put him down, love,' added the bus driver.

Reluctantly, Brooke boarded the bus, annoying the other passengers because it took her so long to find her purse in her huge backpack. She felt warm, sleepy and rumpled from a night of passion. At last, she sat down in a seat at the front and took out a book – it was going to be a long journey. After a few minutes, she dozed off.

Two hundred miles away, in Kirklochy, Jennifer Grant looked round the elegant foyer of Ardnashell Lodge, proud of her vision: she'd spent an eye-popping fortune on having the hotel re-decorated, lovingly faithful to its era. It was mainly due to her efforts that it had recently been upgraded to a five-star rating. Her parents had taken off for the summer, travelling in Canada and Alaska to celebrate their pearl wedding anniversary, and now she was in charge. She breathed in deeply and smiled to herself in exhilaration. Glancing in the mirror, she took in her sleek reflection: her discreet make-up, her shiny dark hair in its French plait, the circles of light her crystal earrings cast, her silver-grey dress. She enjoyed its soft swish and the clack of her heels as she crossed the foyer to inspect the arrangement of lilies, cream and gently freckled with pink, that the village florist had delivered earlier. Just then, the door opened and an elderly couple walked in, the husband struggling with two cases. Jen immediately switched on her warmest smile. 'Mr Finch, Mrs Finch – welcome back to Ardnashell Lodge. I do hope you enjoy your stay.' It was a part of Jen's deluxe service to remember all the guests' names. Briskly, she rang the bell for assistance and checked the couple in.

'Jason, if you could take Mr and Mrs Finch's bags and show them to the Buttercup Room.' She nodded at their expensive looking, but tattered, old suitcases and watched as the Australian effortlessly lifted them.

'The hotel's looking quite wonderful, Miss Grant,' said Mr Finch. And it was, Jen silently agreed. It really was.

Chapter 2
The Whole 9½ Weeks

According to local folklore, no one born in Kirklochy ever truly leaves the village: they always come back in the end.

Amy emerged from the coach, breathing in the fresh country air, as her cases were unloaded from the hold.

'This is toadally, like, awesome,' said an American voice from behind her.

The narrow street was bathed in evening light, and there was the sound of seagulls shrieking, and surf pounding onto the beach. The grass verge at the edge of the road was starred with buttercups, forget-me-nots, purple orchids and pink campion. A mountain range rose in the background, dwarfing the tall, straight Scots pines.

Although she'd never expected to return, Amy felt the familiar spell of the village begin to weave around her. Good weather was rare, with some years skipping summer altogether, and so the villagers tended to make the most of any sunny day. All the tables outside the Claymore Inn were occupied. A bunch of teenagers, boys in logo'd tee-shirts and surfing shorts and girls in coloured vest tops and frayed denim mini-skirts, sat on the seawall, flirting and showing off, vying for the attention of a very beautiful young woman, the only one wearing a dress, which lent her a sophistication beyond her years. It was subtly sexy in what it suggested, rather than what it revealed. With a start, she recognised that the girl was Evie Martin – she'd been a child of about eight when Amy last lived in the village, refusing to be parted from her beloved Hello Kitty, but she was all grown up now – she must be sixteen or seventeen. Amy smiled to herself at the self-consciously sensuous way she was licking her ice cream. Claiming her suitcases, she pulled out her mobile phone and called the local taxi driver, who said, in his usual unhurried way, that he'd be ten minutes. She stretched, enjoying a slight breeze which ruffled her hair, and noticed a few more familiar faces.

'Well, I never saw the like, Muriel. I feel sorry for her poor mother, that's all I can say – ' drifted over from where Mrs Crombie was standing with a bunch of cronies, wearing a tweed hat despite the heat of the evening. Amy wondered, not for the first time, where she purchased her coats, of which she had a selection in pastel coloured crimplene. Idly, she considered whom they might be discussing. Evie Martin, she guessed, judging from the dark looks they were throwing at the girl as she crossed her long legs and tossed her hair over her bare shoulders.

'Absolutely no respect. When I was a girl – ' Mrs Crombie went on. *The youth of today*, Amy always hoped she'd add.

'Amy, you're back.'

Hearing a man's voice behind her, she spun round. 'Hi, Cal.'

Amy couldn't remember a time when she hadn't known Callum Buchanan, the local vet. Tall and broad in the shoulder, he looked relaxed, tanned, out-doorsy and wonderfully healthy. With him was his constant companion, a yellow Labrador bitch called Nutmeg.

'Great to see you, Ames.' Callum pulled her into a tight hug, and she leaned against him, feeling much better. There was nothing like the friends whom you'd known forever, grown up with, shared so much. Nutmeg barked sharply.

'Great to see you,' Amy murmured, her face against Cal's tee-shirt. Then she disengaged, so that she could pat Nutmeg on the head.

A horn tooted beside her as the taxi drew up. Callum loaded her cases into the boot.

'See you soon, Cal,' Amy said, as she climbed into the taxi. 'We should totally catch up.'

Callum waved as the taxi pulled away. Amy looked out of the window as the familiar scenery slid past. She really was home.

She dropped her cases just inside the door of Ardnashell Lodge. Previously, the décor had been somewhat tired and passing itself off as faded grandeur, but, since her last visit, the hall had been repapered and freshly painted. The fragrance of lilies drifted over.

Her sister was standing behind the reception desk, tapping at the computer keyboard, her hair immaculate, her eyes shrewd behind round glasses. Amy suspected that Jen didn't really need these – her vision would have to be perfect, like everything else about her – but wore them just to add to her air of brisk efficiency. She'd been an entrepreneur since she was twelve years old and had set up her own dog walking business. She was wearing a simple grey shift dress, which practically had "classy" embossed into the material. Despite her youth, she favoured sharply tailored trouser suits, fitted white shirts, pencil skirts and sleeveless dresses straight out of *Breakfast at Tiffany's,* all in grey, black, navy or taupe. She was in charge and looked the part.

'Hey, Jen.'

'Hi, Amy. Good journey?' Jen tapped across the floor to hug her.

'Not bad.' The "screaming bairn" quotient on the coach had been mercifully low, but, on the downside, the toilet had been out of order since Inverness and, for the first leg of the journey, she'd been sitting next to a very large man who took up more than his half of the seat so that she'd had to perch uncomfortably on one buttock for more than an hour. 'Oh, come here, you,' Amy added, in a burst of warmth for her little sister. She held her closely, rocking her slightly, feeling her body tense. 'Honestly, it's like hugging a tree.'

They disengaged. Jen was smiling now. 'I need to show you round.' She was practically rubbing her hands with excitement. The sisters went into the small room which had, until recently, been home to several muddy pairs of boots and ancient waterproofs. Now, it had been converted into an office.

'I've totally overhauled our website,' Jen said, minimising the spreadsheet on the screen and clicking the mouse to reveal stunning views of the countryside, then a virtual traverse of the interior of the hotel. Amy noticed that she'd had a French manicure. There was nothing about her sister that wasn't immaculate.

'I can't tell you the plans I have for this place,' Jen said, launching into a fifteen minute monologue.

'This week, Dreichndrookit, next week the world, hey, Jen?'

'That's the plan,' said Jen. In the background could be heard a crash which sounded like breaking crockery.

'Marcel?'

Jen nodded. Amy had crossed swords a few times with the head chef, a Parisian so devilishly, darkly handsome that he made Jean-Christophe

Novelli look like a troll.

'I'm surprised you haven't sacked him already.'

Jen bit her lip. 'I'm thinking about it, but he's so popular with the female guests. And quite a few of the men, too.'

Marcel's smouldering, brooding persona, coupled with his husky, broken English, only seemed to enhance his appeal. Women always seemed to like a bad boy. Amy shook her head. Way too high maintenance, the fantasy so much better than the reality. 'I don't believe in artistic temperament,' she said. 'It's just an excuse to behave badly.'

'And this is *French* artistic temperament, which is on a whole new level.'

A gorgeous aroma of coffee wafted over. Jen poured out a cup each. 'Cheers,' she said, knocking her mug against Amy's. 'You know, Ames, I'm really sorry you lost your job, but I think it's serendipity that it happened just when I need a chef. Because of the recession, lots of people are holidaying in the British Isles this year and business is booming.'

Amy smiled. It was also serendipity that Lewis was back in Kirklochy. Her heart raced at the thought of seeing him again.

The girls finished their coffee and Amy followed her sister up the stairs. Everywhere was repapered and newly carpeted, the décor quiet and sophisticated.

'It really is gorge, Jenny.'

'I must show you this,' Jen said, producing a key. She unlocked the room at the end of the corridor, which directly overlooked the sea. 'Honeymoon suite.'

The room was dominated by a vast four-poster bed swathed in gold and deep pink netting, the counterpane strewn with rose petals. The pillows, piled with scatter cushions in wine and gold, looked to be satin. The carpet was gold and thick enough to paddle in. On an antique table were twenty-four red roses in a crystal vase and beside them a box of Belgian chocolates. In the en-suite bathroom, the champagne was on ice, and two flutes stood ready on a shelf beside the bath. The air was heavy with the scent of the roses, both real and synthetic, the Glade air fresheners carefully kept out of sight. It was like stepping into a fairytale.

'Brooke's design,' said Jen. Brooke was as dreamy and romantic as Jen was hard headed and business-like. 'Really corny, hey? But the guests love it.'

'I'm sure.' Amy felt a tingle run right through her as she entertained a brief fantasy of being alone here with Lewis, the door locked behind them, and him undressing her and laying her down among all those rose petals…

'And, last but not least – ' said Jen, over her shoulder, as she relocked the door and began to march along the corridor. She pushed open a glass door, and Amy followed her into a spa which wouldn't look out of place on *Cribs*. There was an aroma room, a steam room, a Chinese salt room, a sauna and a jacuzzi.

'Hot stones, monsoon showers, mud wraps…Jenny, this must all have cost a fortune.' Standing in the middle of all this luxury, Amy felt a dart of fear. The hotel books must be not just in the red but bright puce.

'It did. Which is why I have to make a success of this place. I'm hoping to promote the hotel as the perfect hen party venue: weddings are back in fashion. I've already got some bookings.'

Hen parties. Amy pictured an eruption of shrieky, leggy girls, in tight tops, sparkly feather boas, "L" plates and short skirts. 'Well, I hope you know what you're letting yourself in for.'

'I do. Everything's under control. Trust me.'

Amy followed Jen as she closed and locked the doors, then strode off along the corridor and down the stairs. She'd definitely perfected the art of sashaying in killer heels.

'Jenny! Ames!'

Just as they reached the foot of the staircase, Brooke spilled into the foyer, in a blue vintage tea dress, bracelets jangling and her shining dark hair floating around her shoulders. Behind her was Gus the Taxi, carrying her bags – she always seemed to bring out the "knight in shining armour" in men. She rushed towards them, slender arms outstretched to enfold them both in a three-cornered embrace and a waft of flowery perfume.

The honeymoon couple arrived at just after nine o'clock. They were twentysomething, handsome and long limbed. They couldn't stop smiling, and hardly took their eyes off each other long enough to sign the register. They gasped in delight as Amy showed them to their room.

Later, she dragged herself up the narrow staircase to the family's quarters on the top floor. It was clear that Jen's revamp hadn't reached up this far, yet there was something comforting about the fact that home never changed. The wallpaper and threadbare carpets were the same as they had always been, the school photo of her and her sisters still grinned down from the sideboard. She sank down on her bed, tiredness at last beginning to catch up with her. Had Jen been too ambitious? Taken on too much? She worried as she brushed her teeth, but then all was wiped from her mind in a wave of excitement as she thought about how close she was to seeing Lewis again.

★

'Jenny, honey?'

Normally, Jen hated endearments of this kind, especially from a man, and would have sharply slapped down anyone who addressed her like this, but she felt so relaxed under Gregor's expert fingers that she couldn't get up the energy to mind. He gave great head massage. 'Mmm?'

'Have you ever thought of ditching the Billie Holiday look? Maybe getting a fringe cut in? It would look so much softer.'

'I like it like this; it's smart and business-like.' Jen surveyed her reflection in the geometrically shaped mirror. She always wore her hair pulled tightly back into a ponytail or a neat French plait. The new, improved, toughened-up Jennifer Grant was firmly in control and didn't do *soft*.

'Oh, well, don't listen to me. I am but a hairdresser,' Gregor sniffed, pretending to be offended.

Jen loved coming to the salon for her six-weekly trim. It was one of her guilty pleasures, the only time she allowed herself to switch off – the ammonia scented air, the girlie giggling and confidences, the nail polishes in every colour of the spectrum, the trashy magazines. She'd just finished an article on how it was now cool to wear socks with sandals. A new issue of *Freak Week* lay on the table in front of her: *OMG! Two-Stone Boobs Nearly Smothered Hubby*, ran the lurid green typescript on the cover – there was a kind of terrible fascination about it.

Gregor's hands had now moved down to her shoulders. 'You're very tense, you know.'

'I am not tense,' barked Jen. 'I'm perfectly calm.'

When she'd first moved to Glasgow to begin her business studies degree, although she'd refused to admit it, Jen had been in culture shock. Glasgow was so big, so noisy, so busy, so polluted. There were crowds of people and constantly rumbling traffic. No one else from Auchenstoorie High was at the business school. Brooke, in her Junior Honours year at Glasgow University, was totally wrapped up in her studies and her Spanish boyfriend, so Jen had spent far too much time and money visiting Amy in Edinburgh. She'd taken a job in a B&B in the Great Western Road, partly to earn money and partly to get more experience of the industry: she had always aspired to be a hotelier like her parents. This was where she'd met Anna, an actress, or, more accurately, a chambermaid, and later her flatmate. When Anna had finally landed a small part in a play at the Tron Theatre, she'd gone along to support her. She'd met Neil in the bar, during the interval, and they'd got talking. Conversation raced. She felt relaxed and excited at the same time, and found herself being witty and vivacious. Neil was a lawyer and ticked all her boxes. He was ambitious, established and intelligent – Jen had always agreed with Germaine Greer's assertion that the brain is the sexiest organ in the body – but could also make her laugh and did voluntary work in his spare time. He was somewhat older than she was, but she'd always preferred older men.

She might have carried on drifting around in her state of ignorant bliss forever, if she hadn't popped into Waitrose at the top of Byres Road one evening for a pint of milk, and glimpsed Neil with another woman. Sharing a trolley, they meandered down the aisles, taking turns to throw in baked beans, bread, butter, everyday items which left her in no doubt of their togetherness.

She'd marched straight over to him and slapped his face – let him explain *that* to his girlfriend – then she'd thrown down her carton of milk and hurried out of the shop and back to her flat. Anna had been out and she'd sat down on her bed, heartbroken, humiliated and furious in equal measure. He'd taken advantage of her vulnerability and homesickness. It had all fallen horribly into place: why she'd seldom been invited to his house, why he worked late so often. Between her studies and her job, she'd had very little free time and this had worked in his favour. How could he be so deceitful, she'd wondered, with another stab of pain. It was less than two weeks since he'd taken her out for a gorgeous meal in the Merchant City to celebrate their first anniversary. He must be one of those people who got off on the adrenalin of living a double life – but what about her feelings? She'd been so in love with him.

But she'd vowed to chalk it all up to experience. She'd never let anyone, least of all a man, make a fool of her again. She had her career and her Rabbit. She'd have sex when she wanted it, on her own terms, when she felt that physical itch, but would not get emotionally involved.

'Coffee?' asked Gregor.

'Thanks.' She settled more comfortably in her chair and flicked through the heavy, glossy pages of *Marie Claire*. When she left, much later, her hair was sitting perfectly in place, her nails were short but shiny, and her eyebrows were perfectly arched. She felt ready for anything.

'I do hope you enjoyed your stay.' Jen flashed her floodlight smile at the gentle, middle-aged English couple who were keen bird watchers.

'To actually see puffins at such close range: marvellous,' said the tall, stately husband.

'Wonderful,' agreed his wife. 'We got closer and closer to them and they didn't mind at all – they're so inquisitive.'

They'd just left, promising to return the following year, when Aura Wallace, one of the kitchen staff, ran across the foyer in tears, followed by Amy. Jen watched as Amy slipped her arm round the girl's shoulders and led her into the office.

Some time later, Aura left, looking marginally happier.

'What happened?'

'She dropped a false eyelash in the soup.'

'Whaat?'

'Relax. We found it.'

'Well, thank goodness for that.'

'Don't be like this, Jen. She's really upset. You'll need to speak to Marcel.'

'Imbecile.' Marcel was fuming, as Jen entered the kitchen. He hurled a plate which smashed against the wall.

'Marcel, you can't speak to people like that; we'll have no staff left.'

She raised her voice above the sound of the pots which the chef was now clattering about.

'You theenk it is OK to put ze eyelash in ze soup?'

'Well, obviously not, but you can't... you're very...intimidating –'

The problem with Marcel was that he was so dark, so devastatingly handsome and so sultry and sensual that it was hard to concentrate. She'd never before known a man who could make black and white chequered trousers and a chef's hat look sexy.

'I work my hands to the bone and for what?' cried Marcel. Oh, no, he was working himself up to a virtuoso performance. 'To be surrounded by morons – ' His voice ran on, interspersed with Gallic swear words. Jen clapped her hands loudly in his face.

'Marcel. MARCEL. Stop. Enough. You're being completely unprofessional. There are guests in the dining room –'

''Scuse me, Chef. The couple at table six want to see you,' interrupted one of the waiters, slightly red in the face. His good humour restored, Marcel smiled smugly and strode out to be praised.

★

After cooking breakfast and looking at all that food, Amy had little appetite. All the guests seemed to want something different and Jen insisted that pleasing all the people all the time was essential if they were to beat off the competition from their great rival, Carlyle Hall, a larger hotel further down the coast. Many of the guests were hill walking enthusiasts who wanted a full Scottish breakfast before setting out, but she'd also served up the meat and dairy-free full Scottish breakfast, the skinny Scottish breakfast (grilled, not fried), the continental breakfast, porridge, cereal, fruit and yoghurt for the healthy, round after round of thick, buttery toast, and salami, bread and cheese for a family of German guests, whose breath must stink at twenty paces. The newly-weds, as part of the honeymoon package, also qualified for breakfast in bed: toast cut into heart shapes, scrambled eggs with smoked salmon, croissants, pastries and Bucks Fizz – all served on silver platters. It was hard not to feel just a little bit envious of them, radiant and loved up in their his-and-hers fluffy white towelling robes.

Leaving Jason, a cheery surfing dude, to finish the washing up, she made her way upstairs to the family's flat. Brooke was having breakfast, chewing a piece of toast and lemon curd, her face hidden behind *Grey Granite*. She groped for the mug of coffee on the table in front of her and sipped from it, never taking her eyes off her book. There was another piece of toast on the plate and Amy grabbed this and bit into it while crossing the kitchen to put on the kettle – she'd done enough cooking for one morning. She made some coffee and then sat at the table, opposite her sister. Finally, Brooke looked up from her novel. With her delicate, heart shaped face, high cheekbones, huge bright blue eyes and long, thick sweep of dark, shiny hair worthy of a shampoo advert, she was definitely the beauty of the family. Nothing – not NHS glasses with thick lenses, naff haircuts, dental braces, freckles or hangovers could disguise this. Even when she'd moved to Glasgow at eighteen and gone through a Goth phase – Amy now believed that, at the time, she'd been unprepared for the effect her sexuality would have on men – it had still shone through. She'd even managed to look gorgeous when she'd misread the instructions on a home dyeing kit and accidentally dyed her hair an unbecoming mustard colour.

Today, she was wearing a cornflower blue silk robe and smelled of freesias. She was intensely feminine, dressing in cropped tee-shirts, soft, angora sweaters and floaty, floral dresses, which she bought from a vintage shop in Byres Road. On the rare occasions she wore jeans, those were low rise and skin tight to show off her flat stomach and slim, shapely legs and coupled with ballet pumps. She laced her trainers with coloured ribbon and was the only girl Amy knew who actually owned a parasol. She was big on underwear, with scented drawers full of frail, frilly, silky sets. Brooke would never wear old chewing gum coloured bras or big knickers, even when there was no one to see them.

'Oh, hi, Amy,' she said, as if she'd only just noticed Amy was in the room. She pushed a delicate, beringed hand through her hair. 'I could have sworn I had more toast. Must have eaten it.'

'I guess.'

Brooke was working on a Phd on Irony and Social Commentary in the Novels of Jane Austen, and much preferred books to real life. During the university vacations, she worked as a chambermaid and waitress and did the occasional shift on reception, although Jen didn't trust her to use the electronic reservations diary. She always hoped a guest would leave behind something intriguing to enliven her days. Once, a couple had forgotten their pink furry handcuffs, which Jen had parcelled up neatly and returned with a compliments slip.

'I've been wanting to have a chat with you, Amy.' Brooke adjusted her glasses and assumed a gentle, caring voice. 'Are you really upset about Stuart?'

Amy considered this, as the sweet voice of Jessie Ware trilled softly in the background: Brooke had always favoured sensitive, female singer-songwriters.

'Not really. I mean, we'd been drifting apart for a while. And we hardly saw each other.'

Amy had worked evenings and weekends in the restaurant, while Stuart had taught maths at an Edinburgh comprehensive. In the end, the relationship had become... comfortable, like a scuffed, worn-in old pair of Levis that fit like a second skin. He was sensible and reliable, which, now she came to think of it, made him sound like a pair of Hunter wellies. Stuart had actually been something of a departure for her – her previous two boyfriends had both been intense, struggling musicians. She realised, now, that she'd been subconsciously trying to recreate her relationship with Lewis – no wonder they hadn't worked out.

'Oh... right. Well, so long as you're not too devastated.' Brooke looked wrong-footed. Whenever she had her heart broken, she was inconsolable, shattered, desolate, and went into a decline that would do Heathcliff and Cathy proud.

'No. I'm fine. Really.'

'Wow, you're so sorted,' Brooke said, a wistful expression crossing her lovely face. No doubt, she wouldn't have approved of the easiness of Amy and Stuart's relationship at its best – the Netflix binges, the walks on the Pentland hills, the cooking together, the Saturday nights sharing a takeaway and a bottle of wine in front of the TV. Come to think of it, Marcel, passionate and creative, was exactly Brooke's type. Mercifully, he had a Hepburnesque girlfriend, so was out of bounds – Amy imagined the Frenchman would crush her sweet, sensitive sister like a clove of garlic.

'We hardly ever had sex, by the end,' Amy added.

Brooke bit her lip. 'That doesn't sound so good, babe.'

No doubt all Brooke's relationships would have to be the whole *9½ Weeks*.

'Why don't we have a girlie night in, you know, to cheer you up?' Brooke suggested. 'We'll do face packs and deep conditioners, we'll paint our nails, we'll drink loads of wine and eat lots of chocolate and ice cream. We'll watch a DVD –' Not *Wings of a Dove* again, Amy thought. 'I know, I brought *Wings of a Dove* with me. We'll watch that.'

'Lovely,' said Amy.

Brooke would probably understand about Lewis, but, for now, Amy preferred to cherish thoughts of him to herself, like a jewel wrapped in tissue paper. She'd never known why he'd picked her out of the crowd, when he could have had anyone, and she'd never taken it for granted. They'd been on the beach, she and a group of friends, sitting on the rocks, chatting, flirting and posing. It had been a rare sunny day, light until nearly midnight. She and Lewis had slipped away and walked along the cliff top path, watching light dance across the Minch, and then strolled under a canopy of trees. As the sun set, the mountains looked as if they were on fire. Of course, she'd fancied Lewis: everyone had. She'd been by no means the only girl at Auchenstoorie High doodling his name, encircled by hearts, on her jotters. At some point, they'd begun holding hands, and they'd walked slowly and talked softly.

Then Lewis had kissed her. Firm but gentle, teasing yet sweet, she felt it deep down inside. Even nearly ten years later, she shivered at the memory. Of course, she'd been the envy of all the other girls. Probably they, too, wondered what she had that they didn't.

She had a memory box which had been hidden at the back of her wardrobe in Broughton Street and had now been transferred to her bedroom cupboard here. As well as some compilation CDs he'd burned for her and photos of the two of them, she had a hideous purple fluffy gonk he'd won her when the fair came to Ewensay, some wild flowers, carefully pressed, which he'd given her; a bottle of the aftershave he always wore, still with a faint trace of its fragrance; a Muse tee-shirt (unwashed) which he'd once left at her house; a yellow plectrum and the train and concert tickets from when they'd gone to see Paul Weller at the Corn Exchange in Edinburgh.

She'd never have been allowed to go away for the weekend with him, but for the fact that she'd told her parents that they would be staying with his aunt and uncle in Stockbridge. Mum and Dad had been reassured by the classy St Bernard's Crescent address – not realising that it was a scruffy student flat-share. One of the flatmates had been at a concert in Hyde Park and she and Lewis had shared his hard, narrow bed. Flanked by Lewis' cousin and his flatmates, she'd had no problem being served alcohol in the Raeburn, their local. On the Sunday afternoon, they'd taught her how to roll a joint, how to inhale. When Mum had phoned to check up on her, Lewis' cousin had pretended to be his uncle and she'd nearly burst in the effort not to laugh out loud. She hugged herself at the thought of it – at seventeen, it had been the wildest, most wicked, grown-up adventure she'd ever had. Probably still was, really.

She hadn't started daydreaming about him again for no reason; there had been a number of factors which had re-ignited her feelings: the night that, dressed as a French maid, she'd seduced Stuart on the sofa, and he'd carried on watching Dundee United play Hibs over her shoulder; the night she'd been in a club in Edinburgh and Lewis' indie band had been playing. Several years had passed since she'd last seen him, but he wore them well, his sensitive face more finely chiselled than before. The bunch of skimpily clad teenagers standing by the stage and gazing at him as if he were Paolo Nutini obviously thought so, too; the night her best friend, Misty, had phoned her up, bursting with excitement, to tell her that she and their old mate Duncan had got together, and she'd known there was no comparison; the night she'd suddenly thought *Damn, I haven't paid my Council Tax*, whilst she and Stuart were making love; the Kirklochy jungle drums beating out the message that Lewis was back.

*

Jen yawned: it had been a long day. Again, she considered dismissing Marcel – no Employment Tribunal in the land would think that unreasonable. But, then again, he cooked like an angel and having a French head chef gave Ardnashell Lodge a certain cachet, not to mention his infamous sex appeal.

The door opened, just then, and a tall man came in, his face hidden by a big, dripping, black umbrella, which closed to reveal Patrick Walsh. For the past few years, he'd been Dad's assistant manager, until family commitments had taken him back to his native Dublin. Just before Mum and Dad had left, he'd been in touch to ask if he could come back. Patrick had almost been part of *her* family, and extremely good at his job, so Dad had agreed instantly, and now he would be working for her.

'Hi, Jenny. Good to see you, and looking as beautiful as ever.'

'Thank you,' Jen said, coolly, well aware that he said this to all the girls. 'Raining out?' she went on. What a stupid remark, but she'd been thrown by seeing him again. She'd forgotten how attractive he was.

'Ever so slightly, Jennifer.' Patrick smiled, his whole face and his greeny-blue eyes lighting up. He was unbelievably charming: he hadn't just kissed the blarney stone – he'd snogged the living daylights out of it.

'Pads, I was so sad when I heard your dad was ill,' she said. Lovely Seamus – old school courteous, but always up for a laugh. He'd totally won her over with his love of the Highlands – the scenery, the birds, the wildlife, the malts. 'Are you all right?'

The flirtatious smile slipped from Patrick's face like snow off a roof. 'Yeah. By the end, he'd… well, he wasn't the man I'd known. I just needed to come back here – too many memories at home. Work always takes my mind off my problems.'

Jen nodded – hard work had always been her saviour when she was in a bad place. The break-up with Neil was due at least some of the credit for her excellent degree and the hotel's 5-star rating. She could feel her eyes welling up, so switched into business-mode to cover her feelings. 'Do you want the good news or the bad news first?'

'The good news.'

'Okay. I've found you a flat. It's above Fratelli's and it overlooks the beach.'

'And the bad news?'

'You can't move in for four weeks. The current tenants have only just given notice.'

'So?'

'We've got a few students in the staff quarters, but the really good news is that I've got a vacancy, so I can give you the Blue Room. You might have to move around a bit, but I'll put you up in the hotel until you get the keys to the flat.'

'Suppose I can rough it for a bit.' Patrick smiled.

'Well, get settled in, then I'll meet you in the bar in an hour to lay down some ground rules.'

'Yes, boss,' said Patrick, raising his hand in a salute.

Chapter 3
Smooth Operator

Brooke sat on the bed in the honeymoon suite, her shoes off and her back against the velvet padded headboard. The newly-weds had left for a snowboarding holiday in the French Alps and no one was booked in for tonight. This was her favourite place. She sneaked in here frequently to think or read, enjoying the peace and quiet, breathing in the scent of roses and trying not to think about the air freshener, discreetly plugged in behind the chest of drawers.

For over a year, she had been seeing her PhD supervisor. How could she not? How could she resist a man who knew so much about books and writing, but couldn't wire a plug or make toast without burning it? He was married, but separated from his wife and living in a grotty, untidy flat in the Maryhill Road, which had all the warmth and personality of a bus shelter. It made him seem vulnerable.

Brooke loved her life in Glasgow. She loved the west end, with its second hand bookshops, vintage clothing emporia, delis, cafés and wine supermarkets. She'd study in the library or her messy bedroom and she'd walk through Kelvingrove Park to the university and her supervision sessions. She and James would sit in his office, small and lined with glass fronted bookcases, which overlooked the West Quadrangle. The discussion would become so fascinating and absorbing that they would break off just long enough to move on to their favourite café, where they'd sit in slouchy leather sofas, their hands curled round mugs of coffee. As time passed, those sessions would extend into dinner or the pub, sitting with their drinks in the quietest corner they could find. The conversation had eventually moved on from the academic to the personal, with James confiding in her about the break-up of his marriage, and about his daughter, Emily. One evening, he'd leaned across the table in the candlelight and kissed her, and she'd kissed him back enthusiastically, although her hair had nearly caught fire. That weekend, they'd become lovers.

Currently, James was on holiday with his daughter, but he hoped to visit her in Kirklochy soon. Brooke longed to see him. She missed his intellect, his dry humour and his quiet kindness.

As she was inclined to confide in her flatmates, blushing slightly, over late night mugs of hot chocolate, soft music playing in the background, she'd learned a lot from him.

Brooke's previous relationships had tended to be brief and passionate. Her piece of rough trade, the ghillie's son, hadn't lasted long since she couldn't contemplate a boyfriend who'd never even heard of Virginia Woolf, and had thought that Charles Bukowski was the new Polish barman at the Claymore. The closest she'd come to her romantic ideal was in her junior honours year, with Javier, a Spanish assistant attached to the Modern Languages Department. She'd shared a single bed in a leaky top floor bedsit in Kersland Street with him for nearly a year, and been devastated, depressed and desolate when he'd returned to Málaga.

Then there'd been the rather too intense relationship with Eloïse, her best friend, flatmate and fellow English student. They were so similar, it was uncanny – sisters under the skin. It would have been a match made in Heaven but for one minor detail – Brooke preferred men. Surprisingly, they had managed to remain friends, and she still liked to think of herself as bisexual, believing it made her a more rounded person.

After a while, she got up and waded across the carpet to look out of the window. She loved Glasgow, but she needed to come back here as well. She missed the sea; the River Kelvin was no substitute. It was a clear day and she could see right across the sparkling water to the Tara Isles, even make out the cluster of white cottages. The pale sand curved round the bay, and she could see families with windbreaks, picnics and beach balls, all out to make the most of their holiday.

*

One of Jen's innovations had been to introduce pre-dinner drinks, which, she felt, added to the sophisticated image of the hotel. Guests could, if they chose, gather in the drawing room to be served dry sherry or malt whisky. This room, long and high and with tall, narrow windows which reached from floor to ceiling, was ideally suited to this gracious ritual. Tonight, as a range of seafood was being prepared in the kitchen, a number of people stood chatting under the chandeliers as violin music played softly in the background. Brooke was drifting around in a black dress, slender and graceful as a ballet dancer, her glossy hair piled up on top of her head, carrying drinks on a silver tray. Patrick was here, too, circulating and exchanging flirtatious banter with the women. Jen watched as he approached an intense, brainy looking young woman, plainly dressed, no make-up, glasses and a ponytail, holidaying alone, who, in seconds, was laughing up at him, her face glowing. Most men who carried on the way Patrick did, Jen suspected, would get a slap in the face more often than not. To be able to pull it off, you had to be as good looking as he was. Patrick had shiny, wavy dark hair and eyes the colour of summer seas, his soft Dublin accent adding considerably to his appeal.

As Patrick went on chatting to the ponytail woman, Jen listened in idly.

'I can't see past Richard Ellman, meself,' he was saying. Spotting the James Joyce book in the woman's hand, Jen grudgingly applauded him for having homed in on her interests – the thinking woman's crumpet.

Jen looked over at Brooke, who was standing with an elderly man, touching his sleeve and listening to him recount his fly fishing adventures with as much attention as if he'd been George Clooney. This was a talent of her sister – to make whomever she was with feel special. Jen could admit, just for a moment, that Brooke did occasionally serve a useful purpose in the business. The combination of her good looks and sweet nature was irresistible.

She reflected that, under her roof right now, were two of the most physically attractive men she'd ever met, yet she didn't feel a spark of interest in either of them: Marcel was a nightmare – volatile and given to sudden explosive burst of temper, or icy cold moods which could last for days.

Patrick, on the other hand, was *too* charming. How could anyone possibly know what lay beneath that smile and all the craic? Who could tell when he was being genuine? She half expected saxophone music to waft over whenever he walked into the room.

Briskly, she began to collect glasses and pile them onto a tray. She prided herself on being impervious to the testosterone which was raging around her. For the foreseeable future, she intended to focus on her goal, which was to double the profit margin of Ardnashell Lodge within the next five years.

'Good evening.' The voice on the other end of the phone was loud, posh and vaguely familiar. 'Hugh McMichael here.'

Jen remembered now. Hugh McMichael had stayed at the hotel the previous summer and again at Hogmanay with his silly, snooty wife, Celie. Pompous and arrogant, he was an Edinburgh advocate, opera lover and wine buff. Celie, pretty, blonde, vacuous and probably about fifteen years his junior, was obviously a trophy.

'Good evening, Mr McMichael,' Jen said warmly. He must be phoning to make a repeat booking.

'Just to inform you that, although I initially gave an ETA of 7pm, we've been slightly delayed, but should be with you around 8.'

'Not a problem, Mr McMichael. We'll be delighted to see you, whatever time,' Jen lied, massaging her tingling right ear.

As soon as she'd hung up, she grabbed her mouse and skimmed through the reservations diary, hand shaking. She'd known, really, that all the rooms were booked, but she'd just had to make sure. There was no booking in the name of McMichael. There was, however, a note scribbled on the edge of a brochure: *McMichael 7pm 18/6*, in Brooke's round, rather childish handwriting. Jen put her head in her hands.

'What's up?' came a soft, Irish voice.

'Oh, Patrick.' Jen looked up, desperation making her confide in him. 'I've just had a phone call from a couple to say they'll be here in – ' She glanced at her watch, 'about twenty minutes, but we're double booked and I haven't got a room for them –'

She quailed at the thought of Hugh McMichael's reaction. He could be extremely difficult. Last year he'd complained about the food, the wine, the accommodation, even the weather, although Jen admitted that this was beyond even her control, to the extent that it was amazing that he'd booked to come back at all.

'He'll probably sue us for breach of promise, or something.'

'Jen, calm down.' Patrick spoke in his usual laid-back drawl.

'How can I? How inefficient is this going to make us look? Just when I'm trying to build up the business. For every customer you let down, six potential customers get to hear about it. And we'll have to send them on to Carlyle Hall. This is a disaster.'

Patrick held up his hand. 'Jenny, a tsunami's a disaster. This, we can fix.'

'How?' barked Jen.

'They can have my room.'

Patrick turned on his heel and marched down the hall, Jen following. They took the stairs to the first floor landing two at a time. Patrick unlocked the door. The Blue Room was possibly the most delightful one in the hotel, barring the bridal suite. Wide bay windows framed a sea view and mountain range. The village florist had visited earlier that day, and the irises on the antique chest of drawers were fresh. Patrick pulled a suitcase from under the bed and emptied a couple of drawers into it, then threw the contents of the wardrobe on top of them. Jen gathered up toiletries and aftershave – Allure for Men, she might have guessed, an iPhone, Bluetooth speakers and a book: *Brooklyn* by Colm Toibin. Interesting, but she didn't have time to think about that now. After closing the case, with some difficulty, they stripped the bed and remade it with fresh sheets and duvet. In the en-suite bathroom they replenished the soap, shampoo and shower gel, replaced the towels with identical clean, fluffy white ones embroidered in blue, and then hurried back down to the reception desk, just as eight o'clock struck.

Mr and Mrs McMichael didn't arrive until 9.40pm.

*

'I suppose I should thank you,' Jen managed, as she and Patrick sat at a corner table in the deserted dining room, eating leftover fish pie (aka Coquille St Jacques).

'Jennifer, it was really nothing.'

Just as well she was immune to Patrick's charm, Jen thought. That smile would have had most women begging for mercy.

She was going to have sharp words with Brooke when she got home.

All brains and no common sense, that girl. Jen bet she was reading some book or day dreaming about her boyfriend when she should have been working. This was on top of yesterday's incident, when her sister had been found fast asleep on the four poster bed in the bridal suite. She had a good mind to fire her, except that being fired would suit Brooke very well. Then she'd be free to float about reading and day-dreaming all day long. Brooke made no secret of the fact that she found cleaning and waitressing about as stimulating as a Finnish computer manual.

'So, I was thinking, you can have Brooke's bed, since this is all her fault.'

'Fair enough.'

'Without her in it,' snapped Jen, surprised at the ice in her voice. 'She can sleep on the sofa.'

The sofa was horribly uncomfortable to sleep on.

Jen had always shared a room with Brooke, but she couldn't stand her sister's mess, her drippy female vocalists, the scented candles and lavender water that made her sneeze, or Brooke's habit of reading far into the night. So the door had barely closed behind Mum and Dad before she'd moved her GHDs, power wardrobe, killer heels and Bose speakers into their bedroom. She had no intention of moving back.

'That really won't be necessary,' said Patrick, but he was grinning and Jen found herself laughing with him. Patrick probably did fancy Brooke. Jen was used to men pursuing her sister. Pretty, slender, fragrant and delicate as a flower, she had that vulnerable, little-girl-lost thing going on, which most men seemed to like, nicely balanced with a first from Glasgow University. Much good it would do him, though: Brooke was besotted with her tutor. On the other hand, many men seemed to feel threatened by dynamic career women such as herself. Not that Jen cared. She had more important things on her mind. It was pleasant, though, sitting chatting over a late dinner, warmed by a bottle of wine.

The next morning, the sisters sat at the kitchen table, eating toast and Nutella.

'Bathroom's free.'

Patrick walked across the room and switched on the kettle. His hair was damp from the shower and he was wearing one of the hotel's fluffy white bathrobes, accentuating his tan, his long, muscular legs on display.

'Ding, dong,' murmured Amy.

'I think I've died and gone to Heaven,' whispered Brooke.

'Grow up,' hissed Jen.

★

'I suppose you had your nose in a book when you were meant to be working?'

Brooke looked down at the carpet, her eyes following the pattern of twining leaves.

'No. The phone kept ringing. Lots of people wanted to reserve a table in the restaurant for tonight and I got distracted. I did write the booking down, but –'

'…you forgot to transfer it into the reservations diary. You must see you can't make mistakes like that.'

'Are you going to fire me?' Brooke asked. 'Please?'

'Don't get wide. How would you have liked to explain to the McMichaels, of all people, that we didn't have a room for them? How embarrassing would that have been, when they'd actually booked? We'd have had to send them on to Carlyle Hall. For every customer you let down –'

'Six potential customers get to hear about it,' mumbled Brooke.

'Good. You're learning. Now, I want a top-notch job done on the bedrooms today. I want them to be absolutely sparkling. I want the bathroom floors to be so clean I could perform open heart surgery on them.'

Knowing Jen, this probably wouldn't be beyond her capability.

'Clear?'

'Crystal.'

'And, another thing, the honeymoon suite's totally out of bounds, unless you're either cleaning it, or have booked and paid for it for the night.'

Out of bounds! This was too much even for Brooke. Jen in this mood reminded her uncomfortably of their teacher at the village school when she was seven and Jen was five.

'Out of bounds? Who do you think you are, Jennifer? Listen to yourself.'

'I'm not doing this for myself. I'm doing it for all of us. For our family's future.'

'Well, you're going about it the wrong way. You've got the personnel management skills of Genghis Khan.'

'I'm not here to be popular.'

'Well, you've got that right, if nothing else.'

Brooke marched past her sister and out of the room, closing the door firmly behind her.

Later, Brooke pushed her trolley, laden with fresh sheets and towels and lemon and pine scented cleaning agents, along the first floor corridor. She unlocked the door of the Blue Room and went in.

It had been left untidy, the bedclothes thrown back, shoes kicked off and some clothes lying over a chair. Most people left their rooms fairly neat, but it would be just like the McMichaels to expect the hired help to do everything. Brooke stripped the bed and put on fresh sheets and an exquisite duvet embroidered with blue flowers. On Celie McMichael's side of the bed was *Epiphany* by Barbara Worth. She had been meaning to read this for ages – set during the French Revolution, it had been shortlisted for the Orange prize. She hesitated, then picked it up: she'd just flick through it for a moment:

> *Dane was the first person she saw. Topaz's mouth went dry: he was well buff, even for a footballer. Check those abs! But, just then, Lexi, his girlfriend, appeared by his side, snaking her arm round his shoulders. Why couldn't he see how cold and calculating she was? She didn't love him the way Topaz did but she wasn't about to give up her WAG lifestyle. Everything from her personality to her hair extensions and her coloured contacts, right down to her painted toenails, was fake...*

This couldn't be right. Puzzled, Brooke opened up the jacket. No way. Hidden beneath it was the cover of *Topaz*, the bestseller by Natalee, glamour model turned reality star turned WAG turned businesswoman turned author. It was well known that she employed a ghost writer to pen her auto-biographies as well as her novels, but that hadn't stopped her books from selling shedloads.

Suddenly, Brooke felt sorry for Celie McMichael, pretending to be something she wasn't so as to fit in with the cultured, Glyndebourne attending, *Telegraph* reading, Radio 3 listening, Tory voting persona that her husband chose to promote. She picked up the dresses from the chair, and began to smooth those out and hang them in the antique wardrobe. Donna Karan, Alice Temperley, Versace. Her mouth watered as she slipped them onto the hangers. It was no good. With a furtive look behind her, although she knew she was alone in the room, she pulled her emerald green uniform shirt over her head and slipped out of her navy trousers and flat shoes. It might be the first and last time she'd ever wear a Versace dress. She slid into it. It was a perfect fit, as were the Louboutins – size four – which had been carelessly tossed aside. Brooke gazed at herself in the long mirror, piling her hair up on top of her head with one hand. The dress was the most beautiful she'd ever seen, tight, strapless, scarlet and beaded along the bodice and hem with crystals. It was like stepping into another world: a world of red carpets and premières and champagne, sliding into the pages of Natalee's book. She could almost see the flash guns popping, hear the excited shouts.

She was jerked back to reality by the sound of a key turning in the door. She jumped, heart thumping and colour rising in her cheeks, folding her arms protectively across her chest. The door opened and Hugh McMichael stepped into the room.

'I th-thought you were in Glenstruan,' she managed to stammer. Over breakfast, the McMichaels had been discussing, in overly loud voices, how they intended to lunch at The Creel, the Michelin starred seafood restaurant in the town, then catch the matinee of *Cat on a Hot Tin Roof* at the Glenstuan Theatre. They never missed an opportunity to name-drop.

'Evidently,' said Hugh. 'We realised we'd forgotten our theatre tickets and came back for them. My wife's in the car.'

'I'm so sorry.' Brooke let her hair fall, spilling around her shoulders, and held out her arms in a gesture of supplication. 'It's just… I couldn't resist. Your wife has such exquisite taste.'

'Her personal shopper does, you mean,' said Hugh briskly.

'Well… I'll just change, and –'

'Not so fast,' said Hugh, striding towards her. He was across the floor in a few paces, towering over her. 'I could put in a complaint about your dereliction of duty –'

'I know you could, and I'd deserve it, but I'm apologising and asking you not to.'

'Actually, it's rather becoming,' said Hugh thoughtfully. 'Yes. Very fetching. Perhaps, this time, we'll say no more about it. But I'll expect a first class service from now on. I hope that is understood?'

'Yes,' Brooke breathed. 'Thank you.'

He lifted the theatre tickets and left. Brooke's hands shook as she put her uniform back on, cleaned the toothpaste spatters off the bathroom mirror, scrubbed the floor and polished the wood. She dreaded to think what Hugh McMichael's idea of a "first class service" was.

'That is a very unhappy young woman,' Patick remarked. He and Brooke were on dinner duty. He glanced over at where the McMichaels were sitting. They didn't seem to be talking much, and were eating slowly.

'Isn't she? Just like Nora in *A Doll's House*,' said Brooke.

'I bet she'd rather be at T in the Park than Glyndebourne.'

Brooke reflected that the women's movement had been set back a hundred years by the rise of the WAG, a new breed of young woman who aspired to marry well.

'I could never marry for money, only for love,' Brooke said. The Finches walked in, then, and sat at a table by the window. She went over to take their order – seafood chowder to start. Brooke feared she wasn't much better as a waitress than she was as a receptionist and was terrified of dropping a tray of soup on the carpet or, even worse, over a guest.

Snap, snap.

'Waitress.' Hugh McMichael's put-on tones carried across the room.

'How can I help you, sir?' She plastered on a smile. He surely couldn't be about to complain about the food again. Marcel's beouf en croute was his speciality, so buttery and tender it melted in the mouth, worthy of a whole galaxy of Michelin stars. He'd already complained about the prawn and avocado starter.

'This fork's dirty. Change it, please.'

'Certainly.' Brooke's hand shook as she reached for the fork, which was, of course, sparkling clean. Celie looked miserable, her face white and pinched, her long fingers, with their large diamond ring and beautifully manicured nails, plucking at the beads on her clutch bag. Brooke went through the swing doors into the kitchen, pausing for a moment to compose herself, then headed back across the room with the same fork. Celie's face was buried in the menu as Brooke handed it back. Hugh McMichael looked speculatively at her, a slight smile tweaking at the corner of his mouth. She could see that he was playing with her – making sure that she was in no doubt that he had a hold over her now.

'I'd like to order a bottle of wine, please. A Bordeaux, I think.'

'Can I be of assistance, sir?' came a voice at Brooke's side. She breathed a sigh of relief.

'I'm looking to order a suitable wine.'

'May I suggest the 2005 Château Margaux?' asked Patrick. 'The perfect accompaniment to beef and with a wonderful bouquet.'

'That would be very acceptable,' conceded Hugh. Brooke hurried back towards the kitchen.

'Just taking a break,' she called to the nearest sous-chef, who was chopping vegetables at incredible speed. She pushed open the side door and stepped outside, leaning against the wall and taking deep breaths of the salty air. She was shaking. She sat down at the table, putting her head in her hands. Why had she let herself get into this mess, given the vile Hugh McMichael ammunition against her? Why did she just follow every impulse, without ever thinking of the consequences? Why hadn't she resisted the temptation to try on Celie's clothes? Jen would freak if she knew she'd gone through a guest's wardrobe. She inhaled deeply and let out a long, shuddering breath, only marginally comforted by the whisper of the tides. She'd have to avoid the McMichaels for the rest of their stay – not easy if she was rostered to clean their room. Then there was Lewis Burns – someone else she'd have to avoid this summer, another time when she hadn't been able to resist. Her stomach ached with anxiety at the thought of it all. She wished herself back to Glasgow with James and her flatmates.

'Brooke?' The kitchen door opened and a rectangle of light fell across the paving stones. 'Are you all right? You've been ages.' It was Aura Wallace.

'I felt a bit faint. I thought the fresh air might help, but –' She let her voice trail away. 'I'm just going to go upstairs.'

Back in the flat, she curled up in her favourite easy chair, relieved that she was alone. She wasn't sure how long she lay there, in a foetal position, before Patrick came in.

'Are you okay?' he asked. 'Aura said you felt faint.'

Brooke looked up. 'I'm all right, Pads.'

'You're not.' Patrick peered at her. 'You're as white as a sheet.' He bustled off to the kitchen, coming back with two steaming mugs of tea, and sat on the end of the sofa nearest to her chair. She sipped the tea, although it was really too hot, and managed a faint smile as he tried to divert her by talking about books.

★

Jen could hear voices from the living room as she strode down the hallway. She opened the door. Patrick and Brooke were in there, drinking tea, Brooke wrapped in a furry throw.

'It was very affecting,' Patrick was saying.

'Makes you think about your place in the world,' added Brooke. 'Paddy's just finished reading the *Kite Runner*,' she went on, turning to Jen. Jen relaxed – her sweet, gentle sister couldn't stay angry with her for long.

'Really?' said Jen, switching on the kettle. She bet this was part of Patrick's repertoire – a phrase he threw in when chatting up brainy babes. She hoped he'd soon be able to move out of the flat. It was just too unsettling to have to share her living space with him, to see him emerging from the bathroom after his morning shower, wrapped only in a towel, or to stand beside him in the cramped galley kitchen, breathing in the smell of his skin overlaid with his aftershave, or to sit opposite him at the breakfast table, looking across at his tousled dark hair, and his sleepy green eyes. Also, Brooke was forever padding around, trailing floral scents, her mass of hair hanging down her back and around her shoulders, in her cute little pyjama sets. Even her feet, the toenails painted pink, and her belly button, studded with a silver heart, were pretty. Jen hated tattoos, but Brooke's – a lily at the top of her arm – was delicate and beautiful. She looked good enough to eat. How could Patrick resist?

Later, Jen marched into the bathroom, closing the door behind her. Brooke looked round in surprise.

'What's going on between you and Paddy?'

'What do you mean?' Brooke turned her huge, short-sighted blue eyes on her. Close up, she smelled of toothpaste and coconut shampoo. It was like trying to have a showdown with Lassie.

'You're always together, whispering in corners. But, I'll tell you now, it'll end in tears. Yours.'

'I'm with James. If you think I'd even dream of seeing another man… oh, I'm going to bed. I've had enough of today.'

She pushed past Jen and stalked back into the living room. Jen felt immensely lighter, relief coursing through her, totally lifting her dark mood. She rubbed her sleeve over the steamed up mirror and looked at her reflection. She'd never be anywhere near as beautiful as Brooke.

Then she sat down on the edge of the bath with a thud. She couldn't be, just could not be, falling for Patrick Walsh.

Chapter 4
Fifty Shades of Grey Matter

Jen stood by the kitchen door as the guests ate breakfast. The trick was to be always available, yet never intrusive. Brooke was serving huge plates of bacon, egg, mushrooms, black pudding and fried potato scones to a group of lads from Bath University, who were here on a hill walking holiday. She managed to look gorgeous even in a tartan dress, apron and white cap. Jen bit her lip – she believed Brooke's passionate denial of any budding romance between herself and Patrick, but surely he'd be irresistible if he really set his sights on her? A group of girls, here for the spa, certainly seemed to find him so, and were throwing him appreciative glances, their plates of bran flakes and sliced banana lying untouched. Why was it always women with the body of Lara Croft who were obsessed with diets and calorie counting? Patrick, though, didn't seem to notice, but, instead, had moved seats and was now sitting with Mr and Mrs Finch, advising them on the best local tourist attractions and how to find them. He really should work for Visit Scotland – he'd make a sightseeing tour of the Gobi Desert seem attractive. Mentally, she slapped herself on the head. She did *not* have feelings for Patrick – he was the biggest rake this side of B&Q.

'Paddy, it's your day off,' she told him, as the last guest left the dining room. 'You're meant to be chilling out. Shouldn't you be at the pub, drinking poteen by the fire and exchanging craic with the locals?'

Patrick shrugged. 'Or chopping peat while reading James Joyce?'

'I mean it. You don't need to hang around here; you should get out and about and enjoy the weather. It's the first summer's day we've had in years.'

'Well, I was thinking of climbing Ben Lochy again – the north face.'

'Will you be all right?' Jen felt a slight frisson of panic.

'Of course; I'm like a mountain goat.'

'An old goat, anyway,' Jen said, going into the foyer. Inevitably, the hot girls and the hill walkers seemed to have hooked up, and they were all either seated on, or leaning against, the big leather sofa, laughing and flirting. The prettiest girl was practically sitting on the lap of the cutest guy. Again, she felt relieved – suddenly she was seeing every woman she met as competition.

It was Jen's afternoon off, and, later, she made her way out of the front entrance and into the garden, pausing to admire the flowers. Delicate sweet peas clung to a trellis and the high brick wall was thick with ivy, hydrangeas grew in every shade of pink, blue and purple, tiger lilies blazed. She'd spoken too soon about the good weather and the colours had been heightened by a recent shower. She breathed in the mingled scents of the flowers, the rain, and the freshly cut grass. Soon, she reached the end of the narrow track that led into the village, and walked along the promenade. The beach was deserted, and Fratelli's, the Italian café, was busy with holiday makers. As she reached the door of Maggie's tearoom, four older women were just going in, but they turned to leave immediately, pushing past her. She gazed after them, perplexed. Most of the younger people in the village favoured Fratelli's, but she was meeting Gregor, who thought that Maggie's was wonderfully kitsch. He was already there, sitting at the window table. For once, there was no slice of lemon drizzle cake in front of him. Apart from two holidaymakers and old Mrs Kinloch, who was engrossed in *People's Friend*, the cafe was deserted.

'Was it something I said?' Jen asked.

'Never mind that. I've got some news,' said Gregor, as soon as the pot of Earl Grey had been served. 'I'm getting married!'

Normally, Jen would've been squealing in excitement, but Gregor seemed so deflated that she couldn't.

'To Robbie?' she asked cautiously.

'Of course to Robbie,' said Gregor. He sounded extremely tetchy, for once not bantering or larking about.

'Congratulations. So when's the big day?'

'Next month,' said Gregor. 'At the registry office in Inverness.'

'Are you sure about this?' protested Jen. 'I thought you'd want a bit of a splash – what about the Hollywood glamour theme you always wanted? And the fireworks? '

'No, I've always wanted to elope – it'll be so romantic. Just the two of us, and a couple of witnesses.'

'Greg, what on earth's wrong?' Jen took her friend's hand, thinking how sad and defeated he seemed. Gregor shrugged and, reaching into his jacket pocket, pulled out a small square of cardboard, tossing it on the table between them. Jen lifted it:

> *"Thou shalt not lie with mankind as with womankind. It is abomination."*
>
> *Leviticus Chapter 18, verse 22*

'What the actual – ?' she cried.

'I found it on the hall carpet. Someone must have pushed it through the door.'

'Who?' demanded Jen.

'I don't know. I can think of a few people who don't think it's right that we're getting married – especially in the church…thank goodness Robbie didn't see it.' Slowly, Gregor poured out a cup of tea. 'I'd mentioned in the salon that we were planning the wedding, and, apart from –' he gestured at the piece of card, 'a couple of people have cancelled their hair appointments with me, and, today, Mrs Crombie and her cronies came in here, but left as soon as they saw me.'

'So that's why you don't want the wedding to be in the village?'

Gregor gave a grim nod.

'I thought Christianity was meant to be about being inclusive and caring about other people,' Jen said. 'Not judging them.' Grabbing the piece of card, she ripped it into shreds, marched over to the bin and threw them in. 'There,' she said. 'Best place for that.'

Gregor again nodded, his expression still sombre.

'I'm sure Tom would marry you,' Jen went on. 'He's pretty cool, and he's not much older than us. He'd never turn you away from the church if you really wanted to be there. At least he's totally different from old Mr Colquhoun – he'd have had a stroke.' She managed a weak smile at the memory of the fire and brimstone preacher who'd preceded the

Rev. McIvor. 'Come on, Greg – you're not going to let a bunch of narrow-minded old harpies dictate how you live your life, are you?'

Gregor shook his head. 'It isn't as simple as that, Jenny. My mum's refusing to have anything to do with it, and Dad's backing her up – buckin' lily-livered bastard. Tom probably would marry us, but I don't want any more grief. This is meant to be a happy time for us. All I want is to make a proper commitment to Robbie.'

Jen remembered how, during their many late-night conversations – just the two of them curled up on the sofa after a movie night, with a tub of Chunky Monkey ice cream and two spoons and a bucket of popcorn – Gregor would confide that he just wanted what everyone else did – to find someone to love who loved him back.

'Why can't people just get on with their lives, and let you get on with yours?' Jen said, in a burst of anger, hating to see her best friend so unhappy. 'What do they expect you to do?'

'Get married to a woman, I guess, or else be alone for the rest of my life.'

Jen held his hand all the more tightly. 'It's so unfair. You and Robbie are so good together, but look at the Morrisons – the way she talks to him! It's as if they don't even like each other. God knows why they got married in the first place. Yet Mrs Crombie and co. seem to think that's all right.'

'Will you be my best woman?' Gregor asked, then. 'I'd like you to be there with us.'

'Of course I will. I'd love to.'

'Robbie's going to ask Phoebe, his sister, to be a witness. She's lovely. After the ceremony, we'll go out for dinner to this wee place I know by the Ness. We went there for our first date. Simple, sophisticated –'

'I think you're both going to be very happy,' Jen said thoughtfully. She paused. 'Greg – I'd like to hold a reception for you both in the hotel. Hollywood glamour, like you said. No pressure: just think about it.'

'Thanks, Jenny.' Gregor smiled wanly and rose to go to the loo. Jen watched his departing back as he walked away – she might not be looking for a relationship, but to be alone for the rest of her life? Never to feel that connection with someone? Never again to fall asleep and waken up in a lover's arms? It sounded so lonely. Patrick's face flashed into her mind and she pushed it firmly away.

Jen was tired by the time she got back to Ardnashell Lodge. They'd had about a gallon of Earl Grey each, then she'd insisted on ordering Prosecco for a toast in a failed attempt to cheer Gregor up. Inside her office, she dropped her bag on the floor with a start. Patrick was sitting on her ergonomic chair, poring over the hotel accounts.

'What the hell are you doing?' she demanded.

To his credit, he didn't try to make excuses. 'Looking over the books.'

'I think you'll find that I am the manager now – and I issue the instructions as to what I want you to do.'

'Listen, Jenny, your daddy asked me to keep an eye on things. I've worked here for a long time, and I'm here for you if you need any help with anything.'

'Whaat?' Jen said, collapsing into a chair. 'He doesn't think I can cope?' Jen was very close to her father. He claimed she was the son he'd never had. Patrick took off his glasses, his expression softening.

'Of course he does. But you're very young –'

'I'm young, but I've been to business school. I know what I'm doing.'

'I'm sure you do. He just wanted me to provide some moral support, in case you needed any advice or –'

'Would you stop patronising me? I'm perfectly capable of running this place on my own.'

'I'm not. You're still in charge, Jen. But I'm right here if you need any support.'

'I don't need your support. I'm managing perfectly well,' shouted Jen. 'And I suggest that, from now on, you just keep *out of my way.*'

'With pleasure,' said Patrick. He turned back to the computer screen. Jen stamped out of the room, her face like thunder.

'Good evening, Miss Grant.'

She turned to see the Finches, back from their daily stroll along the promenade. Immediately her face smoothed out into a high wattage smile.

'Good evening, Mr Finch, Mrs Finch. I do hope you've had a pleasant day. Will you be dining with us tonight?'

'Of course. We wouldn't go anywhere else.' Mrs Finch took her husband's arm and slowly they made their way to the dining room. Jen marched up the stairs. She couldn't believe that her parents and Patrick were treating her like a child after all the effort she'd put in. Still, lots of people hadn't taken Karren Brady seriously when she first became managing director of Birmingham City. Ha. Karren was Jen's idol, and she'd been about the same age as Jen was now when she started out on her career.

In the living room, Brooke was watching *Stranger Things* on Netflix, drinking red wine and painting her nails all at the same time. Jen sank down on the sofa beside her. She needed her sister's sweet, undemanding company. She needed warmth and comfort.

'After you, Jennifer.' Patrick's voice was icily polite. Amy glanced up. He was holding the kitchen door open for Jen, looking ridiculously hot in his white dressing gown. In contrast, Jen was wearing a trouser suit, killer heels and full make-up, as if to deny any vulnerability.

'No, after you,' she said. It was remarkable that anyone could get so much biting sarcasm into those three little words. The flat was really too small for the cold war which had been waging between the two of them since yesterday evening.

After some clattering around, Patrick emerged with a mug of coffee in one hand and a piece of toast in the other, and stalked out of the room.

'What's up with Jen?' asked Amy. 'She's been like a bear with PMT since last night.'

'She fancies Paddy,' said Brooke, from behind *Random Acts of Heroic Love*.

'I do not fancy Paddy,' said Jen's furious, disembodied voice from the kitchen. The woman had the ears of a lynx. 'He's a traitor and a low-down snake.'

'See, fancies him,' Brooke said, peering round the edge of her book.

'Actually, it's not me that's in lurrve: it's Amy,' Jen said, joining them at the table.

'Ooh, Ames, tell us.' This was enough to merit Brooke putting down her book.

'With Lewis Burns,' said Jen. 'Not much gets past me.'

'Oh, Amy. Your first love. That is so romantic.' Brooke beamed and pressed her hands together.

'Well, he's not going to come knocking on your door. You've got to come up with a strategy to reel him in,' Jen said, obviously anxious to divert the attention from herself.

Dreamily, Amy sipped her coffee. Maybe no one could ever compete with that first love experience, but none of the few other men she'd dated had ever come close to Lewis. Paddy was undeniably attractive, but he was more like a brother to her and she'd always preferred Lewis' sensitive, soulful looks: his intense blue eyes and wavy black hair, his beautiful hands with their long slender fingers. Sitting on his bed, they would compose songs together, he writing the music and she the lyrics, watched over by a poster of Jimi Hendrix, and she'd loved it, the buzz of creativity. Then, afterwards…

'Your first sub-task,' said Jen, adjusting her glasses, 'is to talk to him. No more than ten minutes, and you *have* to be the one to end the conversation.'

It must seem strange to Jen, who was so proactive – to use her own word – that Amy had yet to approach Lewis, although she had been here for some days now. It was fear that made her hesitate – fear that he wouldn't cherish the memory of their teenaged romance as she did. Perhaps he had long consigned it to the past as adolescent and imma-ture. A man like him must have had many girlfriends since they'd split up. But Amy had always felt that she could never truly lose touch with someone to whom she'd once been so close: there had been no one else, no slow ebbing away of their passionate interest in each other or their excitement in each other's company, no slowly drifting apart. Lewis had gone to Manchester to study music and performing arts. Amy had visited as often as she could, taking the night coach, the cheapest but most uncomfortable mode of transport available. When she'd moved to Edinburgh to train to be a chef, and they were drawn more and more into their studies and new friendships, the visits, phone calls and PMs had gradually tailed off.

'I hope you've got something gorgeous to wear.' Brooke's voice broke into her thoughts. She nodded, thinking of the bright red skinny jeans she'd bought in Top Shop in Princes Street, which were low-rise and so sizzling hot that she'd all but scorched her legs as she tried them on. Stuart, she remembered, had always claimed that he liked her to look natural, to dress down, not to call attention to herself. Jen would probably say he felt threatened. She'd never have flourished if she'd stayed with him.

Straightening her back, Jen swept past Brooke and Patrick, who were sitting in the foyer, and went into her office. A moment later, there was a knock at the door.

'Jen? Can we come in?'

She opened the door and they marched in. Brooke sat on the other chair in the room, so that Patrick was forced to sit on the sofa, which meant he was practically horizontal. This was good – it gave her the psychological advantage.

'How can I help you?'

'Paddy's got a brilliant idea for the business,' Brooke said. Jen had never known her to take much interest in the running of the hotel before but today her eyes sparkled and her cheekbones were slightly pink. She looked lovely. Come to think of it, she'd been quite subdued lately, spending even more time with her nose in a book, which Jen had put down to her dislike of waitressing and cleaning – it was a relief to see her looking brighter.

'Amaze me.' Jen crossed her legs at the ankle and looked coolly at Patrick over her glasses.

'Well, I was having a drink with my mate, Sean, at lunch time, and we came up with the idea of painting holidays. Bound to be a winner with the scenery around here, and Sean could teach –'

Hell: it *was* a brilliant idea, but Jen didn't want to seem too enthusiastic. 'Where would all those people stay?' she objected.

'The chalets,' Patrick said, at once.

'But, I don't know that they'd be habitable – I had to miss them out in the refurb 'cause I'd run out of overdraft.'

'I had a look at them this afternoon. A good clean and a coat of paint and they'll be fine,' said Patrick. 'Artistic types won't expect anything too luxurious. They'll want to rough it a bit – part of the experience.'

'I also thought of residential creative writing courses,' said Brooke, no longer able to contain herself.

'I don't know anything about creative writing,' protested Jen.

'I'll organise it all, I promise,' Brooke said.

'You really need to bring in more money, Jenny. You're seriously over-extended,' Patrick added.

'Who would teach those classes?' Jen asked.

'I know just the woman,' said Patrick.

'I bet you do.' Jen's mouth closed in a tight line.

'Niamh Malahide,' went on Patrick, as if she hadn't spoken.

'Niamh Malahide,' breathed Brooke, as if he'd said "J. D. Salinger". 'Wow. I just love her books – I've read all of them, over and over. How do you know her?'

'We were at Trinity together,' Patrick said. 'We, ah, kept in touch. I think I can persuade her.'

'I'm sure,' Jen said, getting to her feet. Suddenly she felt depressed. It was obvious that this Niamh Malahide was an ex-girlfriend of Patrick's. One of many.

'So we'll do it?' Brooke glowed with anticipation.

'Yesss.'

'You're so not going to regret this.' Brooke jumped up and threw her arms round Jen's neck, her hair silky smooth against her face.

Brooke was on fire. She'd even drawn out a critical path analysis, Jen noted, approvingly, although at this point it was fairly basic: update website, sort out chalets. This was split into two sub-tasks – clean and paint. While Jen herself updated the website, adding yet more photos of the scenery surrounding the hotel and biogs of the two tutors, and placed advertisements in a range of quality magazines and writing periodicals, Brooke organised all the cleaning and catering staff and paid them double time to go down to the chalets and scrub them from top to bottom.

The following day, all their friends from the village turned up to help paint. The only person excluded from Jen's three-line whip was Amy, who was providing snacks throughout the day and was also cooking for the riotous party which would take place that evening, when all the work was done; boxes of wine and six-packs of beer were piled up in the storeroom in readiness.

A thorough check of the chalets had proved that, although they were cluttered, dusty, cold and dingy, there was no evidence of damp. As Jen entered the one nearest to the hotel, she saw that the team which had been in yesterday had done a wonderful job – the windows sparkled, wooden surfaces glowed, the carpets were brushed and rugs beaten. The windows had been left open to disperse the musty smell. Gregor, somehow managing to look stylish in a tight tee-shirt and paint-smeared dungarees, a cloth tied loosely round his neck like a scarf, was shaking his booty to *Just Dance*, as he sloshed on the paint. Beside him, Callum was brushing it on with short, careful strokes.

'Just slap it on, Cal,' teased Jen, raising her voice over the music. 'You're not painting the Sistine Chapel.'

Misty and Duncan were here as well, but they were making slow progress as they were completely loved up and kept pausing to gaze at each other or to share a kiss.

'Put some welly into it, guys,' called Jen. Really, it was exhausting, trying to keep everyone in order, she thought, as she finally began stroking gloss paint onto a window frame. Apart from Brooke and Callum, the only person who was really putting any effort in was Gregor, and even he kept stopping to chat or to boogie to the playlist he'd made up especially for the occasion: now he was swinging his snake hips and singing along to *The Shape of You* by Ed Sheeran.

But gradually it all came together, despite everyone downing tools at lunch time to tuck into a big vat of lentil soup and some warm crusty bread and cracking open the beer and wine at six o'clock sharp. The walls were all painted in a warm apricot colour, the woodwork in a fresh, dazzling white.

'Cheers,' Jen called, raising her glass. 'Good work, guys.'

Amy, having brought from the hotel kitchen homemade pizza slices, chunky chips, garlic bread, a huge pan of vegetable chilli and another of mushroom risotto, was sitting on a two-seater sofa with Callum, talking and laughing softly. They were so annoying, Jen thought, their conversation so thick with in-jokes and shared memories that other people could barely understand it. It was almost as if they were talking their own private language. She poured herself another glass of wine and wandered over to chat to Gregor, who was selecting yet another playlist, a disco compilation. He turned up the volume and began to moonwalk across the floor, something Jen could never emulate, no matter how often he tried to teach her. Everyone refilled their glasses, the evening morphing into a party.

The next morning, a posse of somewhat hungover men turned up to complete the finishing touches. Gregor and Robbie took charge immediately. Since the refurb, the chalets had been used as a dumping ground for unwanted pieces of furniture from the hotel, so there was plenty to choose from. Jen watched in admiration as they directed the men where to place chairs, sofas and coffee tables, then whisked around hanging paintings and curtains, placing ornaments and lamps and arranging rugs, cushions and throws. In each chalet, there was a working fireplace in the living room, and it was hoped that, of an evening, the students would sit in the ancient, but deep and comfortable, sofas, drinking whisky and exchanging stories as the fire crackled and glowed.

'Thank you, Rob – you should totally have your own daytime TV show,' said Jen, as she sat at the long, scrubbed pine table in the kitchen of Marmion, the first chalet, watching Robbie take mis-matched china from a box and arrange it artistically on the Welsh dresser. Gregor was down at Waverley, the second chalet, doing likewise. It looked amazing. If she had tried that, it would just look like the bric-a-brac section of a charity shop.

Showing surprising enterprise, Brooke had borrowed a horse box from Galbraith's Farm, and Patrick, Callum, Duncan and a bunch of farmhands were loading it up with the excess furniture. Jen nodded to herself – she'd make a businesswoman of her sister yet.

Jen knocked on the door of Brooke's bedroom, which was still being occupied by Patrick. There was no answer, so she let herself in, closing the door softly behind her. Patrick's distressed Diesel jeans and size ten boots and trainers looked incongruous against the ultra-feminine background: Waterhouse and Monet prints covered the only wall not shelved and given over to books. There were necklaces hanging over the dressing table mirror, a row of floaty, floral dresses in the wardrobe, something silky pooled on a chair, a fluffy dressing gown on the back of the door and a jam jar full of wild flowers which perfumed the air.

Lying on the white lacy duvet was the tee-shirt Patrick had been wearing yesterday. Jen lifted it to her face and buried her nose in the fabric, smelling traces of his aftershave. Suddenly, she was overcome with a wave of longing so strong that she had to sit down on the bed, still holding the tee-shirt, which had clung to his body, caressed his skin... briskly, Jen rose and walked over to the bookshelves. She reasoned that her feelings for Patrick were like an illness – the flu, maybe. She would recover inside a couple of weeks: it was simply a case of mind over matter.

For someone so ditzy, Brooke had her books amazingly well organised: not only were they in alpha order by author, but they were also sub-divided by year of publication. It therefore only took a few seconds to locate Niamh Malahide's books, squeezed in between Mailer and Mantel. Jen selected the earliest of those, *Awakening*, and padded out of the room.

Although it was early afternoon, it was quite dark in Jen's own room: the weather had broken and mist and sleet formed a sequinned veil over the window, blocking out the view of the hills. Switching on a lamp which cast a warm pink glow, she wrapped herself in a soft, cosy old dressing gown and curled up at the top of her bed, leaning against the padded headboard.

"A major new talent" – *Irish Times*

"A remarkable début" – *Daily Telegraph*

"The voice of her generation" – *Herald and Tribune*

"A cracking read" – *heat* Magazine

"Wonderful – the best book I've read this year" – Marian Keyes

Jen's heart sank as she read the glowing testimonials on the back cover of the book. Then she turned it over, opened it, and began to read.

'Jen.'

Jerking back to reality, she had no idea how much time had passed. Brooke was standing before her with a tray. 'Tea?'

Jen nodded and Brooke, her pink tongue jutting slightly between her red lips, carefully placed the tray on the bedside table, then sat on the bed, her arms wrapped round her knees. 'Good, isn't it? Admit it: it's a much better read than *Who Ate My Cheese*, or whatever it's called.'

'A remarkable début.'

'Isn't it?'

Jen reached for her mug, and took a sip, although the tea was very hot. 'Brooke?'

'Mmm?'

'Do you think Gabriel is Patrick?'

'I've really got no idea.'

'Well, it's autobiographical, isn't it?'

'To some extent. I mean, it's based on her life, but it isn't necessarily true in every detail. It's fiction.'

After Brooke had gone, Jen read until it was dark outside, and she realised that, apart from a bowl of porridge at the crack of dawn and one digestive biscuit, she had barely eaten all day. Still holding the book, she made her way downstairs to the kitchen. She'd have to scrounge some leftovers from dinner, but that wasn't so bad, as they'd be French cuisine leftovers. After reading for so many hours, she felt drowsy, but unsettled also. Gabriel, with whom Orla, the heroine, has her first passionate affair, was Patrick, or Patrick was Gabriel, she was sure of it. Patrick had met Niamh at Trinity. And the desperate yearning which Orla/Niamh had felt for him was just the same as the way she felt.

Later, she let herself into her office. Her hands shook slightly as she booted up her computer and logged into Niamh's website. In her fevered imagination, Niamh was a raven-haired, light-eyed, Celtic beauty. After some minutes, she was looking at her homepage, *All About Niamh*. A photo of her, obviously taken in some sunlit garden, showed her to be a raven-haired, light-eyed, Celtic beauty. Quickly, Jen ran her eye over some biographical details: born in County Donegal twenty-nine years ago, oldest of seven children, studied at Trinity College, Dublin. *Awakening* had been written when she was still a student, and published when she was just twenty-four. In addition to her three novels, she'd also written several scripts for *Temple Bar*, a kind of Irish *Cold Feet*, which Jen had loved when it was screened a year or so previously, and was said to be working on a new screenplay. *Awakening* was to be made into a film, with Keira Knightley hotly tipped to play Orla, and Dervla Kirwan the lecturer with whom she has her first lesbian experience. Jen switched off her computer, feeling depressed.

★

Jen parked outside Kirklochy train station, drumming her newly French manicured nails on the steering wheel. She was a few minutes early.

'How will I know you?' Niamh had asked on the phone the previous night, in her soft, husky Irish accent.

'I'll hold up a banner with your name on it.'

'Right.'

'I'm joking. Trust me, you'll know me. It won't be that busy.'

Jen had gone to a great deal of trouble to prepare for her first meeting with Niamh Malahide. Apart from the manicure, she'd had a facial, her eyebrows threaded, her eyelashes permed, her hair French plaited, and a professional make-up. She reckoned that the only woman who'd had more care lavished on her face than she had this morning was the Mona Lisa. It was important to look her best. It was time: Jen sprayed on yet more perfume and walked, as steadily as she could, into the station.

Chapter 5
All About Niamh

Many guests remarked on how charming Kirklochy Station was. Behind a board with the name of the village in both English and Gaelic was the whitewashed station master's house, and pansy-filled pots stood at regular intervals along the platform. The train rattled in right on time. Only three people alighted: an elderly local couple, and a young woman who, from her photo, was Niamh. 'Jennifer?'

Jen walked towards her, understanding, now, why people often called make-up "war paint". Knowing she looked immaculate gave her confidence.

'Niamh. Good to meet you.' She held out her hand to shake.

Niamh was several years older than Jen, but she wore it well, the barely-there wrinkles at the corners of her eyes and around her mouth adding character. She was dressed in faded Seven jeans and a leather jacket, the tattoo on her right hand, between forefinger and thumb, making her slightly edgy, as did her bitten and discoloured nails. Her hair hung over one shoulder, as black and shiny as gloss paint. Deep, sensitive and troubled.

Terrific – Patrick's ex was a cross between Sally Rooney and Daisy Lowe.

Jen stowed Niamh's laptop, suitcase and backpack in the boot of the car and they set off on the short journey back to the hotel.

'This is gorgeous,' Niamh said, as Jen stopped driving to allow some sheep to cross the road. She glanced out of the window, seeing the scene through a stranger's eyes: the wild flowers on the grass verge, the sheep studded fields, the loch, calm and blue, the tall, straight Scots pines, the bracken-stained mountains.

'Thought you were a country girl, too. County Donegal, isn't it?'

'Mmm. It's a long time since I lived there. Another life.'

Jen drove up the drive of the hotel, parking with care, determined to prove that she had as much spatial ability as any man. 'I'll show you to your room,' she said, once inside the foyer. Niamh had been allocated the Rose Room, a small, but beautiful, room on the ground floor, with the added advantage of floor-to-ceiling French windows which looked out onto the rose garden. The carpet was deep pink and the wallpaper cream with tiny rosebuds scattered across it. The duvet was also cream, and the bed piled with plump pillows and cushions in shades of pink and wine. A vase of pink roses stood on the bedside cabinet.

'Wow.' Niamh dropped her laptop onto the bed and stood looking out of the window, seemingly transfixed by the view. 'It's so quiet. I see what you mean about the tranquillity.'

She was interrupted by the sound of a plate smashing against a wall, and a stream of Gallic cursing, which Jen chose to ignore. 'Let's go and get a drink,' she suggested, leading the way into the corridor.

'Paddy,' Niamh cried. She ran towards Patrick, who had just come out of the office. Jen watched as he lifted her into the air and birled her round, as if she were weightless.

'Must have been quite a session,' Jen said. After dinner the previous evening, Niamh and Patrick had gone outside for a nightcap. There was a paved area in the centre of the rose garden where a table and chairs were set out. The evening had been dark but warm and heavy with the scent of the flowers and a full moon had dappled the grounds. Strategically placed outdoor lighting turned the garden into something enchanted: a lovers' bower. Jen had lain in bed awake, occasionally catching the sound of soft laughter from down below, imagining the two of them in such a romantic setting.

She picked up an almost empty bottle of Jack Daniel's and a glass which had fallen on its side, bleeding the last few amber drops onto the table. Another glass lay on the paving, among pale pink petals.

Through the window, she could see Niamh still lying in bed, one slender arm and a sweep of dark hair hanging over the edge. Brooke touched her arm.

'Jen, Niamh told me last night that she split up with her husband last year. She and Paddy are old friends. She probably wanted to talk it through with him.'

'And you're telling me this because –?'

'I know you like him, Jenny. You don't need to put on the tough-girl act with me.'

'Patrick is free to be with whoever he likes,' Jen said firmly, not at all reassured by her sister's comments as Niamh was officially on the rebound.

She'd hoped Patrick would have the most agonising, dry-mouthed, splitting-headed, nausea-inducing hangover since time began, but, infuriatingly, when she got back upstairs, he was in the kitchen, cheerily frying bacon and eggs. His white robe didn't meet across his chest and she glimpsed lightly tanned flesh.

'Top of the morning to you,' he said, accentuating his Irish accent.

Jen ignored him and poured herself a mug of strong, black coffee from the pot on the counter.

She didn't have much time to dwell on what she dreaded was Patrick and Niamh's rekindled romance. Niamh spent most of each day holed up in her room reading samples of the work emailed by her prospective students, only emerging to walk with Patrick in the hotel grounds. In the evenings, they went to the Claymore Inn, to have intense discussions – or so Jen imagined – over a few pints of Old Sheepshagger. Jen herself was fully engaged in making the arrangements for the hotel's first hen weekend. She'd entered into an agreement with the family who owned Bannockside Castle, a little way down the coast. Despite being unbelievably posh, Finlay and Harriet Gilmour were flat broke, struggling to manage the colossal heating and maintenance bills which their stately home required, especially since the recession. Jen was determined to capitalise on the fact that, after losing popularity for a while, marriage was now back in vogue, and on the high profile weddings which had taken place in Scotland. The arrangement was that the bride and her friends would stay at the hotel for a few days prior to the wedding, enjoying extensive use of the spa and beauty facilities, the marriage ceremony itself would be held in the castle, then the bride and groom would spend their wedding night in the honeymoon suite. On discovering that most of the roof of the west wing needed to be replaced, the Gilmours had been only too pleased to apply for a licence to host weddings.

Jen had been awaiting the hen party with some trepidation, but refused to admit it – it was important to come across as calm and in control, but it was just as she had feared it would be. Eight leggy young women in high heels, tiny skirts and sparkly pink cowboy hats exploded into the elegant foyer, all with the obligatory hair extensions, ridiculously white teeth, false eyelashes, French manicures and butterscotch tans: sprayed on, Jen assumed. She'd yet to meet a Glaswegian who didn't get sunburn just from opening a fridge.

It was easy to see which girl was the bride: on her left hand, she sported a diamond that, sold on, could have paid off the budget deficit.

'Ms McCracken?' Jen stepped forward, wearing her professional smile and holding out a hand to shake.

'Not for much longer,' the bride-to-be said, smiling and tossing a couple of yards of blonde extensions over one tanned shoulder. 'In a few days' time, I'll be Mrs Tiara McGaughey.'

'Congratulations,' Jen said. 'Jaden's by far the most prominent Rangers' player since Ally McCoist.' She spoke confidently, although, until half an hour ago, when she'd Googled him, she had never even heard of Jaden McGaughey.

'Tiara, hen, could you ask if somebody can bring wur bags in?' asked a tall, willowy girl with hair of an unlikely colour of red.

'Jason, would you mind?' Jen turned to the Australian, still smiling; it was a wonder she didn't suffer from lock-jaw, she reflected. Tiara tossed the keys to him and he caught them neatly and strolled out of the front door.

'Now, I'll show you all to your rooms. Dinner is served from seven o'clock onwards in the dining room. I recommend the salmon en croute –'

'Is there a McDonalds anywhere near here?' interrupted another hen, a stunning brunette.

'Unfortunately not,' Jen said. By this point, she knew, her smile was a little strained. 'But I'm sure everything will be to your satisfaction.'

As soon as the girls had been checked in and were getting settled in their rooms, Jen hurried along to the kitchen, which was steamy and busy. Marcel was barking orders at a couple of sous-chefs who were chopping vegetables at tremendous speed. Working for Marcel, especially at busy times, was only marginally less stressful than dodging sniper fire in a war zone. Jen approached him with a flutter of nerves.

'The wedding party has requested, er... burgers,' she told him, keeping her voice firm and calm.

'You expect me to make bur-gerrs?' Marcel demanded, throwing down the knife he was holding, his face like thunder. Excellent – he seemed to be in a good mood. Jen studied her nails. 'Well, if it's beyond you, I'll get Amy to do it.'

'Ees not beyond me,' Marcel sniffed. 'Ees beneath me.'

'So you'll do it?' Jen knew that Marcel could never resist a challenge. He nodded. Jen left, aware of quite a frisson in the kitchen now that the wedding party was here.

Later, after several drinks in the bar, the hen party walked elegantly into the dining room. Several guests turned around in their seats to admire the glamorous procession. Tiara led the way, her walk rhythmic and sexy, her head held high. She wore a sparkling gold dress. Aura Wallace was an avid reader of *Caledonian Celeb*, and she'd explained that the willowy redhead in plunging black silk was Lacey Lafferty, currently dating Vladimir Ashkenazi, the Rangers' striker, and the brunette walking behind her was Jorja McIntosh – professional ex-girlfriend and star of hit Scottish reality show *Fly Me To Dunoon*. She was wearing a pair of high heels which Jen could see, from the red soles, were Louboutins and were to die.

'My feet are pure killing me in thae shoes,' she remarked, as the hens took their seats.

Jorja even had that essential accessory – a wee yappy dog with its hair tied up in a pink ribbon, which was peering out of her handbag, Jen noted with disapproval.

The WAGs were absolutely appalling, she had to admit, as she cleared up much later on. They'd continually snapped their fingers at waiting staff, eaten little of the cordon bleu burgers, but drunk masses, shouted and argued, shrieked with laughter. Someone had spilled a full glass of vodka and Irn Bru over the linen tablecloth and down the wall, and Jorja and her dog had both had to be carried upstairs by Patrick. Jen's heart burned with envy – what a pity Jorja had been too unconscious to appreciate it.

Almost asleep on her feet, she loaded up the dishwasher – it was gone two in the morning and she really couldn't expect any of her staff to work this late.

The next morning, Jen drove the short distance to Bannockside Castle. Standing amid acres of land, it was in the Gothic style of architecture, with turrets of golden stone and many-paned windows. The main selling point was the sweeping staircase down which Tiara would float before the ceremony. Even Jen was unprepared for the sight of the Great Hall, which had been made to look like a vast ballroom, with massive three-tiered chandeliers. Round tables covered in white satin and surrounded by brocade chairs were set out all round the room.

'Tell me there's not going to be a Sleeping Beauty theme, like in *Fly Me to Dunoon*,' she asked a designer who was half way up a ladder, adjusting an ornate lamp. 'That would be just too tacky.'

'No, no, there isn't,' he confirmed.

'Well, thank goodness for that,' Jen said, looking around her. The room was scented with the fragrance of lilies and the ancient wooden floor was so smooth and beautiful that it looked as if it had been hand polished with an electric toothbrush.

'Actually, it's a Cinderella theme.'

*

Jen walked into the spa. She'd had a few sleepless nights worrying about how much it had cost, and, every time she came through the door, she felt slightly sick as she thought about how much she still owed on it. She just prayed it would turn out to be worth it, bringing in more – and wealthy – clientele. The height of quiet sophistication, it was immaculately done out in sea green and gold and incorporated steam rooms, Chinese salt room, a sauna and a hot tub, with adjoining beauty rooms. The lighting was subdued and whale music played in the background. A dog-eared copy of *Freak Week* was lying on the coffee table: *Filler horror! – My face is so swollen I look like the Elephant Woman!* read the copy on the cover. Discreetly, Jen dropped it into the bin – this was not the image she wanted to convey. No doubt, one of the WAGS had brought it in. She concentrated very hard on the profit this wedding was going to accrue. The girls should certainly be satisfied customers. Jen had done everything – absolutely everything – in her power to please them, including going to the village store herself when one of them had demanded a Bombay Bad Boy. She strolled down the softly lit, tiled corridor, breathing in the fragrance of the scented candles, and pulled open the door into the thermal room.

'He's a pure bastard.' That was Lacey's voice, rising above the music. 'And that lassie's nothin' but a hoor.'

'She came ontae my Kayden wanst,' added Jorja.

Between the two girls, Tiara was huddled up on the sofa, tears streaming down her face. Jen hurried towards the group. 'What's going on?' she asked. Seeming distraught, Tiara carried on sobbing. 'Lacey?' Jen pursued, turning to the redhead. Her face grim, and with some difficulty on account of the length of her false nails, Lacey swiped at the screen of her pink-encased iPhone.

'Ti's agent's just phoned her. There's a story in the paper about Jaden.'

Tiara's sobbing redoubled as Jen took the phone, her heart plummeting as she read:

RANGERS ACE PLAYS AWAY

HE SCORES WITH STUNNA

Below was a photo of Jaden McGaughey, handsome and blue-eyed, relaxed and smiling. Standing beside him was a girl in a cream coloured dress, carefully tousled dark ringlets flowing over deeply tanned breasts, and teeth so white they must surely glow in the dark. Jen read on, sick to her stomach. The tabloid had obviously saved this prize piece of gossip until a few days before the wedding, when it would have the maximum impact.

The *Red Top* can exclusively reveal that Rangers' top goal scorer, Jaden McGaughey, has scored with stunning escort Lucille McGovern, known as Juicy Lucy, just weeks before his wedding.

LAP DANCER

And the randy Rangers' player, who recently denied rumours of an affair with a high class lap dancer, paid £1,200 for one night with the glamorous escort.

SEX ROMP

And sources close to the footballer say that he bedded sexy Lucy, 22, five times in one steamy session. The pair met in a swanky Glasgow night club following an Old Firm game, in which he had already scored several times.

FULL STORY: Pages 4 – 7 The *Red Top* Comments Page 16

Jen finished reading and glanced up to see Lacey and Jorja both looking at her. 'Oh, my God,' she said.

'Aye,' said Lacey, her face stony. Behind the two girls, Tiara was still crying.

'Can I do anything?' Jen asked, deeply uncomfortable at such a display of naked emotion. 'I could call Dr McLuskie. She's had a terrible shock.'

'Me an' her'll look after Ti,' Lacey said. 'Don't you worry, hen,' she added, turning to Tiara. 'At least you've goat your pals.' She went to sit beside her, Jorja sinking into the adjacent sofa.

'Okay,' Jen conceded. 'Just let me know if you need anything.' She hurried down to reception, head spinning. Just as she reached the foot of the staircase, the front door opened and a tall, exceptionally good looking, young man marched in. He was wearing sunglasses – pretty optimistic, as it was grey and dreich outside. Having seen his photo in the paper not ten minutes ago, Jen immediately recognised Jaden McGaughey. Despite being unshaven and dressed in jeans and a hoodie, he exuded glamour. As he strode across the foyer towards her, his phone began to ring.

'No comment. Lea'e me alane.' His broad Glaswegian accent was at odds with his appearance. No sooner had he terminated the call than his phone again began to ring. 'No comment!' he barked. 'Bastards,' he added, switching the phone off. Now he was standing in front of her. 'Ah need tae see Tiara McCracken.'

'I'm not sure that Ms McCracken wants to see you,' Jen said, tartly.

Jaden took off his shades, revealing piercing blue eyes. His face crumpled. 'I need tae see my fiancée. I need tae tell her it's all lies.' He swallowed. 'I met this lassie, like, once, at a club, for about five minutes. She must've sold a story. She's told them…ah need to talk to Tiara, like, now. I've flew up from Glasgow on the red eye. Missed training. Got a taxi all the way from Inverness.' He pushed his hands through his hair in distraction. 'Bastards. How can they no' leave us alane?'

'I'll go and find out if Tiara will see you,' Jen said. Jaden McGaughey exhaled deeply, a measure of the tension he must have been feeling. 'Meantime, I'll have someone bring you some coffee while you wait.' She directed him to the bar, rang for assistance and then began to make her way back upstairs and along the thickly carpeted hallway towards the spa. Tiara was now sitting up, sniffing, a tall glass of peppermint tea sitting, untouched, in front of her, and wrapped in a fluffy robe. She'd managed to stop crying, but was staring vacantly into space. With her face scrubbed of make-up, her wide blue eyes and her flaxen hair, she looked sweet, innocent, and very, very young.

'Tiara, Jaden's here to see you. He needs a little chat.' Jen kept her voice quiet, but firm.

'Aye, well. Mibbee she doesnae want tae see him,' Lacey said.

'If that's the case, I'll ask him to leave.'

'No,' Tiara said, her voice low and pain-wracked. 'We need to talk.'

'He's waiting downstairs for you.'

Half an hour later, Jen escorted Tiara into the bar. She'd changed into a pale pink Juicy Couture jogging suit and scraped her hair back into a ponytail, but was wearing absolutely no make-up. Perhaps she wanted Jaden to see just how much pain he'd caused her, visible in her puffy face, shrunken eyes and reddened nose. To Jen's relief, Patrick was there, standing by Jaden's chair with a coffee pot: he'd evidently just been refilling the footballer's cup. Jaden stood up. 'Ti, babe. Thank God.'

'Don't you call me that. You've goat no right to call me that noo.' Her voice was rough and broadly Glaswegian. She marched across the room and slapped Jaden on the face. He reached out and took her by the shoulders, looking down at her. 'Tiara, darlin', you've got to hear me out. I've come all this way to explain.'

'Hiv ye, aye? Well, it better be good. Ma hert's broke in two. We were meant to be getting married in a few days. Ah thought you loved me –' At this, she broke down again. 'Ah've never been so humiliated in my life,' she sobbed. Jaden put his arms round her and began stroking her back.

'Ah do love you. Ah've loved you since forever. There's never been naebody else. You know that.'

'Ah don't know onyhing onymare. Why is this girl saying you went wae her?'

'Listen and ah'll tell you. Me and some of the lads were in The Ivy, having a bit of a celebration. We'd beat Celtic three-nil. Then me, Darius and Mikey went onto Arta. This girl came over and asked fur wur autographs. Ah spoke to her for, like, five minutes, and, the next thing ah know, she's sellt a story.'

'Why would she do that?'

'Well, for the money, obvs – and because she wants to be a celebrity.' Tiara seemed to relax somewhat. 'They're all jealous, babe. They all want what we've got. Ah'm playing fur the team ah've supported since ah was a wean, and, on tap ae all that, I'm just about to marry the most beautiful girl in Scotland.'

Tiara began to cry again. Jaden fell to his knees before her. 'Tiara, darlin', ah swear to you, nothing happened between me and that lassie, apart from being papped standing next to her for a few minutes – say you'll still marry me.'

'Ah don't know,' Tiara blurted, ending on a sob. 'You need to gie me space. Ah need tae think.'

'Come on, Tiara.' Jen's voice was gentle as she put her hand on the small of the girl's back and guided her out into the corridor. Breakfast had been cleared away, so they went into the dining room, sitting down at a corner table.

'Ah don't know what to do, Jenny,' Tiara cried, as soon as Jen had fetched her a glass of water. 'Ah love him. Ah've never even looked at another boy since I was fourteen. That's when we got thegether – at high school. Ah thought we were forever. Ah couldn't wait to get married to him –'

'But now you don't know if you can trust him?'

Tiara shook her head, more tears spilling out. 'But ah don't know if ah can live without him.' She swallowed. 'Ah'm just going to go for a wee walk, try to clear my head.' She stood up and began to trail towards the door. Jen looked at her departing back, her fragile frame. Even her ponytail looked dejected.

'Even if Tiara decides to call the wedding off, it's too late for them to get a refund. Thank God,' Jen said, fervently, pacing up and down. She'd called an emergency summit, and she and her sisters were sitting in her office, sipping coffee. She'd diverted her phone calls to reception. There was still a lot riding on the possible cancellation: she felt quite sick at the thought of the chaos that would result – several cases of vintage champagne to be returned to the wine merchant, for instance, all the staff they'd drafted in for the occasion – half the village – to be told their services were no longer required, the coachman, the horses, the florist... Jen's head hurt just thinking about it. Even worse, *Caledonian Celeb* had exclusive rights to cover the wedding, and they'd lose the free advertising and publicity for the hotel – and the whole area – that this would have generated. She'd been hoping it would put Kirklochy on the map, bringing in more well-heeled tourists.

'But how can she marry someone she can't trust?' Brooke asked. 'How could he? Tiara told me she's been going out with him since they were at secondary school. They were childhood sweethearts.'

'We don't know for sure that he did,' Jen said. 'He says it's all lies – and some people will do anything for money. And to get noticed.'

Brooke looked sceptical. 'Do you really believe that?'

'I honestly don't know,' Jen said. 'He certainly came across as devastated. And the *Red Top's* not exactly an unimpeachable source.'

'Then again,' said Amy, 'he's Jaden McGaughey. He's surrounded by adoring fans, he has beautiful girls throwing themselves at him, desperate to take Tiara's place. He's come to think that he can do anything he wants, and have anyone he wants.'

And what about the prostitute, Jen wondered. Perhaps she misguidedly thought that, if she consorted with the likes of Jaden, some of the glamour and celebrity would rub off.

'You didn't see him, Brooke,' she said. 'He really did look absolutely shattered. I think he honestly does love her. Maybe he *was* telling the truth, and this Lucy girl did make it up. She wouldn't be the first.'

'Either that or he's just upset about being caught out,' Amy said. There was silence as they all contemplated this.

'Oh, God,' Jen said, another thought dawning on her. 'What if the Gilmours pull out after all this hassle? This is our first joint venture. What if they decided they didn't want to work with us again? Plus we're going to lose out on all the bar takings – which would have been massive, if the hens are anything to go by. Basically, the whole village'll be out of pocket – Fratelli's, Maggie's, The Claymore –'

She took a few deep, even breaths, trying to calm down.

'Still, until Tiara actually cancels the wedding, we don't have a problem,' she added.

There was a knock at the door.

'Come in.'

Aura Wallace sidled into the room. 'Jenny, the phones are going mad. Everyone's heard about Jaden. I've had Fern on saying that she's already ordered the flowers – should she cancel them? Even the laird's been on, asking if we still need Daybreak and Seaspray for the horse-drawn carriage. Lauryn says do we still want her and Evie to work that night, because they're saving up to go to Ibiza.' Suddenly she gasped. 'Oh, no. I've been dying to meet Darius McClurg. I'll be gutted if –'

'Aura, the wedding hasn't actually been cancelled yet. Just tell everyone I'll get back to them when we know more.'

Outside the window, she caught a flash of pink as Tiara walked by.

'Poor wee soul,' said Amy, following her gaze. 'I can't imagine how she must be feeling, to be betrayed like that, never mind when all the wedding preparations are in place and she was just about to take her vows.'

Again, they all fell silent, watching as Tiara sat on a bench and put her head in her hands.

Jen checked her phone and found that she had 31 new messages. She didn't intend to answer any of them.

Tiara, fragile – worryingly fragile, actually, walked robotically through the back entrance of the hotel and sat on the chaise longue in the foyer, crying. With her face still devoid of make-up, and her soft fine hair pulled back, she looked sweet, doe-eyed and incredibly pretty. Jen was struck again by how young she was. She couldn't be any more than twenty.

Through the banisters, she watched Patrick approach her and sit down beside her. She saw him slip his arm round her slender shoulders, feeling a stab of jealousy so acute that she was in physical pain.

At first Tiara just sobbed into the front of his shirt. Quietly, Jen walked downstairs and sat on her other side.

'You know,' Patrick said at length. 'I don't believe anything I read in the *Red Top*, and you've also got to remember that tomorrow it'll be lining dog baskets.'

Tiara sniffed, the sobbing starting to give way to long, shuddering gasps.

'I had a long talk with Jaden this morning, and I can see he's absolutely heartbroken at the thought of losing you, and he wants to marry you more than anything.'

Tiara glanced up and Jen saw a spark of hope flare in her eyes.

'But, if you're at all unsure about him, then you shouldn't go through with the wedding. It's not too late to call it off. Everyone would understand.' Patrick's voice was soft and calm. 'Do you honestly feel you can trust him?'

'I don't know,' Tiara said, her voice high and thick with tears.

'If he's betrayed you once, he may do it again.'

'I know, I know.'

'Tiara, you need to think very hard about this. Only you can decide what to do.'

'All my family and friends. My dress. All my bridesmaids. The flower girls. The cake. The castle. We were going to have a carriage and two white horses. It was going to be like a fairytale –' Tiara began to sob again as she considered the implications of calling off the wedding.

'You've been together a long time,' Jen tempted. 'You've got a fabulous life. The house in Loch Lomond and the flat in Glasgow Harbour –'

Tiara dashed the tears from her cheeks with the back of her hand. Patrick said nothing, but gently stroked the girl's back.

'He's swore it's all lies,' she said. 'He says everyone wants a piece of him. They're all jealous of what we've got together. Th..that girl – the bitch. She made it all up. She did it for the money, and because she wants to be famous.'

'The *Red Top* always gets everything wrong,' added Jen. 'It's been sued so often, it's a wonder it's still in business.'

Suddenly, Tiara raised her head and bunched her little hands into fists, in a gesture of determination.

'I will marry him. He's my man and I love him.'

'Okay, okay. It's your call, Tiara.'

Patrick helped Tiara to her feet and hugged her briefly. Jen watched as she wearily approached the staircase, her head bowed.

'Thank goodness she decided to go ahead with the wedding,' Jen said, later, as she and Brooke were drinking tea in their living room.

'Jenny, really –' Brooke looked distinctly uncomfortable. 'It's all so awful for her.'

'Business is business. You can't let sentiment get in the way,' Jen told her. 'Anyway, she totally should marry him – then she can divorce him in a few months. She'd be awarded a ton of money in lieu of her humiliation.'

'You're all heart, Jennifer,' Patrick said, coming in from the kitchen. His voice was instant frostbite. 'That wee girl's in bits down there, but God forbid that that should get in the way of your plans for world domination.'

He stalked out of the room. Jen glanced at Brooke, who was looking reproachfully at her. Why did Patrick have unlimited time for everyone else, but none for her?

'I'm going to bed,' she said. Suddenly, she felt flat and depressed.

Chapter 6
The Devil Wears Primark

'Is *he* here yit?'

The woman standing before Jen, hands planted on her hips, wore Primark's finest: a wrap-around leopard-print dress, gold stilettos and a slim fitting faux leather jacket. Her hair fell in peroxide curls below her shoulders; she obviously modelled herself on Madonna.

'I'm sorry, Madam, who are you referring to?' Jen's smile didn't waver.

'Michael McCracken. That useless scumbag of an ex-husband of mines.'

Ah, the mother of the bride.

'He doesn't appear to have checked in yet, Mrs McCracken.'

'Ms Suttie,' snapped the woman. 'This is my partner, Davie Sweeney.'

Davie Sweeney was a very handsome boy, with close cropped black hair, blue eyes and regular features, his good looks marred by a swallow tattoo on his neck and sovereign rings like knuckle dusters. Jen held out a hand to shake.

'Will I show you to your room?' she asked.

'Aye, you do that, hen. And get somebody to bring wur bags.'

At Jen's signal, Jason lifted a fake leopard skin suitcase, hot pink vanity case and a tatty sports holdall, leading the way to the Buttercup Room, which was done out in sunny yellow.

'This place is dead posh, Rita, isn't it? Check thae chandeliers – pure mental, man,' said Davie, as they made their way upstairs. He sounded nervous.

Leaving the couple prowling around their room, Jen hurried back downstairs.

More wedding guests were checking in in the foyer, a bunch of clones – dead straight bottle blonde hair, tattoos and tans the colour of Irn Bru for the girls, shaven heads, tattoos and tans the colour of Irn Bru for the boys. As Patrick and Brooke took the new arrivals to their rooms, Jen returned behind the desk. Every room was booked out for the next two days, with the exception of the Lilac Room. This had been allocated to Tiara's cousin, but she had pulled out as she was appearing in *Love Island*, and was determined to grab every nano-second of her fifteen minutes of fame with both hands, which meant that Patrick could finally move out of the flat.

'Is the old witch here yet?'

Jen looked up from the bookings diary to see a man who bore a striking resemblance to the actor who'd played Grant Mitchell. Michael McCracken, she presumed, the father of the bride.

'The wife,' he explained. 'Marguerite McCracken.'

'Your, eh, Ms Suttie and her partner have checked in, yes.'

'Partner,' scoffed Michael McCracken. 'He had to dog school to come along the day.' He cast a sidelong glance at the blonde clinging to his arm. She sniggered.

'Dad,' cried Tiara, running towards him. Michael McCracken's only daughter was also obviously his only weakness. Dropping the blonde, he enfolded her slender body in a leather jacketed embrace.

'It's okay, Princess,' he said. 'Daddy's here.'

All-out warfare between the McCrackens was averted that night, as Michael and Kayla, his girlfriend, had decided to eat out, going in search of traditional Glaswegian fayre – chicken tikka masala with naan bread. The next morning, at breakfast, Jen planned to seat the two couples at polar opposite ends of the dining room.

'Jenny, Jenny, Jenny, you've really done it this time,' Patrick said, shaking his head in sorrow.

'I've put Kirklochy on the map,' Jen retorted.

'For all the wrong reasons. Those two, Mick and Rita, will kill each other, given half a chance. And, as for the crack dealer –'

'Pads, Davie isn't a crack dealer. He works in Asda.' Brooke's voice floated over from where she and Niamh were sitting at the dining table. 'Actually, he's very shy and a really sweet guy. I was talking to him in the dining room.'

Brooke and Niamh had been holed up here for much of the day, working their way through piles of word processed sheets which had been submitted by Niamh's prospective students.

Niamh was an absolute nightmare, Jen had decided – neurotic, moody, brooding, highly-strung and prone to long, solitary walks when she was meant to be working. She claimed she was suffering from writers' block. Jen had little patience with this, but Brooke had a massive girl-crush on her, and the two women were forever sloping off to the Claymore to talk about love, life and literature.

'She's a tortured soul,' Brooke had told Jen in admiration.

'So am I, after a couple of hours in her company,' Jen had answered.

Now, she was flicking through today's *Red Top*. All the tabloid press had latched onto the story of how Tiara was standing by her man – this story totally eclipsing the minor matter of a security leak at Whitehall. *Caledonian Celeb* had produced an entire supplement on it. Lucy McGovern was said to be "revelling in her new found celebrity" – shopping in the designer outlets in the Merchant City and turning up in all the smartest bars and restaurants in Glasgow, surrounded by paparazzi. She'd sold her story to the *Red Top* for a reported £50,000.

'Celebrity,' scoffed Jen. 'Notoriety, more like. It's still prostitution, however much you get paid for it.'

'Jenny, I think you're being really unsympathetic,' Brooke said. 'You don't know anything about this girl's life, or how she became an escort in the first place. She must have been desperate – and I bet she really hates it, and wishes she could do something else. Don't be so judgemental.'

'What I don't understand –' Patrick turned to Jen with a look that would crack ice, 'is how you keep going on about how the likes of Tiara have set the Women's Movement back a hundred years, how you despise women who can do nothing for themselves, but you still encouraged her to marry that slimeball. You were like a devil sitting on the poor girl's shoulder.'

Thank goodness Patrick was moving out of the flat that night.

'Now who's being judgemental? You don't know for a fact that he did cheat on her, and, anyway, she's madly in love,' Jen protested, although she thought "mad" was the operative word.

'And what would you know about that, Jennifer "Heart of Glass" Grant?'

'Look, I'm trying to run a business. I can't afford to let emotions get in the way.'

'You've become very hard since you took over the running of this place, Jenny,' Brooke said, and her large blue eyes were sad. 'Very cynical.'

'Just as well it wasn't left up to you to run it, anyway,' Jen said. She couldn't stand Brooke's disappointment.

'Guys, could we dial it down a bit, please?' Amy said. 'At the end of the day, it was Tiara's decision to go ahead with the wedding, no one else's.'

'Thank you,' said Jen. She stood up, looking around at the others. 'Does that conclude the case for the prosecution? Or does anyone else have anything to add?'

Patrick, Niamh and her sisters looked back reproachfully at her, but said nothing.

'Good. I'll go and get on with my work.'

She left the room, closing the door firmly behind her.

The next morning, Jen rose early to check out some guests who had a flight to London to catch – part of her luxury personal service. After they'd left, she hurried along the corridor to her office, coming face to face with Niamh, who was padding back towards her bedroom.

'Hey, Jen.' Niamh beamed at her, the argument of yesterday seemingly forgotten. She was barefoot and wore the thick, white, fluffy dressing gown that came with the room, her hair long and loose around her shoulders.

'Hi,' Jen muttered, taking refuge in her sanctuary. She booted up her laptop and tried to concentrate on the staff payroll. Why had Niamh been prowling around in a dressing gown at this hour of the morning? But she knew, really, that she'd spent the night with Patrick – the Lilac Room was just a couple of doors down from her room. Distracted, she only just stopped herself from paying Aura Wallace £60,000 for one evening's overtime.

All day long, as she tried to focus on spreadsheets, ordering of supplies, juggling bookings and discussing menus with Marcel, she kept imagining Patrick and Niamh in bed together, slim and tanned against the ivory coloured Egyptian cotton sheets, their slender fingers and limbs entwined, their dark hair tangled on the duck down pillows. She kept having flashbacks of Niamh in her white robe, floating down the corridor, her face glowing. It was as if someone had stuck a knife between her ribs.

Even Jen had had to admit that Jaden McGaughey was gorgeous. He and Tiara, with her slender blondeness, made a stunning couple. His daily training schedule ensured that there was not a spare ounce of flab on his six foot two inch frame. His hair was dark and glossy, his blue eyes dreamy. He had amazing bone structure and a tush like an apple. His hands were beautiful, making him look more like an artist or a poet than a premier league footballer.

'Haw, darlin',' he called, snapping his fingers at Jen. 'Going to get us some champagne? Nane of that cheap stuff, neither.'

Inwardly seething, Jen smiled so hard that her jaws hurt. She'd need to book a Botox treatment by the time this wedding party left. Simultaneously, Jaden had managed to commit two of her most hated crimes. 'I assume Laurent Perrier will be to your satisfaction, sir?' she managed to say, although it nearly choked her. Jaden curtly nodded his approval. He'd dropped his penitent act pretty quickly as soon as Tiara had accepted his story and agreed to go ahead with the wedding.

The McGaughey and McCracken families were having dinner together on this, the eve of the wedding. Patrick expertly opened the champagne and poured it into outstretched flutes.

'Can I just get a beer?' Davie Sweeney was asking. He looked pale and anxious, barely out of his teens and totally out of his depth.

''Course you can, love,' Brooke said, touching his shoulder. Jen shot her a sharp glance; she'd had to have words with her sister before about over-familiarity with the guests.

Yet another gorgeous woman floated across the room, then, her hair piled up on top of her head in intricate coils, showing off cheekbones you could hang a coat on.

'Miami,' she bawled. 'Pack it in!'

A child of about four, who was wearing candy pink nail polish and matching lipstick, was charging around the room, giggling and ducking in and out of the white damask shrouded table legs. Jen watched as Patrick crouched before her so that their eyes were on a level and spoke quietly to her. To her amazement, the little girl walked back over to the table and climbed onto her chair. Good grief – it seemed that all females, even the devil-child, were under his spell.

The only consolation was that Hugh and Celie McMichael, sitting in the corner picking at coq au vin, looked absolutely furious. 'Riff-raff,' Hugh muttered as she hurried to the haven of the kitchen.

Inside, she paced restlessly up and down. How could Jaden McGaughey just strut into the family celebration, with no trace of contrition, flashing around his money, as if nothing had happened? How could anyone be that arrogant? Because he was Jaden McGaughey, she admitted, and every man wanted to be him while every girl wanted to be with him. She lifted a dirty glass, gripping it so hard that it shattered in her hand.

'Careful,' said Patrick from somewhere above her, as she stooped to clear it up, but it was too late – a narrow shard of glass had cut into her thumb. She bit her lip as the blood seeped out. Patrick had grabbed the dark green first aid box from its shelf and helped her to her feet. She could hardly breathe as he took her hand and held it under the cold tap, waiting for the bleeding to stop, and as he gently cleaned the cut, the pain forgotten in the excitement of being this close to him. She could feel the heat of his body, smell the spicy aftershave he wore, see the stubble on his jawline, the criss-cross shadows his long lashes cast. All too soon, he'd stemmed the blood with a blue bandage. 'All right?' he asked.

'Yeah. Thanks. Thanks, Pads,' Jen murmured.

Patrick allowed himself a brief smile. Jen's heart relaxed slightly – at least he didn't seem to hate her anymore.

Niamh was definitely having sex – and plenty of it, Jen concluded gloomily, the next morning, as she watched her demolish a full Scottish breakfast, two rounds of toast and a gallon of fresh orange juice. She looked absolutely shattered, but while her eyes were bruised with exhaustion, they also sparkled. Her face glowed and she buzzed with energy. She was cool and sophisticated in a black broderie anglais dress, her hair tied back with a piece of black lace, striking with her light eyes and scarlet lips against the monochrome. Jen glanced at Patrick to see if he seemed in a similar state of bliss but he was as inscrutable as ever.

'You look lovely,' Jen heard Brooke say.

'T'anks,' Niamh said. 'You could say I've got me mojo back. I haven't slept all night,' she confided. 'But it was worth it.'

'We'll talk about it later, babe,' Brooke said, throwing a resentful glance at Jen. 'After my shift's finished,' she added pointedly.

It irritated Jen that Brooke always made out she was such a slave-driver. Brooke didn't have a clue what was involved in managing the hotel. Jen also had to work family members at least as hard as everyone else, or she'd be accused of nepotism. She stalked out of the room, her head held high. She told herself that she was a businesswoman and not some pathetic, sappy female out of the pages of a romantic novel – she was too busy to be interested in Niamh's true confessions.

Despite being fake-baked, buffed, exfoliated, waxed, cleansed, mois-turised, coiffed, styled and made-up to within an inch of their lives and with more spare parts than Halfords, Tiara and her six bridesmaids hit the beauty rooms early the next morning, along with her mother and her granny, who resembled a low rent Bette Midler. Gregor, beside him-self with excitement, had been drafted in to help with the hair styling. Jen walked around, breathing in the perfumed air, hoping against hope that there would be no last minute hitches.

She could hear blood-curdling screaming – one of the hens having a Hollywood wax – said to be the most excruciating pain this side of childbirth. Two other girls were sitting side by side, wearing fluffy turquoise robes, mud packs and eye pads.

'... Irish guy, he's fit as,' Jen overheard. 'I just love that accent.'

'I bet he fancies hisself, but.'

'Oh, he does,' Jen said grimly.

'Ah'll never been in a relationship again; it's just too painful,' wailed Jorja McIntosh, her hands splayed in front of her as the nail technician fixed on glittery talons. The champagne had been flowing freely and seemed to have made her maudlin, as she, once again, lamented her lost love. 'I'll never again find someone so –'

'Rich,' Jen muttered to herself.

'...right for me,' said Jorja, ending on a sob.

'Better off without him, hen,' said Rita. 'I was pure gutted when I split up wi' my Mick, but Davie's way hotter.'

'Kayden was the only one for me,' protested Jorja.

'Girl power, Jorja,' said Jen. 'Hold your head high, look fabulous and show you don't even care about him.'

The last thing she needed was for the girl to have some kind of meltdown just before the wedding. It was all stressful enough as it was. If she decided to sell another story, the tabloids would be all over it like wasps on a jam sandwich.

'I was absolutely bealin'. I told him where tae go –' another voice floated over.

Jen slipped away.

Jen had expected the wedding to be the most tacky, tasteless and ostentatious occasion in the history of time, as if planned by a committee chaired by Barbie and comprising Elton John, RuPaul, and the fairy from the top of the Christmas tree, but she had to admit that it was all rather beautiful. According to Aura Wallace, the hotel's showbiz correspondent, Tiara had attended dance classes since she was a toddler and the Cinderella theme commenced with a short ballet with her as the principal. Jen watched as, dressed in her dusky pink, patched and ragged "Cinders" outfit – which had actually been created and handmade by one of the top Scottish fashion designers, she danced, almost floating, like a leaf blown here and there on the breeze. It was sheer pleasure to watch her move, so supple and fluid, to see the beautiful lines of her body. After ten breathtaking minutes, she ran lightly out of a side door.

Next, Jaden McGaughey and his best men, all in full Highland regalia, approached the altar. Meanwhile, in a side room, Tiara was changing into her wedding dress. She would then board her carriage – drawn by two white horses, and be driven a short distance along the coastline, the guests adjourning outside to await her return.

There was great excitement, especially for the journalists from *Caledonian Celeb*, which had sole rights to cover the wedding. The dress, also the work of a top Scottish designer, was the most closely guarded secret since the identity of the Third Man. Silvana Stuart, the wedding director, had everything scheduled to the nano-second and a violin quintet struck up *All of Me* by John Legend at three o'clock precisely, as Tiara and her father began their slow, measured walk down the aisle. Again, Jen was pleasantly surprised – she'd expected the dress to be the last word in over-the-top vulgarity – an overblown meringue that even Barbara Cartland would baulk at, or perhaps a skin-tight corset dress which would be more suited to a French bordello. Instead, Tiara wore an elegant gown in ivory, her slim golden shoulders rising from a hand-embroidered bodice. Rather than the up-do usually favoured by brides, her corn coloured hair had been left loose and softly curled. She wore just one jewelled pump and a crown of summer flowers. For a moment, Jen imagined herself in such a dress – understated, simple, so that it showed off the bride rather than the dress. Then she shook herself mentally – aye, right. Like she was ever going to parade about in white lace and promise to obey some man. As Tiara walked stately past her, she glimpsed her serene, perfect profile through her veil.

There was a brief pantomime while Tiara sat on a seat at the front of the hall and Jaden slipped on her other shoe, then they rose to take their vows.

Jen let out her breath sharply as the minister proclaimed the couple man and wife – she hadn't realised she'd been holding it.

'You may kiss the bride.'

As Jaden leaned forward, pulled Tiara into his embrace and kissed her on and on, the photographer from *Caledonian Celeb* went wild, his camera whirring and flashing, the couple's stock having risen since the Juicy Lucy debacle.

All decorum was forgotten only minutes into the reception. The entertainment was being provided by Jaden's friend, hell-raising Scots rocker Richie Girvan, who was more than a little the worse for wear. The girls ran around shrieking and flicking up the kilts of the men, people were eating little but knocking back gallons of champagne cocktails. Tiara's granny fell over during the slosh and broke her kneecap, and Miami was sleeping peacefully under a table. Jaden McGaughey and a couple of his team mates were playing football with a hatbox they'd found.

Much later, Richie Girvan's music had been replaced by banging tunes at ear-bleeding volume. Fascinators were lop-sided, make-up was smudged, and high heels had been kicked off and replaced with trainer socks. Jen was bone weary, but she'd need to stay up until even the most diehard guests had staggered off to bed.

The next day, from behind the reception desk, Jen watched the wedding party leave. Tiara and Jaden, beautiful and golden, were bidding farewell to their guests, prior to flying out to the Bahamas to carry on the honeymoon. Patrick and Jason were taking their Louis Viutton suitcases out to their car. Would Tiara be truly happy? Did extreme good looks, celebrity, wealth, exotic holidays, Club Class travel, head-to-toe designer clothes, a flat in Glasgow Harbour and a pair of Louboutins in every colour of the spectrum – their "fabulous life together" as Jen herself had put it – compensate for being with a man who'd probably been unfaithful to her and might well be again? Whom she couldn't really trust? How much fun would it really be to be constantly under the scrutiny of the tabloids and pursued by paparazzi? And how many of the guests had been true friends – old, close friends with whom they'd shared highs and lows, been there for each other – rather than teammates and other "C" List celebrities?

Her eyes rested on Patrick as he made his way outside with yet another suitcase. He'd been so kind to Tiara – while all she had done was to try to convince her to go ahead with the wedding. And what would she do without him? When a furious argument had looked likely between Jaden McGaughey's – heavily pregnant – younger sister and one of his cousins, he'd managed to diffuse it before they came to blows, as well as overseeing all the arrangements for the reception. No. Even if they could never be together, there was nowhere she'd rather be than right here, with Patrick.

Later, she wearily climbed the stairs to the flat. She'd taken the afternoon off – the first break she'd had in several days. Amy was in the kitchen, prepping the food for tonight's dinner, while Brooke was in the spa clearing up the flotsam of discarded champagne flutes, glossy magazines, shredded gold paper, twisted wire, corks and Godiva chocolates left by the girls. They could really put it away – it would be viable for them to open their own recycling plant. Brooke was under strict instructions to restore the spa to its usual pristine state for the next group of guests, so Jen had the place to herself. Thankfully, she kicked off her killer heels and slipped out of her tight dress.

After a long, hot shower, she put on her pyjamas, fluffy bed socks and slippers and settled on the sofa with the latest *Freak Week*, a secret guilty pleasure. *My Sisters Are Also My Cousins*, screamed the front cover. With enjoyment, she opened it and began reading an article about a woman who believed that her three year old son was the reincarnation of Elvis Presley.

The door opened. In one fluid movement, Jen slid the magazine under the sofa and grabbed the nearest book, a Lee Child thriller, from the coffee table.

'I've been looking everywhere for that,' Patrick said, 'I've been dying to get back to it.'

Jen was furious that he'd caught her in ancient pyjamas and slippers and with her hair loose and messy and her face bare of make-up. Only Brooke, with her milky complexion, startling blue eyes, long, curling lashes, high cheekbones and curving red lips, could make that a good look. She and Brooke were alike; anyone could tell they were sisters, but Brooke was like the deluxe version, the way Jen would look if she'd been airbrushed.

'Would you like a cup of tea?' she heard herself ask.

'Sure, if you're making.'

Jen shuffled into the kitchen. She had absolutely no chance with Patrick now, she thought, but, at least, they could hang out as mates, she could spend some time with him.

'Thank goodness they've all gone,' she said, collapsing beside him on the sofa.

'I don't know, I kind of miss them,' said Patrick. 'Like when you've had a tooth extracted.'

After three mugs of tea and a Caramel Log, Jen felt warm and relaxed.

'I knew there was something I'd forgotten to tell you,' Patrick said. 'You know Rita and Mick?'

'Unfortunately, yes. I've been trying to expunge them from my memory, but it's not easy.'

'Well, spending some time together's made them realise they're made for each other. Their divorce hadn't come through, so they're still married –' His green eyes shone with fun. 'But they've decided to have a blessing and renew their vows, wait for it –'

'Here?' whispered Jen.

'In the rose garden –'

'With all their friends and family?'

Patrick nodded again.

'What about Davie and Whatsit… Kayla?' Jen protested.

'Sorted. Davie asked Kayla out.'

'You're joking.'

Patrick shook his head. Jen began to laugh, throwing her head back. How long was it since she'd had a really good laugh? Too long, she decided. Patrick joined in and they leaned against each other, tears running down their cheeks.

'You're not so bad,' she told him, when she was composed enough.

'And you.' Patrick's eyes were close to hers. 'You can seem almost human, sometimes.'

Brooke's hand shook as she knocked on the door of the Blue Room. If only she hadn't been on duty when Hugh McMichael had phoned. Her heart was racing; she prayed that Celie would be there. The door opened and she swallowed as she glanced around. He was alone.

'R-r-room service,' she faltered. She placed the glass of Talisker, on its silver tray, on the nearest surface and began to sidle away, reaching, behind her back, for the doorhandle, but he was coming towards her.

'Where's Celie?' she blurted.

'The spa. She's having a massage. She'll be a while yet.' Now, he was standing right in front of her. He reached out and touched her cheek. 'I don't know why you're so nervous, beautiful girl.'

'I just need to…I'm on duty. I have to –'

Hugh McMichael gave a brief shrug. Brooke took a step backwards, but now she was cornered, pressed against the wall. He put a hand on either side of her head then stooped, his face up close to hers, then forced his tongue between her lips to open her mouth. She struggled, but he was too big and strong. Suddenly, a phone rang, cutting across the sound of his breathing. Distracted, he stopped kissing her. Frantic, she managed to duck under his arm and grab the door handle and, next moment, she was running along the corridor, her footsteps muffled by the thick pile carpet.

Back in the flat, she could hear voices and laughter. She went into the bathroom and cleaned her teeth, then gargled with mouthwash, desperate to wash away the taste of him.

'What's wrong?' Jen asked, as soon as she walked into the living room. She sat down and burst into tears. 'Brooke, what *is* it?' She was aware of her sister standing up, then crouching before her, Jen took her hands. She managed to stop crying, taking long, shuddering breaths.

'It's Hugh McMichael,' she managed to say, at length. Neither Jen nor Patrick spoke, waiting for her to go on. 'He... he phoned for room service, but, when I went up, Celie wasn't there. He was on his own. He pushed me against the wall, so I was trapped, and kissed me. It was horrible.' She shivered. 'His phone rang and that distracted him for a moment, and I managed to get away.'

'Oh, Brooke.' She almost broke down again at the concern in Jen's voice. 'What a horrible thing to happen. But he won't get away with it. I promise.'

'You'll.... he caught me trying on Celie's clothes one day and he said he wouldn't make a complaint, but he wanted a first class service in return. He's been sort of... playing with me, making sure I knew he had something on me. ' Brooke looked down at her and Jen's entwined hands, so similar. 'I know it was bad of me – I shouldn't have gone through her wardrobe –'

She glanced up to meet Jen's eyes. Her sister's face was flushed, her neck mottled red. She bit her lip.

'I can't believe I intimidate you so much that you didn't feel you could talk to me. I'm so sorry, Brooke. You must've been terrified. I should've realised there was something wrong – you haven't been yourself lately.'

'If I'd not tried on the dress – '

'Brooke, whatever you did, it's Hugh McMichael who's at fault here.' Patrick spoke for the first time. 'It's sexual assault and I think we should report him to the police.'

'Please don't, Paddy,' Brooke whispered. 'I don't want to go through it all again. I just want to put it behind me.'

'Okay.' Patrick's voice was soft. 'I'm going to ask him to leave, right now. He'll be gone by dinner time, trust me.'

After he'd left, Jen pulled Brooke into her arms, stroking her back and hair. 'You'll never have to see him again, I promise.'

Brooke blinked back a few more tears into Jen's fluffy dressing gown. They stayed like this, holding each other, until Patrick returned.

'What happened?' Jen asked, still keeping an arm round Brooke's shoulders.

'I pointed out that it would be better if he left, so he's packing. I nearly offered to do it for him. I think he's going to tell his wife that he's been summoned back to Edinburgh for a big case – but, whatever. I've given him one hour to get the hell out.'

'Thanks, Pads,' Brooke breathed, feeling marginally better now that Hugh McMichael's threat was no longer hanging over her.

'I'm going to take the night off,' Jen announced. 'We've been so busy, we never get the chance to just spend time together. But, tonight, we'll have a really good talk, just the two of us.'

Chapter 7
Amy in Wonderland

Amy had seen the village hall in many guises, but, tonight, great effort had been made to turn it into a night club. It wasn't exactly Madison Square Gardens, but she was very much looking forward to the evening ahead. Her stomach knotted with anticipation at the thought of seeing Lewis again – she was so excited that it was actually painful. Fairy lights had been wound round the rafters and tea lights placed along the window sills. Jen looked amazing, she reflected, dressed like the young girl she was for once in a very little black dress with criss-cross straps teamed with over-the-knee black suede boots. She'd left her hair loose and it tumbled down her back, glossy and luxuriant. Patrick was wearing old jeans and a grey tee-shirt, his beauty needing no adornment.

'Where's Niamh?' Jen was asking him, in a carefully casual voice.

'Working.'

'I thought she was suffering from writers' block, or whatever it is.'

'Not any more. She's been locked away in her room all day, writing. She's like a woman possessed.'

'No change there, then,' muttered Jen to Amy, as the first act, Dead Beat, shuffled on stage, a bunch of local teenagers in skinny jeans, Converse and beanie hats. Not so long ago, the noise they'd made had been so dire that they'd been forced to rehearse in one of Farmer Galbraith's furthest away barns, but all the practice seemed to have paid off and tonight, wisely forsaking their own compositions, they kicked off with Paolo Nutini's *Ten Out of Ten*, which they followed up with a series of equally catchy cover versions which had everyone singing along and dancing in the aisles.

Next up was an ageing seventies throw-back, whose grey hair was still worn long and who sported flares extended with curtain material, but he was an accomplished guitarist who, this time, had everyone swaying with their eyes closed to the songs of James Taylor and Neil Young.

The final performer before the interval was Evie Martin. Amy watched as the teenager walked on stage, slim as a blade in a floral dress and biker boots, her long, tawny curls flowing down her back from under the cutest denim hat. No wonder most of the young boys, and several of the girls as well, had such a crush on her. She was a revelation, as, accompanying herself, she began to sing. The hairs stood up on the back of Amy's neck. Not since the days of Rowan Galloway – Kirklochy's most famous export – had such a beautiful voice been heard in the village. Note perfect, sweet yet husky, pure and clear, she sounded like a young Sinead O'Connor. She could sing anything, switching from blues to ballads, from jazz to pop with ease, moving her audience almost to tears one minute, making them dance, clap and stamp the next. When she bowed slightly to signal that she'd sung her last song, everyone cheered and shouted for more. Evie obliged, ending with *Amoureuse*. Beautiful song, Amy thought, and absolutely believable performed by such a fresh, lovely young girl. She'd always loved this song – it made her think of Lewis and the very first time she'd ever made love.

There was an interval before Lewis, who was the headline act, came on stage, when everyone surged towards a trestle table piled with cans of beer and boxes of wine. Amy splashed some plonk into a polystyrene cup and fought her way through the crowd of teenagers surrounding Evie. 'Well done; that was absolutely gorgeous.'

'Thank you,' said the girl, meeting her eyes with a cool confidence far beyond her years. She tossed her hair over her shoulders and went back to talking to her friends.

Amy's hand shook so much at the thought of finally seeing Lewis again that she slopped beer all over her jeans – purposely old and faded, so that she wouldn't seem to be trying too hard. At last, it was time. Brooke touched her arm as he walked on-stage, just him and his guitar. Gracefully, and so relaxed, he sat on a stool and began to play. Mesmerised, she gazed at his beautiful artist's hands on the strings, as he began an acoustic version of Bruce Springsteen's *Fire*, his voice deep and smoky. They used to listen to this all the time, lying on his bed, talking softly and lazily, breath against breath, hands touching, holding, clasping.

'Get a grip, Amy, you look like a love-sick cow,' hissed Jen, nudging her sharply.

'Shut up, Jen.' Brooke's voice on her other side was surprisingly fierce.

Amy barely took in her sisters' whispered conversation; she was too lost in memories of herself and Lewis. Both living with their parents, and in a village where privacy was impossible, they had had little opportunity for sexual adventure. The purchase of condoms had been even more fraught for Lewis than it was for most teenage boys, since his aunt was the village pharmacist and a stalwart of the Free Church, which meant that he'd had to travel as far afield as Ewensay, where he wasn't known. She shivered as she remembered one May bank holiday weekend. Brooke and Jen had been dragged off to Eriskay to visit family, but, since Amy was seventeen, she'd been allowed to stay behind to concentrate on revising for her Highers, but, instead, had smuggled Lewis, who'd told his mum he was going camping, into the hotel flat. Even after all this time, she shivered at the recollection: how, after days of longing for him, she'd thrown herself on him as soon as he'd come through the door and dumped his backpack, tent and ever-present guitar on the floor, kissing him hungrily while scrabbling at the buttons of his jeans. Nothing since had ever come close to that passionate love-making, the thrill of feeling his skin hot against hers, of being so close to him. She remembered his blue eyes, intensely fixed on her face as he gently pushed back her hair, the talk, their conversation sparkling with recognition, the silences, the knowledge that there was nowhere else she'd rather be than this shabby flat in grey, rain-soaked Kirklochy, as long as Lewis was with her. There was always music in the background, the soundtrack to their romance.

But she'd never believed that he was totally hers. He was too beautiful, too talented, too soulful. She had never been confident that she would keep him.

She snapped out of her daydream as loud applause broke out. Evie Martin – the wee minx – and a bunch of other girls, had pushed their way down to the front of the hall, indulged because of their youth and prettiness, and were standing right by the stage, gazing up at Lewis. She hadn't been mistaken; he was better looking even than when she'd known him before, his chiselled features more finely honed.

He'd learned how to work an audience, his between-songs patter causing spurts of laughter, and he incited them all to sing along ever more loudly. All around Amy, people were bellowing out the words, clapping, dancing, as shards of light spun across their bobbing heads from the silver disco ball suspended from the ceiling.

For part of the set, Lewis sang some of his own compositions, his performance so intense that she wondered if his guitar might break.

To a room which was completely silenced, he finished with *This Guy's in Love with You*. Up until this moment, Amy had considered this to be the most cheesy, cringeworthy song ever written, even if Noel Gallagher had covered it, but now she found herself transported by the simplicity and sincerity of his rendition, and even more by his bewitching, wicked smile as he finished, to rapturous applause. Surely every woman in the room must have been moved.

Jen grabbed Amy's arm. 'Promise me you'll play it cool.'

She felt sick with anticipation as she made her way out of the main hall, surrounded by people buzzing from a great night out. There was a group of teenagers behind her.

'That was minted,' one of them said.

'Evie was, like, totally amazing.'

'Awesome.'

'That was the bomb.'

'Verrrry enjoyable evening,' boomed Robert Kingsley, a local roué, gallantly steering his new "laydee", through the crowd. Amy could swear she felt her hair lift slightly in the riptide generated by his voice. A leading light of the local Am Dram Society and RADA trained actor, he was used to projecting across full theatres. By all accounts, he'd once been very handsome, and had played Hamlet, Macbeth, Julius Caesar and Romeo. He also gave good leer, she thought, in distaste. Patrick and Jen were standing in the corridor.

'Great night,' Patrick was saying.

'Awesome,' agreed Jen.

'You look different.' Patrick lifted a hank of her hair and twisted it round his fingers, and Amy saw Jen's face light up in a smile.

'Careful, Jennifer, you're in danger of actually having a good time.'

His voice was soft. Amy began to sidle away, feeling that she was intruding.

'Hey, Paddy.' Evie Martin had appeared out of the cupboard being used as a dressing room, and seemed to have no such reservations. She gazed up at Patrick through her eyelashes, her sensuality somewhat laboured, and with the knowingness of an older woman. She really was gorgeous, Amy admitted: long limbed, dewy skinned, with huge brown eyes and hair so long and thick that she didn't really need a jacket. So much time spent outdoors had sprinkled her nose with freckles and this small imperfection served to make her look even more attractive.

'Hi, Evie.' Patrick turned to her. 'You were brilliant tonight.'

'Thanks, Paddy,' Evie said, favouring him with another luscious smile.

'Let's go for a drink,' suggested Patrick.

'I'll catch you up in a bit,' Amy said, watching them all leave in some relief.

Of course, there was no stage door at the village hall. Amy made her way down the narrow corridor and slipped into the small, chilly bathroom. There was a tatty, bleach-stained brown towel and the knitted toilet roll cover which had been there ever since she could remember. She washed her sweaty hands yet again on a piece of cracked pink soap and sprayed on more perfume – Angel, which she used to wear when she and Lewis were together. She hoped the smell of it on her skin would bring back happy memories. She gripped the wash-hand basin as she regarded her face in the mirror: she felt quite queasy. She'd spent most of the afternoon working on her casual, not-trying-too-hard look: lightly tanned skin, clear lipgloss, a touch of brown mascara. Her hair was carefully arranged into a messy side ponytail, curled tendrils framing her face. Her jeans were old and faded, but showcased her flat stomach and long legs, her ancient blue tee-shirt deepened the colour of her eyes and hugged her waist. Her boots had a modest heel, but added a couple of inches to her height. Taking a deep breath, she pushed open the door, squeezed round it, and carried on towards the dressing room.

Lewis' head was bent as he zipped up his guitar case, his wavy hair falling forward.

'Lewis?' Amy's heart was racing so fast that she thought she might pass out.

'What?' He sounded distracted, but then glanced up, his face breaking into a smile. Amy's nerves vanished, to be replaced by an intoxicating feeling of rightness.

'Hey, Amy,' he said. 'Come in.'

Then she was standing before him.

'It's been a great night,' she told him. 'You were fantastic.'

'Thank you,' Lewis said simply, adept at accepting a compliment. 'I'm still buzzing. It's the best feeling, being up on stage performing and watching everyone having a good time.' His deep blue eyes were fixed on her. She hadn't forgotten the way he had of making her feel desired, intensely female and wildly sexy – she hadn't forgotten anything.

'Lewis.' A voice floated down the corridor. 'Haven't you got a home to go to?' It was the caretaker.

'We're just leaving, Frank.'

They went outside. It was quiet, but for the ever-present sound of the surf and a faraway babble of conversation, carried on the soft breeze, from the tables outside the Claymore Inn. The sun was setting, an orange ball sliding down the indigo sky and setting the sea on fire.

'The others are all in the pub. D'you want to go?'

'No.' Lewis looked at her, his eyes searching her face.

They sat down on the seawall. He was still gorgeous to look at, even more so, his face more lived-in, with more character. He still smoked and, in his hands, it was an art form. He'd taught Amy to smoke, too, but she'd given it up, with great difficulty, when she'd met Stuart. Lewis had corrupted her, teaching her about love and sex, and she'd been more than happy for it to be that way.

'So,' Lewis said. 'We always said we'd never come back to the village –'

Amy nodded, smiling, strings of memory tugging. They'd both been desperate to leave, desperate for the bright lights, the freedom of the city. They'd sit on this very same wall and talk about their dreams for the future, and those had always involved their being together.

'So, are you back for good?' They spoke in unison, then stopped and laughed, their eyes locking.

'Are you?' Lewis asked, gently, blowing smoke into the warm air.

Amy shrugged. 'For the foreseeable future.'

'How come?' Lewis was looking closely at her, his head slightly tilted to one side.

'The restaurant I managed in Edinburgh closed down. Wild Mountain Thyme in Broughton Street. I was renting the flat upstairs, so I had to move out of there, too.'

'Aw, wee shame.' Lewis began to stroke her bare upper arm with the ball of his thumb. Despite having shared a bed with Stuart for so long, it was the most sensual experience she'd had in years.

'I'd just split up with my boyfriend,' she added. It was important that he should know this. 'So there wasn't really anything to keep me there –'

'Why?' Lewis' voice was soft.

'He wasn't –' She just managed to stop herself from saying *He wasn't you*. '*We* weren't really going anywhere,' she amended. 'Then Jen offered me a job at the hotel.'

It was hard to concentrate: she couldn't stop looking at his mouth, remembering how it had felt on hers, what a perfect fit it had been. The leaving of Edinburgh now didn't seem such a tragedy. A memory ambushed her of slowly making love on his bed, on one of the rare occasions they had had the privacy to do so, the sound track their own special iPod playlist which they'd compiled together.

'Anyway, are *you* back for good?'

'Who knows? For a while, anyway.'

'Why did you leave?'

'Tensions in the band. Musical differences. I needed some space to write.'

Amy divined that this wasn't a favourite topic of conversation.

'Where were you staying?'

She'd wondered about this ever since she'd seen his band perform, her head full of questions about what he was doing now and with whom.

'Bruntsfield Place.'

'Nice.'

'It was excellent. There was a bookshop, an off licence downstairs and a chippy across the road.'

'What more could a boy want?'

Their eyes met again in a searching look.

'Come on,' Lewis said. 'I'll walk you home.'

Standing up, he took her hand and helped her to her feet. They walked slowly along the coast road towards the hotel, talking quietly as they had done so many times before. They were still holding hands and it felt natural.

'We should totally get together for a proper catch-up,' Lewis said, as they reached the imposing gates at the end of the hotel's drive.

Belatedly remembering Jen's advice, Amy managed not to blurt out *What about tomorrow?* 'Thursday's my night off.' She kept her voice casual.

'Thursday,' Lewis said. 'Seven-thirty, the Claymore?'

Amy nodded. 'Good for me.'

Lewis kissed her.

When Amy floated, radiant, into the flat much later, Brooke and Jen were sitting on the sofa in their dressing gowns, drinking hot chocolate. They both turned to her, their blue eyes accusing.

'Amy, you didn't. Tell me you didn't,' Jen pleaded.

'Of course I didn't. We just kissed.'

But what a kiss it had been, deep, sweet, teasing, full of promise, her back against the rough stone, her hands twisted into his hair. She could hear the swish of the tide, smell wild flowers on the night air, Lewis' aftershave, faded by then, and the unforgotten scent of his skin.

'What part of "play it cool" didn't you get?'

'Shut up, Jen. She's in love, can't you see?'

Amy drifted off into her bedroom, looking at her reflection in the mirror: her tousled hair, her flushed cheeks, her sparkling eyes.

On Thursday night, Amy and Lewis lasted for one drink each at the Claymore, before jumping up and hurrying down the coast road to his flat. On the landing, he began to kiss her, then they stumbled through the door and into the flat itself. Amy had the impression of jewel coloured rooms as he led her to his bedroom. It was dazzling white inside, like a bright, snowy winter's day. Lewis' long fingers deftly unbuttoned her dress. She shrugged it from her shoulders and it slid to the floor. Moments later, she was lying on the white duvet, while Lewis parted her legs with his knee. Jen was full of rules about dating, which, as far as Amy could see, could be summed up as *Treat Him Mean to Keep Him Keen*. Those included how long you should make a man wait before going to bed with him – but surely they didn't apply to the man she'd been in love with for the best part of a decade? It was far from their first date. She forgot about Jen, however, as Lewis began kissing her again, this time more urgently.

Much later, she lay on her back, gazing up at the white ceiling. She felt as if she was floating, completely blissed out. She'd remembered everything about him – his smell, his taste, the pattern of freckles and moles on his skin. He'd remembered that she liked to be kissed all over, that any part of her back was an erogenous zone. She moved closer to him, her head on his shoulder, thinking, contentedly, that in Lewis' hands, everywhere was an erogenous zone.

Even losing her virginity had been wonderful. Lewis had been so gentle and patient. Her initial shyness and anxiety had given way to ecstasy. Being curled up with him, naked, had seemed so right. Whatever happened, nothing could take away that beautiful memory.

How could she have lasted so long without this kind of passion?

Their teenage sex had usually been hurried, risky, often outdoors, always thrilling, but now it was different – they had all the time and privacy in the world. The explosive chemistry between them was still there. Now that Lewis had his own flat, they could take all night, slowly explore each other's body, there was no fear that anyone would burst into the room, no need to clap his hand over her mouth to stop her from crying out. The flat next door was a holiday let, currently unoccupied.

'That was amazing,' she said.

'Really?' Lewis leaned on his elbow and looked into her face, his eyes teasing – he couldn't fail to have been aware of her ecstatic response. Then he moved, so that he was lying on top of her, and she felt deliciously crushed.

'Ames?'

'Mmm?'

'Why did we ever split up?'

Amy considered this. 'We didn't,' she said. 'We were just on a break.'

Lewis laughed and began to kiss her again.

*

The next day was Amy's day off and she didn't return to the hotel until mid-morning, drifting slowly into the grounds, pausing several times to smell the flowers. Brooke, on one of her many breaks, was sitting at the table in the small courtyard outside the kitchen, sipping coffee.

'You're a dirty stop-out, Ames,' she said fondly.

Amy pulled out a chair and sat beside her sister, unable to stop smiling. 'It was so amazing, Brooke.'

It wasn't just the sex: in between they'd lain skin against skin, gazed into each other's eyes, clasped hands. He'd played with her hair and stroked her back and held her close. He'd kissed her, long and deep, after they'd made love as well as before. They'd leaned back on the padded headboard in the half light, talking and laughing softly, sharing memories. When they'd finally fallen asleep, she'd been wrapped in his arms, and still was when she woke up.

'Just... be careful.' Brooke looked seriously at her.

'I'm always careful.'

'I didn't mean it like that. I meant...well, it's early days.'

'Hardly.' Amy was annoyed with her sister for refusing to share her buzz. 'Brooke, I've been in love with him for ten years. No matter who else I was seeing, I couldn't get him out of my mind.'

'I know, I know.' Brooke reached out and touched her arm, her face breaking into a wicked smile. 'I'm probably just jealous. I hate sleeping on my own; it makes me really crabby.'

Amy, looking at her reflection in the bathroom mirror, knew she had never looked so good – her eyes sparkled, there were roses in her cheeks and her skin glowed. Her newly washed hair was soft, scented and gleaming. Forget Botox, fake bakes and collagen – what a girl really needed was the desire of a man like Lewis. In a short, floaty floral chiffon dress, and coral coloured shoes, she felt beautiful and feminine.

Out in the hall, she nearly crashed into Brooke, who was trying to walk and read at the same time, but, instead of being annoyed at her sister's hopelessness, she just laughed.

'Oh, sorry,' Brooke said. 'Are you going out? You look fantastic.'

See? Brooke had noticed it, too.

As she walked along the front towards the Claymore Inn, even the teenagers mooching around by the bus shelter looked on appreciatively.

It was quiz night and the pub was busy. She spotted Gregor and his hairdresser colleagues and four of the Fratelli brothers laughing and chatting in an alcove. There was no sign of Lewis, so she bought herself a drink. As she hovered, looking around for a free seat, Misty raised her hand.

'Over here, Amy.'

She wove through the tables and took a seat beside Misty and Duncan. Also sitting with them was Callum. He raised his glass to her in silent toast. They'd all been at Auchenstoorie High together.

'Hi, Ames, on your own?' Misty asked.

Amy shook her head. 'I'm meeting Lewis.' She couldn't help smiling, even just speaking his name. 'Did you know we'd got back together?'

'Amy –' began Misty, but then was interrupted by a screech of feedback.

'Welcome to the Claymore Pub Quiz. The prize money is now standing at £75,' boomed Murdo, publican and quiz master, through the microphone.

'Round One, Question One: Music. Of which band is Fyfe Dangerfield the lead singer?'

'The Guillemots,' hissed Callum. Like most men Amy knew, his head was a mine of trivia, much of it pertaining to music.

Lewis was late, but, often, if he'd become deeply involved in a composition, he'd forget the time, or want to get the chords down on paper before they went out of his mind. Or maybe he had become carried away, working on lyrics, which he always said were just as important to him as melody.

'What links Liverpudlian lasses Thelma Pickles and Maureen Cox?' Murdo was asking.

'They dated two Beatles each,' said Amy and Callum simultaneously, and high-fived each other. She was enjoying herself, relaxed and comfortable with her old school friends and a glass of red wine.

'Hi,' said a soft voice at her side. Lewis had pulled up a chair. 'Sorry I'm late.'

His eyes, deep and blue, were close to hers. She breathed in the smell of him, took in his long lashes, his curving mouth.

'It's all right,' she murmured.

Lewis took her hand under the table.

Chapter 8
Write On

Brooke rose early on the first day of the creative writing course. She'd been blue ever since the incident with Hugh McMichael, but now she felt a spark of excitement about the day ahead, her spirits rising and his spectre receding somewhat. As she soaped her limbs under the shower, she wondered if, in the next few weeks, she and Niamh would discover a new Jenni Fagan or Chris McQueer.

Much later, they sat on the "rustic" bench (B&Q's finest) outside Marmion, the chalet allocated to the creative writing classes. Brooke sipped her coffee, enjoying a light breeze which ruffled her hair and gave some relief from the heat of the sun. On days like this, she felt that she truly loved this part of the country and belonged here: the fields rippled, sun dappled the mountains, the loch was deepest blue, sheep bleated. Niamh was gazing broodingly into the distance.

'Are you nervous?' Brooke asked. The students were due within the hour.

Niamh shrugged. 'Ah, no, I'll be grand.' She lapsed into silence again.

Brooke certainly felt that they knew the students already – they'd all submitted examples of their work and included: an intellectual feminist, a romantic novelist, a woman who wrote raunchy bonkbusters, a sci-fi writer, a crime writer, a girl who wrote chick-lit and another who wrote sensitive, contemporary women's fiction and a young man who was writing a series of gritty dramas set in a Glasgow scheme. Over the next few weeks, they would pretty much have most genres covered. She and Niamh had become ever closer, confiding in each other over several late night conversations as well as working together.

'Beautiful day,' Niamh said, at length.

'Yeah, we can have the barbecue after all,' said Brooke. This had long been planned as a party to welcome the students, but, this being Scotland, it had seemed unlikely that it would ever take place. Of course,

Jen had formulated a fall-back plan – but this was much better.

Niamh was looking in good shape today. After cracking her writers' block, she'd told Brooke that she was inspired, and that she'd spent several days and nights in a feverish writing frenzy, barely stopping to eat, drink and bathe as the words seemingly poured out of her. She'd looked elated but shattered, her eyes bruised with exhaustion. Now she'd had some sleep, however, she looked beautiful, with her alabaster skin, pale blue eyes and long black hair flowing over her shoulders from below a wide-brimmed hat. Niamh didn't do suntans. Brooke had always admired this kind of beauty in other women – cool, dark, sultry – almost as much as she admired Niamh's voice which was husky and as rich, sweet and dark as treacle.

Just then, a car drew up beside them, leaving tyre marks on the grassy slope. A young woman jumped out and marched confidently towards them, her hand held out to shake.

'Carolyn Masterson.'

This, thought Brooke, as the woman took her hand in a firm grasp, was the Glasgow solicitor who wrote the worthy, intelligent, feminist novels. She had a strong, clever face, framed by a sharp, dark bob which was pushed back from her forehead by a pair of Gucci sunglasses. She wore a simple pair of what looked to be diamond earrings. Despite the heat of the day, she had on well-cut navy trousers and a cream silk shirt, although she had taken off her jacket in concession to the high summer.

'Howya,' Niamh was saying. 'I'm Niamh Malahide and this is Brooke Grant.'

'Pleased to meet you,' said Carolyn. If she was impressed by Niamh's literary fame, she gave no sign. 'Sorry I'm a little early,' she added. 'Rather over-estimated how long it would take to drive up here.'

'No worries. Let's go inside, and we'll show you round.'

Besides the bedrooms, there was a large kitchen with, in the middle, a round table of scrubbed pine and a living room with a huge L-shaped sofa. Both those areas would be used for reading, critiques, one-to-one meetings with Niamh, and writing exercises.

As soon as Carolyn had been shown round and was sitting at the kitchen table sipping iced water, Brooke heard another car screech to a halt, followed by the sound of slamming doors. She hurried outside.

The woman who had emerged, or exploded, from the car – a shocking pink Beetle – had shocking pink hair and wore vintage shades with heart shaped frames. Her lips were a scarlet slash. Her dress was in an extravagantly rose patterned fifties' style, with a sweetheart neckline and a huge, circular skirt, frothing with deep pink petticoats. High heeled purple sandals, a purple dolly necklace and a handbag like a tea cosy with handles completed the outfit. Tall and slightly plump, she was as subtle as Times Square at New Year. Brooke bet her life savings – £24.80 – that this was Pearl White, tabloid journalist and aspiring chick-lit writer.

'Hiya, I'm Pearl.' The woman advanced towards Brooke.

'Brooke.'

As they shook hands, Brooke was aware of a thumping sound. Another woman was approaching, dragging behind her a suitcase on wheels. With her left arm, she was clutching a Tupperware box to her flowered chest. 'Hello, dear,' she began. 'Have I come to the right place for the creative writing retreat?'

'You certainly have,' Brooke said. What a lovely woman: everyone's ideal granny. She must be over seventy, with thick, snow white hair. She wore a floral summer dress and had a lilac coloured cardigan – handknitted by herself, Brooke was certain, draped around her bony shoulders. Close up, she smelled of faded Tweed perfume, home-baking, and freshly ironed cotton.

'Brooke and Pearl,' Brooke said.

'Lily McVey,' said the woman.

Within the next half hour, most of the rest of the students had turned up and were sitting around the kitchen table, drinking tea and eating scones which Lily had brought with her.

'I'll take the register. I think there's someone missing,' Brooke said, picking up her clipboard. She marked off Carolyn, Lily and Pearl, then began to read.

'Alan Govan.'

'Here.'

Alan Govan was a young man in black jeans and – he must be sweltering – a leather jacket. Brooke remembered he was the extremely talented writer of grim, gritty short stories set on a council scheme in Glasgow, which were laced in equal parts with horror and black humour. A purist, fiercely proud of his working class roots, rabidly socialist, vegetarian and a lover of James Kelman, she imagined.

'Bruce Paxton.'

'Yes.' Bruce Paxton, who was writing an adventure story about pirates for young adults, was a nerdy looking man wearing glasses and an anorak.

'Clare Loveheart.'

'Yes.' The speaker was a balding, middle-aged Yorkshireman in a tank top. He had gentle, chocolate brown eyes which peered out from behind thick glasses.

'That's me pen-name, like,' he explained. 'Me real name's Keith Grimshaw.'

Okaaaay. The romantic novelist.

If Clare Loveheart wasn't quite what she'd been expecting, Colin McCulloch, the sci-fi writer, absolutely was, in M&S jeans and a Microsoft tee-shirt. His dark eyes sparkled with intelligence.

Brooke was just looking at her watch and wondering if they should wait for the latecomer or just head off for the barbecue when a slim, pink-faced girl burst into the room.

'Lanie Scott?' Brooke asked.

The girl nodded, her face growing pinker. 'Sorry I'm late. I got a bit, kind of, lost.'

'Don't worry about it,' Brooke said, sensing a kindred spirit.

Brooke followed Niamh as she led the way up to the rose garden, where the barbecue was being held. It looked beautiful in summer. The gardener had trained some yellow roses over an arched trellis, and some pale pink ones up the side wall. In the centre was a square, slabbed area laid out with tables and chairs where guests could have a meal or a drink al fresco. This was surrounded by rose beds. There was also a paved border all the way round the outside, on which benches were set out. Two of those had been moved today to accommodate the barbecue. As she followed Niamh through the arch, Brooke could see Patrick, who never, but never, cooked, happily turning burgers, steaks, sausages and kebabs over the flames. Although he was wearing surfer shorts and an apron, he still managed to look ridiculously sexy. Beside him was Jason, who was buttering burger buns and rolls.

Jen was presiding over the table bearing the plates, cutlery and napkins. As always, she looked immaculate. Unlike everyone else, she was cool and unflushed, and her make-up hadn't run in the heat – it wouldn't dream of it. Why did she keep insisting she wasn't sweet on Patrick, Brooke wondered, as her sister's eyes yet again rested fondly on him.

Amy had brought out bowls of delicious looking salads: potato salad garnished with parsley, pasta salads, beetroot salad, three-bean salad and colourful fruit salads. She was ripping the clingfilm covering off those, hampered by the fact that Lewis, standing behind her, had his arms round her waist and was kissing the back of her neck and her bare shoulders. She looked transported, her hair tousled and her make-up sticky. Amy was totally in thrall to her undeniably attractive boyfriend. With a spark of fear, Brooke caught Jen's eye, and, once again, pushed out of her mind the hot, sultry Glasgow night and her own brief dalliance with him.

After they'd been served, everyone sat down at a long table, chatting, munching and swigging ice cold drinks. Brooke found herself in conversation with Pearl White, who was a scream, full of scurrilous gossip about the Scottish celebrity world. Carolyn had made a bee-line for Jen and the two women seemed to be competing with each other as to who worked the longer hours and who was under more pressure, before moving on to a discussion about the last series of *The Apprentice*.

'Jaden McGaughey got married here, didn't he?' Pearl's voice was studiedly casual, obviously hoping for a story.

'They got married at Bannockside Castle,' Jen said. 'Great venue, if you're planning a wedding in the near future.' Jen never missed an opportunity to get in some PR.

'Who is this man?' asked Carolyn.

'Rangers' striker. Drop dead gorgeous and the most gifted Rangers' player since Ally McCoist,' explained Pearl.

Jaden carried on the proud tradition of such as George Best, Ryan Giggs and Wayne Rooney, men who played as hard as they played.

'Never heard of him,' said Carolyn.

'Wonder how long it'll last?' Pearl mused. 'The *Red Top's* running another kiss and tell exposé at the weekend. Couple more girls he slept with – both at the same time – have come forward.'

'And been paid well for it,' Patrick observed.

'Tiara'll stand by him. She loves him,' Brooke said.

'And the lifestyle,' said Bruce Paxton. 'She wouldn't be able to buy designer clothes, eat in the best restaurants, travel and stay in five star hotels without him. She'd still be living on a council scheme. Those girls know what they're getting into but they'll turn a blind eye for the money. It's a trade-off.'

Despite his nerdy appearance, Brooke felt that he had a sharp, unpleasant side to him. 'Not in this case,' she cut in. 'He and Tiara met at school. They've been going out since they were fourteen. Long before he was rich and famous.'

'It's dreadful,' Carolyn said. 'I can't believe that, in this day and age, it's again become acceptable to aspire to marry well. I'd rather make my own money.'

'I'd never marry for money, I'd only marry for love,' Lanie Scott agreed. Brooke smiled at her.

Inevitably, the conversation turned to books.

'I loved *Epiphany*, by Barbara Worth,' Carolyn said, referring to the worthy epic and Orange Prize winner.

'Marvellous book,' said Brooke.

'I preferred *Handbags and Heartache* by Paige Turner. Cracking read,' Pearl said.

'I don't think I know her,' sniffed Carolyn.

'She's only the bestselling author of the year so far,' said Pearl. 'Chick Fic at its finest.'

'Nothing I'd be interested in, I'm sure.'

'You're dismissing her because she's popular? How patronising is that?'

Brooke's heart was racing – she hated conflict and dreaded that the two women were going to have a full-scale row. It was obvious that they were both strong personalities and as opinionated as each other.

'I met Lee Perks at the Edinburgh Book Festival last year. Great bloke,' cut in Keith/Clare, referring to the cockney music journalist and publishing lad-lit phenomenon. His last title, *I Don't Fancy Yours*

Much, had sold more than a million and a half copies. His new book, *Get Your Coat, Love, You've Pulled,* just out this month, was expected to do equally well. Brooke threw Keith a grateful smile for keeping the peace – for now at least.

Brooke was thoroughly enjoying helping Niamh with the creative writing classes – it beat cleaning toilets and waitressing all hands down. She felt much happier – diverted from her worries about Lewis and how much she missed James. The students ranged in age from 24 to 74 and came from all walks of life, the writing varying from Pearl's glitzy, racy chick-lit, to Keith's bodice rippers, to Carolyn's legal thriller, to Colin's fantastical tales, to Alan's gritty, hard-hitting short stories. She had no problem getting up early now, to set out for the chalet and the first class of the day.

As she pushed open the door, a delicious smell drifted out. In the kitchen, Lily was placing a tray of flapjacks on the table to cool, beside a Victoria sponge cake. She must have been up for hours. She straightened up, a striped apron on over her floral dress.

'Lily, you don't have to do this,' Brooke exclaimed.

'Yes, I do,' said the older woman. A wistful look crossed her face, but only for a moment. 'This is the first time I've looked forward to anything, or enjoyed anything, since my husband died.'

'When was that?'

'A year ago but sometimes it feels like just a week.' A look of great sadness crossed Lily's face. Terribly moved, Brooke put her arms round her narrow shoulders. She might have been having a tough time lately, but it was nothing to what poor Lily had been going through. 'Let's go in,' Lily said, after a moment. 'I'm on this morning. And I want to check my Facebook first, to see if my granddaughters have PM'd me.'

Each morning, two of the students had their work subjected to an in-depth critique. Everyone took their places on deep sofas in the living room, as Alan kicked off:

> *'... the close bloomed with damp and graffiti. The door hung from one hinge, damaged in a fracas some weeks ago, but never repaired. Outside, the sky was like a bad mood. On a lamp post, a symbol to show*

> *a dealer was holding. Johnny walked past the boarded-up tenements, the knife cold in his hand…'*

Alan was a writer of tremendous power and passion, Brooke thought, and Lanie Scott, gazing at him with her cheeks slightly rosy and her lips parted, obviously had a passion for him. Brooke again felt an affinity with the girl. Assisted by pots of Earl Grey tea, flapjacks and Victoria sponge, the group spent an intense couple of hours analysing his work, then it was Lily's turn. Her novel called to mind the blockbusters of the 1980s: the novels of Barbara Taylor Bradford, Jilly Cooper or Judith Kranz, wonderfully incongruous from a Fort William housewife. Brooke was enthralled by it.

> *'…Reaching the bottom of the sweeping, gilded staircase, her scarlet Rifat Ozbec ballgown floating around her shapely ankles, her titian hair gleaming like copper in the light of the chandelier, Flame came face to cruel, green eyed, chiselled, jaw clangingly handsome face with Oliver Knight, tall, lean and impeccably dressed in black Armani. This was her tormentor – the man who had bought the agency, taken her job, humiliated her beyond words. The man she hated with a passion. The man who was so achingly sexy that her nipples shot up like rockets and every inch of her scented body was an erogenous zone. She thought she'd explode into flames at his nearness. The man who, five minutes later, was throwing her onto the bed in his luxurious suite, and ripping off $3,500 worth of couture. The man she loved with a passion…'*

'This is brilliant,' exclaimed Pearl, when Lily had finished reading.

'Is it really possible to have sex on an ironing board?' Niamh asked, looking perplexed.

'Oh, yes, dear,' confirmed Lily.

After Lily's work had been dissected, it was lunch time. Niamh's mobile phone rang just then and she nipped outside, as everyone sat down to bread, cheeses, meats, olives and hummus, which Amy had delivered earlier. She returned a few minutes later, her face glowing.

'That was my agent,' she said. 'I've been nominated for an award for those scripts I wrote for *Temple Bar*. I've to go to this big bash in Dublin.'

'Genius.' Brooke stood up to embrace her friend, as everyone else spontaneously began clapping.

Chapter 9
Aspects of Love

ROMANCE: with aspects to Saturn, you will feel closer to your partner than ever. Lucky in love, a romantic encounter is heading your way.

LIFE: You'll be bursting with creativity and desperate to pursue a new project. Capitalise on Venus' alignment with Mars to crush any negative feelings. Positivity is your greatest ally.

Lucky day: Wednesday　　　　　*Lucky number: seven*

It was not her own horoscope that Amy was reading, but Lewis'. Of course, complex and captivating, he had to be Pisces, that most emotional, artistic, creative and sensitive of signs. Amy was Scorpio, another water sign, which meant that they were totally compatible.

'What're you reading?' Jen glanced over her shoulder on her way to the kitchen for a coffee. 'Horoscopes?' Her tone was mocking.

'Okay, I know you don't believe in them.'

'Of course I don't. We Virgos are very practical.'

Actually, Amy didn't set too much store by the horoscopes in the *Kirklochy News* either. It was a little known fact that her friend Euan Buchanan, staff writer, editor, sub-editor, web engineer and star photographer, was also "Madame Zara", and cribbed them from the internet. Occasionally, he would make up a particularly scary prediction for any villager who had seriously annoyed him.

'But, Euan,' Amy had protested, when he had confessed to this, 'that means a twelfth of your readers now think they're about to go bankrupt, get divorced, be betrayed by a friend, lose six sheep, and be run over by a tractor. That's eight people whose week you've totally ruined.'

'Ooh, never thought of that,' Euan had admitted.

An even less well known fact was that, hiding behind the pseudonym

Sarah Michelle Cox, Euan also covered women's issues, although Amy acknowledged that he'd made a pretty good fist of writing about this season's handbags today. Not long ago, when there wasn't much happening in the village, he'd even tried to introduce an agony column, *Ask Annie*, under yet another alias, but had had no interest – because everyone knew everyone else, the locals were too embarrassed to share their marital, adolescent, sexual or professional problems. To save face, Euan had had to make those up anonymously, triggering much intrigue and speculation, rumour and counter-rumour, among his readership, especially Mrs Crombie and her gossipy cronies.

A romantic encounter is heading your way.

Amy smiled to herself: that was one of Madame Zara's predictions which would definitely come true. Today, Wednesday, was *so* going to be Lewis' lucky day.

For Amy, one of the greatest pleasures – as Callum had predicted – of being back in Kirklochy was spending time with her old friends. She, Misty, Euan, Heather, Duncan, Callum and, of course, Lewis, often met up, sometimes at the Claymore Inn for Quiz Night, other times to sit in their favourite alcove chatting easily over pints of Old Sheepshagger. On warm, dry nights, they would walk along the cliff path to Hermit's Point, taking in the breathtaking scenery, or picnic on Jamie's Cove, the quiet, sheltered strip of beach they considered their own. Sometimes, it would just be herself and Misty, sitting for hours in Caffe Fratelli sipping vanilla lattes, or having a manicure at the salon, sometimes it would be just herself and Euan, working together for the *News*, as he'd asked her to write a weekly cookery column, and often it would be herself and Callum, out walking and talking. Of course, she and Stuart had had good friends in Edinburgh, but there was nothing like the friends she'd had forever, who totally knew and accepted her. She could throw on her oldest, most comfortable jeans, her Uggs and sou'wester, pull on a beanie hat, go out wearing not a scrap of make-up, and they'd all talk about anything that came into their heads.

Later, she pulled on her hot, red skinny jeans. She seemed to have lost a few pounds – cooking so many fry-ups every morning would do that to you – and they fitted perfectly, clinging to her hips, showing off her flat stomach. She teamed them with a grey vest top and warm hoodie as protection against the brisk westerly wind. She didn't bother with make-up other than red lipstick – she was glowing with good health and happiness.

The sea breeze whipped her newly washed hair into disarray as she made her way to the flat Lewis was renting above the outdoors shop.

Since she and Lewis had got back together, her life had been totally cinematic. Everything seemed bigger, brighter, more sparkly, more significant. She was tired but alert. She'd walk down the hill from the hotel and along the front, sometimes in the sun but often in the spray of the waves as they crashed onto the beach. On such days his flat was a cosy cocoon and they'd stand at the window, his arms round her, and watch the waves leaping over the seawall to splash on the pavement. They'd sit on the sofa, he noodling on his guitar, and write songs together. Sometimes, he'd play her melodies he'd written for her. She'd been horrified by his diet and had begun teaching him to cook. Barely numerate and hopelessly impractical, he excelled at being creative and he'd learned quickly. They'd spent many happy hours experimenting: chopping. slicing, dicing and frying, the air heavy with the aromas of tomato and garlic, while music blared in the background. They'd eat their sweet, sticky desserts in bed. They'd have baths together by candlelight. They'd lie beneath his duvet, her back against his chest, her buttocks against his stomach, her legs hooked over his, as the rain rattled down on the skylight window, their voices lazy in the darkness. They'd make love for hours on his big sleigh bed, the sofa or the floor, always accompanied by their very own playlist.

Lewis' flat was beautiful. The living room, dominated by a huge purple velvet sofa strewn with silk cushions, was done out in deep pink, turquoise and gold, the colours of Morocco, more character coming from a scattering of North African artefacts. The kitchen, in deep saffron, had pots of herbs along the window sill, several well used copper pans and cookery books of Mediterranean, Thai and Caribbean cuisine. The bedroom was painted completely in white, both walls and floorboards, the duvet cover ivory, the only splash of colour coming from an abstract painting above the bed.

This had nothing to do with Lewis personally, but was due to the fact that the flat belonged to Valissa Lavender. Valissagate was the biggest scandal since the Profumo Affair: at Easter, the flamboyant queen of the Am Dram Society had eloped with Struan Lorimer, twenty-two years her junior. Mrs Crombie and her busybody entourage must have had a field day. Opening the door off the promenade, Amy smiled at the thought of Valissa, with her fondness for purple, who dressed as if she were about to receive an Academy Award even when taking out her bins. Her mouth was dry with excitement as she hurried upstairs.

'Hi.' Lewis greeted her knock, stooping to kiss her cheek. As always, a wave of longing swept over her as she breathed in the familiar scent of his skin, his aftershave and the smell of clean, raw sweat.

Lewis had added nothing to the decoration of the flat except stained coffee cups, dirty ashtrays and pieces of paper, some of them scrumpled up, with snatches of lyrics and chords written on them.

The other unwelcome addition to the room was Evie Martin, who was sitting on the sofa. She wore a dark blue dress with delicate straps and sprinkled with tiny white flowers, which echoed the freckles scattered over her shoulders. A silver heart-shaped pendant nestled in the hollow of her throat. She had the sheen of extreme youth, and her long, tawny hair was held back by two simple plaits. Her pretty feet were bare, the nails painted crimson. She smiled a secretive, cat-like smile.

'Evie and I've been working on a new song,' Lewis said, by way of explanation. 'Do you want to hear it?'

Amy nodded, still jolted by Evie's unexpected presence in the room. She sank into an armchair.

Evie and Lewis took up their guitars and began to strum, their voices harmonising in a delicate melody about love and loss. The sharing of their gift for music made Lewis and Evie seem so intimate, all of a sudden, their voices, Evie's both gravelly and sweet, blended so beautifully, the lyrics were so poignant.

'That's all we've got so far,' Lewis said, after just a couple of minutes.

'It was lovely,' Amy managed to say, badly wanting Evie to leave. There was something so compelling about her: young, beautiful, talented and confidently looking forward to a bright future. She combined the poise of a much older woman with the idealism and passion of youth, when everything seems possible.

'I should go, Lewis,' she said, slipping her feet into her Vans and pulling on a denim waistcoat. She stood up.

'Bye, Amy.' Evie turned to her. Was it her imagination, or did she read a challenge in that faint smile?

'Bye, Evie,' Amy said, in relief, beginning to relax somewhat.

Lewis saw Evie to the door and returned after a muttered conversation.

'Hi,' he said, softly, crossing the room and taking her in his arms. Amy closed her eyes, her head spinning with the intensity of his kisses.

'I read your horoscope this morning,' she said, when they finally came up for air. 'It said you're heading for a romantic encounter.'

'Really?' Lewis said. Amy shivered deliciously as he nibbled her ear, kissed her neck, pushed the strap of her top aside and bit her shoulder.

'Yeah,' she breathed. 'Today's your lucky day.'

'It certainly is,' Lewis said. Amy groaned as he slid his hand under her vest. 'Because we're both water signs, we're totally compatible,' she murmured, then let out a gasp.

'Maybe we should have sex in the shower,' Lewis suggested.

Amy giggled as he took her hand and led her to the bathroom.

She woke early next morning, to the sound of the window panes rattling. For a few moments, she luxuriated in the warm comfort of Lewis' bed, thinking how good it would be if they could stay here, just the two of them, shutting out the cares of the cold, stormy day. Lewis was lying on his side, clutching the pillow. She watched him sleep, his skin golden against the white of the sheets, his dark hair tousled. She felt carefree and relaxed, as if the overly scented, minxy spectre of Evie Martin had left the building, the door firmly closed and locked behind her. Surely Lewis' kisses would not have been so ardent or his love making so passionate if he harboured feelings for the girl?

Carefully, she eased herself out of the bed, trying not to wake him, slipped his dressing gown around her and tiptoed into the kitchen. There was nothing in the fridge apart from beer so she made a cup of instant coffee and sat at the table.

'What time is it?' Lewis was standing in the doorway, wearing only boxer shorts, his hair standing on end. He was too skinny, Amy reflected, despite her best efforts. He smoked too much and didn't eat enough. No doubt, a diet of nicotine, alcohol and caffeine fitted his musician's persona and enhanced his voice, giving it that raw, husky edge.

'Six.'

'Aaagh.' Lewis yawned widely. 'That's the middle of the night.'

'I know, but I'm on breakfast duty at seven.'

'Couldn't you just stay here? We could go back to bed.'

Amy drained the last of her coffee and smiled. 'Of course not; some of us have to work for a living.'

A shadow of annoyance passed over Lewis' face. 'I work,' he said. 'I work very hard. What do you think this is?' He gestured through the open door into the living room, at the guitar and the sheets of paper garlanded with musical notes spread across the sofa.

''Course you do, babe,' Amy said, crossing the room and kissing him on the mouth. Lewis wasn't really suited to the working world, she remembered. His uncle had once tried to enlist him into his electrician's business, but had had to sack him for the safety of the public. There were still a few houses in Kirklochy where, if you pressed the light switch in one room, the bulb would come on in another. It was just as well he was such a talented musician.

'Anyway, Jen would kill me if I was late.'

'Scary woman,' Lewis agreed.

Regretfully, Amy left and set out through the wind and rain to the hotel.

'Round 5 – General Knowledge. Question 1: Whereabouts on a horse would you find a frog?' Murdo boomed, over the microphone.

'The hoof,' whispered Callum. This was an easy-peasy question for a vet. Amy scribbled down the answer.

'Question 2: What is the link between novelists Margaret Drabble and A.S. Byatt?'

They're sisters, Amy wrote, surprising herself. Some of Brooke's knowledge seemed to have rubbed off on her. At last they'd got a couple of correct answers, but were still lagging way behind.

Beep. Beep. Beep.

Callum groped for his jacket and pulled his pager out of the pocket. 'Sorry, Amy, I've got to go. I'm on call.' He stood up.

'Can I come?' Amy asked, on impulse.

Callum shrugged on his jacket. 'Why not?'

They hurried out of the warm pub into the still light evening. A few minutes later, Amy was sitting beside him, high in the Land Rover, as he negotiated the narrow country lanes towards Galbraith's farm. He drove skilfully, fast yet cautious. He was always capable, calm, in control.

At the stables, Amy slid out of her seat and onto the soft ground. The pregnant horse was obviously in agony. She could hear desperate neighing and grunting. The poor animal's limbs were thrashing around as she heaved in pain.

Opening the back of the Land Rover, Callum slipped quickly into overalls and pulled on wellington boots. Amy looked down at her Uggs – the straw was sodden with blood and urine.

'Put these on.' Callum indicated a pair of purple Hunters, which she assumed belonged to Sheena, his girlfriend, also a vet. Gratefully, she stowed her own boots in the van and pulled on the wellingtons, following Callum, who'd grabbed his bag and was hurrying towards the farmer.

'I think the foal's twisted,' Farmer Galbraith shouted. Amy stood aside as Callum approached the mare, talking gently to her, stroking her muzzle, trying to calm her.

Pulling on a glove which covered his whole arm, she watched him, with great patience and concentration, right the position of the foal.

This was one of the strangest, but best, nights of her life, she thought, as she watched Callum, calm and efficient, deliver the foal, then clean it with a hank of straw. It was so adorable, with its big eyes, as it tried to stand on spindly legs. It was incredible to watch him, as gentle and caring as he was capable, to see him in a new light.

Callum seemed elated also. 'It never becomes routine, the creation of a new life,' he said.

'Would you and your girlfriend like to come in for a cup of tea?' Farmer Galbraith's wife was asking.

'Love to,' said Amy, suddenly realising she was ravenous. 'But I'm not his girlfriend. We're... just good friends.'

'Less of the "just".' Callum threw his arm around her shoulders, hugging her to his side.

'No, you're right,' Amy said. Suddenly, the moment was slightly charged. 'My friends are so important to me.'

'Good.' Callum ruffled her hair and they walked into the farmhouse, his arm still loosely round her. Soon they were sitting at a large, battered pine table in the kitchen, drinking strong tea and eating chunks of apple tart with thick, fresh cream.

'That was amazing,' she told him, much later, as they drove back into the village, listening to Ben Howard. Hastily, she sat up straight, her head having slipped onto his shoulder.

The next day, Amy was in the kitchen, chopping, frying, saute-ing and spicing. She had invited Lewis over for dinner and was determined it would be the best meal he had had all year. He was due at seven o'clock. Everything was on schedule as she checked the food, slipped into a silky little black dress, sprayed on *Allure*, put some music on low, and lit the scented candles. The usually shabby room looked completely different, bathed in flickering light.

She'd been looking forward to this, being alone with Lewis, all day, but, after half past seven had come and gone, then eight o'clock, she was possessed by a sick, panicky feeling. She tried his mobile, but it was switched off.

'Ooh, that smells gorgeous.' Jen had walked into the room. 'Isn't he here yet?'

Amy shook her head, turning slightly away so that her sister wouldn't see the glimmer of tears in her eyes.

'No. He must have got held up. You might as well have it.'

Jen sat down at the table, candlelight glinting off the crystal glasses, and Amy served the delicious food that she'd prepared with such care, but it was a struggle to force it down. Where was he? The fear that he would leave her assailed her again, and she just couldn't bear it. She watched miserably as Jen polished off the dessert, licking chocolate sauce from her spoon.

'Death by chocolate,' she mused. 'But I prefer something much more unpleasant –'

There was a knock at the door. Amy hurried into the hall. 'Where have you been?' she hissed. 'It's nearly ten o'clock.'

'Your dinner's in here.' Jen patted her washboard stomach and threw Lewis a look that would freeze nitrogen.

'I'm so sorry, Amy.' Ignoring the evils that Jen was throwing him, Lewis took a step towards her and held her hands in his. 'I was working on *Me Without You*. I fell asleep on the sofa. I've just woken up.'

Relief swept through Amy. *Me Without You* had a delicate, haunting melody, and was her favourite because they'd co-written the lyrics. He looked dishevelled, his wavy hair uncombed, stubble on his jawline. He bent down to kiss her, totally unfazed by Jen's malevolent presence.

Amy clung onto him, his stubble grazing her cheek, his hair soft against her face, breathing in his scent.

'I'm starving,' he said, when he finally broke off. 'I haven't eaten all day.'

'The kitchen's over there,' Jen said. 'Baked beans, tin opener.'

She threw Lewis a look that, by rights, should have turned him to stone, and stalked out of the room.

'Is she always that scary?'

'Yes,' said Amy. Taking his hand, she led him into the kitchen. Now they were alone, he kissed her again, deep, devouring, his hands running up and down her back. 'Hey, Ames?'

'Mmm?'

'What's the difference between Jenny and a Rottweiler?'

'I don't know.' She wriggled ecstatically as he began nibbling her earlobe, then kissed her shoulder.

'A Rottweiler doesn't wear lipstick.'

'Shut up,' said Amy, but she was laughing. Quickly, she knocked together a tomato pasta dish and sat opposite him in the candlelight, sipping wine.

'Can I stay the night?' he asked, much later.

'Of course.' Excitement coursed through Amy. Lewis had never spent the whole night in her bed before – only snatched hours here and there when the rest of the family had been out. Although they now barely spent a night apart, they always stayed at his flat.

'I like this,' he told her, touching the black satin rose on the bodice of her dress. His long fingers caressed the contours of her body through the thick, silky fabric. Her mouth was dry with desire.

'It's for Gregor and Robbie's party,' she gasped, as he located the zip under her left armpit and slowly pulled it down. 'Have you got something to wear?'

Lewis' look was grungy in the extreme, and, however much it suited him, it would never be right for Gregor's party. Everyone was looking forward to the rare opportunity to get dressed up. She leaned up and kissed the corner of his mouth. 'I'd love to see you looking glamorous, for once.'

He looked gorgeous in ripped jeans, faded old band tour tee-shirts and a battered leather jacket. She could only dream of how he would look in a suit and with a proper haircut.

'Oh. I…. Amy, I can't make the party.'

'What? Why not?'

'I've got a gig at Inveralan Arts Centre.'

'But… Gregor's one of our oldest friends. Everyone's going to be there.'

'I know and I'm sorry, but I can't turn work down.'

'But you've known about the party for ages. It's his wedding reception.'

'I'm not just doing it for me. I'm doing it for both of us, for our future.'

Amy was speechless for a moment. It was the first time Lewis had ever mentioned their having a future together. He put his arms round her, holding her close, rocking her slightly.

'I won't enjoy it without you,' she muttered, at last, into his shoulder.

''Course you will. Like you say, everyone's going to be there: Cal, Euan, Heather, Duncan, Misty –'

'I suppose.'

Lewis slid his hand inside her dress, stroking her hot skin. The trouble was, she couldn't stay angry with him for long because she always wanted him so badly. She was hurting deep down inside from her need of him. 'Let's go to bed.'

'I'm so going to make it up to you,' Lewis murmured, burying his face in her neck.

The next morning was warm and sunny, the rose garden looking its best with the velvety red blooms bathed in golden light. Several guests had decided to eat their breakfast *al fresco* and were lingering over it. Jen walked around, refilling coffee cups, the delicious aroma mingling with the scent of the roses. As she passed Niamh's room, she couldn't help noticing that she'd forgotten to close her curtains last night. She couldn't resist glancing in: the room was uncharacteristically neat, the coverlet of the bed as smooth as a game show host and still turned down at the corner with the gold wrapped Godiva chocolate perched in the middle. Jen's sunshiney good mood vanished and she felt chilled to her core: Niamh's bed hadn't been slept in.

A few hundred yards away, Brooke woke up and wished she was still asleep. A ray of sunshine stabbed into her eye. It was hard to say which part of her body was in the most pain: her queasy stomach, her sandpaper dry mouth which felt as if it had been re-upholstered in angora, her splitting head, or her aching throat. She didn't even know where she was. Slowly, she eased herself into a sitting position, resting her back against the padded headboard of the bed. She groped on the bedside table for her glasses and put them on. She was wearing only a pink vest, a black lace thong and an assortment of bracelets. Slowly, the events of the previous evening drip-fed into her consciousness: there had been a furious argument between Pearl White and Bruce Paxton. They'd never got on, and there had been a number of verbal skirmishes between them. Last night, their mutual dislike had come to a head – Pearl's vintage fifties' white gloves were well and truly off. She was on a short fuse at the best of times, but she'd also decided that her stress-free country break was the ideal time to give up smoking. Her arm was patched like an urchin's trousers and she'd had to have a nail replacement. Suffering from the double whammy of nicotine deprivation and PMT, she'd totally lost it. Bruce, in a cold fury, had vowed to catch the first train back to Glasgow, with a defiant Pearl offering to help him pack. There had been a slightly shell shocked evening meal, then everyone had gathered in the living room to finish off the wine. Brooke, Niamh and Lanie

Scott had gone outside to smoke and Niamh had slipped back to the hotel and fetched the duty free bag from her room and they'd caned a bottle of Jack Daniel's. They'd had an intense, putting-the-world-to-rights conversation, which had now been completely erased from her memory, and she'd decided that Niamh and Lanie were soulmates and the closest friends she'd ever had. She hadn't been that drunk since the all-night party that one of the students she supervised had thrown for his twenty-first birthday just before Christmas. The combination of Ciaran's birthday, Christmas spirit and post-exam relief had been an explosive one and she hadn't got home until lunch time the next day.

She and Niamh must have crashed in the room vacated by Bruce Paxton: she now recognised the magnolia walls and the leaf-patterned Ikea curtains and matching duvet cover.

'Hey.' Niamh pushed open the door with her hip. Wearing a Nike tee-shirt which Bruce must have left behind and which revealed her long, shapely legs in their entirety, she looked sexy in a tousled, slutty way, her hair wild and mascara smudged under her eyes. She carried a tray bearing Nurofen, two glasses of water and two mugs of black coffee. Placing this carefully on the bedside table, she rejoined Brooke on the bed and passed her a glass and two tablets.

'Thanks, babe,' Brooke managed to say, sluicing down the tablets with water and feeling very slightly better as it hit her parched throat.

She sipped her coffee slowly, waiting for the painkillers to take effect. Mercifully, it was her day off – the last thing she needed today was to spend the morning scrubbing out toilets.

'So, last night, did we… you know?' she managed to tease feebly.

'Hardly. You were dead to the world,' Niamh said.

'Thank goodness for that,' Brooke croaked, sipping her coffee. 'I've done some pretty mad stuff when I've been drunk.'

'Thanks, love,' Niamh said, her tone dry. 'Although I thought you liked a bit of girl-on-girl action.'

If Brooke hadn't already been corpse-white, she might have blanched. What had she been saying to Niamh and Lanie last night? She shook her head, wincing at the pain, so that her hair fell across her face, obscuring her expression somewhat.

'I do. I mean, I did. And it's not like you're not totally gorgeous, and

I'd like to… be with you, it's just that I'm seeing James now, so it isn't possible –'

Niamh put her hand over Brooke's. 'Babe, chill. I was only joking.'

'Oh.' Brooke looked down at their hands.

'Will we go back to sleep?' suggested Niamh, her voice gentle.

'Okay,' Brooke said meekly. Gratefully, she slid back down the bed.

Much later, feeling marginally better, Brooke pulled on her hotpants and sandals and walked back down to the hotel, slightly uplifted by the fresh air. Horrors! Lewis was walking in the opposite direction, out of the back gate, rail thin in his tight jeans and an old blue tee-shirt, his hair tousled and his face rough with stubble.

'Hey, Brooke,' he called, as she approached. As always, he was wearing headphones. Lewis was absolutely the last person she wanted to see. The only good thing about having a hangover was that it absorbed all her attention and took away from the awkwardness somewhat. She closed her eyes and leaned against the wall.

'Heavy night?' Lewis asked, sliding back his headphones.

'Mmm.' Brooke groaned. Suddenly, she had a flashback – Lewis kissing her, gently biting her neck, stroking her hair.

'I would like to talk to you,' she said, 'but I'm too knackered. I need to get back to bed. Soz.' She hurried past him.

She crept in by the back entrance and peered warily down the corridor. The coast was clear – go go go. She held her breath as she tip-toed past Jen's office. She really didn't feel equal to a sharp lecture from her young sister about lowering the tone of the hotel by wandering about in last night's – unsuitable – clothes, hungover to the teeth, wild haired and scuzzy eyed. She really was old enough to know better. It was with relief that she reached the flat without meeting any of the guests and pushed open the door. She showered, scrubbed her teeth, gargled with mouthwash, crawled into her bed, and slept for five hours.

Jen could hear voices and laughter from Amy's bedroom as she entered the flat. She pushed open the door. Inside was a happy, girlie scene. Amy was sitting on the bed, in skinnies and a faded old Libertines tee-shirt which belonged to Lewis, her hands curled round a large mug of tea.

Not a good look, Jen thought, but she guessed Amy liked to wear Lewis' clothes, as if it made her feel close to him even when they were apart. Brooke was curled up in an armchair under a fluffy throw, also cradling a mug of tea and delicately nibbling a Hobnob. Niamh was standing by the full-length mirror, wearing Amy's posh frock. Even though she had on Doc Martens and no make-up, she looked stunning. Jen had never seen her wear anything but black but the flame colour suited her to perfection. It was a beautiful dress, but Niamh really made it glow.

'You'll look amazing with make-up and the right accessories,' Amy was saying. She turned to Jen. 'Niamh's going to borrow my dress to wear at the awards ceremony.'

Jen had heard all about Niamh's awards ceremony. Niamh had even been schooled in what facial expression to wear for the camera should she not win (resignation combined with delight for the victor).

'It's perfect,' Brooke said.

Jen watched, rigid with envy, as Niamh carefully unzipped the dress and stepped out of it. What a figure! Her breasts, encased in a black lacy bra with a hole in it, were both full and firm, round and creamy. Her waist was tiny, her stomach flat and her legs seemed to go all the way up to her armpits. How could Patrick resist? And how could Jen ever compete?

Chapter 10
Do it Like a Prude

Gregor and Robbie were safely married. Jen had driven her friend to Inverness for the ceremony. It had been a beautiful day, and they'd spent the journey with the windows open, looking out at the sun-dappled countryside, catching up, and singing along to a disco playlist Gregor had put together specially for the occasion. Another card had been put through his door, this time with a floral cross on the front, but they were both in high spirits, relishing the feeling of freedom as Jen's car powered along, the wind in their hair.

'All right, Thelma?' Jen had asked.

'Awesome, Louise,' Gregor had answered.

They'd come out of the registry office still bathed in sunshine, walked along the banks of the Ness, and then adjourned to Robbie's favourite restaurant for a delicious meal and much chatting and laughter. She'd felt relaxed and happy – she hadn't realised how much stress she'd been under at the hotel for the last few months until she'd taken this break. She knew that the lodge was in safe hands with Patrick, but couldn't help wishing he was here with her to share in the day, and wondering what he and Niamh were getting up to in her absence. Again, she tried to push those thoughts firmly to the back of her mind.

She'd decided to throw a dinner party for Gregor and Robbie in lieu of a wedding reception, in keeping with their desire for stylish and sophisticated. Gregor was enamoured of Jane Russell, Lana Turner, Joan Crawford and Betty Grable, who, to him, epitomised a lost age of true glamour, so the theme was Hollywood – the Golden Era. She'd spent many rainy Saturday afternoons ensconced on his sofa with him, a box of Milk Tray, a pot of Earl Grey, plenty of paper hankies and a black and white matinée. The dress code for this evening was monochrome. She ran her hand down her dress's soft velvet bodice. Backless, floor-length and pewter grey, it was stunning. She also had long, silver-grey satin gloves which covered her elbows and a black wrap and shoes: glamorous enough even for Gregor's exacting standards, she hoped. All the girls were excited about the occasion and the rare opportunity to get dressed up to the nines – or even the tens, as Gregor would say.

In the flat, Brooke was sitting on the sofa wearing a dove grey silk petticoat and drinking peppermint tea while painting her nails with silver polish. She somehow managed to look gorgeous although she had her rollers in.

Jen made herself a coffee and wandered downstairs. The conservatory dining room was closed to the public for tonight and she wanted to have one last look. Once inside, she leaned against the wall, sipping. There were monochrome stills from Gregor and Robbie's favourite films all round the room. Silver helium balloons floated above the long table, and, later, Aura Wallace and Jason would have the job of lighting all the silver candles which stood the length of the table and along the window sills. She'd even rolled out the red carpet, knowing this would tickle Gregor.

She was passing through reception, on her way to put a vase of freshly cut white roses in the centre of the table when the main door opened and three women walked in – Mrs Crombie, the village battleaxe, flanked by her long-suffering sidekick, Muriel, and Martha Martin, Evie's mother. Carefully, Jen placed the vase on the desk. The trio marched towards her.

'What is this... pantomime in aid of?' Mrs Crombie demanded. 'The MacPherson boy?'

Jen met the older woman's cold, fishy eyes and smiled coolly. 'For Gregor and his new husband, yes. He's actually Gregor MacPherson-Forbes now.'

'I can't believe you'd condone this... travesty of a marriage, Jennifer Grant. And every decent and right-thinking person in the village agrees with me.'

Jen had been aware of an unpleasant undercurrent in the village, with a few people requesting that a stylist other than Greg cut their hair or sitting as far away from him as possible in the tearoom. At least she'd been able to have a drink with the boys in the Claymore Inn without fear, Mrs Crombie being staunchly tee-total. The Claymore was, to her, the equivalent of stairs to a dalek.

'Really?' Jen said, crisply. 'I'd like you to leave now.'

'Oh, we'll leave,' Mrs Crombie said. 'But we'll be standing right out-side the gates.'

Jen noticed then that each of the women held a pile of cards.

'It was you who put those cards through Gregor's door,' accused Jen. 'Well, it might please you to know that Gregor was extremely upset, and you've spoiled what should've been a very happy time for him and Robbie. And they're devoted to each other.'

'According to the Bible, homosexuality is a sin.' Mrs Crombie was unrepentant, her sour face puckering up with distaste, as if even speak-ing the word offended her. 'Don't you agree, Martha?'

'Of course, Mercy,' said Martha. How on earth had this drab, insipid little woman managed to give birth to the beautiful Evie, Jen wondered. No wonder the girl took every opportunity to rebel.

'It also says: "Let he who is without sin cast the first stone",' said Jen, the phrase popping into her head from the days of old Rev. Colquhoun – she could still hear his booming voice. 'And, what's more, it's my belief that Tom McIvor would've been happy to marry Greg and Robbie if you hadn't driven them out of the village. It's called Christianity. He would never turn anyone away from the church who genuinely wanted to be there.'

'It's not natural,' Mrs Crombie said, and she actually shuddered.

'In your opinion, which is purely subjective,' cried Jen. 'It's natural to Gregor. He and Robbie are in love. They're a lot happier together than half the couples in Kirklochy.' She fixed Martha Martin with a cold stare, holding her gaze until Martha dropped her eyes.

'I might have guessed you'd take that attitude, Jennifer Grant – going off to Glasgow and coming back all high and mighty and full of fancy ideas.'

Mrs Crombie often boasted that she had never been to Glasgow, which she believed to be the Gomorrah of the central belt.

'It's not that at all.' Jen felt slightly frantic. She wasn't getting any-where. She must get rid of the three women before Gregor, Robbie and their friends arrived – this was meant to be her wedding present, and she wanted everything to be perfect. Gregor had already suffered enough. Also, she couldn't afford an altercation in front of the hotel's guests, some of whom would soon be assembling in the drawing room for pre-dinner drinks. It was against everything the lodge stood for. She fell back on simple sincerity. 'Gregor's my friend and I want him to be happy.'

Mrs Crombie folded her arms and stuck out her chin. Jen nearly fainted with relief as she saw Patrick come out of the office and walk into the foyer. She tried to catch his eye, but he seemed to have gathered immediately what was going on, and, in an instant, was by her side.

'Sure, but you're a handsome woman, Mrs Crombie,' he said, his expression sincere.

'Well, I suppose I was quite a toast with the lads in my young day –'

'I'll bet you were. I bet the young bloods in Kirklochy were all over you.'

Mrs Crombie allowed herself a trace of smugness. 'I had my moments.'

'I bet you broke a few hearts when you got married.'

It was hard to believe that Mrs Crombie had once been married, although the name "Mrs Crombie" was something of a giveaway. Jen had no recollection of there ever having been a Mr Crombie. He must have died before she was born. No wonder the old bat always looked so constipated – she probably hadn't had sex for about twenty-five years. Mrs Crombie nodded, as if mesmerised by Patrick's sea-green eyes.

'And you and –'

'Hector,' said Mrs Crombie, still looking up at him.

'You and Hector were very happily married? You were madly in love? You were made for each other?'

Good grief. Jen couldn't believe he was coming out with all this stuff. And, was it her imagination, or was his brogue softer and more pronounced than usual?

Mrs Crombie nodded again. 'Of course.'

'Well, then, would you deny a young man the chance to be as happy as you were? Would you say he had to be alone for the rest of his life?'

'I –'

'I know you're a compassionate woman, Mrs Crombie. A good Christian.'

OMAG. Jen clamped a hand over her mouth as Mrs Crombie groped in her coat pocket for a hankie and dabbed at her eyes. Poor, cowed Martha Martin was looking at her shoes.

'Come on, Mercy, dear,' soothed Muriel. 'Let's go and have a nice cup of tea. I've got some chocolate biscuits in.'

Jen exhaled deeply as the three women turned to leave.

'My work here is done,' Patrick said.

'Thank you, Father Walsh.' Feeling that she had every excuse, Jen threw her arms round him and hugged him tightly. She felt his arms go round her and hold her closely. She breathed in the smells of his aftershave and shampoo, feeling warm and protected. All too soon, she heard Gregor and Robbie's excited voices in the foyer.

She opened the doors of the conservatory with pride.

'Fabulous,' cried Gregor, which was the greatest compliment he could pay.

'To die,' agreed a falsetto voice behind him.

'Hi, Ali,' said Jen. Gregor's friend, Ali, was the love child of Charles Hawtry and Kenneth Williams. He, Gregor and Robbie shrieked for some minutes about how fabulous everything was – from the chandeliers right down to the napkin rings.

'You look gorge, darling,' Robbie told her.

'You, too,' Jen said. Robbie *was* a good looking man, but too bland for Jen's taste, with his perma-tan, regular features, square jaw, dark brown eyes and teeth so white they could be seen from the moon. He looked a little like a Hollywood star himself. Still, he was both gay and married, so he wasn't terribly available anyway.

Amy had prepared a feast: prawns in chilli and coriander, smoked salmon with cream cheese, chicken flavoured with honey and mustard, garlic mushrooms, salads of every colour and texture and baby new potatoes sparkling with butter and herbs. Jen's mouth watered even more at the sight of the desserts: mint chocolate-chip cheesecake, a delicate lemon mousse, exotic fruit salad with fresh cream, chocolate fudge cake and tiramisu.

Watching everyone eating with relish, knocking back the wine, which had been sourced by Patrick and was cheap but very good, talking their heads off and laughing uproariously, Jen felt she could relax for a while. Aura and the other waitresses had everything well under control.

'Lovely meal.' Patrick was complimenting Amy, who was sitting opposite.

'I suppose I should thank you for earlier,' Jen said. She'd made sure that he was seated next to her.

Patrick grinned. 'Yeah, we saw them off just in time.'

'You did, you mean. Mind you, I haven't got all the brogue and the blarney.' She didn't have mesmerising turquoise eyes, tousled dark curls or ripped abs, either, she might have added. Niamh leaned across the table. Jen had to admit that she looked stunning, wearing a black silk trouser suit which made the most of her long legs. Under the skin tight jacket she wore nothing but a push-up bra, showcasing black lace and much pearly cleavage. Round her neck was a heavy onyx pendant. No prizes for guessing whom she was trying to impress.

'Fair play to you, Jen, you certainly know how to throw a party. And, Amy, you're some cook,' she said. She was still infuriatingly glowing and happy.

'All in a day's work,' Jen said.

When the last, delicious bowl of dessert had been scraped clean and the table cleared, Jason and Patrick pushed it against the wall to create a space for dancing, and Gregor and Robbie took the floor. Gregor was a trained ballroom dancer and Robbie a match for him, and everyone stood watching them in admiration. Amy found herself standing next to Lauryn and Ross, two cousins of Gregor's who were part of Evie Martin's friendship group.

'Great nosebag, Ames,' said Lauryn. 'It was totally worth missing Evie's gig for.'

'Evie's got some gigs?' Amy asked.

'Yeah. She's playing at the arts centre in Inveralan tonight. She had to get there earlier to do a sound check.'

Both teenagers looked impressed, their expressions saying: "How cool is that?"

'She should totally go on the X-Factor,' Ross added, a slight blush suffusing his pale cheeks.

'Good for her. I just have to... check on something in the kitchen.'

Amy hurried across the room. Once in the kitchen, she poured a glass of wine and slipped out of the back door, away from the hubbub of Aura and the others washing up and gossiping about the evening. She sank down on the bench which was used by her staff at break times.

Why had Lewis neglected to mention that Evie was also performing at the arts centre tonight? Did he have something to hide? Again, she thought how well suited he and Evie were: music-obsessed, writing songs together with such soulful, poignant lyrics, talking for hours about their favourite albums, no detail too trivial to mention, rehearsing together, their sweet, raw, smoky voices blending to perfection. Lewis was nearly ten years older than Evie and Amy was aware that she saw him as a mentor. Then there was the beauty that made them stand out. How could Evie not be attracted to Lewis?

Amy drank down half her wine in one gulp.

How could Lewis not be attracted to Evie?

She lost track of time as she sat there, thinking. It wasn't easy, being Lewis' girlfriend. There would always be other women – women who fancied beautiful, intense musicians with hypnotic blue eyes and artists' fingers and husky voices, who wanted to be name-checked on album sleeves, who wanted songs written just for them. Women who jostled to stand near the stage and gaze up at him. What would happen if he did find the fame he craved? He'd be public property.

'What are you doing, skulking out here?'

'Oh, Paddy.' Amy started. 'You gave me a fright.' She drained the last of her wine. Patrick sat down beside her.

'That was a fabulous meal,' he said. 'Everybody's talking about it.'

'Mmm.'

'Ames, are you all right?'

'Yeah. I just shouldn't drink champagne. It makes me –' To her horror, she felt a tear creep over the edge of her eye and slide down her cheek. '... makes me over-emotional and maudlin.' She dashed it away with the back of her hand.

'What's going on, Amy?' Patrick's eyes, fixed on her, were serious. 'Do you want to talk to me about it?'

Suddenly, Amy realised that she did. Patrick was only a few years older than she was and she'd known him for a long time – he was the big brother she'd never had.

'Everyone keeps asking me where Lewis is,' she explained. 'All our friends are here but he couldn't do this one thing for me and come.'

'So where is he?'

'In Inveralan. With Evie Martin.'

Patrick raised his eyebrows, but said nothing, inviting her to go on.

'They've got a gig at Inveralan Arts Centre. But he never told me Evie was going to be there – I only found that out today. What if there's something going on between them? What if... Paddy, what if he's going off me?' She finished speaking on a sob, the thought of losing Lewis to Evie too terrible to contemplate. She opened her tiny clutch bag, pulled out a paper hankie, and began to mop her eyes. Patrick put his hand over hers.

'Sure, why would he want to do that?' he asked. 'Has he done anything to make you feel that way?'

'I suppose not,' Amy admitted. She still stayed at Lewis' flat most nights, and his habitual lateness was due to his absorption in his music. The night he'd stayed in her bedroom at the hotel, their love-making had been more passionate than ever. They'd moved her bed, as they used to do as teenagers, so that Brooke, who slept next door, wouldn't hear the headboard banging against the party wall. Afterwards, she'd lain in his arms, absolutely content, and they'd slept wrapped around each other. They were still as close as ever; he hadn't distanced himself from her, they still fascinated each other as they always had.

'If the party hadn't been on the same day, you'd have been with them,' Patrick pointed out.

'You're right.' Amy managed a smile. 'I'm just being para.'

Patrick got up and pulled her to her feet. 'Let's go and get drunk,' he suggested. They went back into the kitchen.

★

Confident that the evening was going well but needing a few minutes' peace and quiet, Jen went out into the rose garden. The warmth wrapped round her like a velvet shawl. Stepping carefully down the crazy paving, she heard voices. Niamh and Brooke must have sneaked outside to smoke. She could detect the acrid smell mingling with the fragrance of the flowers.

'I never could resist him.' That was Niamh.

'I'm not surprised,' Brooke was saying. She had an exceptionally soft voice but a light breeze carried it over to where Jen was standing. 'He's gorgeous. And that Irish accent does it for me every time.'

'He totally gets me,' sighed Niamh. 'And the sex is still amazing.'

Brooke giggled drunkenly. 'Okay, now you're just showing off.'

Jen gripped her wine glass so hard it nearly shattered. Woodenly, she made her way back into the hotel, the girls' voices now inaudible, and sat down on the sofa in her office without switching the light on. She tried to tell herself that she'd already known that Patrick and Niamh were having mind-blowing sex, already come to terms with it, so it shouldn't be such a shock, but somehow, hearing Niamh actually say it, it was. Yet again, she imagined their long, slender bodies entwined on her Egyptian cotton sheets, their fingers inter-locked, their breath and dark hair mingled. It was some time before she felt composed enough to return to the wedding party.

Brooke drifted, somewhat unsteadily, down the corridor towards the bathroom, where she used the toilet, washed her hands in the expensively scented soap, and looked at her reflection in the mirror. She had her hair up and wore dangly, diamanté earrings. Her black dress was gorgeous – a lucky find in a charity shop in Byres Road. She felt as sophisticated as a Bond Girl in it. It was wildly sexy – floor length and backless, the narrow bodice held round her neck by a frail, diamanté studded ribbon. She'd received many appreciative glances throughout the evening, but what was the point if James wasn't here to see it? James' soon-to-be-ex-wife had gone on a cruise with her new – and very flash – boyfriend. She would be away for several weeks over the summer, and had decided that it would be a good opportunity for James to spend "quality time" with their daughter. Roughly translated, Brooke felt, this meant that it would be a good opportunity for Joanna to spend "quality time" with her new man and without the company of a truculent, caustic fourteen year old. Emily had refused point blank to stay in the grotty Maryhill flat, so James had returned to his marital home in Newton Mearns for the summer vacation and Brooke had hardly seen him. Emily was, of course, called after Emily Brontë. Therefore, the name had conjured up, for Brooke, a sweet, old fashioned girl, but the real Emily, whom she'd met for lunch in Stereo, had been a Mosher, a Goth or an Emo – who knew, with icy blue eyes, long hair dyed an unnatural shade of blue-black, and a good line in sarcastic comments – when she deigned to speak at all. Mostly she'd been monosyllabic or lapsed into a sullen silence.

The meeting had been a disaster.

Sighing, Brooke freshened up her make-up, sprayed on more perfume, and hurried back to the conservatory in search of more wine.

★

The sedate dinner had morphed into a party and was an undeniable success, but Jen felt depressed as she leaned against the wall and surveyed the room. Most of the guests were still here and didn't look like leaving any time soon – people were mingling, sipping drinks, chatting and laughing. Niamh was nowhere to be seen and neither was Patrick. Jen tried very hard to concentrate on the profit she would make on the bar this evening.

Amy walked into the room, much cheered up by the anaesthetic of a bottle of red wine, and was immediately swept onto the dance floor by Ali. It was getting dark outside, the room now lit by flickering candles which were reflected against the glass. She and Ali waltzed around the floor – it was sheer pleasure to dance with someone so expert.

'Hey, Ames.' Callum was walking towards her, clapping. She'd known he was going to be late, since he was on duty.

'Hi, Cal. Ali could totally be on *Strictly*, don't you think?'

Callum nodded. She could hardly take her eyes off him, as he looked so different tonight. He normally wore Hunters, an ancient green Barbour and old jeans. Off duty, he swapped the wellies for Nikes and the Barbour for a beat-up leather jacket.

Tonight, he was wearing a grey suit and lilac shirt. He had a fine body, Amy caught herself thinking, broad in the shoulder and tapering to a narrow waist and long, muscular legs, probably due to his passion for hill walking. He'd had his hair cut, also, which drew attention to his deep-set brown eyes.

'You can be quite good looking, when you try,' she told him, tugging on his wine coloured tie.

'You're pissed,' he said, breaking the spell.

'And you've got a lot of catching up to do.' Amy fetched him a glass of wine. Callum had just finished bringing her up to date with Farmer Galbraith's horse, now returned to robust health, and her foal, named Poppy, when she heard a soft voice in her ear.

'Hey, Ames.'

Her heart soared. Lewis was by her side, as elegant as ever although he was wearing ripped jeans and a Nirvana tee-shirt. He pulled her into his arms and kissed her thoroughly, not caring that there were several people in the room. She clung on to him. He put his arm round her waist as they carried on chatting to Callum. As always, Lewis was charmingly attentive and he laughed frequently at their friend's stories, but Amy was desperate to drag him upstairs to bed and be further comforted by his lovemaking.

Chapter 11
Smells Like Teen Spirit

'James!' Brooke ran towards her boyfriend. She'd missed him terribly and was desperate to snuggle up into the warm circle of his embrace and flood him with all her news. He'd make it all better, she knew. But Emily was standing beside him, throwing her evils, so she had to settle for a tight hug.

'Emily. Good to see you again,' she murmured. The teenager, dressed head to toe in black and with a scarf patterned with skulls around her neck, looked thoroughly disenchanted to be here. Her eyebrow and top lip were pierced and her hair dyed to the colour of liquorice. She wore masses of black eyeliner. She bet that, looking the way she did now, Emily would be totally unrecognisable to the teachers at the exclusive Glasgow private school she attended.

'Let me show you to your rooms.' Brooke led the way along the corridor which overlooked the rose garden.

'Thanks, Brooke,' James said, as she unlocked the door to his room. He smiled, which instantly made him look handsome and much younger. She'd always thought that he looked foreign – Spanish, maybe, and remembered how disappointed she'd been to learn that he came from Paisley.

'You're just next door, Emily,' Brooke said, her voice taking on a hearty, aunt-like tone. The room was charming and full of late afternoon sunshine, but, determinedly unimpressed, Emily pulled out a state-of-the-art, top-of-the-range iPhone, and began checking her messages.

'Well, I'll leave you to settle in.' Brooke's voice now took on a cooler note. 'Dinner is served from 7pm onwards –'

'Hey, hun,' Emily interrupted. 'Yeah, hmm, it's, like, totally boring. The back end of beyond. Nowheresville-on-Sea. I think I'll just shoot myself now –'

Good plan, Brooke thought grimly, but, of course, she couldn't say so.

'WTF, Zo!' Emily said. She sat down on the bed, as if settling in for a long chat. 'What did Kyle SAY?'

Brooke left the room, closing the door firmly.

Yet another handsome, glowing, loved up honeymoon couple floated into the hotel's foyer. Holding hands, they walked slowly, unable to stop gazing at each other, and paused to share a kiss. *Pur-leeze*, Jen felt like saying, but, of course, she couldn't.

'Mr and Mrs Richardson?' she said, instead.

'As of yesterday,' agreed Jemima Richardson, in ringing Home Counties' tones. She smiled fondly up at her new husband, showing too many excellent teeth, which gave her a somewhat sharky look. She simpered as she signed the register in her new name, the white gold double band on her left hand catching the light.

'I'll show you to your room,' Jen said, as Jason lifted their matching new Louis Vuitton suitcases.

'It's *amazing*,' Jemima cried, as she followed Jen into the rose-scented honeymoon suite. As always, the champagne was on ice, two dozen, deep, velvety red blooms were arranged in a crystal vase, a tray of Godiva chocolates and fresh, exotic fruit stood on a table by the window, and two thick, fluffy snow-white dressing gowns hung side by side in the en-suite bathroom.

'I think we'll have dinner in our room. Olly?' Jemima threw a suggestive look at her new husband.

'Of course, madam,' Jen said.

Everyone was completely loved up at the moment, she reflected, sourly, as she sat at her PC, typing with a verve and precision that would put Tokio Myers to shame: the Richardsons, Gregor and Robbie, Amy and Lewis, Brooke and James, Patrick and Niamh. Even Robert Kingsley had phoned earlier and booked a table in a "secluded" corner of the dining room, in which to romance the soignée Annalie.

'You're not still working?' Patrick put his head round the door.

'I've just got a few things to sort out.'

'Niamh and I are going to the Claymore for a drink later. Why don't you come with us?'

Jen couldn't stand the idea of playing gooseberry to Patrick and

Niamh of all people, of him taking pity on her. She'd rather work all evening. 'No thanks, Pads. I've really got to finish this.'

Patrick shrugged. 'Suit yourself, Jenny No-mates. We'll see you in there later if you change your mind.'

Brooke was definitely on a promise, she thought, as she cleaned her teeth much later. The bathroom was full of steam and the fragrance of the Origins products which her sister only used on very special occasions because they were so expensive. Overcome by a wave of exhaustion, she slapped moisturiser onto her face and then shuffled off to bed.

Brooke crept downstairs, her bare feet sinking deliciously into the deep pile of the carpet. She was wearing a coffee coloured silk nightdress and matching robe. She'd left her hair loose and it floated around her shoulders, silky and scented.

'Room service,' she said, softly, as she tapped on the door. She'd made absolutely certain it was the right room, remembering an incident in Amsterdam which still made her blush. The door swung open and she transferred the *Do Not Disturb* sign to the outside, moving straight into James' open arms. He kissed the top of her head and stroked her hair.

'I've missed you so much,' she murmured, breathing in his familiar smell. They sat on the edge of the bed, his arm round her, while she poured out everything that had happened since she'd last seen him – including her horrible experience with Hugh McMichael, as she'd been longing to do for weeks. As always, he listened without interrupting.

'Brooke, why didn't you tell me all this before? I don't like to think of you bottling it all up.'

'I didn't want to talk about it on the phone. I wanted to see you.' Now that he was with her, his arms around her, the memory began to recede a little. He began to kiss her, gently at first, but then blazing up into passion.

In the early morning, the room was bathed in gold light. Brooke leaned up on her elbow and watched James as he slept. Going to sleep with him and waking up with him had been wonderful after so long apart: the feel of his skin against hers had been intoxicating. After the first time they'd made love last night, she'd cried. It had been slow, intense, absorbing. He'd clasped her hand and looked into her eyes throughout. He hadn't been entirely dry-eyed, either.

Now, she felt too warm and happy to move, but she would have to – she was on breakfast duty. She slipped out of the bed and pulled her nightdress over her head, then wrapped her robe around her shoulders. She crept across the room and out into the corridor, closing the door quietly behind her. Then she froze, the carefree smile wiped from her face. Emily was approaching her. Why did she have to be the only teenager in the hemisphere who didn't sleep in until early afternoon? As she drew near, Brooke noted how young she looked, with her face stripped of its metalwork and make-up. Her skin was pale and scattered with freckles. She'd be quite a pretty girl but for the bored, sullen look that she perpetually wore.

'Hi, Emily.' She tried a light, cheery tone. 'You're up early.'

'Couldn't sleep,' Emily growled. 'It's too quiet here.'

'Well, why don't you go back to bed for a bit?'

Emily didn't move, but stood before Brooke, her face stony.

'You're sleeping with him,' she accused. Her expression showed a kind of amazed horror, as if she'd just spotted a tarantula climbing up Brooke's nightdress.

'Of course I'm sleeping with him; he's my boyfriend,' Brooke said, but gently. 'Emily, listen –'

'You're disgusting.'

'Why don't we go out later, just the two of us? We'll have a coffee and a chat about everything –' Brooke spoke softly and considerately, not least because Jen would totally kill her if she was heard brawling within the hotel and disturbed the other guests.

'Aye, right,' Emily said. 'Like I'd want to talk to you about anything. All this is totally your fault.'

'What do you mean?' Brooke suddenly felt cold.

'If you hadn't been having an affair with Dad, he and Mum would probably still be together.'

'I was *not*,' hissed Brooke. 'Your dad had split up with your mother long before I started seeing him. Long before. I wouldn't... I would never do anything like that.'

Emily gave an exaggerated shrug. 'Well, you would say that, wouldn't you?'

'Of course I would, because it's the truth.'

'Whatever.' Emily stalked into her room and banged the door shut.

Emily's upset that morning didn't seem to have affected her appetite, Brooke reflected, as she watched the girl hoover up a full Scottish vegan breakfast and four slices of toast.

'I ordered coffee, not tea, Dolly Daydream.' A voice broke into her thoughts.

'I'm so sorry, Mr Bassett.'

'Don't worry about it. I won't tell anyone if you don't.' Brooke knew that the loud-mouthed Englishman fancied her. He winked at her in an exaggerated way and she smiled. Then she caught Emily looking over at her and became para that the teenager would think she'd been acting flirtatiously and cast her all the more firmly as a man-eating home-wrecker. She couldn't bear to think that Emily held her responsible for the break-up of her parents' marriage. But, then again, maybe she had just said so to upset her.

'I can't believe I'm missing Lottie's party,' Emily moaned later, into her phone, as she mooched by, ear buds in place as always. Brooke didn't understand why she kept complaining about being bored, when her iPhone contained every form of entertainment she could ever need: her Spotify playlist, e-books, games, email, myriad apps, films, TV programmes and every kind of social media, and she also spent inordinate amounts of time murmuring down it to her friend Zoë or texting, her deft thumbs working furiously.

Brooke had never been bored as a child or a teenager. From a young age, she'd read constantly, curled up in a worn old easy chair by the electric heater in the living room, escaping into other worlds: the adventures of a duffle coated teddy bear from deepest Peru, hidden gardens, secret cousins, talking horses, boy wizards and girl private eyes, rival junior pirates, travelling in her imagination to Civil War era Massachusetts, 1940s Cornish boarding schools, the 1920s Lake District, solving mysteries alongside a bunch of child detectives sustained by lashings of pop. She'd been captivated by the bizarre imagination of Roald Dahl, possessed by the dark world of Harry Potter and engrossed by the care home misadventures of Tracy Beaker. Later, she'd graduated to the shelves of blockbusters in Mum's bedroom: Judith Krantz, Jackie Collins, Jilly Cooper, Barbara Taylor Bradford. It had been easy to leave the village behind, travel far away in her imagination.

Brooke had the next day off and she wandered into the village. She had a major chocolate craving and her plan was to hole up on the comfy sofa at the back of Fratelli's with her book, thereby keeping out of the way of Jen and the 101 "wee jobs" that would be sure to need done if Jen could find her. In an attempt to set a good example to Emily, she'd given up smoking that morning and felt shaky, twitchy and crabby from nicotine withdrawal.

As she walked down the coast road, slightly uplifted by the fresh breeze, she noticed Emily sitting on the seawall, looking out across the water.

'Mind if I sit down?'

Emily shrugged but said nothing, resuming her contemplation of the horizon. Brooke sat beside her, looking down at their dangling feet – Emily's big, black DMs and her own strappy pink sandals. It didn't seem that long since the teenaged Brooke had sat here reading D. H. Lawrence or George Orwell, or listening to angry music on her iPod while gazing broodingly out to sea.

'I was just going to go for a coffee, if you want to come?' she ventured. No one could say she didn't try.

'No thanks.' Emily didn't even look at her.

'Are you meeting your new pals?'

'What's it to you?'

'Emily, could you please drop the attitude? I was only asking.'

'Yeah, because, with me out of the way, you think you can sneak off back to bed with Dad. So don't try to make out you care.'

'Pity's sake,' Brooke shouted. 'I didn't say I cared. I was just asking.'

'*Wooh,*' said Emily, finally turning to face her. She was smirking, delighted to have got under Brooke's skin.

Brooke was instantly ashamed of her flash of temper. 'I can talk to you as an adult, can't I?'

Emily shrugged. 'Patronise me, you mean.'

Brooke clenched her fists, but managed not to snap. 'You shouldn't feel so threatened by me –' she began, then immediately realised this was a mistake as Emily's face tightened in anger. 'I honestly want us to get on. You might actually like me if you ever give me a chance and get to know me.'

'Dream on,' Emily said, scrambling to her feet. Brooke stood up also.

'Hey, Em,' said Evie Martin, appearing at the top of the steps which led from the beach.

'Hi, hun.'

Evie walked towards Emily, her arms outstretched. The two girls embraced fondly and at length. Brooke slunk away.

Each day, Brooke had to clean and tidy Emily's bedroom. It was remarkable that anyone could make such a mess with so few possessions. Today, Brooke had fallen over Emily's Doc Marten boots as she let herself into the room. Every garment she'd brought with her, apart from the clothes she stood up in, seemed to be scattered on the carpet. Make-up was spread across the dressing table and all the towels were wet and tossed on the bathroom floor. Despite the French cuisine available downstairs, a half eaten Pot Noodle stood on the bedside table beside a Red Marlboro packet. She'd also left her straighteners on. Brooke unplugged those just as they were about to burn a hole in the carpet.

On the bed were sheets of paper covered in a big, round, childish scrawl, which looked like either angst-ridden poetry or song lyrics. Brooke mentally filed this away – she believed that everyone needed a passion in life, and maybe she'd found Emily's.

On the way to Fratelli's to meet Niamh, Brooke passed Emily sitting on the seawall, more animated than she'd ever seen her and flanked by Craig Peden and Evie Martin. They were all smoking, Evie in what she probably imagined was a very sophisticated way, but Brooke decided to turn a blind eye to this as a rite of passage. A few other teenagers mooched nearby, shoulders hunched, hoods up and hands shoved into the pockets of their skinny jeans.

'It was, like, the most random night ever,' Emily was saying. 'We all piled into a taxi and ended up at this party in the west end. We were mad with it.'

Brooke presumed that she was enjoying patronising the other young people, showing off her big city sophistication.

Sitting at the window table of Maggie's Tearoom was Lily McVey, the raunchy granny from the creative writing classes, with her new friend, Ava Hunter, who was one of the students on the art course. They looked totally engrossed in their conversation, Lily's hand on Ava's arm. The two older women had really hit it off, finding many shared passions, including music and ballet, and had already arranged a trip to Sadler's Wells next month to see *Sleeping Beauty*. "I'm very close to my grand-daughters," Lily had told Brooke. "But I needed a life of my own, too."

Theirs wasn't the only new relationship formed: Lanie Scott was now seeing Alan Govan. So shy that she was virtually invisible, Lanie had blended into the background, until she began to read. Then every-one had seen the wit and emotional intelligence, her true personality coming out. She would never turn heads, but, close up, she had pretty, delicate features and lovely grey-green eyes.

Brooke felt a quiet satisfaction with the way the classes had gone. Even Niamh, despite her initial misgivings, felt that she had learned so much from the students. Pearl had filed an article on the course, which was due to appear in the *Herald* Arts Supplement.

Once inside Fratelli's, Brooke crossed the chequered black and white floor and fed some coins into the genuine 1950s' jukebox in the corner. Pulsing with coloured light, the jukebox had been there as long as anyone could remember. The art-deco Italian café, with its smell of pastries, its rainbow coloured selection of ice cream, its Knickerbocker Glories, its dozen fragrant kinds of coffee, its hot chocolates and its hot waiters, was the hub of the Kirklochy youth social scene. Brooke selected the Teddy Bears' *To Know Him is to Love Him,* then went to join Niamh.

'Cheers,' she said, slipping into the seat opposite her friend. Her usual order, caramel latte and double chocolate muffin, was already waiting for her. Niamh was sipping espresso from a tiny cup, and intermittently shoving chunks of brownie into her mouth.

'You look as if you could do with a sugar rush,' she remarked. 'How's it going with James?'

'Good,' Brooke said. 'Emily hates me, though.'

'I'm sure not. She's just being fourteen, all angsty. I should know. I've got a sister that age.'

'Oh, she does, Niamh,' Brooke said, breaking off a piece of muffin. 'She accused me of splitting up her mum and dad.' How could she even contemplate trying to be a step-mother to Emily? She was barely ten years older.

'She's hurt and angry and she's taking it out on you. Try not to take it so much to heart.'

'Easy for you to say.' Grimly, Brooke chewed a chunk of her muffin.

'Maybe you need to spend more time with her, take an interest.'

'Yeah, well – she can't stand being in the same room as me. But I've found out she's into music –'

'Maybe you can build on that, then. If you want James, you've got to want Emily, too. They come as a package.'

Niamh put her hand on Brooke's wrist. 'Do you want another coffee?' she asked.

'Yeah, but I'll get it.' Brooke placed her order and then sat down again, gazing out of the window across the sparkling water to the horizon. Niamh seemed deep in thought.

'Diarmid phoned me last night,' she said suddenly.

'OMG,' Brooke said. 'What did he want?'

From her many intense, wine-fuelled, late-night conversations with Niamh, Brooke had gathered that her brief marriage had been a passionate emotional rollercoaster, exhilarating, dizzying, turbulent and as addictive as a class "A" drug, with bitter fights and ecstatic makings-up.

'To talk. He wants me to meet up with him in Dublin.'

'And will you?'

'Of course not. I told you, sleeping with him was a mistake. It should never have happened. It's just…. he looked so good, I was drunk and I was all hyped up from winning the award. I just couldn't resist.'

'We've all done it,' Brooke said.

Niamh crooked an eyebrow. 'Had an affair with an ex-husband?'

'I mean, we've all had great sex with an ex. In the past, I mean. Not since I've been with James.'

'Really?' Niamh's tone was dry.

'It's practically the law,' reassured Brooke. 'The last time I went to

Spain, I looked up Javier and we ended up in bed. It just seemed natural, since we used to live together. It would have been weird not to.'

'Trust me, Brooke, it wouldn't work.'

'You'll meet someone else,' said Brooke. 'I was absolutely devastated when I split up with Javier. I thought I'd die of a broken heart.'

'I'm not ready to meet someone else: it's all too raw. I'm putting men on hold for a while. I want to concentrate on my work. I've got a deadline. You know, I really think this new novel might be the best thing I've ever done.'

'For sure,' said Brooke, who'd read several chapters. 'But aren't you missing out one tiny wee minor detail?' She smiled. 'Sex?'

'That would be a terrible waste,' said the waiter, gallantly, as he placed a fresh cup of coffee in front of each of them.

'Shut up, Rocco,' said Niamh, but she was laughing. She traced the black gothic "J" tattooed on the inside of Brooke's wrist with her index finger. 'Is that what the "J" stands for, then, Javier?'

Brooke nodded, biting her lip.

'Good move, Brooke – now you can only go out with men with the initial "J".'

'Well, fortunately, I don't really see myself ever being with anyone else but James.'

'Wow. That sounds heavy. Maybe it'll be you getting married next.'

Brooke spluttered into her coffee. 'No need to go that far. Anyway, Emily would hate it.'

Brooke and James walked along the beach. She and her friends had pretty much had this little-known, narrow length of sand to themselves as teenagers. They'd spent many long summer evenings here, flirting, showing off, drinking cheap cider, barbecuing sausages, eating hot dogs and licking the ketchup from their fingers, the soundtrack from Gregor's boombox, or often an acoustic set from Lewis. James had told her that Emily was going out with Craig Peden, and, since then, she'd seen the teenagers making out in the bus shelter and holding hands as they walked along the beach. Brooke presumed that, at seventeen, in a band and with a driving licence, Craig must seem like a mature man of the world to Emily. No doubt, she was relishing telling all her friends back in Glasgow about him. She'd probably already changed her Facebook status to "in a relationship", Brooke thought, with a giggle, and put up a load of black and white shots on Insta of the two of them gazing moodily into the middle distance. Idly she wondered if the fact that Craig had had his tongue pierced would enhance his kissing technique. James was relaxed about the liaison, believing, perhaps wrongly, that the young couple couldn't get into too much trouble in such a small village, where everyone knew everyone else. Tonight, Emily claimed to be spending the evening at the Pedens' cottage, "listening to music", which, as everyone knew, meant the same as "doing homework", teen-speak for lying on the bed and kissing until your lips bled. However, with Craig's mum, dad and granny in the next room, she didn't think the teenagers would get too carried away. She shivered: it had been a fine night when they'd set out, but had now turned chilly and she was seriously underdressed in her pristine white vest, sandals and floaty sea-green Monsoon skirt. She marched moodily on, feeling a cold breeze and smirry rain on her face. She'd always planned to bring James here, as well as showing him other places from her personal history: the hollow at the foot of the cliff where she would sit for hours reading, the walks she deemed most scenic, her favourite view of the village, her primary school. But with Emily as a reluctant and malevolent chaperone, it hadn't happened.

'Brooke, talk to me.'

She stopped walking and spun round to face him. The wind was rising and her hair kited around her shoulders.

'When we made plans for this holiday, I didn't know you'd be bringing Emily.'

'Neither did I,' protested James. 'I didn't know about the cruise then.'

'I just thought we'd have more time together,' Brooke said. Even she thought that she sounded whiny and peevish. 'And I thought we were meant to be looking for a flat, but you haven't mentioned it since the end of term. I suppose you think it would upset Emily?'

James took hold of her goose-pimpled upper arms. It was raining heavily now, and she could feel the seaspray from the incoming tide.

'We will look for a flat.'

'When?' Brooke demanded, her sharp cry flung aside as the wind rose.

'As soon as you get back to Glasgow. And, Brooke, you wouldn't think much of me if I didn't want to be with Emily, or I didn't care about her feelings.'

'Did she tell you that she holds me responsible for you and Joanna breaking up?'

'Of course you're not. I'd moved out months before we started seeing each other.'

'I know that. But does Emily? Or is she just trying to upset me?'

'She's jealous and she's hurting, but she shouldn't take it out on you. I'll take her for a drive tomorrow, and we'll talk it all through.'

'Thank you,' Brooke muttered. She remembered Niamh's advice – James and Emily came as a package, but no one could say she hadn't tried to get through to the girl, although she didn't seem to be getting anywhere.

'I know how hard you've tried to get on with her,' James said, as if reading her thoughts. 'And you're equally as important to me.'

'Good,' Brooke said, feeling calmer. 'We can have some quality time tonight, anyway.'

'If that's what you want to call it –'

James steered her away from where the waves were washing in, dangerously close to her turquoise sandals, until they were standing in the relative shelter of an outcrop of rock, although it hardly mattered, since, by now, her vest was soaked through and her drenched skirt was clinging to her bare legs. It was raining even more heavily now. James stooped to kiss her, his mouth warm on hers, his stubble grazing her cheek. Brooke kissed him back with all her strength, pulling him as close as possible, feeling the hard heat of his body against hers as the rain poured down and the tide swept in. Time seemed to stand still. Brooke was oblivious to the rock against her back as he peeled her vest from her wet skin. She arched against it, then shuddered as he bunched up her skirt in one hand. She threw her head back, groaning deep in her throat. Her wild cry echoed round the narrow stretch of beach as she was soaked again by a wave crashing just a couple of feet away.

The next night, Patrick, James, Niamh and Brooke had decided to form a team to compete for the prize money – now standing at £100 – in the

Claymore Inn's weekly quiz. The others had gone on ahead and Brooke would join them when she'd finished her shift.

It was a warm evening and she felt summery and airy as she walked along the coast road in her floral sundress and sandals. As she drew near the bus shelter, she could see Emily and Craig, deep in conversation, and taking it in turns to swig from a large bottle of coke. Despite the lovely summer's evening, Emily looked like the angel of death in her head to toe black. Craig was wearing the grey beanie hat which seemed to be welded to his head.

'That's Dad's girlfriend,' Emily said.

'Brooke Grant?' said Craig. 'She's a total babe. No wonder your dad fancies her.'

'Shut up, you creep,' cried Emily, and, the next moment, she'd slapped him hard across the face, the sound echoing round the quiet street.

'Pack it in,' said Craig, rubbing his cheek. 'Psycho,' he added, throwing Emily a dark look.

'Emily, Craig, cut it out. Now,' Brooke said, running towards them, her sandals slapping against the road, aware that she sounded like a primary school teacher. Craig turned towards her, looking slightly sheepish, glazed and flushed. Emily took to her heels and ran off down the road, narrowly missing being run into by a cyclist.

'Emily, don't be stupid, come back.' Brooke gave chase, gathering up the floaty folds of her skirt in her right hand. Emily climbed over the seawall and ran across the beach, her Doc Marten boots sinking into the damp, ribbed sand. Brooke hared after her, her breath rasping in her throat. At last, Emily stopped running and leaned on a breakwater. As Brooke approached, she was violently sick.

'Had you guys been drinking?' Brooke asked. The bottle of coke had obviously been liberally laced with alcohol: vodka, most likely.

'No,' wailed Emily, wiping her mouth on the back of her hand.

'You are coming back to the hotel with me right now,' Brooke told her. Emily was a pitiful sight. Her mascara was smudged and two tears were sliding down her cheeks. She must be feeling rotten. She smelt of Patchouli oil, vomit and stale smoke. Brooke put her hand on the girl's shoulder. Emily shrugged it off, but fell into step with her with surprising willingness.

Back in the flat, Brooke phoned James and told him that she and Emily had decided to hang out and so she wouldn't make the quiz. He sounded pleased that they seemed to be getting on better after his and Emily's chat that afternoon, and was probably imagining cosy girl talk, although, as they spoke, Emily was hunched up on the sofa beside her, white as a sheet, and trying to keep down a glass of water.

'Why don't you have a shower?' Brooke asked. 'You'll feel so much better.'

Emily did look better, later, when she came slowly back into the room, wrapped in Brooke's fluffy bathrobe, her face wiped clean of tears and make-up. She sank down on the sofa, smelling of toothpaste and mouthwash.

'Better?' Brooke asked.

Emily sniffed, but nodded.

'You probably won't feel too clever in the morning,' Brooke said, crossing her fingers behind her back. 'But just say it's a 24 hour bug. That's what I always said. And you shouldn't smoke, either. It's so bad for you –'

Emily rolled her eyes. '*Sooo* hypocritical.'

'It's do as I say, Emily, not do as I do,' she said. Horrors – she was turning into her father.

Brooke's own teenaged rebellion had come late in life – she'd been eighteen, nearly nineteen when she'd moved out of her hall of residence into a small, shabby bedsit in Kersland Street. How she'd loved her wee room, with its sagging, but very comfortable, bed, threadbare sofa, easy chair, patterned square of carpet, linoleum, beautifully carved antique chest of drawers and MDF wardrobe. It might have been small and ugly but it represented freedom. Her own space. Her own name on the door, written in a flowing italic script and surrounded by flowers. It had absolutely everything she needed: a desk and angle-poise light, bookshelves, a double bed, a kettle and a toaster. There was an ancient, but wonderfully deep, claw-footed bath in the chilly bathroom at the end of the draughty, lino'd corridor.

She'd been very responsible: going on the pill, and spending some of her tiny salary on an iron. All her waitressing experience had paid off and she'd got a job in a café in the west end which sold more than

100 different kinds of tea and held poetry readings on a Friday night. There was no one to worry that she virtually lived on porridge, toast and peanut butter, preferring to prioritise her income on second hand books, Red Marlboro and Gold Blend. She could eat on dates and at parties, anyway, and there were lots of those. There was no one to pull her up for coming home drunk, or for not coming home at all. In those days, she could club all night, knock back a mug of black coffee, and still go straight to her classes.

After growing up in the village, the anonymity and freedom of the city were intoxicating. Only her passion for literature and some straight talking from her advisor of studies had stopped her from careering drastically off the rails.

Feeling something crackle behind a cushion, she pulled out the new issue of *Freak Week*, out today. This was Jen's guilty pleasure, but it wasn't quite as secret as she liked to think. *OMG!! IMPLANT TERROR! MY BOOBS EXPLODED AT 30,000 FEET,* read the shocking pink headline on the cover. Brooke smiled and, after a moment, Emily did, too. It served to break the ice somewhat.

'Brooke?' Her voice was low and muffled.

'Hmm?'

'I suppose it *was* nice of you to cover for me with Dad.'

'Don't get too carried away, Emily, you're embarrassing me.'

'No, I mean, like, thanks.'

'That's all right.' Brooke smiled. This was the first time Emily had ever said a civil word to her.

'I know you didn't really split up Mum and Dad. Dad explained everything. I just –'

Emily was wearing a silver ring in the shape of a skull. She twisted it round and round her finger. It occurred to Brooke that, completely blissed out in her relationship with James, she'd never truly taken Emily's feelings into account before, or realised how miserable she was.

'You're like really beautiful. And clever. Dad's mad about you.'

'Well, I hope so.' Brooke gingerly slipped her arm round Emily's thin shoulders. Although she and her new friends were forever hugging each other and she'd seen Emily and Evie fondly absorbed in playing with each other's hair, she was afraid she'd be rebuffed. 'But he's your dad;

he loves you. There's room for both of us.'

Lessons from the Book of Life! Brooke realised that she sounded as if she was quoting from the script of *Friends*. However, since she and Emily were Scottish, it lost something in the translation. Hastily she changed the subject.

'You play the sax, don't you?'

Emily nodded. 'And the guitar.'

'Who do you like? Fit As?'

'Aye, right,' Emily scorned. 'Bland, bland, bland. Wallpaper music. I want to be a singer-songwriter, like Ellie Goulding.'

'My sister's boyfriend's a musician,' Brooke said, an idea beginning to take shape.

'What's his name?'

'Lewis Burns.'

'Never heard of him,' sniffed Emily.

'Well, you won't have, but I promise you he's really good. He's very well respected in the Dreichndrookit area.'

Emily again rolled her eyes.

'He once supported Lisa Hannigan at King Tut's,' Brooke tried. Emily looked marginally more interested.

'Anyway, he's doing a song writing workshop in the arts centre. Do you want me to see if you can go along?'

To Brooke's surprise, Emily nodded. 'Okay,' she said, and smiled.

Brooke could hear Amy singing in the kitchen. 'What's that?' she called, from where she was sitting on the sofa, reading.

'*Me Without You*,' Amy said, crossing the floor with a mug of coffee in each hand. 'It's our song. Lewis wrote the melody and we worked together on the lyrics.' She sat next to Brooke and placed the mugs on the coffee table. It was a beautiful day outside and there was a broad stripe of sunlight falling across the carpet, but Brooke's stomach again twisted with anxiety so that she was actually in physical pain.

'It's lovely,' she said, trying to push aside the toxic guilt. 'I'd buy it, anyway.'

'Thanks, babe.' Amy looked radiant and glowing. 'It's not so shabby, being a muse.' She paused for a moment. 'We got such a buzz out of working on it together. It was amazing, creating something new that's just ours.'

Brooke lifted her mug and made to sip from it, although it was still too hot. If only she could've known that Amy and Lewis would both end up in Kirklochy and back together, she'd never have dreamed of kissing him. Keeping a secret from her sister was like a shadow falling over their relationship. How could she have betrayed Amy, her best friend, her true north? She tried to push down the feeling of panic and sound normal. 'Ames? I need to ask you a favour.'

Amy raised an eyebrow. 'What's that?'

'Well, it's Lewis, really. I need you to ask him if he can squeeze Emily into his songwriting workshop.'

'You can ask him yourself,' Amy said. 'He's coming over later.'

'Okay.' Crap.

'I've been teaching him to cook. We're doing his favourite tonight: vegetable moussaka. You can eat with us if you like.'

'Thanks,' Brooke managed. Of course, she'd seen Lewis around the village and with Amy, but she really didn't want to have to spend the evening with him.

They'd met up by chance on a hot summer night in Glasgow, more than a year ago. She and her flatmate had gone to a gig at King Tut's and Lewis' band had been the support act. They'd been standing near the stage and he'd smiled over and then dedicated the next song to her. Pretty cheesy, she thought, now, but at the time, she'd been royally drunk. She and her flatmate had shared a bottle of vodka before they even left the flat, to get into the mood, then carried on drinking.

At the interval, she and Lewis had slipped outside to smoke, grateful to escape from the sweaty atmosphere in the club. They'd always got on well and chatted easily – about books, music, mutual acquaintances, their inspiring English teacher in school and the culture shock of living in a big city after the village, their smoke drifting lazily on the warm air. He'd looked at her with his head slightly tilted to one side, as if he were truly interested in what she was saying – he'd always been a good listener. She'd been in a happy, hazy drunken bubble. Perhaps she should have stopped him when he leaned in to kiss her – he was her sister's ex, but her groin didn't seem to know that. She was curious to test out his kissing technique for herself; she'd heard a lot about it. She gripped the collar of his denim jacket, then her arms curled round his neck, her fingers twining into his soft hair. He'd tasted of tobacco and beer, smelled of danger and spicy aftershave. They'd kissed on and on as traffic swished past, the tail lights bright against the dark sky, Lewis' mouth moving from hers to her ear, her neck, her shoulder, the hollow of her throat. She'd slid her hands under his tee-shirt and caressed his strong, hard back.

They'd missed most of the headline act by the time they went back into the club, hot, sheepish and rumpled. In the ladies' she'd repaired her smudged make-up, combed her tousled hair and rebuttoned her dress. The next morning, she'd had a killer hangover, a sore throat and a stubble rash from her marathon snogging session. Those hadn't lasted long, but the guilt had never gone away.

'Hey, Brooke.' Lewis followed Amy into the room, a carrier bag in each hand. One seemed to contain food; she could see an aubergine sticking out, while the other, clinking, obviously had bottles in it. Was it her imagination, or did she see a spark of panic in Lewis' eyes also? If so, he'd covered it up quickly.

'Brooke's having dinner with us – she's going to sample your cooking,' Amy said.

Brooke settled back in the sofa, reading and sipping from a glass of red which Amy had brought out to her. She could hear laughter and talk over the chopping and sizzling from the kitchen, and sometimes all was quiet. She presumed Amy and Lewis were kissing, or simply standing stock still and gazing at each other. A delicious aroma wafted across the room. Amy and Lewis seemed to be inseparable, just as they'd been when they were teenagers. Maybe he'd only been attracted to her that sultry night because she reminded him of Amy. Her spirits rose marginally. Surely Lewis wouldn't want to tell Amy what had happened between him and Brooke, threaten what he had with her? She relaxed slightly, but then panic surged again as she thought that perhaps he'd want to be honest with her, have no secrets from her. What if he did decide to confess? Would Amy be hurt? Angry? Both? How could they carry on sharing the flat?

Amy put on some Elbow and they sat at the table. Brooke again sniffed the air as Lewis served up each of them a generous portion. 'This is lovely,' she said.

'Cheers,' said Lewis. 'But I had a lot of help from Ames.'

No one could mistake the connection between them – the lingering looks they kept exchanging, the way they'd finish each other's sentences and laugh at the same time, or suddenly fall silent, the way Lewis would gently touch her back or her shoulder whenever he passed her chair.

After they'd eaten, he took a swig of wine and fixed his piercing blue eyes on her. 'What did you want to talk to me about?'

'I need your help.'

Lewis raised his eyebrows quizzically, but said nothing.

'I've got my boyfriend's daughter staying at the hotel just now. She's fourteen and she's… hard work. Way too much attitude. She's been seeing one of the boys in the village, going out drinking –' She took a huge gulp of her wine.

'I'm sure you're a very good influence on her, Brooke,' teased Lewis.

'I just can't get through to her, but she's into music –'

'And?'

Lewis looked at her closely and she remembered, now, this knack he had of making her, and presumably every woman, feel as if there was no one else he would rather be with, and like the most attractive girl in the room.

'Can you get her onto that songwriting workshop you do?'

Lewis shrugged. 'Sure.'

'Thanks so much,' said Brooke, in relief. She wouldn't put Lewis in charge of a window box. Frankly, she doubted that he could tie his own shoe laces, but he was a very talented musician and he never had any disciplinary problems with teaching teenagers, as all the boys looked up to him and all the girls fancied him.

Lewis smiled, leaning back with his arms folded behind his head, a sure sign of relaxed confidence. 'No bother.'

'Thanks, babe.' Amy put her hand on his knee.

'I'll give you both a lift into Inveralan on Saturday morning; it's the least I can do,' Brooke said. She wouldn't have to be alone with him – Emily would be there all the time.

'Is that a threat?' Lewis teased. Brooke managed a smile – she was a notoriously bad driver.

'I'm just going to get off now,' she said. 'I've got a few things to sort out. I'll tell Emily the good news.' She rose in some relief. 'Thanks, Lew. I'll see you on Saturday.'

She tiptoed gratefully out of the room.

*

Brooke was polishing the already gleaming wood surface of the reception desk when Lewis rocked up. He sauntered across the foyer, his long legs encased in tight, faded jeans, giving a whole new meaning to the term "morning glory". Just then, Emily came shyly down the stairs. Yup, there they were – the inevitable Doc Marten boots and black leggings, but over those she wore a delicate grey dress with a floral pattern. She had obviously made a great deal of effort to look her best. With her make-up applied with a much lighter touch than usual, and her hair black, glossy and newly washed, she looked young, fresh and pretty.

'Nice dress.'

'Yeah?' Emily said. 'It's Mum's. *She's* got taste.'

'Emily, this is Lewis Burns, who's going to be taking the workshop today. Lewis, Emily Carlin, my –' Brooke let her sentence fade out at this point, being quite unable to think of how to explain her relationship with Emily.

'Hi, Emily.' Lewis stood up.

'Hey,' Emily mumbled, her cheeks slightly rosy.

'Will we go?' Brooke asked. 'I told Evie I'd pick her up at nine.'

Emily's face fell at the revelation that Evie Martin would be accompanying them. They went outside and Brooke unlocked the doors of Patrick's car, which he had lent her for the day, with a pleasing bleep. She appreciated Patrick's faith in her driving, as his car was very flash and very sporty. Jen often teased him about how it was a babe lair on wheels, with champagne flutes in the glove compartment and R&B permanently on the iPod. She pressed "play" and Marvin Gaye's *Let's Get It On* slithered around the car. She giggled.

Evie was just coming out of her gate as they pulled up outside the

Martins' cottage on the outskirts of the village. She wore a demure, navy blue dress patterned with gold stars and ending well below her knees and her hair hung over one shoulder in a thick plait. Her parents, both elders in the Free Church, were notoriously strict and Brooke knew that she would change into her skin tight, ultra short denim hotpants, vest and Converse as soon as they arrived at the arts centre. As far as she was aware, Evie wasn't allowed to: wear make-up, dress sluttishly, dance, date boys, smoke, drink alcohol, or tidy her room on a Sunday, but seemed to delight in leading a double life which would befit a Cold War spy, going to great lengths to do all the above – apart from the latter – while maintaining a front of innocence and purity for her parents.

She knew all this because she'd once had a summer fling with Isaac – or, as he had rebranded himself – Zac, Evie's older brother. It hadn't been love, but it had been exciting: secret meetings, stolen kisses. Once, she'd had to climb out of his bedroom window. She bit her lip in remembered pleasure – all that repressed sexuality. After a while, she'd hit on the idea of "borrowing" the keys to one of the disused chalets in the hotel grounds and meeting him there. Neither set of parents ever questioned their frequent disappearances – it didn't seem to occur to them that it was possible to have sex during daylight hours.

She jerked back to the present as Evie jumped in and closed the door smartly. The car filled with the scent of Ghost perfume. Brooke drove off down the coast road.

'Catch you,' said Emily, in quite a friendly tone, as she, Evie and Lewis got out of the car. Brooke watched as they walked up the path to the converted church, the stonework sandblasted to honey gold. Once again, she admired the huge stained glass window, also beautifully restored, which dominated one wall. When the sun shone through it, it scattered the old stone floor with patterned jewel coloured light. Brooke got out of the car and began to walk to the town square, past the maritime museum, passing some of Lewis' other students – two young men with guitar cases on their backs, skinny jeans, long neat beards and their hair in buns, and an older man with a bald head, a tattoo on his neck, earrings, several facial piercings and a beard which was dyed pink. She strolled along in the sunshine, window shopping.

There was her favourite café, the Spinning Jenny, just across the road. A tinkling bell announced her entrance and she sat down at a window table, covered in an antique embroidered linen tablecloth. The centrepiece of the room was a Welsh dresser showcasing a collection of willow pattern plates. Brooke ordered Lady Grey tea with lemon and a chocolate éclair which she ate with a dainty cake fork, watching the people, mostly tourists, passing in the street outside. She felt relief that she was getting on slightly better with Emily now, that she was safely at the workshop, for today at least. If anyone could handle her, Lewis could. She sighed. Once again, she felt a slight cloud pass over, a shiver of apprehension, as she thought about her fling with Lewis. It didn't really even qualify as a fling, not even as much as a one night stand, and they'd both been single at the time, she told herself, yet again. Or, at least, she had and he'd claimed to be also. The same thoughts kept chasing relentlessly round her head – it was clear that Lewis really cared about Amy, so he surely wouldn't rock the boat by telling her what had happened between them. Amy would never know. But *she'd* know, and she was finding the guilt hard to bear. If she told Amy, it might make her feel less guilty, but would also hurt her sister. Best to draw a veil over it.

But then, Lewis was serious about Amy. What if he did decide to confess? If he decided that he wanted a clean slate? She couldn't be sure he wouldn't, and she couldn't very well ask him. Brooke sighed, thoughts going round and round in circles.

'Hi, how did you get on?' she asked, much later, as Lewis, Emily and Evie came out of the arts centre. Lewis had loomed so large in her thoughts that day that she half expected him to have grown horns and a forked tongue – but he looked just the same as ever and seemed relaxed. Her heart eased slightly.

'Good,' Evie said languidly, tossing her plait over her slender shoulder.

'Awesome,' said Emily. 'And I suppose you were glad to see the back of me, so you and Dad could get it on.'

'Emily –' Brooke pushed her hands through her hair in distraction.

'Not at all, Em,' said Lewis. 'And I'm very glad you came. You've got something. It's a raw talent, but it's there. You've got a real sense of melody.'

'I do?' Emily glowed, breaking into a smile. Again, a blush crept over her cheeks.

'For sure. You should play the song you've been working on to your dad and Brooke later.'

'Okay,' Emily said, shy now.

Brooke threw Lewis a grateful glance.

Emily played her début gig in front of a small, but select, audience of Brooke and James, Lewis and Amy, Patrick and Niamh. Emily approved of Niamh and it wasn't hard to see why – Niamh looked just like Emily all grown up.

'It was a pretty, like, organic process,' she was explaining, as Brooke hid a grin behind her hand.

Emily took up Lewis' guitar and began to play, the anger smoothed from her expression and replaced by absorption as she strummed and began to sing. Brooke could see that Lewis had been right: the tune was rough and needed work, but there was a definite hook to the chorus.

Everyone clapped uproariously when she'd finished.

'See? What did I tell you?' said Lewis.

'I'm hearing a touch of Ellie Goulding,' James said.

Emily glowed. Patrick went out for fish and chips all round and the evening turned into a party. Emily looked rosy and happy, other than when Lewis pulled Amy onto his lap and wrapped his arms round her. Underneath the killer smiles and the flirtatious banter, he was genuinely kind, Brooke thought, feeling a wave of warmth for him; he really did care about Emily, and he really did love Amy. 'Do you want to ask Craig over, Em?' she asked.

Emily shrugged.

'Not seeing him anymore?'

'Just as a mate. He's pretty immature, really.'

'Lewis is hot, though, hey?' Brooke lowered her voice so that only Emily could hear. Emily blushed furiously. 'Yes,' she whispered, then giggled.

Brooke ate her last chip – crispy on the outside, fluffy on the inside. She wanted to savour this moment, when Emily had spoken to her like an equal, rather than a home-wrecking, wicked stepmother.

Chapter 12
Crazy in Love?

'This is going to be a top girls' night out,' Amy said. Brooke high-fived her, giggly and excited from drinking a glass of wine while she was getting ready. Amy pulled her jacket more closely round her: it was freezing in the station.

'Heyyy,' Gregor yelled, the length of the platform. He hurried towards them, closely followed by Misty and Aura. They were going into the next village to a gig. Misty and her younger sister looked alike, but whereas Misty favoured the natural look, Aura was wearing hair extensions, bordered on orange and was heavily made up and with false eyelashes so thick and heavy they looked as if they had come courtesy of Vileda. Brooke looked beautiful as ever in a floral playsuit which showed off her long legs. Her hair was piled up in a beehive and she wore bright red lipstick.

Amy watched in anticipation as, with some difficulty, Gregor eased the hot pink tickets out of the back pocket of his leather trousers and handed them out. Priced at £10 each, they promised an evening with Beyoncé impersonator Flora Jean and her tribute act Destiny's Step Child. A complimentary glass of pink fizz was included in the price.

'Flora Jean's awesome,' Gregor told Amy. 'She got four chair turns in *The Voice* last year.'

Just then, the Inveralan train pulled up and they all climbed gratefully aboard into the warm. Once they were seated and the train had chugged slowly out of the station, Brooke produced a bunch of pink plastic flutes and a bottle of sparkling wine from her capacious handbag.

'OMG,' squealed Gregor, fit to break a window, as Misty held hers out. He clapped his hand over his mouth. 'You're engaged.'

'Yesss,' said Misty, high-fiving him.

'When? Tell me, tell me.'

'Last night.' Misty's face softened. 'We were walking along the beach, the sun was setting and he proposed. It was so romantic.'

'*This is the 6.55 train to Auchenstoorie, calling at Strathduncan, Ramshorn, Inveralan and Ewensay. This train will terminate at Auchenstoorie,*' interrupted the tannoy. 'Did he get down on one knee?' Brooke clamoured.

'Yes.' A faint blush stained Misty's cheeks.

'He wasn't wearing his Ted Baker trousers, was he?' Gregor frowned slightly.

'No. No, he wasn't,' Misty said, looking slightly distracted.

'Let's see your ring,' said Amy. Misty held out her hand. The ring was a narrow white gold band set with a sapphire and two diamonds. Gregor splashed more Cava into each flute.

'Misty and Duncan!' he cried, draining his.

'Misty and Duncan,' chorused Amy, Aura and Brooke, bumping their glasses together.

'We do a fantastic wedding package at Ardnashell Lodge,' Amy said. Jen would totally kill her if she didn't grab this Heaven-sent PR opportunity with both hands.

'Of course we'll have our wedding at your hotel, Ames. Like, in a year or two. We've only just got engaged.'

'Tickets, please,' said the guard. They all began to hunt in handbags and pockets. Gregor had looked slightly miffed at the interruption, but his face broke into a smile when he realised how "buff" – to use his own word – the guard was.

'You were giving him the eye,' giggled Aura, before the guard was out of earshot.

'Was not,' Gregor spoke with dignity.

'Don't know if you can top Tiara and Jaden's wedding, though,' Amy said. She was having fun. She had got used to spending all her spare time with Lewis, but maybe it was healthy to spend an evening apart, reconnect with her friends, she thought, as she chomped a handful of M&Ms, and washed them down with more fizzy wine. She never tired of the view on this train journey: long, golden beaches curving round the foot of the cliffs; flower-starred grass verges; blue-grey water; mountain ranges in the background.

In comparison to Tiara and Jaden's glamorous celebration, Amy's dream wedding was a quiet, intimate affair with just family and close friends in the hotel's rose garden. She imagined a simple ceremony with lots of music amid the heady floral scent, followed by a sumptuous dinner she hadn't cooked herself.

'When's Lewis going to make an honest woman of you, Ames?' Gregor said, as if reading her thoughts.

'Oh… we're just living in the moment. Lewis isn't really into marriage,' she said.

'I bet he isn't,' said Gregor, his tone meaningful.

'What do you mean?' Amy asked, stung, and noticing the look of unease on Misty's face.

'Just that he's a free spirit. Not, you know, bound by convention.' Gregor's face was smooth and innocent.

'*Next stop Inveralan,*' boomed a Glaswegian voice over the tannoy. '*Please remember to collect all your luggage and personal belongings before alighting from this train. Scotrail wishes yous a pleasant evening.*'

The train drew into Inveralan Station just then, and everyone began to pull on their jackets and gather up their possessions. Already a little drunk, Amy stumbled slightly in her high heels as they followed what looked like a hen party, a noisy, shouty bunch of girls clacking along in pink glittery cowboy hats and sparkly feather boas, shrieking and trailing the scent of strong perfume in their wake.

The theatre in Inveralan Arts Centre was totally transformed. Pale pink helium balloons floated on either side of the stage. Rows of bottles of cheap, fizzy rosé wine stood on a table by the door. Amy allowed a girl in a red bodycon dress to fill up her glass.

As Flora Jean and her band sang their way through the Destiny's Child back catalogue and strutted their stuff on stage, the girls and Gregor sang along, bellowing out the words, dancing wildly and downing several more glasses of the sickly sweet plonk. The hen party was boogying in a line, waving pink feather boas aloft. Amidst all the fun, it was easy for Amy to dismiss Gregor's comment on the train.

The evening flew by and it seemed that little time had passed before the theatre was full of the sound of stamping and chanting as the audience begged for an encore. The band obliged with a couple more hits and then it really was time to go.

After the sweaty heat of the arts centre, the drizzly cold outside hit them like a shock. Amy shivered, her vest top and thin jacket totally inadequate protection against a Scottish summer. 'What time is it?' she asked.

Gregor switched on his iPhone. 'Oh, crap. It's quarter to twelve. We've missed the last train.'

What were they going to do? There was a taxi service in Inveralan, but the hen party had claimed it. Amy tried to phone Gus the Taxi, but he also seemed to be unavailable. Lewis couldn't drive, Gregor's husband was away at a conference, and Duncan had planned to spend the evening at the Claymore Inn with a few friends, catching up over several pints of Old Sheepshagger. Inveralan had closed down for the night. Walking home was out of the question: at the best of times, it would take most of the night, but in high heels it would be near impossible.

'Maybe we should see if there are any vacancies at the Corrie Head?' Misty suggested. The somewhat ramshackle hotel, beloved of hill walkers, was at the top of the main street.

'We could, I suppose,' Amy said. Maybe she was spoiled from living in the "elegant 5 star boutique hotel, in the heart of the beautiful Highlands", as the website had it, but she didn't really fancy spending the night in the Spartan Corrie Head. It was said to be freezing in winter and boiling in summer, the only air-con a broken window.

'No good,' Gregor said. 'We're working tomorrow, and the first train isn't until half nine. Anyway, I haven't got my hair wax with me.'

'Or a toothbrush,' added Amy.

They huddled in the doorway of the arts centre. The rain had gone off, but it was bitterly cold. Brooke was shivering dramatically in her denim waistcoat. Gregor ran his hands up and down her arms, trying to warm her up.

'I'll phone Cal,' Amy said, taking out her iPhone and scrolling down through the numbers.

The phone rang out for some time, but at last Callum answered, sounding sleepy. Perhaps she had woken him, as it was past midnight now. 'Hi, Amy.'

'Hello. Did I get you out of bed?'

'No. No, it's fine. What's up?'

Quickly, Amy explained her predicament.

'Well, just sit tight, and I'll be with you as soon as I can.'

'Thanks, Cal,' breathed Amy, instantly comforted. 'You're a star.' Cal never let her down.

'What a Milk Tray hero,' Gregor exclaimed.

'I know,' agreed Amy.

'I knew he would come,' Gregor went on. 'Of course, you do realise he's got the hots for you, girl?'

'Don't be so ridiculous, Greg.'

'I think you'll find I'm right,' Gregor said, tossing his head. 'You can't be a hairdresser for the best part of ten years without learning quite a bit about the human psyche.'

'Rubbish.'

'It's true,' protested Gregor. 'Everyone confides in their hairdresser. The secrets I could tell –'

Everyone's spirits had risen at the news of their imminent rescue.

'Callum's lovely,' Misty said. 'You could do a lot worse.'

'I'm so not having this conversation,' Amy said. She just couldn't think of her oldest friend, whom she'd known since she could speak, in terms of romance. 'Anyway, he's got a girlfriend,' she added, to strengthen her case.

'Wrong,' carolled Gregor. 'He and Sheena have split up. And I got that from his mum. She was in getting her roots done today. Personally, I think that colour does nothing for her, but –'

'Why?'

'It's too dark for her complexion. As you get older –'

'No, Greg,' Amy said patiently. 'Why did Cal split up with Sheena?'

'Because she's gone back to Glasgow to work in a small animal practice and they didn't want to do the long distance thing. So, he's up for grabs.'

'Gregor, *I* have a boyfriend.'

'Ah, yes,' Gregor mused. 'The lovely Lewis.'

Amy threw him a sharp glance, but his expression was bland. 'If you've got something to say about Lewis, just come out and say it, instead of making all those insinuations.'

'Insinuating nothing,' Gregor said, inspecting his nails.

Callum's Land Rover wasn't the most stylish mode of transport, with the über-glamorous Aura looking particularly out of place as she clambered aboard in her gold stilettos, seriously straining her skin tight trousers, and sat down on a tartan travelling rug which smelt of dogs. Brooke wrapped a pet blanket, patterned in paw prints, around her shoulders and snuggled into it. Everyone was in high spirits to be out of the cold and on the way home and they sang along at the top of their voices to the soft rock which was being played on Kirklochy FM. Amy was yawning copiously by the time they'd dropped the others off and were driving up towards the floodlit hotel. Courteous as ever, Callum got out of the van to help her and Brooke down.

'Thanks, love,' Brooke murmured, embracing him. Amy felt unreasonably irritable – he was meant to be *her* friend.

'I owe you one,' she said, as he hugged her also.

'You certainly do,' Callum said, but she could see his smile in the dim light.

'I'll cook you dinner tomorrow night, if you're not working.'

'I'm not.'

'Okay. I'll see you tomorrow, then, about half past seven?'

She leaned up and kissed him on the cheek, before following Brooke up the stairs to the flat. As she went into the living room, she felt her phone vibrating with a text inside her bag. She pulled it out.

Sorry 4 being a bi-atch 2nite. Cu 2morrow. Sweet dreamz, G X, she read.

Gratefully, she kicked off her shoes and then briskly cleaned her teeth. Her bedside lamp was on, and, in its rosy glow, she could see Lewis lying in her bed. Quickly, she edged down her jeans and pulled her vest over her head, her heart warming. He must have missed her tonight, he must have wanted to be with her. She switched off the light and slid under the duvet, cuddling into him. The bed was too narrow to be anything but close. He smelt of stale beer and faded aftershave.

'Lew?' she murmured.

'I certainly hope so,' Lewis said, still half asleep.

The next day, Misty wasn't working and came to the hotel for a second-hand afternoon tea – Amy had rescued some cakes left over by the guests: tiny cheese scones and a selection of éclairs and marzipans better suited to a dolls' tea party. This was accompanied by Lady Grey tea with sliced lemon.

'Very posh,' Misty remarked, helping herself to a cheese scone garnished with tomato.

Amy shrugged. 'One of the perks of working here.' They sipped their tea for a few moments. 'Mist, how did you know Duncan was The One?' Amy asked, on impulse.

'I always liked him, I guess, but we were in the Friend Zone and I'd never seen him as boyfriend material,' Misty said. 'Then, one night, the two of us went out for a walk – no one else was up for it – and we met Mrs Kinloch. It was terrible – the poor old soul was wandering about, freezing in a nightie and slippers and she was completely lost. She's an old friend of my granny's but she didn't even recognise me. We took her back to her daughter's house to make sure she was safe. Dunc was brilliant – so kind and gentle – that it made me look at him with new eyes.'

Amy smiled – they'd all grown up together, known each other forever – it had only taken the couple about 22 years to get it together. 'Are you sure you're not rushing into anything?' she teased. 'I hope you're going to have a really long engagement.'

Misty grinned at her, but then became thoughtful. 'We know each other inside out and he totally accepts me,' she said, at length, then her face broke into a bewitching, cheeky grin. 'And I fancy him something terrible.'

'He's very handsome,' Amy said, although Duncan's sporty, outdoorsy good looks – red-gold hair, tanned skin and light blue eyes – didn't really do it for her. She preferred her men dark and soulful. Misty and Duncan were a joy to spend time with, Amy reflected – best mates as well as lovers, always in tune, their high spirits infectious.

'Your birthday's coming up, isn't it?' Amy said. 'Why don't we have a little do for you here? We can celebrate your engagement at the same time.'

Amy stood in the kitchen of the flat, tasting her carrot and orange soup. The next course was salmon in a delicate watercress sauce, fresh baby vegetables and new potatoes. For dessert, she had made the much more sinful banoffee pie. Because Callum wasn't driving, she'd bought some wine from the village store, class in a glass at a fiver a bottle – a fraction of the prices of the wines sold in the hotel's restaurant.

Callum was bang on time and they took their seats at the dining table. She'd put floating, scented candles and fresh flowers in the centre.

'This is nice. Very civilised,' Callum said. Amy was aware of a slight awkwardness between them, probably because of the sophistication of the setting and the meal. Usually, when they ate out, it was fish and chips on the quay or a barbecue on the beach. On the other hand, she and Lewis often cooked delicious meals together and they always ended up eating the chocolate pudding off each other's stomach.

'Thanks for rescuing us last night,' she called from the kitchen, as she ladled the soup into two bowls and added parsley, a swirl of fresh cream and some croutons.

'No bother.'

'It was, really.'

'This looks amazing, Ames,' Callum said, as she placed his plate before him. Having been up since the crack of dawn caring for sick animals, he was starving and had seconds of everything. By the time they'd polished off the first bottle of red, Amy felt warm and relaxed and they talked easily about work, family, local gossip and *Killing Eve,* of which Callum had just watched the box-set.

They took the banoffee pie, a pot of coffee and the second bottle of wine over to the sofa. Amy picked up the remote and pointed it at the television, which flashed into life. The camera panned over high rise flats and graffiti laden, boarded up tenements, heralding the beginning of *Mean City,* a gritty police drama set in Maryhill. Last week's episode had ended with a body being pulled out of the Clyde. Amy leaned back in the shabby, but extremely comfortable, sofa with enjoyment, savouring the rich, sweet taste of the pie.

She put her feet, encased in Shaun the Sheep slippers, up on the coffee table. It was so nice to be able to chill out – to pull on old grey jogging pants and a hand knitted sweater, to let her hair dry into unbecoming kinks, to wear absolutely no make-up, to demolish a second helping of pudding. She loosened her waistband and splashed more wine into both their glasses.

'*His psychological profile suggests –*' said DI Ashley McArthur, aka

Rowan Galloway, the Laird's daughter and Kirklochy's star turn.

'*Sometimes, there's no substitute for good, old fashioned policing,*' said the bitter, twisted and recently divorced DCI Jack McNab.

'*With all due respect, sir –*'

Amy sipped her wine. 'She's so photogenic. The camera just loves her,' she mused. She was a fine actress also, her Glaswegian accent flawless. Callum didn't respond and she glanced at him to see he'd fallen asleep. She shrugged and looked back at the screen, where DCI McArthur was now interviewing a suspect. Amy hadn't known Rowan well, as she was one of the landed gentry, the golden youth, and she'd been away at boarding school and then Cambridge University. According to Mrs Crombie and her gossipy cronies, Rowan was both bisexual and promiscuous, relishing her power, having "relations" with anyone she considered beautiful and charismatic enough, both men and women.

Had Lewis slept with Rowan? With a sick lurch of her stomach, Amy was sure he must have. She drank down more wine. What did it matter now that she and Lewis were together? Of course she knew he must have had other relationships in all the years they'd been apart. Even she'd had a few.

She watched the programme until the end, by which time two other bodies had been discovered, there was a whole shoal of red herrings and DI Ashley McArthur was frantically trying to escape from a burning tenement. Callum jerked awake at the burst of the theme tune.

'Cal?' she asked, over the music. 'Gregor told me… he said you'd split up with Sheena. Are you okay about it?'

If this had been a female friend or one of her sisters, they would have spent all evening in in-depth analysis of the relationship and every nuance of the break-up, and would have recounted the dialogue word for word – typical man, bottling it up.

'I'm fine,' Callum said. 'I mean, she wanted to go back to Glasgow, but we weren't really going anywhere anyway. She's a great girl, but there wasn't any… spark anymore.'

'That's exactly how it was with me and Stuart, in the end,' Amy said, with a flash of recognition. 'No spark.'

Callum looked sharply at her. 'And that's really important to you, is it, Amy?'

Amy considered this, a little thrown. Because Callum was a man, they didn't usually discuss relationships. 'Well, yes. I mean, it isn't everything, but there has to be passion.'

'And you have that with Lewis?'

'Of course,' Amy said. Even the mention of his name made her tingle. 'Cal, I've been in love with Lewis since I was sixteen. No matter who else I was seeing, I couldn't stop thinking about him –' She broke off. Maybe nothing could compete with that first love experience, but she'd always felt that Lewis had meant too much to her to become lost in the past.

'If you say so.'

'Cal, what's all this about? You're bound to be upset about Sheena and I'm sorry about that, but Lewis and me –'

'Can't you see he's no good for you?' Callum raised his voice almost to a shout and she jumped at the unexpectedness of it.

'No, I can't,' she shouted back. 'And if you're going to diss my boyfriend then I think you should leave before you say something you'll regret –'

Callum jumped to his feet. 'Here's the thing – I don't regret it. I should have said something weeks ago.'

'No, you shouldn't.' Amy was on her feet also and yelling. 'Because it's NONE OF YOUR BUSINESS.'

'It is my business.' Callum's voice softened. 'You're one of my best friends and I don't want to see you get hurt.'

'I'm not hurt,' Amy said, slightly calmer. 'I'm in love. I've never been so happy.'

'He really messed up my cousin,' Callum said, going into the attack again. 'I've never seen anyone in such a state.'

'I feel sorry for her, honestly I do. But maybe they just weren't right for each other,' Amy said. 'Is she all right now?'

'Yes.' Callum's face was grim. 'But it took her years to get over it. She left the village because of him.'

Callum's family was very close.

'I'm sorry,' Amy said, again. She meant it. She could hardly contemplate the pain of breaking up with Lewis.

'He treats you like dirt,' Callum went on. 'How many times have I seen you sitting on your own in the pub, because he's late or has stood you up yet again?'

'Sometimes when he's writing he forgets the time,' Amy defended.

Callum shook his head. 'Writing? Who does he think he is, Noel Gallagher?'

'Actually, he's very talented,' Amy hissed.

'I bet he is,' Callum said, with a very uncharacteristic sneer.

'You are so out of order.'

'He's twenty-six, Amy. How much longer does he feel that he can doss around, smoking weed and day-dreaming about being the next Ed Sheeran?'

'You wouldn't understand.'

'Oh, what – because I actually work for a living?'

'You're such a man of substance,' Amy sneered.

'Yeah? Well, the only substance Lewis ever has is illegal.'

'Now you sound like my dad.'

'And he flirts with every woman he meets.'

'So what if he's a bit of a flirt?' Amy said, her voice rising again. 'It doesn't mean anything. It's me that gets to go home with him.'

Callum threw his hands up in despair. 'Listen to yourself, Amy. Look, I'm going.'

'Yes, I think you should.'

Callum took a few steps towards the door, then spun back round to face her. 'When it all ends in tears – which it will – then don't come crying to me.'

'Don't worry. I won't,' Amy shouted.

'I mean it, Amy. You're on your own. And that means no more phoning me up in the middle of the night whenever you and your mates need to be baled out. Get *Lewis* to do it –'

Amy said nothing.

'… oh, no. I forgot – he can't drive, and he's always off his tits.' Callum marched towards the door, closing it sharply behind him.

'Good grief. Where's the fire?' came Brooke's surprised voice from the hallway.

Amy collapsed onto the sofa and burst into tears as Brooke came into the room. 'What's going on?' she asked.

'We had a row.'

'Well, I'd gathered that much.'

'He was so horrible,' Amy said, as if they were children again. She reached out her hand and Brooke put a scented, lacy white hankie into it. She mopped at her eyes. Brooke put her arms round her and she breathed in the familiar fragrance of irises. She was going to miss her sister when she went back to Glasgow at the start of the new term.

'You'll make it up in a couple of days,' Brooke said. 'Cal isn't the type to sulk.'

'No,' Amy agreed. She managed a smile. 'We haven't fallen out since we were eleven,' she said. 'I dared him to jump out of Farmer Galbraith's hayloft and he broke his ankle.'

'I think I remember that.' Brooke chuckled. She went into the kitchen, returning a moment later with a large plate of banoffee pie with cream and a clean glass.

'I just love your desserts,' she said, splashing some wine into the glass. She dug enthusiastically into the pie. Remarkable that such a delicate, frail looking slip of a girl should have the appetite of a fifteen stone builder. Then again, Amy suspected that she didn't eat properly when she was at the uni, preferring to prioritise her pitiful income on Red Marlboros and Merlot.

'Callum's really quite sexy, don't you think?' she asked, when she'd finished. She sipped her wine.

'He's about as sexy as Grey Hippo.'

Grey Hippo was a childhood soft toy of Brooke's, somewhat tattered and worn, who still sat in state on her pillow. It was quite impossible to feel desire for a man she'd known since they'd first met at a playgroup in the village hall, and he'd bashed her over the head with a plastic fire engine; since his favourite outfit had been an Angry Birds tee, long before his voice broke. They'd played Pass the Parcel, jumped around on bouncy castles and gone hunting for tadpoles together.

'No, he is,' Brooke insisted. 'He always seems so sorted and controlled, but I bet he's burning with passion underneath.'

'You're mad.'

'See if I'm not right,' said Brooke.

Chapter 13
Whisky Galore

Sometimes, Amy truly yearned for the anonymity of Edinburgh, the rattle and hum of Broughton Street. She was sitting on a bench in Inveralan Station, which was otherwise deserted. She debated whether to go to the loo again, but decided not to for fear of missing the train. She'd made a brief visit to Inveralan, the time between trains being just long enough to go to the chemist and then have a cup of tea in the Spinning Jenny. It had been very busy with its usual clientele of twittery women, and their small talk had made her irritable. The Kirklochy train drew into the platform and she climbed gratefully on board and collapsed into the seat nearest the door, the pregnancy test kit now safely tucked into her handbag. Her nerves were in shreds – it had taken a few days to get the time off work to make this trip. There was no way she could have bought the test kit in Kirklochy – Lewis' aunt was still the village's chemist. Neither did she feel comfortable seeing Dr McLuskie, whom she'd known all her life. He'd delivered her and both of her sisters.

There was a toilet in the passage just behind her and she was sorely tempted to do the test there and then – but it would be just too sordid to find out if she were bringing a new life into the world in a dirty, paper towel festooned public lavatory on a train.

The wind was chilly as she walked along the coast road to Lewis' flat. It was a relief to close the door behind her and shut out the cold, but she felt sick with nerves as she climbed the stairs. The front room was in disarray – scrumpled up pieces of paper strewn across the sofa, empty coffee cups and becrumbed side plates on the mantelpiece, copies of NME on the floor, mingling with CDs out of their cases. The greasy pages of the *Kirklochy News* which had wrapped their chips a couple of nights ago still lay crumpled on the coffee table. There was a faint smell of vinegar and cannabis.

Lewis didn't seem to be here. Her heart eased slightly – she had some time to herself. She took the pregnancy test kit out of its bag and ripped at the cardboard packaging, fumbling with clumsy fingers, then unfolded the instructions, biting her lip as she tried to follow them. Then she heard Lewis' key in the door.

'Hi. What're you doing?' He climbed over the back of the sofa and sat beside her. Her first instinct had been to try to hide the test and its packaging, but Lewis was her partner – they should be in this together.

'Amy?' Lewis picked up the box from where she'd dropped it on the carpet. 'Have you done it yet?'

She shook her head, unable to speak.

'Well, you better do it now.'

His voice was sharp – sharper than she had ever heard it. She got up and hurried into the bathroom, locking the door behind her.

'Amy? Let me in,' Lewis said, a few minutes later, rattling on the glass. Carefully, she laid the white wand on the edge of the bath and unlocked the door. Maybe he'd give her a cuddle and rub her back and she'd feel better.

Lewis ran his hand distractedly through his hair. 'I really do not need this,' he said.

'Well, maybe I don't need it either.' Amy's voice rose. 'And I didn't do it on my own. It took both of us. *And* I've had all this worry for a week already.'

'I thought we were being really careful.'

'We were. Well, I was –'

Lewis snatched up the white stick and looked intently at it. 'You're not pregnant,' he said.

'Let me see that,' Amy said, peering at it. He was right. There was no blue line in the second box. It occurred to her that this probably wasn't the first pregnancy test he'd witnessed. Lewis exhaled sharply, lifting the hair from his forehead. His face broke into a smile of relief. 'Good grief, Amy. Any time you want to give me heart failure –'

'Oh, I think you're already suffering from that.' Amy pushed past him. 'Don't touch me,' she warned. She needed to be on her own, but didn't want to leave the flat – there was too much to be said. She went into the bedroom and closed the door.

She threw herself down on the bed in the dazzlingly white room, staring up at the ceiling and listening to the tide rushing in. Time passed, but she had no idea how long it was before Lewis tapped on the door: 'Can I come in?'

She sat up as he entered the room. She leaned forward, letting her hair hide her face, but felt the bed subside slightly as he sat down beside her. 'I'm sorry,' he murmured, his voice husky. 'It's just that it was a shock, you know?'

'It was a shock for me, too.'

'I know.' Now he did hug her. Strange that someone who kept such an untidy house and dressed so carelessly always smelled so delicious: of citrusy aftershave and fresh, clean cotton. Gently, he rubbed her back. 'It's just... there's a lot going on for me at the moment. Those tracks we've laid down sound really good. This could be my big break.'

'Again?' Amy said.

Lewis chose to ignore this. 'So are we all right?' he asked.

'I don't know.' Amy was crying now. Lewis pushed back her hair and kissed her face: her brimming eyes, her wet cheeks, her trembling mouth. Then he parted her lips with his tongue and kissed her deep and hot and hard, his hands twisting into her hair.

'Lew,' she whispered, when she'd at last been able to break away. 'If I had been....you know. We would have been a family, wouldn't we?'

'Of course we would.' Still holding her hair, he tilted her head up so that he could look in her eyes.

'You eat vegetable, you cook vegetable and you *are* vegetable,' roared Marcel.

Amy had believed that, after so many of the Frenchman's outrageous insults, she was immune to them, but, tonight, she marched straight out of the kitchen door into the small courtyard outside. She didn't feel equal to an argument with Marcel at the moment: she was too fragile after the events of the last few days. Also, Callum normally phoned or texted her daily but he hadn't been in touch since their falling out. She missed him terribly but wasn't willing to be the first to apologise – it was he who had been in the wrong. 'I'm taking my break,' she called, over her shoulder.

Brooke was sitting at the table outside, reading. She wore a white and green print dress and a big, floppy retro hat to protect her pale skin from the last rays of the sun.

'Good grief. That man is beyond obnoxious.'

'Marcel?' Brooke said, not taking her eyes off her book.

'See? You instantly knew exactly who I was talking about.'

'Mmm.'

Amy pulled out the heavy wrought iron chair opposite her sister and sat down.

'Are you okay?' Brooke asked, finally putting her book down and sipping from her glass of Merlot.

'Yeah. How are you, anyway?'

Because of everything that had been going on, conflicting shifts and the hotel being so busy, she felt she hadn't had a chance just to hang out with Brooke for some days.

'I'm good,' Brooke said. Her face broke into a smile. 'James has found us a flat. It's a basement in Hillhead Street, right beside the library.'

'Sounds fab,' Amy said, although, privately, she thought that a basement flat would be dark and cheerless in winter. Brooke would never think of that, though, only seeing the romance of it all.

'It is.'

Reaching down and searching in her handbag, Brooke produced her phone and began to scroll through various shots of the property. There was a small, slabbed area to the front, full of pretty ceramic pots blazing with pansies, and hanging baskets on either side of a door painted glossy dark blue. Inside, the flat seemed very small, but the vendors had made the most of the space by painting it in neutral colours throughout and keeping it simple and uncluttered, the floorboards stripped and varnished.

'This is Emily's room,' Brooke was saying.

The second bedroom looked truly tiny, but was redeemed by sunflowers peering in the window, natural wood bookcases and shelves lined with coloured baskets for storage in turquoise, pink, yellow and acid green.

'The Wild Child's going to be staying?'

'Yup. Every other weekend.'

Amy wasn't sure that the flat was large enough to accommodate the teenager's attitude problem.

'We've been getting on a bit better, actually. She phoned me the other night.'

'Emily phoned you?'

'Yeah. To say she'd read *Awakening*, you know, Niamh's book, and she thought it was "awesome".'

Amy could imagine that Niamh's youthful first novel, a treatise on teenage angst, would appeal to Emily. 'Well – great.'

'Also, I think I went up in her estimation when I introduced her to Lewis. It gave me a load of street cred. Apparently, Lewis "really gets what she's trying to say". I think she's got a bit of a crush.'

'I'm sure.' Amy had meant to sound light, but instead sounded sharp and cold. 'Evie Martin as well. He's got quite a fan club.'

She still felt uneasy at the thought of Evie's knowing, secret smile.

'Are you guys okay?' Brooke looked concerned, cradling the bowl of her glass in her slender, beringed hands. Her nails were perfect ovals, painted in pearl colour.

'Yeah, of course,' Amy said. Their make-up sex had been amazing, well worth her nail-biting wait. Lewis had never been so tender. He'd clasped her hand and looked into her eyes throughout. They'd both cried afterwards. They didn't go to sleep until sunrise. Down in the street below, she'd heard Shamie Morrison opening the shutters of his newsagent's shop. When she'd woken up later in the morning, Lewis was already awake and gazing at her, his blue eyes serious, his fingers twisted into her hair.

'I thought I was pregnant,' she heard herself say.

Brooke would understand. Scatty, dreamy and absent minded, she'd had quite a few scares during her undergraduate days, although, in truth, it was hard to think of Brooke ever engaging in such a messy pastime as sex. Even now, she had a pink, heart shaped post-it stuck on the bathroom mirror, reminding her to take her pill. She'd always confided in Amy because Jen, of course, never made a mistake. Brooke glanced sharply at her. 'But you're not.'

'No.'

'Are you disappointed?'

'Nooo,' Amy said. 'Well, yes. Maybe a wee bit.'

The sisters looked balefully at a four-by-four with a pink, fluffy and sparkly *Princess Mia On Board* sign in the back window.

Of course, she'd never have planned a baby so early on in her rekindled relationship, but, when it had seemed a possibility, she couldn't help her heart warming, and felt a surge of excitement at the thought of it. A beautiful, blue eyed baby – hers and Lewis', a little boy who looked like Lewis, an extension of their passion. It had somehow seemed fitting.

'Babes, I don't know that Lewis is ideal father material.'

'Amy,' called Aura Wallace, from the kitchen door.

Amy stood back to inspect her handiwork. Instead of a traditional birthday cake, she'd made sparkly cupcakes with pink icing and arranged them on a gold stand.

'That looks amazing,' Brooke said, coming up behind her.

Misty and Duncan were popular in Kirklochy and the party had veered somewhat out of control, with just about everyone in the village having been invited.

Misty had stipulated that there must be no alcohol served as her favourite aunt, Morna, was a recovering alcoholic and she didn't want to expose her to temptation.

'Of course. That won't be a problem,' Amy had said.

Patrick, the hotel's resident mixologist, had been having fun dreaming up a menu of mocktails and sparking grape juice would be served in place of Prosecco. The minibar in Morna's room would be emptied and refilled with Perrier water.

The honeymoon suite hadn't been booked, so Amy had arranged for Misty and Duncan to spend the night there after the party. She planned to make it perfect. She would cut the deepest, reddest and dewiest roses from the hotel's garden, set out a tray of strawberries dipped in white chocolate, scatter rose petals across the counterpane, hang up newly laundered, fluffy white bathrobes and arrange Jo Malone products and scented candles in the bathroom. The air would be rich with the scent of roses. The champagne would be on ice – she hoped and presumed that this was one place where Misty's aunt wouldn't be invited.

The party was being held in the conservatory, which was beautiful, full of fresh flowers and white fairy lights. Brooke had decorated it for the occasion. She didn't have a practical bone in her body, but she excelled at all artistic pursuits and her eye for colour was incredible.

After a scrumptious buffet, Amy watched as Lewis, whom she'd persuaded to provide the musical entertainment, rose from his seat near the front. Even she was unprepared for his beauty. Usually, he dressed as if he were going on a fishing trip but, today, he wore smart black trousers and a snowy white shirt. He'd had his hair cut also, accentuating the lean line of his jaw, his chiselled cheekbones and his deep blue eyes. She caught her breath. Next to her, Gregor was looking smug.

'Your handiwork, I suppose?'

'But of course,' said Gregor. 'And his hair wasn't the only thing I wanted to chop off.' He made a snipping movement with his fingers.

'*Sweetie,*' reproved Robbie.

'Shush,' hissed Amy, as Lewis had taken up his guitar and begun to sing. It was a stripped back, acoustic version of Christina Perri's *1000 Years*, absolutely right for Misty and Duncan. He followed this up with Emeli Sandé's *Next To Me*. Finally, he put down his guitar and sang Robert Burns' *My Love is Like a Red, Red Rose*, a cappella.

Amy wasn't the only person in the room in tears.

Everyone had respected Misty's wish to have no alcohol at her party, but they still seemed to be in high spirits. The night would be long and light and Euan, as local DJ, had turned up with several boxes of vinyl records – an eclectic selection.

Now everyone was on the dance floor. Amy and Lewis shuffled around, holding each other closely. He'd been brilliant lately – they'd talked everything through and, when her cramps had finally come on, he'd run her a hot, scented bath and then massaged her aching stomach. Over his shoulder she could see Morna sitting with Robert Kingsley. She'd always thought that he was a shade sleazy, but there was no doubt that he could be extremely charming, and perhaps his "lovely laydees", hand kissing and extravagant compliments were just what Morna needed to help rebuild her confidence.

Misty said that she'd had the best time.

Breaking away from Lewis for a moment, Amy approached the

podium where Euan was standing behind his decks, his ear-phones on, mixing and scratching energetically.

'Hi,' she bellowed, above the music.

'Do you want a request?'

Amy requested *Uptown Funk*, a favourite of hers and Misty's, and turned back towards the dance floor, nearly bumping into Callum, who was coming in the opposite direction.

'Hey, Ames,' he said, softly, putting out a hand to steady her. He smiled, patted her arm, then was gone. Suddenly, Amy felt better. Her heart relaxed. Maybe they could find a way back to their former easy friendship – so long as he accepted that she was with Lewis. She wouldn't listen to any further criticism of him.

Horrors! Mrs Crombie, her ample figure clothed in a floral blouse and matching skirt, a string of pearls round her neck and a pair of navy court shoes on her feet, had just walked in with her friend, Muriel, a vision in dung brown.

What was she doing here? Mrs Crombie wasn't exactly a socialite – the Free Church was the highlight of her week. She was pathologically stingy, so maybe the free buffet was a draw, or perhaps she approved of the fact that the party was to be teetotal. Then again, probably she was looking forward to being deliciously scandalised by the antics and state of undress of the young team.

'Over here, Amy.' Gregor beckoned her into a shadowy corner. Glancing around furtively, he produced a stylish, slender hipflask in matt silver.

'Greg, we're not meant to have any alcohol.'

'It's only a wee nip. Here.'

Amy took a cautious sip, feeling the whisky burn the back of her throat and warm her right through.

'Bet that hit the spot.'

'It did, but don't let anyone else see.'

'I won't.' He stowed the flask safely in his inside jacket pocket.

Amy turned round to see Aura walking somewhat unsteadily across the dance floor, partly because she was in towering high heels and partly because she was inebriated. 'Lewis,' she hissed. 'Help.'

Lewis was nearby, talking to another guy about music, but he turned towards her at once.

'She's trolleyed. We need to get her out of here.'

Lewis slipped his arm around the girl's shoulders, her head flopping against him. 'Which room are you in, love?' he asked, when they were out in the foyer. Although Aura had worked in the hotel kitchen since leaving school, it was the first time she'd stayed as a guest. 'Bet you say that to all the girls.'

'Which room?' said Amy, much more sharply.

'Top of the stairs.'

It took some time to manoeuvre the teenager up to the first floor. But, eventually, they were standing outside her door – but then her key didn't work.

'Wrong one,' said Amy wearily. 'Think, Aura, what colour is your room?'

'Yellow,' said Aura, leaning against the wall.

'Buttercup. That's upstairs.'

Some time later, Amy unlocked the door of the Buttercup Room. Aura staggered in and lay flat on her back on the bed, her flaxen hair extensions fanned out over the pillow. 'The room's spinning,' she said.

Lewis went into the en suite bathroom and returned with a glass of water. 'Drink this,' he said. 'All of it. You'll feel better, honest. Then get to bed and sleep it off.'

Not for the first time, Amy thought how kind he could be.

'I will if you come with me,' Aura said, but she sat up obediently. Lewis held the glass to her lips so that she could sip from it.

'I feel as if I've died and gone to Heaven,' she said, looking him full in the face and managing a flirtatious smile.

'You'll feel as if you've died and gone to Hell in the morning,' Amy said tartly. Then she relented, pushing back some damp hair from the girl's forehead. 'Get some sleep and phone down to reception if you need anything.'

Out in the corridor, she leaned heavily against the wall. 'Misty asked me specially to make sure there was no drinking. I feel as if I've let her down.'

'You haven't.' Gently, Lewis rubbed her back. 'Come on.'

'Thanks for helping me with her,' Amy muttered. She supposed

Lewis had had more than his fair share of nights on the razz. He held out a hand to her and they went downstairs.

Back at the party, several people were dancing, but several others seemed to be going out of one door, while others came in the other. It was like a French farce.

'I'm just going outside for a smoke,' Brooke was saying, picking up her dinky handbag. 'Are you coming, Niamh?'

Niamh nodded, and the two women disappeared through the French windows. A bunch of other people came back in, chatting and laughing, while another group left.

'Good idea,' Lewis said. Amy followed him.

Brooke and Niamh were sitting on a bench talking intimately and swigging from a bottle of Chardonnay like a couple of down-and-outs. Brooke had been delighted that her new friend, inspired by the peace and quiet, had decided to stay on and work on her novel after the writing retreat had come to an end. Jen had agreed that she could move into the chalet, now vacant, for a knock-down price. Brooke passed her the bottle and she took another gulp.

'Where did you get that?' Amy demanded.

'We hid it in the fountain this afternoon,' Brooke said. 'You know, to keep it chilled.'

'Very clever,' Lewis said, his lips twitching.

'It's not funny,' Amy snapped. 'Misty specifically asked that there shouldn't be any alcohol. Of all the juvenile –'

'I'm sorry, Amy.' In her vintage Laura Ashley dress, her large blue eyes cast down, Brooke looked the picture of innocence and abject apology. However, Amy knew from long experience that she was always charmingly apologetic, but also that her behaviour never changed.

'Well, I just hope Morna doesn't find out. Who could blame her for being tempted if she knew you all had a stash of booze?'

'She won't find out,' put in a cousin of Misty's, who'd been giggling nearby with a glamorous gaggle of girls.

'You're sure about that, are you?'

'Yeah, because they've set up the bar in the Gents'. No way she'll ever go in there. Or Misty.'

Amy pushed her hands through her hair in vexation – this evening was becoming like something out of *Whisky Galore*. 'I give in.'

Back inside, Euan was still sweating behind his mixing desk, and swigging from a bottle of spring water – or, more likely, gin and tonic, Amy thought, sourly.

Misty and Duncan were bidding everyone goodnight.

'Thanks, Ames. This has been my best birthday ever,' whispered Misty, pulling her into a tight embrace, and making her feel more guilty than ever. It was some time before she and Duncan tripped happily upstairs, hand in hand, as they kept stopping to chat to everyone they passed.

Most people were now somewhat the worse for wear, but trying to cover up the fact that they were pie-eyed, even the young minister, who'd obviously been plied with drink all evening.

'Are you all right, Mr McIvor?'

'Call me Tom.' His speech was slightly slurred.

'Are you all right, er… Tom?' She nudged Lewis sharply. 'Do you want Lewis to see you home?'

Lewis looked horrified for a nano-second, but then his face smoothed out into a charming smile.

'No, it's fine. The manse isn't far away.' He wove towards the door, none too steady on his feet. Robert Kingsley took Morna's hand, raised it to his lips, and kissed it. 'Enchanté, Morna,' he boomed, giving it the full Laurence Olivier. 'This is not goodbye: it is but au revoir.'

What a plank – but he had brilliantly succeeded in distracting Morna, and Amy was grateful to him for this. Suddenly, he winked at her.

'You see?' Mrs Crombie said. 'It is possible to have a wonderful evening without alcohol.'

'I need a drink,' groaned Amy.

'Can I stay the night?' Lewis asked, after even the most hardcore guests had swayed out into the darkness.

She and Lewis lay wrapped round each other, just managing to fit into the narrow bed, talking and laughing softly about the events of the evening, their voices soft and lazy in the darkness, her head on his chest and her hands clasped in his.

The next day was Amy's day off and she felt she'd totally earned it. She and Brooke apologised to each other for their little spat at the party and, since it was a fine day, they decided to go into the village for coffee and cake at Fratelli's. As they walked along the promenade, the sun was blazing out of a blue sky, tempered by a brisk breeze, water frothing around the rocks. Suddenly, Amy's sunhat blew off and, giggling, the sisters chased after it, climbing over the seawall and onto the beach. She heard the clanking of the ramp and the roar of the engine as the ferry began the short trip to the Tara Isles, gulls shrieking as they swooped down, hoping for food. The boat was crowded with tourists, making the most of the good weather and hoping to see some of the many puffins on the island, or even some grey seals. Families were out, enjoying the sunshine, children darting in and out of the shallows, or eating Fratelli's ice cream and building sandcastles, mums and dads watching contentedly from tartan travelling rugs. Two wee girls were searching for shells. A bunch of teenagers were playing volleyball, laughing and calling to each other. Narrowly missing demolishing a sandcastle, Amy managed to grab her hat. As another gust of wind arose, she held it to her chest instead of putting it back on, looking out to sea as the sun sparkled across the waves. Two men were surfing: Amy identified Jason from the hotel kitchen, who was forever chasing the perfect wave, his blond ponytail flapping behind him.

'Wow,' said Brooke, who was now standing beside her. They watched for a while, entranced by the skill of the two men as they climbed, and then rode, a huge wave, bending forward on their boards, falling in and remounting. At one point, Jason was thrown high into the air, crashing back into the water. Finally, they let the tide carry them back onto the beach.

'Who's the hottie?' Amy heard. Two pretty girls, both guests at the hotel, had also strolled over to spectate. Both had enviable figures, much in evidence as they each wore bikinis which were little more than four small triangles of cloth – one in scarlet, the other in bright yellow. 'Hey, Jase. You looked amazing out there,' called the girl in red. 'Who's your friend?'

Amy felt Brooke nudge her. 'It's Cal,' she said. Sure enough, walking up the beach behind the Australian, was Callum, in a turquoise and black wetsuit. They were both grinning in exhilaration, their teeth very white in their tanned faces.

'This is Callum,' said Jason. 'Cal – Jessie and Rachael.'

'Hi, Jessie, hi, Rachael,' Callum said, smiling at the two girls. He unclipped the surfboard from his ankle and briskly began to rub at his hair with the big towel. He unzipped his wetsuit and peeled it from his torso, revealing broad, tanned shoulders and defined abs, then tied the sleeves at his waist, the muscles in his arms rippling. Then he lifted his board and drove it into the sand. *Aidan Turner, eat your heart out*, Amy caught herself thinking. The two girls began to giggle and flutter their eyelashes, vying for his attention. Sooo obvious, Amy thought, scornfully, but her mouth was dry, and deep down she felt a flutter of butterflies. Cal *was* hot. Why had she never noticed it before? But she knew that really. They'd been in the Friend Zone forever, and she just hadn't thought of him as a real man.

Chapter 14
Virgin on the Ridiculous

'Woo-hoo.'

Jen glanced up from the reservations diary.

'I'm back. Have yous missed me?'

'Of course,' Jen lied smoothly. 'Hi, Tiara.'

Bearing in mind that a couple of the sleazier tabloids had just printed lurid accusations that Jaden McGaughey had fathered a "love child" two years previously, Tiara seemed to be in remarkably good spirits. Tanned to the colour of a Caramac bar, she wore skinny jeans and a sparkling white tee-shirt, the simplicity of her outfit lifted by an enormous blue and gold handbag. Jen could smell the leather – the scent of luxury – from where she was standing. Even she knew that this was the *Fabiola*. It was featured in all the celebrity magazines and cost what, for most young girls, would be about six months' salary. It was made in Milan and there was a waiting list at Harvey Nichols for it. Tiara could afford such luxuries. As a result of her high profile marriage, she was beginning to carve out a career for herself as a lingerie model and *Caledonian Celeb* columnist, sharing her style and beauty secrets and gossiping about the other "celebrities" she met during her frantic partying schedule. This was heavily ghosted – Jen reckoned that signing a birthday card was the height of Tiara's writing ability. She was accompanied by her cousin and close friend, Chanel, who was head to toe in Primark.

'So – how's married life?' Jen asked, feeling that it was expected.

'Oh, it's brilliant.'

'Jaden not with you?' Jen crossed her fingers behind her back.

'No. Playing away.' Tiara spoke without a trace of irony. 'He's went tae Spain tae play against Athletico Madrid.'

'Oh, I love Spain,' said Chanel. 'My best holiday ever was in Benidorm.' She smiled reminiscently. 'Happy days. My first ever pregnancy test.'

'You remember my big cousin, Nell, don't you, Jenny?' Tiara said.

'Of course. Good to see you again, Chanel.' Once seen, never forgotten! Tall and broad, her thick make-up bumpy over her cheeks where she'd tried to cover up her spots, Chanel had peroxide blonde hair scraped tightly back into a ponytail, a style known as the Maryhill facelift. Her wrists jangled with many gold bracelets – Argos' finest, and she had three gold earrings in each ear, all of them big enough for a budgie to perch on. Her voice was like a foghorn. She did, however, have a sweet smile.

'Hey, Jase,' Tiara called, spotting the Australian. 'Could you be a pal and get wur bags?'

'Jase! Ma man! Great tae see you again,' greeted Chanel, in a voice that could have been heard on the other side of the Minch. 'Looking fit as. I'm a pure pushover for a man with a tan.'

Poor Jason. Jen hid a grin. 'So, how are your mum and dad?' she asked, as Jason staggered back into the foyer, weighed down by four Burberry suitcases, a vanity case and a hat box. Good grief – anyone would think that Tiara was flitting, rather than just staying for a few days. She rolled her eyes. 'See since they've got back together? They've been like a couple of newly-weds. Cannae keep their hands off each other. It's well embarrassing, making out at their age.'

'Their blessing's going to be such a beautiful ceremony,' Jen gushed, trying to push this unwelcome image from her mind. It was planned that the renewal of vows would take place in the rose garden, weather permitting, or else in the conservatory dining room.

'Aye, I'm looking forward to it.'

'C'mon, Ti, let's go tae wur rooms and freshen up,' said Chanel. 'Then I'm going to hit the bar and have a wee voddy before my tea.'

Jen groaned inwardly. A "wee voddy" probably meant that, in the proud tradition of the McCracken family, the girl would have to be carried up to her room in the small hours.

'I pure love this place. It's the bomb,' Chanel said, as the two girls followed Jen upstairs. They'd been allocated the Blue Room and the Heather Room which was next door. The honeymoon suite was, of course, reserved for Michael and Marguerite.

'Yeah, it's brilliant,' said Tiara. 'Me and Jaden's going to come here for wur first wedding anniversary. I'm going to book the honeymoon suite today. There'll be the best party ever.'

Jen clenched her fists – was there to be no end to this torture? She focused on the large amount of money that Jaden McGaughey – perhaps in unspoken atonement for his shenanigans – had paid out for his in-laws and their family to stay here and celebrate together.

Jen unlocked the door to Chanel's room. The Heather Room, decorated in shades of purple, pink and deep wine, was charming and Jen's personal favourite. Chanel bounced on the large double bed a few times, her earrings and bracelets jangling, then wandered into the en-suite bathroom. Who wouldn't love the monsoon shower, thick, fluffy towels and dressing gown, handmade soap and Jo Malone products?

'Ooh, I feel just like wan a thae Kardashians. Noo all I need's a hot guy,' she said, returning to the bedroom. She waded through the thick carpet over to the window, looking out at the beach. 'It's so quiet here,' she said, and, for the first time, a wistful look crossed her round face. 'No wee neds hanging about, no jakeys, no junkies, no helicopters, no burnt out cars –'

Suddenly, Jen found herself warming to this big girl with the booming voice and the larger-than-life personality. 'Well, I'll leave you to freshen up. Dinner is served from seven o'clock onwards, and you're welcome to join us for a drink in the drawing room beforehand.'

Always prepared, Jen had made sure that there was plenty of vodka and gallons of Irn Bru as a mixer, as this was Tiara's favourite tipple.

'There's something I need to talk to you about, Jenny,' Tiara said, as soon as Jen had let her into the Blue Room. 'Ooh, this is minted.'

The room did look enchanting with the sun slanting in the window, especially the arrangement of fresh flowers, all in shades of blue. Tiara darted over to the tray of chocolates and fresh fruit which sat on a table by the window and grabbed a large strawberry, eating it delicately and then licking the juice from her fingers and her plump lips.

'If I can be of any assistance –'

'Oh, yeah. Right. Well, what it is is – my Uncle Rab, right, he was married to my Auntie Bella, who's my mum's sister, and my Uncle Tam, he was married to my Auntie Sadie, who's my mum's other sister, right?'

Jen nodded.

'Then, Uncle Rab, he got Auntie Sadie pregnant, and him and my Auntie Bella, they split up. But then, my Auntie Bella started going out with my Uncle Tam, and Uncle Rab, he's seeing my cousin Summer the now –'

'Right,' Jen said, her heart sinking. She must have looked nonplussed, for, to her amazement, Tiara pulled a gold pen and a brochure for a spa from her designer handbag and, leaning on the dressing table, began to scribble a diagram on the back of it, detailing the complicated inter-relationships among her family.

'Bit of a ladies' man, is he, your Uncle Rab?'

Tiara nodded.

'What about your Aunt Sadie?'

Tiara looked uncomfortable. 'She's in a relationship with… another wumman.'

'So you want us to separate the three couples?' Jen squinted at the brochure. 'Rab and Summer, Bella and Tam and Sadie and…. Johnina.'

'Aye, you've got it.' Tiara seemed impressed that Jen had grasped the complexities of her relatives so quickly. 'You're a pal, Jenny.'

'No worries,' said Jen, far less confident than she sounded.

'Uncle Tam was a pretty useful boaxer in his day.'

'This is my pulling dress,' Chanel boomed, as she made her way, somewhat unsteadily, into the drawing room.

'It's a great colour,' Brooke said, with her usual diplomacy. The dress was an emerald green, sequinned number, cheap, shiny and shoddily made, the hem uneven and drooping at one side. It was also a size too small and several inches too short, revealing legs which were streaked from an inexpert fake tan. There was a bald patch on the front, where the sequins had rubbed off.

'Where'd you get it? The Barras?' asked a hatchet faced blonde. 'Hauf the sequences've fell aff, look.'

'Shut up, Summer,' snapped Chanel. She threw a sideways glance at the tattoo on her cousin's upper arm: *Night, night, papa – sleep tight. Your forever in my heart.* 'That's no' how you spell "you're".'

'I know that,' sniffed Summer, drawing herself up to her full height – about six feet two in those heels. 'The tattooist was dyslexic,' she added, with dignity. 'An' at least ah'm no' wearin' a baldly dress.'

Jen took note – Uncle Rab's girlfriend. Suntans seemed to be the height of fashion in Glasgow – Summer was orange, with a full sleeve tat on both arms. She wore an outfit which looked supremely uncomfortable – white body-con dress and pole dancers' shoes. Rab had the look of a prosperous bookmaker, which, Jen had gathered, he was. His hair was black and very obviously dyed and swept back – Jen was sure – to cover a bald patch. Also deeply tanned, he stank of Paco Rabanne and wore a heavy gold bracelet. His unlined forehead was testimony to a devotion to Botox. There was something very off-putting about a man who clearly took so much trouble with his appearance, Jen thought.

'This is Jaden's wee sister, Demi,' Chanel said, as a teenager with her fair share of the famous McGaughey dark good looks waddled across the room towards them. Jen remembered her from the McGaughey-Mc-Cracken wedding but now eyed her with some trepidation – she was heavily pregnant and surely must be about to pop.

'I'm no' due for another two weeks,' she protested, as if reading Jen's mind.

'Thank you.' Another guest, outwith the wedding party, was lifting a glass of champagne from the tray of a passing waitress. He raised his glass to the woman with him. 'I always find champers quite an aphrodisiac.'

'What's that when it's at hame?' asked Summer.

'Makes you horny,' explained Chanel.

'Chanel.' Jen took the girl by the arm and drew her aside, breathing in a cheap perfume which could strip paint. 'Where's Tam?'

'Him and Bella's went to the bar.'

Jen breathed more easily. The crisis was averted for this evening, she hoped, having arranged to seat each couple in a discreet alcove in the dining room.

Later, everyone seemed to be gathered for dinner except the bride and groom. The older women all had hair dyed to a state of matt dryness, either barmaid blonde or brunette shades far too harsh for their complexions, and to be wearing dresses which were rather too low cut, revealing acres of tanned, crinkled cleavage.

'Isn't she cute?' Brooke asked, as a wee blonde girl raced past in a flouncy pink dress and matching furry cape, a silver tiara on her curls. 'She looks like a Disney princess.'

'Miami,' bellowed a peroxide woman, giving chase, 'gaunnae do what I tell you for once?'

Two older women were now passing, one with a green feather sticking out of her head, the other in a grey hat which was attached precariously to her beehive like a satellite dish to the outside wall of a council flat.

'Mick and Rita's done us proud,' said the woman in green.

'Aye, they have, Maureen. Isn't it nice to see both the families together?'

'Aye, hen. The only one that's not made it's wee Jeannie – you know: her that had the hert attack in the toilets at The Forge.'

'This is like something out of *Still Game*,' sniggered Brooke.

'See if yous werenae all here?' Maureen went on. 'It would be –'

'Cheaper,' muttered Jen.

'Jared! Seth! Caleb! Gaunnae pack it in?' bawled another super-glam girl, with pumped up lips, tottering over to split up three wee boys who were rolling on the floor, fighting.

Jen stood by, watching, as the happy couple strolled in hand-in-hand, fashionably late. Dramatically slimmed down, Rita was wearing floor length, plunging zebra print. With dignity, they walked towards the central table which had been reserved for them.

'She's been doing Slimming World,' someone remarked.

'Thae weans are my world,' said another voice.

'Aye, Faliraki, all inclusive. I won five hundred on the bingo.'

As the evening wore on, people seemed to loosen up and the conversation was lively, accompanied by much throaty smokers' laughter. The McCrackens' choice of main course of steak with all the trimmings seemed to be a popular one. Jen congratulated herself on a very successful evening.

'Have yous got broon sauce?' said Mick.

'Can ah just get some ginger?' asked Demi, using the generic Glaswegian term for soft, fizzy drinks.

Late in the evening, when the black forest gateau had been eaten and everyone was lingering over coffee and brandy, the kitchen door opened and Chanel, expertly swinging her hips and carrying a pile of dirty dishes, came in.

'Nell, you shouldn't be doing this,' protested Jen. 'You're our guest.'

'Oh, aye, so ah am,' said Chanel, not at all abashed. 'Force of habit. Ah'm a waitress mysell.'

'Well, go and sit down, and let us wait on *you*.'

But Chanel's eyes had lit on Marcel. 'Haw, are you the chef?' she asked, although the checked trousers and tall white hat were something of a clue. 'That steak was scrumptious, mah man, and so are you.'

For once, Marcel seemed to be speechless.

The next day, Jen sat, relaxed, in Sascha's salon. She and Patrick had been invited to the blessing and she was determined to look her best. She planned to out-Brooke Brooke and look as pretty and feminine as she knew how.

'You have no idea how long I've been waiting to do this,' Gregor said, advancing towards her with a pair of scissors, the shiny blades catching the light. First he cut in a soft fringe, then trimmed the ends, then, grabbing a pair of straighteners, set her hair into rippling curls. Jen looked in the mirror, enchanted. She looked so different, and, as Gregor had promised, softer.

'I'm sure you'll catch the eye of the lovely Paddy now,' Gregor said.

'Not interested,' said Jen.

'If you say so, sweetie,' said Gregor. 'He's a total hottie. And nice with it. Why does he have to be straight? What a waste.'

Playfully, Jen slapped his hand. 'Greg, you're married.'

'True, but I suppose I've got no chance, anyway.'

'Me, neither,' Jen muttered to herself.

'So, what's your dress like? I'm guessing subtle, but sexy.'

'Red silk,' Jen said. Subtle but sexy was exactly the look she was aiming for – her dress left everything to the imagination, but clung to every curve. With her pale complexion and her dark hair, it suited her to perfection.

'And of course you'll be wearing your Louboutins.'

Jen nodded. She had just one pair of Louboutins and they were her most treasured possession. She'd saved up for them for a long time – who knew how many pints she'd pulled and lattes she'd mixed to afford them – and bought them for herself as a reward when she passed her final exams. Brooke called them her Madame Bovary shoes. She felt like a model in them – they made her much taller, her legs longer and more shapely. They made her feel beautiful, sexy, in control.

After Gregor had finished styling her hair, Sascha painted her lips and her nails, both fingers and toes, scarlet, gave her smoky eyes and long lashes, and shaded her cheekbones in pink.

The weather had turned out good enough for the ceremony to be held in the rose garden as originally planned. Jen walked across the crazy paving, stepping carefully in her high heels, her skirt flirting pleasingly around her calves, her toes with their red nails peeping out from her shoes. The hotel's resident hairdresser and beautician must have been busy – all around were full-on slap, elaborate up-dos, beehives, plaits and curls, all topped off with a fascinator.

Standing at the end of a row, she noticed Chanel facing her. With a cheery grin, the girl lifted her hand and waved. She was wearing a dress of a virulent turquoise, tight across her chest and stomach, and a pair of white stilettos. There was a buzz of excited conversation among the guests as Rita and Mick made their way, hand-in-hand, towards the minister.

'Ooh, it's her wedding dress,' someone behind Jen murmured. It was now clear why Rita had been on such an extreme diet – she had been determined to get into the dress she had first worn at nineteen. It was a monstrosity in white satin, with the padded shoulders which had been popular in the 1980s, a square neckline and a ruched skirt which looked like a pair of bathroom curtains Jen's granny had once owned. It may have been the height of fashion at the time, but it now looked like something which had been lying, forgotten, on the floor of the *Dynasty* wardrobe for thirty-odd years.

Behind them walked Tiara and her brother Kian, Tiara floating with her dancer's grace, Kian clumping along beside her.

After the first hymn, the Rev McIvor read those beautiful words about love from 1st Corinthians, the gathering absolutely stilled. There was only the mellifluous sound of his voice and the distant swell of surf:

> *'If I speak in the tongues of men or of angels, but have not love, I am
> only a resounding gong or a clanging cymbal. If I have the gift of proph-
> ecy and can fathom all mysteries and all knowledge, and if I have a
> faith that can move mountains, but do not have love, I am nothing. If
> I give all that I possess to the poor and give over my body to hardship
> that I may boast, but do not have love, I gain nothing... And now these
> three remain: faith, hope and love. But the greatest of these is love.'*

He spoke a few more words, then it was time for the McCrackens to make their vows, which they had written themselves.

'Marguerite,' said Mick, turning to his wife and taking her hands. 'What can I say? We lost our way. Drifting in a cold, cold sea – but I love you and you love me. Two herts that beat in time, I am yours and you are mine. Together we are one, wur future has just begun.'

'Aw, that's pure beautiful,' said the woman standing next to Jen, dabbing at her eyes with a lacy handkerchief.

'Michael,' Rita clasped her husband's hands more tightly, gazing up at him. 'I regret every minute we've spent apart, lonely without my husband, my lover, my best friend, my soulmate. I love you and know that I have finally come home.'

Behind her parents, Tiara was weeping.

The couple's speeches were cliché-ridden and spoken haltingly, as if they were both playing customers in a double glazing ad, and, in Mick's case, heavily influenced by Lionel Ritchie, but Jen was convinced of their utter sincerity, and she found herself blinking back a tear – her mascara wasn't waterproof. Patrick caught her eye at that moment, and threw her a wicked smile. After the final hymn, the guests began to file out of the garden.

'Aw, that was dead romantic.' Jen overheard.

'Ah know. The tears were tripping me.'

★

Because the McCrackens had married in 1986, the theme of the reception was the eighties. Posters of a young Madonna, a dreadlocked Boy George, Spandau Ballet, Mr T, Arthur Daley and Terry McCann and other idols of the decade had been laminated and hung all round the room. *Desperately Seeking Susan* – Rita's all-time favourite film – was showing on a huge monitor behind the bar. The waitresses all wore ra-ra skirts, lace gloves and legwarmers. The McCrackens had brought with them Mullet Malkie, a favourite DJ at their local social club in Linthouse. Rita and Mick took the floor for the first waltz, *Crazy for You*, by Rita's heroine, Madonna.

Later, Jen, sipping a Malibu and pineapple, had to admit that it was turning out to be a wonderful evening. She was beginning to wish she'd been around in the eighties – the music was the bomb. Along with all the other guests, she bellowed out a song about not needing to take your clothes off to have a good time.

'Lovely girl,' Patrick said, joining her. She followed his gaze to where Chanel was sitting with yet another cousin, a painfully shy, spotty boy of about fifteen, managing to coax a smile out of him, motherly despite her own youth. Jen nodded. Earlier, she'd seen the girl discreetly helping one of her great-aunts to the lavatory, and, earlier still, playing with some of the younger kids, making them laugh and beg to be allowed to stay up longer.

'And now another blast from the past,' said Mullet Malkie. 'It's the Human League with *Sound of the Crowd*.'

Tiara grabbed Jen by the hand and the two girls ran on to the dance floor, stepping into a kaleidoscope of flashing colour. They danced until they were breathless and exhausted. Some time and several Malibu and pineapples later, Jen was in physical pain, her ribs aching from laughing so much at Chanel's chat and antics. Having announced loudly that she fancied him, she was now virtually sitting on the knee of Garry, Kian's best friend. Great girl, Jen thought, a little hazily, but as subtle as a whoopee cushion. Patrick was nearby with a bunch of neddy looking boys, chatting about football. She noticed, not for the first time, how easily he fitted in, his ability to mix with and be liked by people from all walks of life.

Everyone surged forward for the buffet. Again indulging Rita and Mick's taste, it consisted of Indian delicacies – chicken and vegetable pakoras, onion bhajis, samosas and poppadums with chutney and yoghurt. Jen ate hungrily, mopping up some of the alcohol.

'This is well generous of Jaden,' said Chanel, dunking a piece of tomato pakora in raita dip. 'A vodka and Irn Bru's £2.20 in my local, and I've had nine the night. That's £19.80. See if the whole 32 of us had the same? It would come to... £633.60.'

Jen blinked in admiration. 'Well, hello, Rachel Riley.'

After this, the evening flew by, a hazy mix of sticky-sweet alcohol and dance music, until Malkie turned down the lights. 'This is your last chance for romance,' he announced. 'Spandau Ballet with *True*.'

This had obviously been a favourite mooney back in the day, as Mick and Rita's friends all surged onto the dance floor, the men being dragged by the women.

'Would you like to dance?' asked Patrick, appearing before her. He pretended to double-take. 'Jennifer, it's you.'

'Funny,' said Jen, but she allowed him to take her hand and pull her to her feet. Secretly, she hoped that he liked the change, even found her beautiful. She slipped her arms round his neck and rested her head on his shoulder, breathing in the spicy, lemony scent of his aftershave. Even in her killer heels, he was still taller than she was, and made her feel protected, his arms round her waist. They didn't move onto the dance floor but stood where they were by the door, barely swaying to the music.

'... happy 'til you came along –' Jen was sure she'd heard those few words above the sax. They must be coming from the corridor.

'Pads,' she murmured, disentangling herself reluctantly. 'Can you hear something?'

Taking his hand, she pulled him towards the door.

'... ruined my whole life.' It was a rough Glaswegian accent.

Out in the corridor, two men, Uncle Rab and a thickset bald man, Uncle Tam, the "pretty useful boxer", Jen presumed, were squaring up to each other.

'Rubbish,' Uncle Rab was saying. 'Yous werenae suited, any fool could see that.'

'I should teach you a lesson you'll never forget.' Uncle Tam's face was white with rage.

'Guys.' Jen stepped towards the two men, relieved to note that, in her high heels, she was taller than they were. 'Could you calm it down, please?'

'No offence, darlin', but what's it got to do with you?' Uncle Rab gave a rictus smile, his teeth unnaturally white.

'I am the manager of this hotel and I will call the police if there's any trouble.'

'You know what he done to me?' Uncle Tam asked. 'He got my missus up the stick.'

'I know,' admitted Jen. 'And that was very … discourteous, but I must ask that you –'

'All I ever wanted was a wean,' Uncle Tam said.

'I'm sorry about that,' said Jen. 'But –'

'It's not my fault if you're firing blanks.' Uncle Rab played his trump card. Patrick grabbed Uncle Tam, pinning his arms to his sides, but he wouldn't be able to hold him for long. 'Jen – call the police.'

Jen pulled her iPhone out of her tiny clutch bag and scrolled down her contacts, searching for the number of Philth, the local policeman.

'Okay. No need to get the polis involved,' Uncle Tam conceded. Jen bet it would be far from the first time either of them had seen the inside of a police cell.

'Come on, guys,' Patrick said. 'You'll need to calm down. It's a party – we don't want anyone to get hurt, do we?'

Uncle Rab turned away and sulkily began to walk down the corridor. Uncle Tam hurled his parting shot: 'And that silly wee tart you've got in tow's just after you for your money. She'll make a fool of you then ditch you, mark my words.'

Jen decided to allow him the point.

'You're some woman, Jennifer, to be sure,' Patrick said. Jen could read respect and admiration in his eyes, and, she hoped, something more earthy. 'You look beautiful tonight,' he added.

Jen closed her eyes as he gently began to caress the back of her neck. They were still standing in the hall, just the two of them. Then there was a bang, a clatter of heels and the sound of sobbing. Jen opened her eyes. 'Who was that?'

'Didn't see.'

The door to the Ladies' Room slammed shut, and they could hear the sound of more desperate crying and then violent retching. Jen dashed in, Patrick just behind her. Only one cubicle was locked.

'Who's there?' Jen called.

'Go away.'

'Is that Chanel? Come on, hun, come out and we'll talk.'

There was no answer – just more snuffling and sobbing.

'Chanel?'

'Come on, darlin', it's Paddy. Come out and talk to us.' Patrick's voice was as warm and comforting as Irish coffee.

After a couple of minutes, the sobbing gave way to long gasps. Slowly, the door opened, and Chanel came out. She looked a pitiful sight, her face streaked with tears and make-up, one false eyelash hanging off, her hair collapsing into a laquered mess. Jen and Patrick led her to a pink, padded chair in the corner.

'Tell us what's wrong,' said Jen, kneeling on the cold floor at her feet.

'It… it's that guy, Garry. He says he doesnae fancy me. Naebody does,' howled Chanel, more tears springing up. How difficult must it be for the girl, Jen wondered, to be the cousin and close friend of the beautiful Tiara?

'You're a nice looking girl, Nell – you've just been hanging out with Tiara too long,' Patrick said.

'I came on too strong. I always do that,' Chanel added, trying to dash the tears away with the back of her hand.

'What's more important is that you've got a heart of gold, you're intelligent and you're funny. I haven't laughed so much in years as I did tonight,' Jen said.

'Aye, that's true enough,' muttered Patrick.

Tiara might be gorgeous at look at, but she had the IQ of a coat stand, Jen thought, but didn't say. 'Why should you drop your sights?' she asked. 'You should wait for somebody who's worthy of you.'

'You're a lovely girl, Chanel,' said Patrick, his gentle Dublin accent as soft as melted marshmallows. 'You just wear your heart on your sleeve too much.'

'Look, why don't we go up to your room, make some tea and have a chat?' Jen suggested. Why was she doing this? Was it just because she genuinely liked Chanel, or was she also trying to prove something to Patrick, show him she had a softer, more caring side?

''Kay,' Chanel managed.

'He's well nice, your boyfriend,' Chanel said, later. She was sitting on her bed, wrapped in her fluffy dressing gown and sipping a cup of tea. Having showered and washed off her hairspray and heavy make-up, she looked sweet, young and vulnerable. 'You're dead lucky.'

'Oh, Paddy isn't my boyfriend,' Jen said. 'We're just colleagues.'

'Oh – I thought yous were together,' Chanel said. 'See me, I've got loads of boy pals and we have a right laugh but they don't want me as a girlfriend.'

'I know the feeling,' Jen said. 'Paddy's seeing someone else, actually.'

'Don't tell me – dead pretty and dead skinny?' said Chanel.

Jen nodded gloomily. 'Long legs, Irish accent,' she added.

'Aw, see the Dublin accent? It's dead sexy, so it is,' said Chanel.

'Well, anyway, we're not talking about Paddy and Niamh, we're talking about you,' Jen said, but her heart was hurting – once again, Patrick had been by her side, helping her to diffuse the tension and probably saving Uncle Rab from being KO'd. They made such a good team. What would she do without him? And he'd been so kind to Chanel: she'd brightened up already. She just couldn't help it – she was falling for him all the more deeply. It had felt so right being held in his arms, feeling safe, feeling excited. What if he'd been going to kiss her? At this thought, the excitement mounted. As if reading her thoughts Chanel threw her an arch look. 'Yous seemed to be getting on pretty well earlier,' she said.

'Well… we… it was nothing. Pads is a total flirt. He just can't help himself.'

'It's more than that, Jenny. Yous get on amazing, you light up every time he looks at you. And I don't hink it's wan-sided.'

'Honestly, Nell. Not going to happen,' Jen said, but she felt a great whooshing firework whizz right through her that her new friend had noticed a connection between them.

'I wouldn't give up hope if I was you.'

Jen refilled the kettle and made more tea. Suddenly, after all this time of holding back, denying her feelings, putting up a front, it was a relief to talk. And who better than Chanel, who was perceptive, sympathetic, and would be back in Glasgow in a couple of days?

Much later, snugly wrapped in her duvet but too wired for sleep, Jen thought about the evening. What would have happened if she and Patrick hadn't been so rudely interrupted? Nothing, she told herself firmly. They'd both had a lot to drink and Patrick was an incorrigible flirt. Actually, it was just as well Chanel had blundered on to the scene, or she might have made a fool of herself, said or done something she'd regret. She told herself this, but didn't believe it.

Chapter 15
From Here to Maternity

When Jen woke up the following morning, she felt dreadful: so unco-or-dinated that she could barely switch off her alarm clock's unwelcome 6am shriek. She seldom drank much – she hated to lose control, but, last night, she'd got carried away and had been drunker than she'd ever been – even as a post-exam student. How late had she stayed up, talking to Nell? She must only have had a couple of hours' sleep. Slowly she got up and, holding her head, made her way to the bathroom. She felt sick and shaky and looked terrible – her hair was a sticky, hairsprayed mess, her face grey and her eyes gloopy with yesterday's mascara. Her red silk dress hung, deflated, over a chair, and her scarlet killer heels had been kicked into a corner.

An hour later, she again stood before the mirror. She'd had a long, hot shower, washed her hair, and, putting on a brave face, was wearing a coral coloured shirt and her sharpest suit. Her hair was again straight, shiny and tied back in a neat ponytail. With deft fingers, she stroked foundation over her grey skin and the dark circles round her eyes, then, almost human again, slicked on some coral lipgloss.

As she reached the first floor landing, she was aware of a fracas going on in the foyer. Uncle Rab and Summer were arguing furiously, suit-cases at their feet. Rab wore that quintessential wealthy bookmaker's garment – a camel coat. From this vantage point, Jen could see that he did, indeed, have a bald patch on the top of his head. She could also see Summer's dark roots. They seemed to be having a tug of war with one of the cases, Summer trying to pull it back towards the staircase while Rab made for the door. Suddenly it burst open, several shirts and a pair of black silk pyjamas falling out. Summer gave those an irritable kick.

'Summer, you daft mare, would you pack it in? Thae P.J.s were from Turnbull & Asser.'

'Can we no stay, Rab?' Summer was whining. 'Everyone else is.'

'No, we can not. I've been insulted in better places than this.'

'No, you havnae. Name one place you've been insulted in that's better than this.'

'C'mon, Summer. Get your stuff together and let's go.'

'Aw, Rab. I want to stay. The girls are going to the spa. I want to top up my tan.'

Jen almost laughed. Summer was practically day-glo as it was. She certainly didn't need a makeover – a makeunder, perhaps, to tone down that brassy, frizzy blonde hair. She obviously didn't do subtle. Her make-up seemingly having been applied by a plasterer, she could do with a few lessons in restraint.

'Aye, you are looking a wee bit peely-wally, right enough,' Rab said, shoving his clothes back into the suitcase. Jen stifled a giggle.

Feeling too fragile to face the couple, she watched as Rab grabbed Summer's arm and tried to propel her towards the door, while Summer dug her heels in like a terrier refusing to go out in the rain. Eventually, to Jen's relief, Rab managed to convince the girl to leave by promising to book her into a beauty salon in Glasgow's west end, buy her a new dress in the Italian Centre and take her out for a slap-up meal and to a casino.

In the dining room, those of the wedding guests who had managed to make it to breakfast at all were in a similar state of collapse to herself, having taken too much advantage of the free bar. Chanel was taking alternate sips from a huge mug of black coffee and a magnum of fresh orange juice.

'Best thing to do is have a fry-up, throw up, and start over,' advised another of Tiara's cousins.

'Classy,' smirked Demi, who, being pregnant, had stuck to soft drinks and so was the only adult in the party not hungover to the teeth. She waddled slowly across the room, stomach thrust out and hand on the small of her back, smiling at the others, and ordered a full Scottish breakfast, which she tucked into with relish. Jen again eyed her warily – she wouldn't be able to relax until the girl was back in Glasgow and within easy reach of a good maternity hospital. Another cousin, green in the face, jumped to her feet and hurtled out of the room.

In the kitchen, Amy was preparing the honeymoon breakfast for

Rita and Mick – a tray laden with scrambled egg and smoked salmon, the toast cut into heart shapes, a plate piled with warm croissants and pastries, a bowl of fresh fruit, a bottle of Bucks Fizz and two flutes, and a scented cafetiere. Jen's stomach rumbled loudly, her hangover hunger at war with the constant feeling of nausea.

According to some guests Jen had overheard chatting, the plan was that the wedding party would have a chill-out Sunday at the hotel, then leave early on Monday morning to start the long journey back to Glasgow. The girls, and some of the young guys, were going to take advantage of the spa, while a group of the older men planned to walk along the front to the Claymore Inn for a darts tournament.

Later, Jen went up to the spa. For once, peace reigned. Chanel, looking like an extra from Dr Who, was flicking through a magazine, her head covered in silver paper. Tiara, with a beatific smile on her face, was having a Swedish massage. The atmosphere was chilled and giggly.

'Thae hot stanes are minted.' Jen heard.

Relieved that everything was under control, she made her way back down the corridor. A *Do Not Disturb* sign hung from the door of the bridal suite. She could hear raucous laughter from outside – it had turned out a fine day and a group of the older women were sitting in the rose garden, sipping tea. Glancing out of the open window, she saw Chanel's mum holding court, her voice carried on the gentle breeze. While the other women were wearing low cut tee-shirts and vest tops, she had on a cardigan and over it the pashmina she'd been wearing last night.

'Aye, Bella, I feel the cold. Always have. See that menopause? Thae hot flushes? Bring it on, says I, I could do with a bit of that. Never had as much as wan.'

The other women laughed.

Just then, Patrick walked by with Niamh, her glossy, raven hair lifting slightly in the light wind. Jen's heart hurt. They weren't touching, but she could read the intimacy in their slow pace and the concentration on Patrick's face as he stooped slightly, the better to hear what Niamh was saying. Niamh had claimed that she was staying on in Kirklochy because she found the tranquillity so inspiring, but it was evident to

Jen that that wasn't the only attraction.

'I suppose Niamh's really happy,' she said, trying to keep her voice as light as possible. Brooke was coming in the opposite direction, carrying a pile of freshly laundered towels. She smiled. 'Very,' she agreed. 'It's so great to see her in a good place, after what happened with Diarmid.'

'Yes,' Jen managed, her already down-trodden spirits plummeting still further. As if it wasn't enough that Niamh had Patrick under her spell, she'd also been married to Diarmid O'Brien, a drop-dead sexy, rascally Irish playwright, whose latest play had just opened in Dublin to rave reviews.

Later, the wedding party re-assembled in the dining room for a light lunch. Jen double-took as Chanel walked into the room. She'd hardly recognised her at first. The hotel's resident hairdresser had coloured her frayed peroxide hair a warm brown and cut it so it now swung just below her chin in a shiny bob. Light, subtle make-up enhanced her fair complexion and big, blue eyes. She'd had a fake tan but her skin was golden rather than the deep mahogany favoured by her friends.

'You look beautiful, Nell,' said Jen.

'She certainly does,' agreed Patrick.

Chanel was beaming, the heartbroken, tear-stained girl of the previous evening long gone. 'I look fit as, daen't I? I'm so going to pull noo.'

'Chanel, have you got time for a quick chat?' Patrick asked.

''Course I have.' Chanel looked surprised, but followed him over to a table by the window. Jen watched as he gestured to the girl to sit down, then took a seat opposite her. Whatever it was that he was saying to her, Patrick was leaning forward, his expression, for a change, serious. Chanel seemed to be hanging on his every word. It was quite some time before she went off to rejoin the rest of her family.

'What was all that about?' Jen asked Patrick, once they were alone together.

'She's a real bright spark, Jen. Have you noticed how good she is at arithmetic?'

Jen nodded.

'Well, she says she loves working with figures but doesn't really get to do it much, except working out six-horse accumulators for her daddy.

And they've got her doing the book-keeping in the restaurant, although she's only paid as a waitress – what a liberty! She's wasted there. She's never had a chance. It never even occurred to her to try for university – no one in her family ever has, but she's more than capable of it. I just wanted to have a talk with her about her future. There's nothing worse than someone not achieving their full potential.'

Jen nodded – once again, she found herself totally in tune with him. 'And?'

'She's going to apply to get on a course in accountancy, and start looking for a better job. She just has to start believing in herself, that she can do it.'

'Ooh – I hope she stays in touch. I'd love to know how she's getting on with it all,' Jen said. She felt horribly guilty about her judgemental attitude when she'd first met Chanel – more than anyone, she was living proof that there was more to everyone than meets the eye.

She plodded on until early afternoon, then went upstairs to the flat. Swapping her power suit for a comfy old nightshirt, she fell gratefully into bed. After a couple of hours' sleep, she felt marginally better, but vowed never to drink alcohol again. A pint of fresh orange juice, two paracetamol, two mugs of strong black coffee and a plate of scrambled egg on toast helped also, and then she felt almost recovered. Changing into a velour jogging suit, she curled up on the sofa with Niamh's second novel (a marvellous tour de force, according to the *Irish Times*). She found herself drawn to Niamh's writing, as if it would give clues to the essence of the woman herself, fascinating because of her involvement with Patrick.

'Jen.'

She'd only read a chapter and a half before the door burst open and Brooke ran in, hair flying, red in the face. 'Demi's having the baby,' she cried.

'What do you mean?'

'She's having the baby. About to give birth. Gone into labour.'

'Okay, I get it.' Throwing Niamh's book aside, Jen jumped up and followed her sister downstairs, where Demi was clinging onto the spars of the banister, howling and sobbing in agony.

'It's probably just Braxton Hicks,' Jen tried.

'It isn't, her waters have broken.'

Jen looked round at Amy, Brooke, Chanel and Patrick, who were standing helplessly in the foyer. 'Well, has anyone called Doctor McLuskie?'

'Of course we have, but he's on another call,' Amy said. 'Mrs Urquhart's having twins.'

Jen turned to Patrick. 'Paddy, you've got a big car, you drive her to Inveralan Hospital.'

'I think it may be too late for that,' Patrick said, as Demi gave another howl of pain.

'I *knew* this was going to happen,' Jen cried.

'What are we going to *do?*' pleaded Brooke.

'I'm phoning Cal,' said Amy, producing her iPhone.

'You're phoning Callum? What on earth for?'

'Well, he's a vet, isn't he? He'll know what to do.'

'He'll know how to deliver a lamb or calf, but not a real baby,' Jen said.

'Look, Jennifer, if you've got any better ideas, I'd like to hear them.'

Jen subsided. Demi's cries were becoming all the more urgent. Although she knew Callum and Amy had had some kind of falling out and he had warned her not to phone him for back-up again, surely this was an emergency, and also, he was too kind hearted to refuse her.

Callum's flat was not far away, and it was only a few minutes before he walked into the foyer. 'What's her name?' he murmured.

'Demi,' Amy whispered back.

'Hi, Demi.' Callum walked calmly towards the terrified teenager, speaking to her in the soft, gentle voice he might use to soothe a frightened animal.

'Are you the doctor?' Demi managed to say.

'Sort of. You're both going to be fine, I promise. Let's get you upstairs.'

The girl sniffed, calmed by Callum's quiet confidence. He and Patrick helped her to her bedroom.

'I'll need to look out the insurance policy. I'm not sure that we're covered for this kind of thing. The carpet's probably ruined,' Jen said.

'*Jennifer.*' Brooke sounded profoundly shocked.

The sisters hovered outside the room. Callum, it seemed, had phoned the nearest hospital, and was being talked through the delivery. As Patrick had predicted, the process was brief, and after much blood curdling screaming, Amy fetched from the flat string and scissors, cleaned in boiling water, to cut the umbilical cord.

Later, Demi was sitting up in bed, holding her new baby girl, wrapped in the softest of towels. She was exhausted, panda-eyed and red-faced, but exuding an aura of absolute radiance.

'Congratulations, Demi,' Amy said.

'I was going to call my baby girl "Destiny",' Demi said, smiling beatifically at Callum. 'But now I'm going to call her after you.'

'Callum?' He sounded perplexed.

'Well, it's something of an improvement,' remarked Jen.

'No,' Demi said, high and giggly. She flapped her hand at Callum. 'Calla.'

'Aw, she's gorgeous,' Tiara breathed. 'Look at her wee hauns.' Leaning towards the baby, she cooed, 'Hi, Calla. I'm your Auntie Ti.'

The baby was indeed beautiful, perfect and caramel coloured.

'I wonder if Oscar de la Renta does babygros?' Tiara said. 'And I've heard of this wumman they say's the best baby stylist in the country.'

'Ti, I think it must've been that boy I met in Ibiza. You know, at Amnesia.'

'Oh, aye,' said Tiara, nodding.

Jen exhaled deeply. It had been quite a weekend.

Dr McLuskie had come eventually and checked Demi out. Now she was wolfing into tea and toast while Chanel and Tiara gazed fondly at baby Calla, now wearing a babygro and ensconced in a cot, both loaned by Aura Wallace's cousin.

'I'm so going to send Jaden McGaughey an invoice for the mattress and the rug. They're completely ruined,' Jen was saying, as the sisters, hyped up with the excitement of the evening, drank coffee with Callum in their living room.

'It was so amazing. A new life,' Brooke said. 'Just think, this is the first birth we've ever had in the hotel.'

'And the last, hopefully,' Jen said. 'No one else would be stupid enough to go on holiday at eight and a half months pregnant.'

'You were brilliant,' Amy told Callum. Exhausted from the massive surge of adrenalin and subsequent comedown, she was sprawled on the sofa beside him.

Callum shrugged. 'It was nothing. Just what anyone would've done.'

'Hardly.'

It crossed Amy's mind to think just how useless Lewis would have been in this situation: he would struggle to deliver a letter, never mind a baby. There was something quiet and strong about Callum – whenever he was around, she always felt at peace. His capable presence was so reassuring, she always felt that she could trust him to make everything right. As soon as he walked into the room, she felt safe.

As soon as Lewis walked into the room, she was weak at the knees.

Jen went downstairs to the bar and returned with a bottle of brandy. Amy felt much happier now that she and Cal were talking again. It was a great evening. The four of them reminisced about their days at Auchenstoorie High, then played Six Degrees of Kevin Bacon. When they were quite drunk, Brooke got out the Scrabble board and convinced everyone to join her in a game. Brooke loved Scrabble.

Before he left, Callum had looked in to see Demi and baby Calla and make sure they were both well. Demi, glowing and fulsome in her thanks, had thrown her arms round him and hugged him tightly.

'Listen, Amy,' he said, as she showed him out. 'I'm sorry about the way I spoke to you... that night. Not about what I said, because that was true and you needed to hear it, but I should have put it better.'

'Thanks for that very gracious apology,' Amy snapped.

'Think about it, Amy.'

'Lewis is meant to be a friend of yours.'

'He is a friend, but that doesn't change what I said.'

'I'm going out.' Grabbing her jacket from its peg by the door she marched off, striding ahead of him along the coast road. Half an hour later, she and Lewis were sitting on his sofa, drinking tea. Lewis sipped his leisurely, much entertained by her stories of the McCrackens and Demi and her gorgeous mixed-race baby. He even managed to do this beautifully, Amy thought, looking at his artist's fingers curled round the mug. It was hand-painted with purple crocuses – very Valissa.

Then she confided in him about her cold war with Callum.

'That's too bad. What did you argue about?'

'You,' admitted Amy, biting her lip. This was dangerous ground, but being drunk took the edge off. 'He thinks you're a layabout and bad news, basically.'

Lewis took the mug out of her hands and laid it on the table, on top of the current issue of NME. Tea splashed on Jake Bugg's face.

'What do you think, Amy, hey? That's all that matters to me.' His incredible deep blue eyes were very close to hers.

'You're all that matters to me. There's nowhere I'd rather be now than here, with you.'

She couldn't quite bring herself to say the "L" word. Lewis pushed the hair back from her face. 'That's all I needed to know,' he said, his eyes still on her. 'Why don't you phone him now? Make it up and you'll feel better. I'll go into the bedroom.' His eyes flickered to where her phone was sitting on the coffee table, beside an ashtray, a yellow plectrum and a paperback copy of *Bright Lights, Big City*. Secure in her love, Lewis didn't feel at all intimidated by her friendship with Callum.

'To be honest, Lew, why should I? I mean, he started it.' She giggled suddenly, realising how childish she must sound, as if they were back at school.

'Hey, Ames, did you just come over for a chat?'

She laughed as he pulled her into his arms, and they fell sideways onto the sofa.

Chapter 16
Vital Signs

'Ardnashell Lodge, Jennifer Grant speaking.'

Jen was expecting a call from a wine merchant, but, instead of his cultured tones, the voice on the other end of the phone was down-to-earth and Glaswegian.

'This is Sister Hepburn from the Royal Infirmary – '

Jen's mind was racing and she felt sick. 'What're you phoning about?' Her voice was sharp. Her parents were in Glasgow. As the culmination of their anniversary trip, they were spending two nights in a city centre hotel and going to the Royal Concert Hall to see Nicola Benedetti guesting with the Scottish National Orchestra. The tickets had been like gold dust and they had been hugely looking forward to it.

'Miss Grant, maybe you should sit down.' The voice was calm and strong.

'I am sitting down,' barked Jen. 'Just tell me what's happened.'

'Your parents have been involved in an accident. Another car crashed into the back of theirs as they were driving through the city centre. They were admitted this morning –'

'But are they all right?' Jen almost shouted. The receiver felt slippery in her hands.

'Your mother is fine, just a few cuts and bruises. She's in shock and we're keeping her in for observation – '

'What about Dad?'

'Your father is still unconscious.'

'But he'll come round. He'll be fine –'

'He's in a critical condition, but he's stable and we're doing all we can.'

'Are you sure it's my dad? Maybe you've made a mistake,' Jen blurted out.

'There's no mistake.' The voice on the other end of the phone was gentle but firm.

'Then… what's wrong with him?'

'He has a head trauma –'

Jen began to shake uncontrollably. 'I'll come immediately.'

Dropping the receiver into its cradle, she ran out of her office, straight into Patrick.

'Where's the fire?' he asked, grabbing her arm to steady her. Then he looked closely at her. 'Jenny, what's wrong?'

Under his concerned gaze, Jen broke down, crying so hard she couldn't speak. Patrick led her over to the chaise longue in the foyer. 'Sit down.'

Jen sank down and Patrick sat beside her. She took the hankie he passed to her gratefully. After a couple of minutes, she managed to compose herself somewhat and mopped at her eyes.

'Someone phoned from the Royal Infirmary. Dad's in a coma,' she managed to say, at length. 'I need to go to him. I need to, oh, no, I need to tell Amy and Brooke.'

'Do you want me to tell Amy and Brooke?' Patrick's voice was soft, barely breaking the silence. Sniffing, Jen nodded.

'Go and get ready.'

Jen nodded again. She got up slowly and made her way up to the flat. In her bedroom, she kicked off her shoes and undressed, pulling on jeans and a fleece, and dug out a pair of trainers from the back of her wardrobe. Her hands were shaking so badly that she could barely tie the laces. Opening a drawer, she pulled out a nightshirt and shoved it into her sports holdall, then added clean underwear and a toothbrush. Frantically, she looked around for her handbag, hardly able to think straight. Then she remembered she must have left it in her office. She ran back downstairs again.

Everything looked strangely the same – her Radley bag on the floor beside her ergonomic chair, the spreadsheet she'd been working on still on her computer screen. It wasn't even half an hour since her world had spun on its axis, changing her life to a lonely, dark and frightening place. Picking up the bag, she emptied out the contents: make-up, perfume, glasses, purse and iPhone onto her desk, and lifted her car keys from the pile.

After knocking briefly, Patrick walked into the room. 'Amy and

Brooke are sorting themselves out. They'll just be a couple of minutes.'

'I need to go *now*,' Jen cried.

'Jennifer, there's no way you're driving to Glasgow; you're too upset.'

'I have to.'

'I'll drive you.'

'Thanks,' Jen managed to whisper.

'Now, give me your phone.'

Jen's whole life was on her phone: numbers, appointments, suppliers, business contacts. She slept with it charging on her pillow, but, now, she handed it over meekly.

'Go and wait for your sisters. I'll make a few calls.'

Normally, Jen hated not being in control, someone else calling the shots, but today she was relieved. Incongruously, the foyer was full of light as late afternoon sun poured in through the windows. Amy and Brooke walked slowly down the stairs. Brooke was crying and Amy looked pale and shell-shocked.

Her sisters sat in silence in the back and Jen in the front beside Patrick. Although it was a fairly warm day, she felt cold and shivery, and was grateful when he turned on the heating.

'I've arranged for Elspeth McMaster from Harbourview Hall to take care of things while we're away,' he explained. 'She's done it before, she can do it again.'

Elspeth McMaster was highly efficient and would do an excellent job, but Jen could hardly bring herself to care.

'And I phoned Anna and she says we can come and stay with her.'

'Thanks,' Jen muttered. Anna still lived in the flat the two girls had shared when she'd been a student.

Jen had often teased Patrick in the past about his big, flash, babe magnet of a car, but she was grateful that it ate up the miles steadily, mountains, pines and lochs sliding past the tinted windows.

The four spoke little, each lost in thoughts which, Jen believed, they were too frightened to express in case it gave them more substance. The scenery gradually became more urban and Jen, exhausted by the emotion of the day, dozed for a while.

'Mum,' cried Jen, as, after walking along what had seemed like miles of pale gleaming corridors, they were shown into the family room. Mum was sitting on a green leather chair, her hair falling forward to cover her face, holding a polystyrene cup. When she looked up, Jen was shocked at how old and drawn she looked – she seemed to have aged ten years in as many weeks. She wasn't alone, though. James was with her. Jen watched as Amy ran forward to embrace their mother and Brooke fell into James' arms. He held her closely, murmuring some soothing words.

Dad was a big man, over six feet tall, rangy and broad in the shoulder. He'd always been so fit and healthy. When he and Patrick had gone hill walking together, Dad had been able to keep up easily with his long, athletic stride, despite the twenty-five year age gap between them. It was almost more than Jen could bear to see him laid low, breathing apparatus covering his face, a drip attached to one of the veins in his hand. Some kind of machine bleeped above the bed.

'Dad,' Brooke breathed, a tear running down her cheek. Instinctively, Jen reached for Patrick's hand. It felt warm and dry. She didn't know how long they all stood there, watching, exchanging a few disconnected remarks. When she could stand it no longer, she turned to the nurse. 'I need you to tell me what's happening, what you're doing for my father.'

'We're doing all we can,' said the nurse. She looked very young. 'You can talk to the doctor when he does his rounds.'

'I need to know *now*,' Jen cried. 'What I don't need is to be fobbed off.'

'Miss Grant, I know you're upset, but –'

'Of course I'm upset. That's my father lying there.'

'Jenny,' Patrick said. He put his hands on her shoulders and turned her round to face him, stooping so he could look her in the eye. 'Listen to me. You're exhausted. You should go to Anna's and get some sleep.'

'I can't sleep.'

'Maybe not, but you can rest. You'll feel better in the morning, I promise.'

'I'll never feel better again,' Jen protested.

'Listen, your mum and Amy are going to stay tonight. They'll phone you if there's any change,' Patrick said. He threw a smile at the young nurse, who agreed willingly.

The sun was rising as they reached the flat.

'Jenny,' cried Anna, throwing open the door. She was wearing a crimson wrap, her blonde curls frothing around her shoulders. She pulled Jen into a tight, Patchouli scented embrace. 'Come in, darling.'

Jen stepped into the familiar hall, with its tatty, patterned carpet.

'And Paddy.' Anna hugged Patrick also. She'd met him a couple of years ago when she'd visited the hotel and, of course, remembered him.

'You can have your old room,' Anna said. 'Mimi's away – she's in a play at the Edinburgh Festival. And Paddy, I've cleared out the boxroom for you.'

The windowless boxroom had been considered by their landlord to be too grotty to rent out, but there was a mattress in there, which had often been used by guests either too skint or too inebriated to get home.

The family worked a rota system, taking it in turns to sit by Dad's bed, day and night, while the others sat in the hospital canteen, drinking yet more coffee. Jen was so drained that she did manage to sleep for a few hours each night, but the sleep was fitful and plagued by nightmares. One night, she got up in the small hours, pulled on a dressing gown belonging to the absent Mimi (so not her real name) and crept into the kitchen. She jumped as she pushed open the door: Patrick was sitting at the table in the half light.

'I couldn't sleep either,' he said, managing a wry half smile. 'Would you like some tea?'

'Yes, please,' Jen said. 'I don't think I could ever drink coffee again.'

Patrick crossed the kitchen, flicked on the switch of the kettle and dropped one of Anna's vile chamomile teabags into a mug. Jen realised that she'd been so wrapped up in her own anxiety that she hadn't thought about how he must be feeling – he'd been close to Dad also. 'I keep thinking,' she faltered, when they were both seated at the table. 'What if he comes round but he's brain damaged?' She presumed they all shared this worry, but no one wanted to say it out loud.

Patrick leaned across the table and took her hands. 'Let's not speculate. It might not come to that.'

'I know, but –'

'Jenny, one of things I admire about you is that you're so brave. You just need to be brave for a bit longer.'

They stayed up, drinking tea and talking softly as dawn broke. Jen went back to bed feeling marginally calmer, slightly more at peace, as if she'd absorbed some of Patrick's strength.

Brooke let herself into James' flat in the Maryhill Road. He'd been brilliant. He would come in and sit with her every evening after work, as well as looking in whenever he had some free time during the day. He would stay up with her when she couldn't sleep, letting her talk if she wanted to, just holding her if she didn't.

She'd come back to the flat for a shower and some clean clothes. There was no change in Dad's condition. She had picked up a summer cold and her throat was constantly sore. She slumped on the saggy old sofa in the kitchen, cradling a mug of tepid tea, still chilled although she was wearing two of James' sweaters.

After a while she heard voices in the close, then the door open and slam, then the voices became louder and Emily and another girl came into the kitchen. Ironically, although it was the school holidays, both were wearing a uniform – tight jeans with more rip than denim and Converse All Stars - purple for Emily and red for her friend. On top, Emily wore a sleeveless black tee-shirt emblazoned with brightly coloured CND symbols, while the other girl had a similar one adorned with gold crosses. They actually looked more like sisters than friends, both with thick, glossy dark hair, masses of eyeliner, and pale lipgloss. Both had various facial piercings.

The girls stopped talking. 'This is Zoë,' said Emily. She didn't introduce Brooke, she presumed because, as the wicked step-mother, or the "brainy bimbo" – Emily's pet name for her – her notoriety had gone before her and Zoë was well aware of who she was.

'Hi, Zoë.'

Emily cleared her throat. 'Eh... sorry to hear about your dad,' she said formally. 'I hope he feels better soon.'

'Thanks, Em. That means a lot,' Brooke said, genuinely touched.

'Come on, Zo.' Emily took two cans of Irn Bru from the fridge and the teenagers hurried out of the room.

Emily stayed with James every second weekend, her bedroom unspeakably untidy. Who knew what lay beneath the silt of music magazines, Top Shop clothes, Converse trainers in assorted styles and colours, dirty plates, the complete works of Sylvia Plath, straighteners, make-up and half a dozen dirty coffee cups and becrumbed saucers. It wouldn't surprise Brooke if the Stone of Destiny were under there. Emily seemed to like it like that, though, as she never tidied up.

After a moment, Emily put on some music – amazing she could locate her speakers. Brooke recognised it as Nirvana's *Nevermind*. It was definitely quieter than the usual ear-bleeding volume, Brooke presumed out of deference to her. In as far as she was capable of feeling anything at the moment, she appreciated it.

*

Outside the hospital, Amy switched on her phone, which buzzed with message after message, variously from Cal, Euan, Misty, Duncan, Gregor, Robbie, and, of course, Lewis. He phoned her several times every day and it was wonderful to hear his voice, but she wished he could be here with her, as Brooke and Jen had their men with them. She was desperate to feel his arms round her. Late last night, they'd talked about it and agreed that, if Dad was no better in a couple of days, Lewis would make the long journey to Glasgow to be with her. She yearned to see him.

Dad's breathing sounded harsh. Jen could hardly stand to see him like this, the drip still attached to a vein in his hand, the catheter and the breathing apparatus on his face. She held his free hand and spoke to him quietly about what had been going on at the hotel over the summer, in the hope that her voice would penetrate, and her words might strike a chord.

'... so you have to come back to work soon. There're a lot of things I could do with your advice on,' she finished. Out in the corridor, she could hear voices, and the rumble of a trolley being pushed past. 'Anyway –'

Jen stopped talking.

She was certain his hand had twitched. She watched him, her mouth dry with tension. Maybe she'd just imagined it, because she wanted it so much. But she wasn't mistaken – his hand definitely moved again. 'He moved his hand. I saw it.'

'I know.' Brooke's face was rosy and her eyes damp.

'But that's… didn't the doctor say that's a really good sign?' Amy said.

'Yes! It's brilliant.'

Jen began to feel a cautious relief, a glow of alertness amid her exhaustion. It was sometime in the afternoon and she was aware of the muted sound of traffic outside, overlaid by the bleeping of the hospital apparatus. Finally, Dad spoke – a single, indistinct word.

'Lorna?' His voice was low and somewhat slurred. Jen burst into tears.

*

Jen pulled on the nightshirt she'd grabbed on leaving the hotel – could it only be a few days ago? – an ancient grey one with a pink elephant embroidered on the front. Her face was grey also, she thought, ruefully, as she cleaned her teeth. She'd eaten her first square meal since coming to Glasgow – scrambled eggs on toast with grated, melted cheese, cooked by Patrick, so delicious that it was worthy of a Michelin star. He'd even made her laugh by addressing her in a French accent, which sounded uncannily like Marcel's. She rinsed, washed her face, went back into the bedroom, sat down on the bed, and burst into tears again. Delayed reaction to the shock of Dad's illness, she assumed, trying to regain control. There was a knock at the door.

'Come in,' she called, frantically wiping her eyes with her hands.

'Do you want to watch *Mock the Week*?' Patrick asked. 'It's just starting.'

'No, I'm going to hit the hay,' Jen said, turning her face away from him.

'Are you all right?'

'Of course.'

'You're not. You look shattered.' Patrick crossed the floor until he was standing before her. Jen let him put his arms round her, breathing in the lemony scent of his freshly showered skin, the smell of clean, raw sweat just beginning to break through. For a few moments, she allowed herself the luxury of leaning on him, resting her head against his shoulder and crying a little into his tee-shirt front.

'He'll be fine,' Patrick said, gently rubbing her back. 'They said he'd be fine, didn't they?'

Jen nodded. 'Sorry,' she said, her voice muffled. 'I'm being selfish. You must be upset, too. You're so close to him and it must be bringing back memories of when you lost your own dad.'

'I'm grand, and Gordon's going to be grand.'

Jen sniffed. Now Patrick's long fingers were stroking the nape of her neck, now her earlobe, now her cheek. In spite of herself, she began to feel excitement course through her veins. 'I look awful,' she muttered.

'You don't. You look beautiful. You don't need all that stuff you put on your face.' He lifted two hanks of her hair and wrapped them round his hands. Jen should pull back, but it was as if they were magnet and metal – she was irresistibly drawn to him and couldn't seem to move away. 'You're not so bad,' she admitted, 'for a smarmy, womanising Irish scumbag.'

'I'll take that as a compliment, will I?' Patrick asked, and kissed her.

Jen's head spun: she'd been waiting for this moment for a very long time, and it was just as wonderful as she'd always imagined. So it should be, she reminded herself, the amount of practice he must have had. Her arms wrapped round his neck and she gave herself up to kissing him, her mouth twisting desperately under his.

'We can't do this,' she said, eventually, somehow finding the strength to break away.

'We're doing all right so far.'

'No, I mean…well, she isn't exactly my favourite person, but what about Niamh?'

Patrick looked genuinely taken aback. 'What about her?'

'She's your girlfriend, if you remember.'

'Niamh's my best mate; she's not my girlfriend.'

'But… you're always hanging out with her.'

'Of course I am. She's my oldest friend.'

'But, but, you're sleeping with her.'

'News to me.'

'What about the morning she came out of your room, then, in her dressing gown, looking as if she'd just won the lottery?'

'When?'

'One morning – early. She was creeping down the corridor from your room, looking totally smug.'

'Or from the garden,' Patrick said.

'What would she be doing out in the garden at seven o'clock in the morning?'

'She's always pacing about out there if she's stuck with her writing. She says it helps her to think.'

'But, but…. you're Gabriel.'

'I'm who? I'm sorry, Jennifer, but you're really beginning to lose me now.'

'In her book? *Awakening*? You're Gabriel.'

'Oh, yeah, yeah. I know what you mean. But I'm not Gabriel. I'm Conor.'

Conor, whom the narrator, lost, lonely and homesick, had met on her first day at university. They'd been best friends all through the book.

'So, who has Niamh been having the affair with?' Jen asked. A terrible thought struck her. 'It's not Lewis Burns, is it?'

'No, of course not.'

'Thank goodness for that. It's just that they're quite similar – sort of arty and highly strung. I could kind of see it, and –'

'She isn't seeing anyone.'

'Huh?'

'She's completely off men at the moment, apart from a wee slip when she slept with Diarmid in Dublin.'

'Her ex-husband?'

'The very same.'

'Why didn't you tell me you weren't going out with Niamh?' Jen blurted out. It would have saved her many a sleepless night if she'd known this. Patrick gazed at her, his expression sincere.

'Jennifer, from now on, I promise to give you comprehensive updates on all the women I'm not going out with. Anyway, you never asked.'

Jen hung her head. She'd been so proud and so scared of betraying her true feelings that she'd pretended to have no interest in Patrick's relationship with Niamh.

'We're best mates,' Patrick said, his voice soft. 'She's my oldest friend. But I don't fancy her, and she doesn't fancy me.'

'She doesn't fancy you? How can this be?'

'If you're going to make fun of me –'

'It's just…. you get on so well, and you always seemed to be together, talking all seriously –'

'Yeah – about her and Diarmid. It's complicated. What happened between them really messed her up. It's taken her a while to get over it. They've both got a lot of baggage –'

This was true – Niamh could fill a whole airport carousel.

'I'm glad she's getting over him,' Jen said.

'Jenny?'

'Mmm?'

'To be honest, I'm not all that concerned about Niamh and Diarmid right at this moment.'

He pulled her back into his arms and began to kiss her again.

When Jen woke up the next morning, Patrick was still holding her. She felt wonderful. She'd slept surprisingly well, feeling safe and protected in his embrace. The bed was a tight fit and they'd had to sleep wrapped round each other, his long legs entwined with hers. In the early hours of the morning, they'd lain close together, just talking, voices soft in the half light of the Glasgow summer.

'Pads, I really was desperately sad when I heard that Seamus was so ill. I was so fond of him,' she'd said, welling up again at the thought of Patrick's lovely dad. 'It's so unfair –'

He'd really opened up to her. Business matters apart, she'd seldom seen him be serious, but, last night, they'd both ended up crying, and she'd kissed off all his tears. Now, she slipped from the bed. She held her breath as he seemed to wake up slightly and stir, but then he slid peacefully back to sleep. For a moment, she luxuriated in watching him, his hair dark and tousled against the pillow, his long eyelashes resting on his high cheekbones. He was beautiful, she reflected. She crept down the chilly corridor to the bathroom and showered as best as she could in a tepid trickle of water, then she dressed in her jeans and hoodie and went into the living room. Anna had already left for work.

Listening to the traffic swishing by out on the Great Western Road, she picked up the phone, a bright red vintage one, and dialled. When she'd been put through to the appropriate ward, a cheery voice told her that Dad had had a comfortable night, and was now sitting up in bed listening to music on his iPod. Relief washed through her again as she leaned for a moment against the wall and then sank down on the sofa. But she was too restless to remain seated and soon she stood up and began to float around the room, butterfly like, looking at all the stills Anna had put up from her favourite films. There was a big, antique mirror above the mantelpiece and she came to rest in front of it, catching sight of her reflection. She looked ridiculous, a big, soppy grin all over her face.

How stupid was she? She'd had sex with Patrick – Jen couldn't stand those sappy women – such as Brooke – who used the term "make love". She was another entry in his little black book, another notch on his bedpost, another scalp on his belt, another conquest.

She'd been completely abandoned, given herself up to him totally.

The really bad news, however, was that she had told him she loved him.

Jen squared her shoulders. The new, improved Jennifer Grant did not lose control. She did not make herself vulnerable to a man, especially one who could give Casanova lessons in the art of seduction.

Time for some damage limitation.

She flicked on the kettle and slotted two pieces of bread into the toaster. She felt ravenously hungry for the first time since Dad's accident. The toaster was temperamental but, with the expertise of long practice, she managed to coax two crispy golden pieces of toast out of it. She had made another round and was pouring herself a third cup of coffee when Patrick walked into the room. She tried to ignore the tingle that shot through her at the sight of his tangled dark curls and his sleepy green eyes, at the sensual memory of his kisses, his skin against hers.

'What's up?' he asked. Obviously, he'd expected her to want to talk about the previous night, about the shift in their relationship.

'Nothing.' Jen's eyes met his in a cool glance. 'I'm just having some breakfast.' To prove this point, she lifted a triangle of buttery toast and bit into it.

'I phoned the hospital; Dad's had a good night,' she mumbled through it.

'Excellent.'

'Would you like some toast? The toaster's a bit temperamental, but –'

'Are you just going to pretend it didn't happen?' Patrick asked suddenly.

'What?'

'What? – last night.'

Jen sipped her coffee. 'We had a one night stand, Paddy. It was fun. Get over it.'

'It was more than that, Jennifer.' Patrick put a hand on either side of her, imprisoning her against the fridge.

'You're very attractive; that isn't the problem.'

'Then what is?'

Jen gazed speculatively at him. 'I don't want to be just another notch on your bedpost.'

The thought of being loved and then left by Patrick was so terrible it made her feel quite faint.

'I don't have a bedpost,' Patrick protested. 'And I don't know what gave you the idea that I'm like that.'

'Oh, come on, Pads. You've been out with half the girls in Kirklochy.'

'Jenny, there *are* only six single girls in Kirklochy. It doesn't exactly make me Russell Brand.'

'Well, I bet, since you moved back to Dublin, you've been through half the single girls there, too.'

A shadow crossed Patrick's face. 'No. Just one.'

Jen didn't like the sound of this at all: it sounded… special. 'What was her name?' she asked.

'Saoirse,' Patrick said, pronouncing it Sair-sha. His face was thoughtful.

'Why did you split up?' Jen ventured.

'Just for the record, she left me. Literally. She got head hunted for a job in New York.'

'What as?' Jen asked. Working in New York was one of the goals on her own ten year plan.

'Television producer.'

'Wow.'

'Jen, we really do have to talk.'

Jen swallowed. If this Saoirse woman had been the one to leave, perhaps Patrick still cared for her. Maybe he was on the rebound. 'Pads, I need some space. I'm going to go out for a walk.'

She pushed past him and walked out, closing the door firmly. She marched down Vinnicombe Street and turned into Byres Road. Genteel west end ladies, well heeled businessmen and scruffy, jeans clad students all stepped aside to make way for her as she strode along past the crowds streaming out of the underground station, two rival buskers playing acoustic guitar in counterpoint and a teenager handing out club flyers. Smart cafés, pubs, delis and boutiques and newsagents, the windows covered in cards advertising accommodation to let, flashed past, until she left Byres Road behind and made her way along University Avenue, slackening her pace slightly to take in the magnificent gothic buildings of Glasgow University.

Eventually, she found herself at the intersection of Sauchiehall Street and Woodlands Road, traffic roaring by on the motorway. Sauchiehall Street was busy, and she liked this – the fact that she could just disappear into this city of a million people where she knew no one, invisible, unnoticed. In Kirklochy, by now, there would be speculation around the cake-stands and at the Rural as to where she was going, why she looked so agitated. Here, she was anonymous.

'Jen,' came a voice from behind her, followed by the clatter of high heels. 'Jennifer.'

Only one person had a voice loud enough to be heard above all that traffic noise. Jen spun round. 'Chanel.'

'Haw, Jenny, hen,' Chanel boomed, with a grin. 'Whit the hell ur you dae'in' here?'

'My dad's in the Royal. He had an accident.'

'Oh, no. Is he going to be all right, though?' Chanel's round face was all concern.

'Yes, thank goodness.'

'Aw, that's brilliant, so it is.'Chanel peered at her. 'You look really different. And you've shrunk.'

'I know,' Jen agreed. She was seldom seen in public in hoodie and jeans and minus her five-inch heels. 'So do you.'

Chanel had maintained the shiny dark bob and the subtle make-up that the hotel's hairdresser and beautician had given her. She wore a smart black suit, sheer black tights and shiny black court shoes. A badge on her lapel proclaimed her to be Ms C. McCracken, Assistant Manager.

'You look great.'

'I know! And I've got a boyfriend now. I met him at the dancing. And wait till I tell you – I've got a new job. I've been promoted within the restaurant.'

'That's great, Chanel. Really great. You deserve it.'

'Know how me and Paddy had a wee chat when I stayed at the hotel? He told me he thought I was wasted as a waitress,' Chanel explained. 'So when the assistant manager's job came up, I went for it. I'm fair enjoying it. I've applied to do accountancy at Glasgow Uni an' all. If I get in I'll go part-time and support myself that way.'

'Well done.' Jen patted Chanel's arm. 'You seem to have it all worked out.'

Her friend again looked serious. 'I owe yous wan. See if I hadnae stayed at the hotel and met the both of yous, I'd never have got up the confidence to go for it in the first place.'

'No worries, Nell. Nothing worse than someone not reaching their true potential.'

'Thanks! Anyway, what are you doing the now?'

'Just going to grab some lunch,' Jen said. Her plan had been to hole up in a corner in Costa Coffee and do some thinking.

'How d'you not come to my restaurant? We do a cracking wee shoppers' lunch.'

'Errr... all right.'

The restaurant Chanel managed was called Fabrizio's, and was in a basement in Bath Street. She pushed open the door and Jen followed her into a welcoming, candlelit room, breathing in the aroma of garlic and tomato. Her stomach rumbled. A very handsome Italian boy was lighting the last of the candles, fat red ones stuck into Chianti bottles.

'Hiya, Enzo, this is my pal, Jenny. Jenny – Enzo Ravinelli.'

Enzo straightened up. 'Ciao, Bella,' he said, kissing Jen on both cheeks. 'How're you doing?' he added, in broadest Glaswegian.

Chanel led her over to a small table in an alcove. She relaxed in her seat. Candlelight played over the red and white checked tablecloth and place mats of Tuscan scenes. Jen tucked into her starter, bruschetta, with relish, all the more so because it was such a treat to be waited on for a change. Enzo was greeting a man and a woman, both clad in smart business suits. 'Buongiorno. I show-a you to your-a table.'

The restaurant was full by the time Jen plunged her spoon into her tiramisu. Chanel placed two cups of cappuccino on the table and slipped into the seat opposite her for a moment. 'Tell me about your new man, Chanel.'

Chanel beamed. 'Ooh, he's lovely. He's called Pascal –'

'Pascal? Is he French?'

'Naw. Fae Drumoyne. I'm telling you, he is fit as. Bit like that Mark Wright.'

'Sounds gorge.'

'So your dad's going to be OK?' Chanel asked, after a five minute monologue about her boyfriend.

'Yeah, thanks.' Jen closed her eyes in ecstasy as she drank her cappuccino. After so many cups of hospital coffee, it tasted inordinately delicious.

'You're not here on your own, are you?'

'Oh, no. I just needed a bit of headspace. My mum and sisters are here.' Suddenly, the desire to talk about Patrick was too much for her. 'And Paddy.'

Chanel's eyes lit up. 'Ma main man. How is he?'

'Good,' Jen said. She sipped again from her cappuccino. She badly needed to confide in someone, and who better to show her vulnerability than Chanel, who lived hundreds of miles away?

'We got together. Last night.'

'Yous got it on? Yous slept together?' Chanel boomed, telling everyone in the room.

'Shhhh. Yes,' hissed Jen, as a few heads turned. Thank goodness she was in Glasgow, rather than Kirklochy, or the news would be all over the village faster than satellite link, passing by only Mrs Havers, and that because she was as deaf as a post. Briefly, she brought Chanel up to date.

'That's pure brilliant,' said Chanel, lowering her voice to the volume of a foghorn.

'I don't know, Nell.'

'What do you mean? He's fit as. And nice with it.'

'I know, but –' Most uncharacteristically, Jen began to fidget, shredding her red napkin. 'What if it doesn't work out? Maybe he's on the rebound from this Saoirse woman. I couldn't bear it if we get together, get really close, and then he ends it.'

'Jen, everyone has that worry. I mean, I'd be gutted if me and Pascal split up. But you need to take a chance. Think what you could be missing out on if you don't go for it. If you want a guarantee, go to Argos.'

'Thanks, hun,' Jen said. Time for a change of subject: she needed some time to herself to mull over their conversation. 'How's Tiara?'

'Great. Jaden's booked to take her to Jamaica for her twenty-first.'

'Sounds fab.'

'Aye. Me and Pascal are quite happy with a wee day out in Saltcoats, but.'

After she'd parted from Chanel, promising to follow her on Twitter, Jen power walked to the hospital to spend an hour with Dad. Later, she walked for a long time in Kelvingrove Park. Eventually she sat down on a bench, half watching a young guy kicking a football around with his two sons and a couple of dogs tearing about. It was getting chilly and she pulled her fleece more closely round her. She would tell Patrick how she really felt – that she did want to have a relationship with him. Visiting Dad had brought it home to her how fragile life could be, and made her realise that she should grab her chance of happiness. Full of resolve, now, she stood up and began to walk briskly back in the direction of Anna's flat. Before long, she was hurrying up the stairs to the second floor.

'Hi.'

Patrick glanced up from the copy of *Red* that he was reading: maybe it was for research purposes. 'Hi, Jen.' He patted the sofa, indicating that she should come and sit next to him.

'Pads, er... about last night –' she began.

Patrick held up his hand, to indicate that she didn't have to say any more. 'That's what *I* wanted to talk to *you* about,' he said. 'Look, I'm sorry, I should never have taken advantage of you when you were so upset about your dad. You were in no fit state and it was wrong of me.' All his blarney and panache seemed to have deserted him and he looked extremely ill at ease, plucking at a rip across the knee of his jeans.

Jen gazed speechlessly at him.

'I didn't mean to... compromise you,' he went on. 'I hope we're still friends?'

'No,' blurted Jen. 'I mean, yes. But it could be so much more –'

The door burst open. 'Hiya,' Anna cried. 'What a day.' She flung herself into a chair, closing her eyes. 'How's Gordon?'

'Fine. He's... fine.'

'That's great. I'm so glad.' Anna had a tendency to be somewhat intense and self-absorbed, but her relief was touching and seemed genuine.

Jen and Anna were total opposites, but Jen was extremely fond of her former flatmate. They'd worked well together, Jen the straight woman to Anna's passionate drama queen.

'It's so good to see you, Jenny – although I wish it was in different circumstances. We had some great times.' Anna turned to include Patrick in her reminiscence.'We were so broke, we used to watch television huddled up under a duvet when the lecky was running low, or we'd scrape together the ingredients for a stir fry between us. Once, we ate nothing but porridge for three days. But we had the best time – we used to laugh and laugh.' She sighed. 'We'll always be friends, won't we?'

'Sure,' Jen said. She could have murdered her.

'Would you like a coffee?' Patrick said, making to get up.

'I would love a coffee.' Anna's eyes were still closed.

'Jennifer?' He turned his green gaze on her.

'Thanks,' Jen muttered, her eyes following him as he went into the kitchen. How could she tell Patrick now that she desperately wanted him to take advantage of her again?

Chapter 17
True Colours

'I need to book four of your best rooms,' said Patrick.

'All my rooms are best,' Jen said. She had felt out of sorts ever since they returned from Glasgow. Lovely to have Dad back, of course, but she'd got used to running the show, making her own decisions, not having to consult anyone.

Dad was worried, too, that, although the hotel had made a great deal of money that summer, the outgoings for the refurb and the spa had been colossal. Jen was further irritated that he had praised Brooke for her business acumen in coming up with idea of the creative writing and art classes, while Jen knew that Brooke had simply been indulging her own passion with the healthy profit margin a happy by-product.

Also, Patrick had backed off completely. He hadn't laid a finger on her since Glasgow, but, also, the teasing banter between them was gone, to be replaced by business-like courtesy. It was sheer hell – despite her caution, she'd been so happy while they were making love, she'd felt so complete. It had been exhilarating finally to admit her feelings and, for the first time, everything had made sense. She'd felt peace, but excitement also. Everything she'd ever wanted had been within her grasp, but she'd ruined it for herself for fear of further pain. She'd rejected him once too often. She'd never get over this. 'What dates are you looking for?'

'Weekend after next.'

Jen's mouse danced briskly over the reservations diary. 'I can give you Iris, Heather, Buttercup and Poppy.'

'Taken,' said Patrick. 'It's Mum's sixtieth birthday,' he explained. 'And she wants to celebrate it here.'

'Three-line whip?' asked Jen, entering his name against each room. Patrick's mother was very much the head of the family.

'Yup. Even Ciaran's coming.'

'All the way from New York?' Jen extravagantly admired Patrick's older brother, who had relocated to Manhattan a few years previously. He was amazingly successful. He had a high powered, kick-ass job on the *New Yorker*, and lived on the Upper East Side, twenty-seven floors up in an apartment overlooking Central Park.

'Yeah.'

'Well, you can be sure of a first class service.'

'I'm glad to hear it.'

For a moment, their eyes met, then Patrick turned and walked away.

'Lovely to see you again, Mrs Walsh,' Jen said, on the eve of Patrick's mother's sixtieth birthday. She'd met all the Walsh family over the years, when assorted members had come to the hotel to visit Patrick.

'Call me Bridie, alanna.'

'I do hope you enjoy your stay, Bridie,' Jen said politely. She hid a grin as she imagined what Chanel's reaction would be if she were here. Patrick had three brothers, and, although, in Jen's opinion, he was the best looking, they were all very handsome men, tall, dark and green eyed. O.M.G! – she'd have a hot flush on the spot. If a device had been invented to measure the testosterone levels in the room, it would have short-circuited by now. Brendan and Anthony were already here, Anthony standing with his wife, a friendly, bubbly woman. Ciaran, of course, was travelling separately. Jen wouldn't put it past him to arrive by helicopter.

'It'll be so nice to have all the family together again,' said Mrs Walsh, but, for a moment, a shadow passed over her face, and Jen felt her sorrow that her husband wasn't here to celebrate with her.

From outside came the sound of tyres on gravel and the slamming of car doors, then in walked Ciaran Walsh. In a Hugo Boss suit and carrying a tablet, he looked as if he'd come straight from a high powered meeting. There was a flurry of good-to-see-yous, how-long's-it-beens?, how-was-your-flights? and how're-you-doings?

'Great to see you, Mum.'

'Ciaran,' said Mrs Walsh, and there was a tear in her eye.

Amid the rumpus, Jen hadn't, at first, realised that Ciaran had brought a girlfriend with him. She, also, looked incredibly high powered. She wore slim black wool trousers, a pale suede jacket which hugged her slender waist and Gucci loafers. Her dark hair was in a side parting, from which it hung in a glossy bell around her shoulders. She looked intelligent, wearing glasses with heavy black frames. Her make-up was subtle, her high cheekbones and lovely bone structure needing little adornment. Jen caught herself admiring her understated style, applauding Ciaran's taste. She seemed slightly nervous, although Jen would have expected her to be ultra-confident – but it must be overwhelming, meeting Ciaran's whole family for the first time.

'Happy birthday, Bridie,' she said, crossing the marble floor.

Jen had been expecting her to have a staccato New York bark, but she had the same gentle Southern Irish accent as the Walshes.

'It's so good of you to come, dear,' Mrs Walsh said.

'Wouldn't have missed it for the world.'

'Welcome to Ardnashell Lodge. I'm Jennifer Grant,' Jen said, holding out a hand. The woman's handshake was firm and cool.

'Saoirse Lynch.'

Jen had to hold onto the reception desk for support. Ciaran *had* brought a girlfriend, but she wasn't his – she was Patrick's.

'What the *hell* is she doing here?' Jen asked, pacing up and down the living room carpet. Ironically, because Saoirse hadn't made a reservation, she had had to book the honeymoon suite, as there were no other vacant rooms. She'd been completely unfazed by this, calmly producing a black AMEX card.

'What are you saying?' Amy asked, appearing in the doorway of the kitchen with a knife in her hand.

'Patrick's ex is here.'

Amy looked confused. 'What, are they back together?'

'Well, supposedly, she's here to celebrate Mrs Walsh's birthday, but, yes, I think she wants him back. Why else would she come all this way?' To her horror, Jen's voice started to shake, and she burst into tears. She tried to mop them away with her sleeve.

'Jen?' Amy laid down the knife and crossed the room. She put her arm round Jen's shoulders and led her to the sofa.

'I love him, Ames.'

'Tell me something I don't know,' said Amy.

'I hate him, the bastard.' Jen began to cry harder.

'Okay, now you're really beginning to freak me out.' Amy held her and rubbed her back until she was calmer. 'Why did you keep pushing him away?'

Jen sniffed. 'I didn't want to get my heart broken,' she said. 'Last time I was seriously involved with someone, it didn't end well.'

'I know, I know,' Amy soothed. She stroked Jen's hair. 'You could be so good together, but you'll have to give him a chance. I think you should tell him how you feel.'

'But what if it's too late and he's back with Saoirse?'

Amy shrugged. 'This isn't you talking, Jen. I thought you liked a bit of healthy competition. Anyway, he might not take her back. Don't forget, she dumped him and then put 3,000 miles between them.'

In the bathroom, Jen cried some more at her ruined face – panda eyes, mascara lanes running down her cheeks, tears making furrows in her foundation, smudged lipstick. What a pathetic sight she was. She washed off her make-up, then patted her face dry and carefully re-applied it, looking her usual immaculate self, but for a slight swelling and redness around her eyes, the only evidence of her loss of control.

Downstairs, the Walshes and Saoirse were dining together. Brendan, who was known to be something of a raconteur, was telling a story, the rest of the family leaning forward, glasses in hand, laughing uproariously. Saoirse was wearing a coral coloured dress, a simple shift, the perfect colour for her pale Irish skin and dark hair. Jen thought that, in any other circumstances but those, she and Saoirse could've been friends – good friends. She was driven, confident, successful and ambitious – just like Jen herself. She dressed similarly – simple, classic, elegant. Suddenly a terrible thought struck her – perhaps Patrick had only come onto her in Glasgow because she reminded him of his lost love?

She couldn't possibly talk to Patrick tonight – she would do it tomorrow.

Jen didn't get the chance to talk to Patrick the next morning, as he had taken his mother out for a "run" in the countryside.

In the afternoon, he went to the Claymore with his brothers, while Mrs Walsh and Saoirse headed for the spa for some intensive pampering. Apparently, this was Saoirse's present to her.

'Mother of God,' exclaimed Mrs Walsh, as the three women entered the sea-green and gold marbled room. 'If only Mary Gilhooley could see me now.'

Saoirse smiled indulgently at her – no doubt, she was no stranger to such luxury. 'I'll leave you in Dawn's very capable hands,' Jen said, glowering in loathing at Saoirse's immaculate back view – glossy, luxuriant dark hair, slender waist and a bottom like a peach encased in soft leather trousers. 'Enjoy.'

She felt sick.

'Happy birthday, Mum.'

The Walshes were all clinking glasses and beaming at each other. Mrs Walsh, looking very smart in a dark blue dress with sequins, pink lipstick, and with her hair set into soft curls, was rosy with happiness. She didn't normally drink, Jen remembered, and was absolutely trolleyed on a glass and a half of champagne. A birthday cake was waiting in the kitchen, as were a selection of gifts in colourful, sparkly wrapping paper.

The craic had flowed as fast as the champagne, with bursts of laughter coming from the table all evening. Mrs Walsh had been thrilled with her cake, in the shape of a shamrock, and even more so with all her presents, and had been helped upstairs at eleven o'clock by Anthony and his wife.

Jen bit her lip as she watched Patrick and Saoirse lift their brandy glasses and head for the French windows at the end of the dining room. Tonight, Saoirse wore cornflower blue silk and had slipped a pale blue pashmina round her shoulders.

Jen hurried out of the other door and down the corridor. The drawing room was in darkness and she walked briskly across the thick pile carpet, wobbling slightly in her heels, without switching on the light. She opened the window a fraction and kneeled down, peering out. Patrick and Saoirse were walking down the path towards the rose garden, engrossed in quiet conversation.

As they passed right by the window, Jen ducked further down, her heart beating fast, her breathing shallow, straining her ears to hear.

'I just really needed to see you, talk to you face to face,' Saoirse was saying.

'You don't have to justify yourself to me,' Patrick said stiffly.

'You're so important to me. I really need you to understand,' Saoirse pleaded.

'I do understand,' Patrick sighed.

'I know I've done a terrible thing, Patrick, but I hope you can find it in your heart to forgive me.'

'You can't just… come out with all this. I need time –.'

Jen bit her lip so hard she nearly drew blood. As they carried on walking down the path, their voices dropped to an indecipherable murmur. She leaned over further, her eyes following them as they sat down on a bench in the garden. She was sick at heart because it was obvious that Saoirse did want Patrick back, was trying to apologise to him for walking away, prioritising her career over their relationship. At first, their body language was stiff and awkward, but then he put his arm round her shoulders and kissed her on the cheek. Jen walked woodenly away from her vantage point, sinking down on an armchair. She wasn't aware of how long she sat motionless in the dark, her mind racing, before dragging herself upstairs.

She was exhausted, but sleep eluded her. She alternated between lying on her back and either side, but felt wide awake, her brain too busy to rest. If only she knew how Patrick had reacted to Saoirse's proposal. Maybe, at this very moment, they were celebrating in the bridal suite, taking full advantage of the four poster bed. Maybe Patrick would relocate to New York to be near her, and she'd never see him again. Her heart aching, she imagined them walking hand in hand through Greenwich Village. She cried for a while, then pulled herself together – maybe pride or anger had stopped him from taking her back, and they were now both alone, miserable and sleepless, Saoirse in that huge bed, Patrick in his flat. She supposed she would know for sure in the morning.

She walked into the dining room as breakfast was being served, careful make-up, a crimson shirt and her smartest suit failing to mask her tired, careworn face. She'd been up for hours. This was the last day of the Walshes' stay and they were having breakfast together in a sunny corner. Patrick and his brothers were devouring a full Scottish breakfast each, while Saoirse, smart casual in Italian jeans and a soft leaf green cashmere sweater, had half a pink grapefruit and a yoghurt. Jen's heart sank as she saw how relaxed, happy and downright radiant she looked – she and Patrick must be back together. She watched as Saoirse sugared his coffee for him.

The plan was that, after a leisurely breakfast, the Walshes would take Bridie to St Luke's Church, as she hated to miss Mass, then they would have a light lunch and chill out for a while before heading off for Inverness Airport.

★

'It's not easy to dress in style while hill walking. Do you think I've pulled it off?' Gregor asked, as he and Jen got out of his acid green Beetle in the parking area at the foot of Ben Lochy. He'd made a pretty good stab at it, wearing Diesel jeans and a red scarf and socks which exactly matched his fleece, the scarf artfully arranged and tied round his neck. He hefted their two huge rucksacks out of the boot.

Jen had phoned him and suggested the walk. She couldn't hang around at the hotel and watch Patrick and Saoirse all lovey-dovey in the bosom of his family. Hill walking always gave her some release and perspective. Problems seemed less serious from the top of the mountain, the village tiny and far, far below. Gregor usually managed to raise her spirits somewhat. They walked along the narrow stony path which made up the first half mile or so of the journey.

'Look,' Gregor murmured, and they both stopped walking to watch a stag with large antlers paddling across the rocky burn which ran alongside them. Once they were ascending the lower reaches of Ben Lochy, she began to confide in him about Patrick and Saoirse.

'What kind of a name's that?' Gregor asked.

'It's Irish,' Jen said. 'Written down, it looks like a Scrabble rack.'

'Of course, I knew you'd fallen for Paddy,' Gregor said. 'But I don't understand why you didn't go for it.'

'He's just so handsome and charming.' Jen tried to explain.

'And that would be bad because –?'

'I thought he was a player and could have any girl he wanted. And I never knew when he was being genuine underneath all that blarney. I was scared I'd get my heart broken.' Jen exhaled sharply. She'd never admitted as much to Gregor before, but it was easier to talk here, striding along with her best friend, not having to meet his eyes, completely alone with him.

'He's a decent bloke, Jen. He *is* genuine.'

'I know that now.' Jen thumped her head with her fist; she'd been so stupid. Images scrolled through her mind, like a montage in a film – Patrick giving up his room to save her skin with the McMichaels, then having to squeeze his six foot two frame into Brooke's childhood bed; breaking up the fight between Tiara's warring uncles; dispatching Hugh McMichael back to Edinburgh after he came onto Brooke; his kindness and humanity to Gregor, Tiara and Chanel when they'd been at their most vulnerable. And, last but not least, the way he'd driven her and her sisters all the way to Glasgow and back when Dad had his accident, and supported her throughout.

Glasgow. Jen had to stop walking for a moment as adrenalin shot through her at the sensual memory of Patrick's kisses roving over her skin, of his face, serious in the breaking dawn, as he moved slowly inside her, as they made love... horrors! She'd morphed into the kind of woman who "makes lurrrve".

'You're not going to let this Sair Arse woman have him without a fight? That is so not like you,' Gregor said, breaking into her thoughts.

'I've got my pride.'

'Aye, well, pride doesn't keep you warm at night.' Gregor paused, a lazy smile crossing his face. 'I would, anyway.'

'Er, actually, you wouldn't, Gregor, because, firstly, you're married, secondly, he's definitely not gay, and finally, you'd have to kill me first.'

'Lewis Burns, though. That's someone who's really bad news. I mean, he's a mate, but I wouldn't want him as a boyfriend,' Gregor mused.

Jen stopped walking for a moment. 'You think?'

Gregor nodded, serious for once.

'Have you spoken to Amy?'

'Of course I have, but she's so besotted, she wouldn't listen. What more can I do? And she now thinks I'm a total bi-atch.'

'So I take it you wouldn't?'

Gregor put his hand on his heart. 'I so would.'

Jen giggled, distracted from her misery for just a moment. 'Anyway, you haven't told me about your honeymoon.'

Gregor and Robbie's holiday had been a rip-roaring ten days in London, staying in Camden Town with their mutual friend, Kirsty, who often came to the village to visit her great-aunt, a neighbour of Gregor's, and was part of the Jamie's Cove Massive.

Gregor took a deep breath, and launched into a description of non-stop partying, schmoozing, clubbing and shopping. They'd gone to clubs in Hoxton, leaving in the daylight, spent a day at an open air concert in Hyde Park, wandered around Camden Market, spent a fortune in Bond Street and listened to indie bands in dark pubs. They'd dined out – every night sampling the cuisine of a different country, and sunbathed in Green Park. Kirsty, with her fashion and media connections, had managed to blag them into: the Groucho Club, the launch party for a new aftershave, a party on a houseboat on the Thames and the VIP area of a wildly hip club called Ice. It sounded as if they'd only got about twenty minutes sleep the whole time they'd been there. As every other shop in Camden was a tattoo parlour, Gregor had had the letter "R" inside a heart tattooed on his right buttock, while Robbie had a tattoo on his forearm which he claimed was "Gregor" in Sanskrit.

'You're mad, Greg. How can he possibly know that?'

Conversation stalled for a moment as they climbed a steep part of the mountain, then paused to admire the view. 'Very cultural trip then, was it?' she asked, when she'd got her breath back.

'Well, we did catch the Damien Hurst exhibition at the Tate Modern,' Gregor said.

Jen wasn't impressed. 'Isn't he the guy who pickled a cow?'

'*Sooo* much more than that.'

Jen had no truck with modern art, although she could appreciate artists such as Sean, who painted beautiful watercolour portraits and landscapes. In fact she had two of Sean's – favourite views of Kirklochy – hanging in the drawing room.

'I bought a couple of Sean's paintings,' she told Gregor. 'They're such a good investment.'

'I've said it before, Jen Grant, you have absolutely no soul.' Gregor pretended to slap her on the cheek, and then turned away to begin the next stage of the ascent.

When they finally reached the summit, they swigged Talisker from a hipflask and hugged each other, Jen's ponytail flapping in the wind, Gregor's quiff rigid from the application of a super-strength, heavy-duty wax. She'd been so right to come up on the hills, away from all the drama far below.

Much later, she and Gregor sat on the seawall, looking out at the evening sun dancing over the water and eating fish and chips out of the *Kirklochy News*. They had never tasted so good.

Jen had hoped to avoid Saoirse, but she was the first person she saw when she got back to the hotel. She was sitting on the chaise longue in the foyer, with a neat little Louis Vuitton – natch – suitcase at her feet. She must be an expert packer as well as everything else, Jen thought, if she'd managed to squeeze in all the fabulous outfits she'd worn during her stay. She tried to cheer herself up by remembering Gregor's nickname for her – Sair Arse.

'Hi, Jen.' Saoirse looked up from *Marie Claire*, a big smile on her face.

'Hi,' Jen managed to say.

'It's been a fantastic weekend. What a lovely place you have here.' Her smile stretched wider. 'And the honeymoon suite's to die.' She winked cheekily, showing a glimmer of the personality behind the alpha female façade.

'Are you and Paddy back together?' Jen blurted.

'Me and Paddy? Whatever makes you think that?' Saoirse looked totally nonplussed.

'Well… I know you used to go out with him, and I couldn't think why else you'd come all this way to see him –' She couldn't very well admit that she'd listened in on Saoirse and Patrick's conversation last night.

'Why do you want to know, anyway?' Saoirse looked curious and a little annoyed now. Jen took a deep breath, remembering her chat with Gregor on the mountain. She wanted Patrick more than anything. She couldn't deny it any longer. She had to take that leap. 'I'm in love with him.'

'You're in love with him?' Saoirse was smiling again, even more brightly than before. 'Oh, this is brilliant.'

'Why?'

Saoirse patted the chaise longue, indicating that Jen should sit down. 'I came here because I had something to say to him, and I felt I owed it to him to tell him face to face, after all we'd been to each other. Ciaran and I are together and I'm moving into his apartment. I've felt so guilty, I nearly bottled it. I booked the flight at the very last moment. I wasn't sure how he'd feel about my new boyfriend being his brother.' Saoirse carried on talking, as if seeking to justify herself. 'When I first moved to New York I was pretty homesick and I didn't know anyone. Paddy suggested I look up Ciaran and he showed me around a bit, took me to all his favourite haunts and introduced me to his friends. We were just mates at first, but eventually, well – '

'And how did Patrick feel?' Jen asked. Maybe it was a mark of maturity or true love, but all she wanted was for Patrick to be happy.

'He was put out for all of a couple of minutes, then he wished us well and said he'd met someone else, too.'

'Really?' Jen stammered. Most uncharacteristically, she could feel a blush creeping over her face. She was a cocktail of emotions – elation, amazement, relief, peace.

'It's you, isn't it?'

Jen beamed. 'I certainly hope so.'

'So now Ciaran and I can go back to New York and get on with our lives knowing he's as happy as we are.'

'Thanks, Saoirse,' Jen murmured. 'I always knew you were a class act.' She found herself hugging the other woman before hurrying upstairs.

In the living room, she dropped her massive rucksack in the floor and threw her jacket onto a chair. She started, then – Patrick was sitting on the sofa, drinking Stella out of the bottle and watching *Mean City*, the Glasgow police drama to which they were all addicted. On screen, Rowan Galloway was emoting for Scotland, having discovered that the teenaged prostitute, whom she had got to know during the course of her investigations, had been murdered.

'*There is no room for sentiment in the job,*' said DCI Jack McNab.

'Hey.' Jen's heart was beating so fast she felt sick.

'Would you ever sit down? You're making me nervous.'

Jen perched beside him on the arm of the sofa. 'I don't know what I was thinking before,' she said. 'But I need to tell you that I love you.'

Patrick looked up at her, his face breaking into a smile, and she was sure she saw a glimmer of tears in his eyes, 'And I love you. You were the main reason I wanted to come back to Kirklochy in the first place.'

'Saoirse said... she told me –'

'So, you truly believe that you can put up with a smarmy, womanising Irish scumbag for the rest of your life?'

'Yes, please. If you can put up with a super-uptight control freak workaholic.' Jen was smiling so hard, her face hurt.

'Just my type,' Patrick said, with his usual gallantry.

Then she was in his arms and they were kissing. It was tentative at first, but then blazed into passion. She threw back her head in ecstasy as he kissed the hollow of her throat. Slowly, he unzipped her fleece, pulling back the strap of her vest and nibbling her shoulder, his kisses straying further down.

'Good grief. Get a room,' said Brooke. When Jen opened her eyes, her sister was standing by the sofa. She was peeking out from between her fingers the way she always did when they were watching a horror film. She hurried back out the door.

'That's not such a bad idea,' Jen said, zipping up her fleece. She stood up and pulled Patrick to his feet. With unseemly haste, they ran downstairs to reception and grabbed the key for the bridal suite. Now that Saoirse had checked out, it was vacant.

'I thought the honeymoon suite was out of bounds,' Patrick said, as they stepped into the luxurious, thickly carpeted, rose scented room.

'It is,' said Jen. 'But, then again, I'm the boss.' Lifting the *Do Not Disturb* sign, she hung it on the outside of the door.

Chapter 18

The High Cost of Loving

Amy let herself into Lewis' flat. What a mess the place was, she thought, fondly: the coffee table was littered with empty mugs and full ashtrays. There was a faint, but unmistakeable, smell of cannabis, not quite masked by the aroma of a scented candle which had been left burning in the hearth. The usual flotsam of plectrums, pens and scraps of paper with lyrics and melodies scribbled on them mingled with becrumbed plates, beer cans and music magazines. Paul Weller gazed up unsmilingly from the front cover of NME. Amy made her way to the bedroom, tugging her tee-shirt free of her jeans – Lewis would be in bed. He kept strange hours, often composing through the night if inspiration had struck, and sleeping in the day.

She pushed open the bedroom door. She was right – Lewis was in bed.

With Evie Martin.

They looked beautiful, lying there, their lightly tanned bodies entwined and their hair mingled, in that blinding white room. Perhaps the hardest thing to take was that they were holding hands as they slept.

Evie was the first to realise that they weren't alone, as if she'd sensed Amy's eyes on her. She sat up, pulling up the clean, white sheet to cover herself. Even now, Amy felt that she could see a flash of the cat-like smile, the challenge in the younger woman's eyes.

'Lewis.' Evie's voice was sharp and ragged. Slowly, Lewis came to, his heavy, sleepy eyes suddenly flaring with panic as he sat up. He also pulled the sheet over his chest, as if he hoped he could hide behind it. Amy stood, frozen with horror, staring at the couple, unable to move or speak.

'Amy, could you give us a moment?' Lewis' voice broke the spell. Amy stumbled into the living room. Suddenly, she felt that her legs would give way if she didn't sit down. She collapsed onto the big purple sofa. A cream broderie anglaise bra slid off it, onto the floor. She hadn't seen that when she came in. Some time later – she had no idea how long, since she was numb with pain, Evie sidled out of the bedroom, now dressed in jeans and a tee-shirt.

'Amy,' she tried, cheeks rosy.

'Get out.'

The door slammed and she and Lewis were alone. He came slowly out of the bedroom, in old faded jeans with a hole in the knee and a khaki tee-shirt with a rip in the shoulder. He crossed the room and knelt on the rug at her feet, looking up at her with his mesmerising blue eyes. Even in her grief she wondered when she would be able to look at him without desire, without tingling with excitement. He took her hands. 'Honestly, Amy. I'd never have hurt you like that. I thought you were at work.'

'I swapped shifts with Marcel,' Amy said, in a low voice. 'How many times?'

'What?'

'How many times have you slept with Evie Martin?'

'This was the only time, I swear,' Lewis said, his blue, blue eyes still fixed on her.

'How old is she? Sixteen? She's a child.'

'She's seventeen,' Lewis said. 'Listen, Amy, we've got a lot in common, with the music. She's turning out to be a good wee songwriter. We'd been working on some tunes together. She's got a bit of a crush on me –'

'Of course,' Amy said.

'I didn't plan this. She came onto me, and…. it just happened.'

'Convenient that it "just happened" while you thought I was working,' Amy said. Sustaining anger had begun to surge through her veins. Suddenly, a terrible thought struck her. 'It… it didn't start when I was in Glasgow with Dad?' She clapped her hand over her mouth, as if she might actually be physically sick. Lewis had a very high sex drive, of which, up until about half an hour ago, she'd whole-heartedly approved.

'What do you take me for? I promise it was only this one time,' Lewis said. His gaze didn't waver.

'Really?' Amy said, thinking of all those times he'd kept her waiting, or failed to show up at all. All those times when he'd "got carried away" composing, or fallen asleep, worn out by the strain of creativity, and missed a date; Evie's secret, knowing looks. She supposed she'd never really know the truth.

'Look, there's nothing going on between me and Evie,' Lewis said. He got up and sat next to her on the sofa. Then he delivered his trump card. 'It's you I love; it always has been.' Gently, he pushed back her hair from her face, stroked her cheek. His voice grew low and husky. 'It's always been you and me, Amy, hasn't it? We've lost so much time already.'

Amy pulled away from him, with a strength she didn't know she possessed. 'Not anymore,' she managed to say. 'It's over.'

It was raining heavily as she walked back to the hotel. Waves crashed against the sea wall, sometimes leaping right over it, to splash at her feet. By the time she got back to the hotel, she was soaked through. Her ears were hurting and her nose running. She'd sobbed and howled out her grief as she walked, her wild cries drowned out by the wind and the waves, her tears washed away by the rain. Just because she hated Lewis didn't mean she didn't love him.

In the living room, Brooke was sitting on the sofa, her head bent over her sewing. Her needle flew in and out of the material as she mended a vintage dress. Her hair twisted into a top-knot, she looked just like one of Jane Austen's heroines, but for the gothic black "J" tattooed on her wrist.

'Hey, Amy, thought you were going to Lewis' –' she heard, as she blundered past. She stripped off her dress, Lewis' favourite, in a rich violet colour, and threw it on the floor. She'd never wear it again, ever – it would be too much of a reminder of this day. She pulled on her pyjamas and a dressing gown which had gone grey with age but was soft and comforting.

'Amy, what's up?' Brooke put her head round the bedroom door. At the sight of her sister's concerned face, she broke down again. Brooke crossed the room in a trice. 'Oh, no. No,' she murmured, as Amy clung onto her, sobbing out her story. She wasn't even sure that Brooke could understand what she was saying, but she'd obviously got the gist.

Eventually, Amy felt as if she was all cried out. Brooke kissed her lightly on the cheek and they went back into the living room. 'Let's have a nice cuppa rosie,' she suggested, in a poor attempt at an East-Enders accent.

As Amy listened to the whoosh and click of the kettle, the pain kept washing over her in shattering waves, like the cold, angry tide. She shivered, the realisation dawning that she now had to get through the rest of her life without Lewis; that it stretched ahead of her, to be trudged through, barren and empty, like the beach on a freezing midwinter day. The life she had planned had veered so much in the wrong direction that she was completely lost. There would be no quiet, intimate wedding, no pretty cottage, no blue-eyed, curly haired babies, no albums dedicated to her.

Another wave crashed into her consciousness, nearly flooring her. Everyone in the village would know. Her humiliation would be public property; the local gossips would have a field day. She couldn't face anyone. She'd never be able to leave the hotel again.

Another wave hit her, sweeping her into icy water. What if she saw Evie and Lewis together – she just could not bear it, while Evie's status among her teenage fanclub would go stratospheric. She'd never again hold him, or gaze into his eyes as they made love, or fall asleep in his arms.

Lewis didn't love her.

'Here we are,' Brooke said, fake cheerily, as she placed a tray bearing two steaming mugs of Earl Grey and a packet of chocolate digestives on the table.

Jen walked into the room just then. 'Good grief. Who died?'

Brooke put her finger to her lips and gestured for Jen to follow her into the kitchen. Amy sipped her tea, although it was too hot, while her sisters held a muffled conference.

'I suppose this is what happens when you play out of your league,' she said, later, as Brooke poured them all yet another cup. The pain was slightly muted by her sisters' comforting presence, but she knew it would hit her again later like a ten-ton truck. The air was hazy with smoke, but Jen hadn't complained once. Perhaps the fact that Amy's life was all but over was mitigation enough.

'Take that back,' snapped Jen.

'I mean, this is what happens when you go out with someone that everyone else wants.'

'No, this is what happens when you go out with a total scumbag,' corrected Jen. 'Anyway, I don't want him. Brooke doesn't.'

Suddenly, Brooke was looking down at her shoes, dainty ballet pumps with bows on the front. Amy had seen that guilty look many times before: the time, as a child, she'd crayoned all over the new living room wallpaper; the time she'd been caught smoking on school premises; the time she'd knocked over Amy's brand new bottle of Allure and spilled it all; the time she'd borrowed her suede jacket and left it on the Auchenstoorie train; the time she'd dropped Jen's mobile phone into a mug of coffee and even a GHD hairdryer couldn't dry it out; the time she'd completely mixed up the reservations diary...

'What?'

'Amy, don't hate me.'

'Why, what've you done?' Amy's voice was sharp.

'Promise you won't hate me first.'

'Of course I won't hate you.'

'Then... I kissed Lewis.'

'Whaaat?' Amy and Jen spoke in unison, both turning to look, appalled, at Brooke, who was still sitting with her eyes downcast, her arms round her knees.

'I kissed Lewis,' mumbled Brooke.

'You wee hoor. And you keep going on about how in love you are with James.'

'Tell us more,' Jen said, her expression still accusing.

'It was a while ago. Obviously. Before I started seeing James. We were both single at the time, or, at least, I was. He said he'd just split up with someone. It was at a gig. We got chatting and –'

'... it just happened?' Amy's mouth twisted sardonically.

'Well... yes.'

'You're meant to be my *sister*.'

'I am your sister.' Finally, Brooke stopped contemplating her shoes and looked up.

'Not any more. Why did you do it, Brooke?'

'He was –' Brooke moved her pretty hands around helplessly. '... captivating.'

'You've always got just the right poncy word, haven't you? Why don't you just admit that you fancied him?'

'What if I did?' Brooke said, with a flash of spirit.

'You knew –'

'Knew what? That you'd gone out with him, like, ten years before?'

'It doesn't matter how long ago it was; there are some things you just don't do.'

'Guys, calm down. Don't you think you're over-reacting?' Jen said.

'Jennifer, shut up,' shouted Amy and Brooke, both at the same time.

'And you didn't think to tell me about this?' Amy went on.

'Well, no. It was a while back, we were drunk, you weren't with him, hadn't been for years. It didn't mean anything to either of us. I did sort of want to tell you but I thought you'd be upset.'

Amy pushed her hands into her hair. 'I just can't deal with you at the moment. Go out, or sit in your bedroom or something. Just get out of my sight.'

'You promised you wouldn't hate me,' Brooke wailed, her eyes shiny with tears. Brooke always looked so sweet and innocent, Amy thought, with another surge of anger, with her vintage floral tea dresses, her lovely, heart shaped face and her big, short-sighted blue eyes peering out from behind her round glasses. But she wasn't – not a bit.

'What about you and Zac Martin?' she said, pain and anger making her want to hit out at her sister.

'What about her and Zac Martin?' asked Jen.

'She seduced him, just because she was bored. An innocent teenager.'

'Hardly –' Brooke protested.

'Well, he certainly wasn't after you'd got your claws into him.' Amy raised her voice. 'You're... rapacious. There's a nice big word for you, *Brooke*.'

'How old are you two? About fourteen?' Jen said. She turned to Amy. 'You can't seriously be this angry with her for getting off with your ex-boyfriend when you weren't even going out with him at the time and you were living with someone else.'

'I mean it, Jen, *shut up*.'

'*Girls.*' Mum was standing in the doorway. 'Amy Louise Grant, what is going on? I could hear you at the bottom of the stairs.'

'Ask her,' Amy snapped, jabbing her thumb at Brooke.

Brooke stumbled out of the room, stifling a sob.

Amy cried until her eyes were bright and shrivelled. She barely slept, torturing herself with memories of Lewis in bed with Evie Martin, and imagining him with Brooke. Why was she so angry with her sister? It wasn't so much that she thought that Brooke had betrayed her, more that she couldn't bear the thought of her being intimate with Lewis.

She began working harder than ever, night after night with no time off, experimenting in the afternoon with new vegan recipes. In this way, she could avoid her family, especially Brooke. In the little time she did have off, she stayed in her room, listening to music, like a sulky teenager. Her concentration had completely gone. She couldn't even focus on *Mean City*, or *The Girls Are Back in Town*, the latest book by chick-lit queen Paige Turner, which Mum had got her from the mobile library.

★

After this, Amy had several visitors. The first of those was Misty, who pitched up on Saturday evening, bringing with her a bottle of Merlot and a chocolate fudge cake from Maggie's tearoom.

'You're better off without Lewis, honestly,' she said, when the two girls were comfortably sitting on the sofa, glasses of wine in their hands.

'That's what everyone says.'

'I know, but it's true. And, if it's any consolation, I don't think it'll last between him and Evie Martin.'

'Maybe what he said was true,' Amy said, with a sudden surge of hope. 'Maybe it did only happen once. Maybe she did come on to him and –'

She had been trying to convince herself of this over the last few days, in an attempt to make her terrible loss bearable. Misty shook her head. 'No, Amy.' She took a gulp of red wine. 'He's an absolute scumbag.' Her expression was grim.

'How do you know so much about it?'

'I slept with him.'

'What?'

'You heard.'

Amy jumped to her feet and marched over to the door, holding it open. 'Get out.'

'No. You're my best friend. I'm not leaving you like this.' As gentle as Misty usually was, she seemed determined to stand her ground this time.

'Best friends don't betray each other.'

'Amy, I'm not throwing away more than twenty years of friendship over a creep like Lewis Burns.'

'Hear, hear,' said Jen, from the hallway.

'For once in your life, Jennifer, would you shut *up* and butt *out*?' Amy yelled, but she shut the door and rejoined Misty on the sofa.

'When?'

'It was a couple of summers ago, before me and Duncan got together. You were in Edinburgh and still with Stuart. I'd been single for ages and I just couldn't resist.'

'Go on.' Amy gulped at her wine, as if to fortify herself against this conversation.

'The next day, he didn't want to know. The bass player in his band told me that he'd just split up with his girlfriend back in Edinburgh. It was a rebound thing. Then they got back together.'

Amy said nothing.

'Do you know why he left Edinburgh?' Misty asked gently.

'Musical differences,' Amy mumbled.

'Musical differences?' scoffed Misty. 'Who does he think he is? Kurt Cobain?'

'Okay. If you know so much, why did he leave Edinburgh?'

'He didn't have anywhere else to go, Amy. The flat he was living in belonged to his girlfriend, who's older than him and one of the sub-editors at the *Scotsman*. When they split up – for good, this time, he crashed for a while at Carly's flat – the girl singer in the band. But I think, maybe, he was knocking her off while he was still living with Rachael.'

Amy vaguely remembered the lead singer of the band from the Edinburgh gig: a drop-dead sexy rock chick with the voice of a fallen angel.

'How *do* you know all this?'

'Euan's still in touch with Lynnette MacLeod.'

'Netty from school?'

Misty nodded. 'You know how she always wanted to be a journalist? Well, she works for the *Scotsman*.'

'Right.'

'It caused a lot of bad blood with the rest of the boys in the band. The drummer had a huge crush on Carly and everyone knew it. So he couldn't move in with them. He had no choice but to come back here and stay with his mum. Then she lent him the deposit for his flat. You know she totally spoils him.'

Amy had been close to Maree, Lewis' mum. She felt another pang: she supposed that that was another relationship she'd lost.

'Plus, I think he wanted to get away from it all, where no one knew what had happened.'

'Except Euan, it seems.' Amy buried her head in her hands. Looking for consolation, Lewis had come straight to her, the girl who had always adored him unconditionally.

'Why didn't you tell me all this? Why didn't you warn me?'

'Amy.' Misty took her hand in both of hers. 'Would you have listened? I don't think so. You were so besotted with him. You had to find out for yourself.'

'Did you know about Evie Martin?'

'No – it doesn't surprise me, but I really didn't.' Misty drained her glass and refilled it. 'Isn't it amazing how a man who writes such sensitive, poignant lyrics can be such a complete tart?'

The perfect family arrived at the hotel one Thursday in the early afternoon. They'd turned up looking like refugees, albeit well heeled ones, having cracked four days into a week's camping holiday. Windswept, bedraggled, soaked to the skin and with sand in every orifice of their bodies, they'd asked hopefully if there were any vacancies and were delighted to be able to book a couple of rooms. Their tent had been flooded, they'd explained, and every stitch of clothing they had with them was wet, except for an emergency change each that they'd been wise enough to keep in the boot of their car, wrapped in polythene.

'I have never enjoyed anything as much as that bath,' declared Perfect Mum, walking into the drawing room, where afternoon tea was being served. Through a haze of pain, Amy watched them: Dad, tall, dark and athletic, Mum, petite, slim and with glamorously golden streaked hair, and two adorable children, a boy of about five and a girl of about three.

'Mr North, Mrs North, would you like to order afternoon tea?' Jen asked. She always made a point of memorising the names of her guests.

'We certainly would,' said Mrs North, in booming Surrey tones. 'I'm ravenous. Trying to cook on a camping stove in a gale force wind and pouring rain isn't for the faint hearted.'

'Oscar, Izzy, what would you guys like?' Jen knelt down – not easy in a pencil skirt and five inch heels – so that her eyes were on a level with the children's. 'What about hot chocolate with marshmallows and cream and some warm crumpets?'

'I only like organic hot chocolate,' said Oscar, in a piping treble.

Jen smiled at the child. 'All our produce is organic. We get it from the farm up the road. The milk's straight out of a cow. You should ask Mum and Dad to take you up there for a look around to see all the animals.'

Amy rolled her eyes. What was with the Supernanny act? Jen didn't even like children. No doubt they were "the customers of the future".

'Sounds fab, but put some brandy in mine,' Mrs North said.

'Hot chocolates all round, then,' said Mr North.

As Amy was sulkily piping skooshy cream onto four mugs of hot chocolate, two of them generously laced with brandy, Jen stalked into the kitchen.

'Enough is enough,' she hissed. 'I know you're upset, but we are meant to be creating a welcoming environment for our guests, not acting as if we were serving up a funeral purvey.' Her face softened slightly. 'You know, living well is the best revenge.'

'If you want to *go on* living at all, get off my case.'

'That's the spirit, Amy. Girl power. Don't let Lewis win.'

Amy let out a growl of frustration.

'Hey, Ames, why don't you introduce a Misery Hour?' said Aura Wallace. 'Joking,' she added, as she skipped across the room, a wet dish towel narrowly missing her head.

★

After lunch on Sunday, Amy had another visitor. She was alone in the flat when there was a knock at the door. Her heart leapt – she still couldn't stop hoping that it might be Lewis. This was the trouble with heartbreak – the only person who could make you feel better was the person who had made you feel so bad in the first place. Maybe he'd come to apologise and explain. Quickly, she ran into the bedroom and glanced at her reflection in the mirror – aaagh – she was wearing an ancient, faded old Nike tee-shirt of Stuart's with a stripy pair of men's pyjama trousers, worn and comfortable. On top of this she had on an old sweater of Dad's, which nearly reached to her knees. She had no appetite and so had lost weight, and her hair hung down her back, limp and unwashed.

'Amy? I know you're in dere.'

So it was Niamh. Amy opened the door reluctantly. She'd been dimly aware that it was quite sunny outside, and Niamh was wearing a black sundress splashed with poppies.

'Can I come in?'

Amy said nothing, but stepped back to let Niamh into the hall. 'Would you like a coffee?'

'Sure,' said Niamh.

Amy brought the coffee in two National Trust mugs into her bedroom. She sat on her bed and Niamh on a tatty old easy chair which had been in the hotel before Jen's refurb and had not survived the cull.

'I just thought I'd see how you were,' she said. 'In a bad way, by the look of it.'

'I suppose you're going to say that Lewis was a big mistake and I'm better off without him?'

'Not necessarily. Why not say it was amazing but it's over now?'

It was true. No one else had a good word to say about Lewis anymore – but he had often been kind and thoughtful, they had had many wonderful times, been completely in tune. They'd cooked together, walked together, written music together, their talk had been intimate and bubbling with recognition, their silence had been comfortable, they'd loved each other's company, felt bereft when they were apart. He'd massage her stomach every month when she had cramps. He'd smooth back her hair, cup her head, kiss her so softly. It hadn't all been about sex. Again she thought about the afternoon she'd lost her virginity to him. He'd been so patient and gentle – it had been beautiful.

'I can't help it, Niamh,' she said, holding out her hands. 'I love him.'

'I know.' Niamh reached out and touched her knee. 'But it was a grand passion – it was never going to last. He wasn't exactly a keeper. In a way, it's good that this has happened.'

'In what way is it good?'

'Because you had to get him out of your system, and now you can move on.'

Right now, Amy thought that the chances of her getting over Lewis and moving on were about the same as her chances of being served a single fish supper by John Lennon down at the chippy on the prome-nade. 'Why did he do it, Niamh?'

Niamh shrugged. 'Because he could, I guess. Every girl should have that *Last Tango in Paris* experience at least once.'

'And did you?' Amy asked, suddenly frightened of the answer.

'Did I have Lewis? Of course not.'

'How come you know so much about it, anyway?' Amy asked, pulling the sleeves of her sweater down over her hands.

'Because it was the same with me and Diarmid.'

'Your ex-husband?'

'Yeah. I just never should have married him. Not that I listened to anyone who told me so at the time. We thought we were outlaws, the two of us and then everyone else.'

Amy was silent, mulling this over.

'And, Ames – sort it out with Brooke. She's in bits about this. Talk to her before she goes back to university.' She paused. 'It must be hard to stay on the straight and narrow when you look like she does.'

'You think I should feel sorry for her because she's beautiful?'

'Now, I didn't say that.'

Niamh stayed for a while and they drank coffee and talked. Perhaps something shifted slightly within Amy, and there was one less chip of ice in her heart.

Chapter 19

The Course of True Love

'Happy birthday, Jen.' Amy put down a tray, which contained a scaled-down version of her trademark wedding breakfast: scrambled egg and smoked salmon piled on heart shaped pieces of toast, a basket full of warm pastries, fresh orange juice laced with champagne and a fragrant cafetiere. She'd been so pre-occupied lately that she'd completely forgotten about Jen's birthday until late last night and had had to improvise. This was the first part of her present. The second, dark chocolate truffles flavoured with Irish cream and dusted with cocoa, was cooling in the fridge.

It was now September, and the north of Scotland was enjoying an Indian summer. Jen and Patrick were sitting in a sunny corner of the dining room. They both looked sleepy, glowing and happy. Jen didn't approve of PDAs but she was holding hands with him. No prizes for guessing what the first part of Patrick's gift had been.

'This looks fab,' Jen said. 'Sit down with us for a bit.'

Since the guests had all eaten earlier, Amy pulled up a chair and poured herself a cup of coffee. Jen looked lovely, prettier than before, softer, radiant. Being in love with Patrick and having that love returned had given her a new contentment and security. Unusually, she was wearing a floaty dress in that season's colours of lilac, dusty pink and amber.

'Doing anything nice tonight?' Amy asked, biting into a pain au chocolat.

'*We* are going out for dinner. The whole family.'

'I'm meant to be working.' After her long incarceration in the hotel, Amy was still reluctant to go out.

'Not any more. Marcel's going to cover your shift. It's my birthday, so you have to do absolutely everything I say.'

'No change there, then,' Amy and Patrick said in unison, then laughed.

'Where are we going?' Amy asked in resignation.

'Carlyle Hall.'

'You're mad. You'll have to take out a mortgage.'

'We're worth it,' Jen said.

Amy suspected that Jen had chosen to visit the rival hotel partly as a fact finding mission, to find out what the enemy was thinking.

'You're not going looking like that, though.'

Amy wasn't at her best – besides her weight loss, she'd bitten her nails right down, she'd given up wearing make-up, and was badly in need of having her hair cut, her eyebrows plucked and her legs waxed. There hadn't seemed any point. 'Say what you think, Jenny. Don't hold back.'

Jen's face softened. 'You're beautiful, Amy. You've just let yourself go. You need a bit of TLC. So I've booked you into the salon. Greg's expecting you at two.'

At two o'clock sharp, Amy pushed open the door of the hairdresser's. Since it had been taken over a couple of years back, it was completely transformed. Everything was black, white and silver, with a chequered black and white floor and mirrors in geometric shapes. A vase of scarlet poppies provided the single splash of colour. On a low table stood a coffee machine, six slim silver mugs, and a pile of thick, glossy magazines.

'Hello, stranger,' trilled Gregor. 'Be with you in a minute.'

Amy grabbed that week's issue of *Grazia* magazine and sunk down on the black leather sofa, breathing in the smell of ammonia, hairspray and nail polish. The salon was the most relaxing place on earth. She began reading an article on 50 Dresses for Under £50, with half an ear to Gregor's chatter as he finished blow drying the postmistress, who'd had a chic crop.

'My husband and I absolutely adore the Cotswolds,' he was saying. Amy stifled a giggle. He sounded just like the queen.

'Oh, that's lovely, Gregor,' the postmistress said, as he moved a mirror from side to side to show her her new cut from all angles.

'Very sophisticated,' Gregor said, as she paid. 'Thank you,' he added, as she dropped several pound coins into the tips jar. 'Does absolutely nothing for her,' he went on, when the door had barely closed behind his client. 'She just hasn't got the cheekbones to carry it off. I did try to hint, you know, subtly.'

'You're about as subtle as a wrecking ball,' Amy said, managing a smile. She did feel a little better, probably due to the passage of time, the support of her family and friends, Gregor's antics and the glorious weather. Catching sight of her unkempt reflection in the nearest mirror, she felt a small spark of excitement at the thought of an afternoon's pampering.

Much later, having had her legs waxed (which was so painful it almost made her forget about her broken heart), her eyebrows threaded into elegant arches, her eyelashes dyed and permed and shiny new nails fitted, she sat in front of one of the mirrors, relaxing as Gregor massaged her head, neck and shoulders. His face, reflected above hers, was, for once, serious. 'You know he's gone, don't you?'

Amy started. 'Gone where?'

Strangely, after a moment of utter panic, she felt a kind of cautious relief: she'd never again have to fear bumping into Lewis in the street, the village shop or the pub, wouldn't have to hear gossip about his love life, or see him with Evie Martin, or another young and gorgeous girl. She wouldn't be able to surrender to her feelings and ask him to come back, however much she wanted to. She would never again tremble before him, longing for his touch.

'London is what I hear.'

'Don't tell me. Maree Burns was in here, having her colour done.'

'Yup. Rich mahogany. Personally, I think at her age she should go lighter, but –'

'Gregor!' Mostly, Gregor's inane babble cheered her up, but occasionally she felt like stabbing him.

Gregor's fingers pressed hard into her upper back. 'My, you're tense.'

'He never even came to say goodbye,' Amy said, suddenly overcome by a terrible sadness.

'He did, but Jenny sent him away.'

'SHE DID WHAT?' Amy shouted, startling Sascha so much that she nearly chopped off her current client's ear.

'Sorry, Annalie.'

'She is so dead, the interfering wee –'

'She did it for the best,' Gregor said, his expression still solemn. 'She thought he would upset you all over again. Or you'd beg him to come back –'

'As if.'

'I believe you,' Gregor said. He clearly didn't. 'Lewis Burns is pretty irresistible, even if he does know it.'

'Amen to that,' put in Sascha.

'Smile, Amy,' Gregor said. 'We've all got your back.'

'I hate being in love,' Amy said, with feeling. 'It makes you sad, vulnerable and mad.'

'It doesn't have to be that way,' Gregor said, his expression in the mirror still serious. 'Whoever said that the course of true love never runs smooth –'

'Who but Shakespeare?' boomed Annalie, the English divorcée. 'Lysander, in *Midsummer Night's Dream*.'

'Well, he's got a lot to answer for. Because it doesn't have to be like that. It can be happy, settled, secure and equal. Your lover should be your best friend –'

Amy raised one perfectly threaded eyebrow. 'And that's how it is for you and Robbie, is it?'

'Yes,' said Gregor, softly, and no one could doubt the truth of his words.

Everyone was in lurrrve at the moment. Even Annalie was still dating Robert Kingsley – only a couple of days ago they'd come to the hotel for afternoon tea and held hands throughout.

'What about Evie?' Amy managed to say.

'She's gone, too.'

'With Lewis?' She felt cold, sick panic rise again.

'No. Honey, you've been out of circulation too long.' Despite himself, Gregor perked up at being able to pass on some gossip. 'There was a scene in the post office. Jared Martin called her a Jezebel –'

'Painted Jezebel,' corrected Annalie.

'… painted Jezebel, and he and Martha have thrown her out.'

'Where did she go?'

'Well, she was moving to Edinburgh to start college anyway, so she's staying with some cousin or other in Marchmont until she can move into her hall of residence. Apparently, he's the black sheep of the family and hasn't spoken to any of them in years.'

Strangely, most of Amy's anger towards Evie had evaporated. She'd been totally captivated by Lewis herself when she was seventeen, and had carried a torch – make that a bonfire – ever since, so how could she blame the teenager for being unable to resist him also? But she obviously didn't mean anything to him. Evie was going to be much better off away from her narrow minded, judgemental parents. In a few weeks' time, she'd have half the boys on her modern musicianship course eating out of her hand.

Donning a pair of fine rubber gloves, Gregor began to apply a red rinse to her hair. Maybe Jen had been right, Amy admitted to herself. When had she ever been able to resist Lewis? Perhaps her sister had saved her from throwing away what little self respect she had left. She opened the latest Paige Turner book as the colour developed, a hilarious, rollicking piece of chick-lit set in a TV studio, a whirlwind of sex, shopping, powerful women and cruelly ambitious men.

Finally, Gregor trimmed and straightened her hair, so that it hung in a gleaming, chestnut sheet down her back, and the beautician applied light, subtle make-up which gave her a golden glow.

*

Patrick wolf whistled as she walked into the foyer later in the evening, in an emerald green silk dress and gold shoes and wrap. 'You look amazing. Just like the old Amy we knew and loved.'

'Thanks,' Amy said. Her ego could be doing with a bit of a boost. 'You, too.'

Patrick was wearing a crisp white shirt and a black suit, simple and classic, the perfect foil for his dark curls and green eyes.

'Is that us?' Jen tapped across the marble floor in her high heels, trailing a discreet, very expensive perfume. She had on one of her trademark Holly Golightly sleeveless black dresses, with a string of large pearls at her neck and her hair piled up on top of her head. Her lipstick and nails were scarlet. She exuded glamour and sophistication.

Amy sat silently in the back seat of Patrick's car, listening to his and

Jen's lively conversation during the short, smooth journey to Carlyle Hall. Their parents and Brooke were travelling separately.

The foyer at Carlyle Hall, painted in Wedgewood blue, was bigger and grander than at Ardnashell Lodge, with a wide, sweeping staircase. An obsequiously smiling waiter escorted them to their table.

'What's he doing here?' hissed Amy, catching sight of Callum sitting next to Brooke at their table by the French windows.

'I invited him,' Jen said.

'Happy birthday, Jen.'

'Thanks, Cal.' Jen smiled serenely. The waiter pulled out their chairs and they sat down as gracefully as possible.

Mum and Dad were holding hands. Some good had come of Dad's accident – it had made them all value him and their family life much more. You were really in trouble, Amy reflected, picking up her leather-bound menu, when your parents were more loved up than you were.

As she ate her avocado and prawn starter, they caught up on family news. It was unusual for them all to sit down together over a leisurely meal because of the long and unsocial hours they worked. Brooke was in high spirits because James had collected the keys for the Hillhead Street flat that morning. Dad was going to drive her back to Glasgow in the week so that she could move in and get settled before the new term at university started.

Jen had some amazing presents: a shell pink cashmere sweater from Mum and Dad; a butter soft leather clutch bag from Niamh, a cornflower blue wrap, which exactly matched her eyes, from Misty and Duncan, a grey silk shirt from Gregor and Robbie and a purple laptop case from Callum. Patrick's gift was a silver charm bracelet, which fitted perfectly round the most slender part of her wrist. A silver shamrock and a "J" studded with tiny sapphires dangled from it. Brooke was skint as usual, but had managed to contribute a silver heart charm which Jen immediately fixed on. Next, she unwrapped, from a mass of tissue paper in various shades of pink, gold lamé baby doll pyjamas, which looked wildly expensive.

'Who're they from?' Brooke asked.

Jen giggled, a little high from the champagne they'd consumed.

'Tiara, of course.'

A pink card fluttered onto the table. *They're for Paddy, too!! LOL, Ti XXX* it read, in loopy, purple writing, the "i" dotted with a heart. Finally, Jen unwrapped a small package with a Glasgow postmark. 'From Nell,' she said, pulling out a gold pendant, half of a heart shape on a chain. It was the most vulgar thing Amy had ever seen. Presumably, Chanel had the other half. Smiling, Jen fastened it round her neck, to hang below her pearls.

'A good haul,' Amy said. The waiting staff had silently melted away during the unwrapping, but now suddenly reappeared to serve the second course. Amy ate slowly. She'd chosen a mushroom stroganoff, and was trying to distinguish each of the spicy, creamy flavours.

Brooke's phone pinged with a text message. She beamed as she read it. 'Emily's invited me to go and hear her rock choir next weekend,' she said, her cheeks colouring slightly. She looked as pleased as if she'd been personally invited to a film première by Chris Hemsworth himself.

By now, the table had become quite riotous. Dad had begun talking about some of the more bizarre and infamous guests who had ever stayed at the hotel, then Callum recounted some of his veterinary adventures. Amy had forgotten how entertaining he could be.

After a while, Brooke got up to go to the Ladies'. Amy followed her. One of the waiters accompanied them, holding open the door to admit them with a shallow bow. Inside, all was black, white and gold, with huge, ornate mirrors on every wall. Maybe a shade ostentatious, Amy thought, critically, right down to the black loo roll. She sank down on a soft white leather sofa. There were bottles of expensive perfume ranged along a marble counter behind the sinks, and velvety soft individual gold hand towels, folded into the shape of shells.

Brooke came out of her cubicle and slowly washed her hands in the gold sparkly soap. She re-applied her lipstick, ran a comb through her mass of hair and sprayed perfume on her pulse points. Amy stood up. 'Brooke, I'm sorry about everything. Freezing you out, refusing to talk to you. I mean, how often does a girl get to have a sister who's also one of her best friends?'

'Not often,' Brooke admitted. Her eyes were full of tears. 'Come here,' she added, her arms outstretched. They held each other tightly.

Amy's cheek was damp with her sister's tears, her body frail in her arms. 'Do you think I betrayed you?' Brooke asked.

'Not really,' Amy said. 'I just couldn't get my head round you being intimate with him, too.'

'I'm sorry.'

'Lewis just isn't worth it,' she said at last, disengaging herself.

'No,' Brooke agreed.

'I'll miss you when you go back to Glasgow,' Amy said.

'I'll miss you, too. But you can come and stay with us on a non-Emily weekend.'

'I will. I'll cook your dinner as a peace offering.' This was a thought. Brooke was a terrible cook, who struggled to make even scrambled egg on toast without burning it. 'What will you eat?'

Brooke grinned. 'Two words: Marks and Spencer,' she said. 'And there's a wicked vegetarian café opened just near our flat.'

Amy felt another stab of pain at that "our flat". Both her younger sisters were happily coupled off. 'At least you shouldn't get rickets again,' she said, to cover it. 'I know you're going to be very happy,' she added, managing a smile.

'Thank you,' Brooke said. Her face was beautiful and serene. 'I think so.'

Amy slipped her arm round her sister as they went back into the restaurant.

By the time they were on the coffee and brandy, Amy found herself sitting alone with Callum. Everyone else had melted away. The sun was setting outside and Mum and Dad had gone for a last walk round the garden, Brooke had slipped out to the terrace to smoke, and Patrick and Jen were networking: they'd spotted their partners in the wedding business across the room and gone over to talk to them. They were both dressed like scarecrows – only the very posh could get away with looking so unkempt.

She people-watched for a while, ignoring him. Sitting at a nearby table was a Shakespearian actor, eating oysters with his famous actress wife. No other diner acknowledged the couple – that would be extremely bad form in such an establishment as this.

'Amy?'

'*What*?'

'I'm sorry about Lewis.'

'Are you?'

'No.'

Amy folded her arms and gazed grimly into the middle distance.

'I'm sorry we fell out over him, though.'

'So am I,' Amy admitted, just as Brooke drifted back over to the table.

A few nights later, a severe shortage of wine forced Amy to leave her sanctuary once more. On principle, she refused to spend more than £5 on a bottle, so the contents of the hotel's cellar were out of the question. It was a warm night and the evening sun had brought out many of the villagers. Several people were sitting at the tables outside the Claymore Inn, enjoying the last pale rays. A couple of teenagers were making out in the bus shelter. She turned her head away so that she didn't have to look at them anymore.

She really didn't know what Lewis was doing those days – she'd been strong and deleted his number from her Smartphone, and also blocked his messages, but she'd been unable to resist looking in his social media accounts. He hadn't really used them much, so there was nothing there to give any clues – just a couple of tweets about live performances from bands he liked and a link to a scene from one of their favourite films. She'd also, in an evening of masochism, played the videos he'd put up on YouTube, looking at his long, elegant fingers on the guitar strings and sobbing as she remembered them unbuttoning her dress, twining through hers, pushing back her hair, caressing her body. She'd had to stop watching – it was torture.

Taking a deep breath, she pushed open the door of the village shop, hoping it wouldn't be too busy: she looked a mess – her hair was scraped back, she had on not a scrap of make-up and she hadn't bothered changing out of her pyjama top, which was pink with a hippo on the front. She'd just pulled on trackie bottoms and trainers and thrown on an ancient jacket over the top. But, in compliance with Murphy's law, there was a queue: two tourists who were buying bottles of Highland spring water – crazy, when you thought how much of it fell from the sky, free of charge. Standing behind them was a bunch of men, including Callum, who were stocking up on beer for the evening – there was a big football match on. Browsing the shelf of tinned puddings was old Miss Dunbar, who had a frozen meal-for-one, a packet of teabags and some cat foot in her basket. For a moment, Amy went cold, having a scary premonition that this would be her in fifty years' time.

The door opened again and a gaggle of teenagers swarmed in, probably to buy mixers for their vodka. Amy turned the corner, heading for the, frankly poor, selection of wines. Her heart sank. Mrs Crombie and her long-suffering sidekick, Muriel, were standing by the frozen food cabinet, deep in conversation. For a wild moment, she considered running away, but – too late – they'd seen her.

'Amy, my dear, how are you?' asked Muriel. 'We heard it was all over between you and the Burns boy.' She pulled a sad face. 'He was always trouble.'

Amy stood, frozen to the spot, terrified that she might burst into tears in the middle of the shop. Muriel tutted. 'Evangeline Martin's a little trollop,' she went on. Amy's mind was racing: did everyone know about Lewis and Evie? The older women's faces blurred. She leaned against the wall, afraid that she might faint.

'When you give yourself too easily, you don't get love in return,' Mrs Crombie said, only just stopping short of pointing her finger.

Callum abandoned his beers on the counter and walked slowly towards the group. 'Come on, Ames. I've got this.' His voice was quiet. He reached for her hand, and led her past the teenagers and out into the balmy evening. His hand on hers was strong, cool and dry and she felt instantly reassured. They walked over to the seawall and sat down. Nutmeg, who had been waiting patiently outside, trotted after them. Callum put his arm round her and she snuggled up to him, hiding her face in his chest. Whereas Lewis had favoured starving-in-a-garret chic, Callum was solid and broad in the shoulder, strong and comforting. Nutmeg shoved her wet nose into the palm of Amy's hand.

'You're shaking,' Callum said, after a few moments.

'I didn't realise everyone knew,' Amy muttered. 'Cal, I think I'd like to go home.'

'Sure.' Callum stood up and helped her to her feet. They walked back to the hotel, still holding hands. She felt his strength, as if it had transmitted into her.

'Thanks, Cal,' she said, as they reached the gates.

'Any time,' said Callum, with a smile. He tucked a lock of hair behind her ear. 'Will you be all right?'

Amy nodded.

'Listen – we've all missed you. We're hoping to have a bit of a party on Jamie's Cove for my bro's birthday on Friday. Are you up for it? No pressure.'

''Kay,' Amy whispered. Since Jamie's Cove was their own private beach, there would be no one there but her friends.

'Good girl.' Callum touched her cheek, then was gone.

Back in the flat, she returned to the haven of her bedroom, put on some music and sat on the bed, pulling the duvet up to her chin. Yet again, she tried to delete from her memory all the times she'd shared this bed with Lewis. But it was impossible to delete a memory – she could still see him lying there, his dark hair spread out on the pillow, see his face break into a smile when he awoke in the morning and realised he was here, with her.

In the end, Amy was very glad that she'd accepted the invitation to Euan's birthday party. She'd decided that her gift would be a sumptuous picnic, and preparing the sandwiches, roasted vegetable and avocado, apple and cheddar, brie and grape, her homemade hummus to be eaten with crusty bread and shiny black olives, had given her something to do. Instead of a cake, she'd made chocolate brownies. All this was packed and stowed in a rowing boat, and, again, she found herself noticing Cal's strong, tanned arms, the way his back rippled as he manipulated the oars. It was warm, but without the heavy heat of the day, and the waves washed onto the shore, turquoise now in the mellow evening light. They all sat on travelling rugs and ate the food, washed down with beer which they'd kept cool by putting it in a rock pool. They'd watched the sun setting – a big orange ball sliding down the darkening sky, then Duncan had built a fire, and they'd sat around the crackling glow, chatting quietly, their faces dappled by the flames, the soundtrack Euan's Spotify playlist. She'd felt quite teary, then, since, by this time usually Lewis would be playing an acoustic set on his ever-present Hummingbird, while they all shouted out requests, hers always including *Me Without You* and Ryan Adams' beautiful *Amy*.

'All right, Ames?' Callum had come to sit beside her. Quickly, she wiped her eyes with the back of her hand.

'Yeah - just having a moment.'

Cal nodded, gently rubbed her back, and didn't leave her side for the rest of the evening, and, despite her tears, she had enjoyed herself, feeling stronger for the support of her friends.

Her next night off was even better, probably because the decision to meet up had been spur-of-the-moment, and they'd all sat on the seawall, looking out across the water to the horizon, their quiet conversation in counterpoint to the whisper of the waves, before piling into the pub in time for last orders.

She and Callum started going out hill walking again, or striding for miles along the beach or the headland. One night, they decided to scramble down steep rocks to explore a narrow stretch of beach. She'd used to love doing this, but she seemed to have lost confidence. Halfway down, she wished she hadn't started, but she had gone too far to go back, so she carried on gingerly, grabbing onto plants and shrubs. Suddenly she slipped. She grabbed frantically for something to hold onto, but it was too late – she was falling. The next moment, she was in Callum's arms. 'It's okay, I've got you,' he murmured. She held onto him, shaking, and then they were kissing. For a moment, she luxuriated in the feel of his mouth on hers. Then he opened her lips with his tongue. Her mind raced and she remembered what Brooke had said about his hidden passion. But then she pushed him away, confused. 'What are you doing?'

'I love you, Amy. I have done for a long time. I'm not just messing about. I wouldn't –'

'Cal, I can't do this. You're my *mate*. I don't know –'

'You need time. I get that.'

Amy turned and began to drag herself back up the rocks, again grabbing onto any plant that would hold her weight, searching for footholds. Somehow, she made it back up to the coast road, Callum a couple of feet behind her, then he walked her back to the hotel. They didn't speak.

★

Amy couldn't sleep. She wandered about in a dream. She made chick-pea curry but forgot to add the chick-peas. She worked an entire shift in odd shoes. She spent a whole day with only one eye made up. She wandered along the beach alone in the moonlight, her thoughts tumbling around her head relentlessly. Callum loved her. She knew that, clear and honest, he wouldn't have said so if he didn't mean it. She couldn't help feeling a spark of joy at this declaration. But how did she feel about him? Was she just flattered, needing the boost to her bruised ego and the salve to her broken heart? Of course she loved him – as one of her oldest, closest friends. They got on amazingly, laughed at the same jokes, had shared so much, had a childhood empathy. She loved his intelligence, his kindness, his strength, the way he totally knew and accepted her, the way he always treated her with respect. Then she thought about his warm dark eyes, his strong, tanned arms, his ripped abs, his passionate, searching kiss, how miserable she'd been when they'd fallen out, how she was missing him terribly even just after a few days. But could she be *in* love with him?

★

She felt her heart leap when her phone rang, accompanied by his face on the caller display. Why was she so tense when it was just her mate, who'd phoned her hundreds of times?

'Do you want to go out for dinner?' he asked. 'With me,' he added, sounding subdued – a far cry from his usual relaxed confidence.

'Are you asking me out?'

'I guess.'

'Okay. It's a date.' She tried to lighten the mood. 'So long as it's not at Ardnashell Lodge, and I'm not cooking.'

She couldn't decide what to wear, her entire wardrobe spread out over the bed. Callum had seen her in everything from a fairy costume to a ball gown. Should she just put on her jeans as she normally would for an evening with him, or should she dress up a bit as for a first date? In the end, she put on her current favourite dress, in mint green lace, which showed off her tan, light make-up and masses of perfume. She left her newly washed hair loose.

'You look beautiful,' said Callum, as she got into his car and settled in her seat.

'Thank you.' They were both unusually shy, and she was glad that she wasn't sitting opposite him – it would be easier to talk if she didn't have to make eye contact. This was totally weird, to feel this nervous with someone who was as familiar to her, as much part of her life, as her sisters. In fact, they didn't talk much, instead listening to his driving playlist and looking out at the scenery – the rust and green patchwork of fields, the bright yellow of rapeseed, a tranquil lochan, reflecting back the sky in deep blue. She opened the window, letting the breeze ruffle her hair. After half an hour or so, they reached Glenstruan. He drove past The Creel, the award-winning seafood restaurant, and, instead, parked in a narrow mews lined with houses in ice cream colours, and led her to Root 66, a vegetarian café.

'This is lovely,' she said, once they were seated at a window table.

Cal smiled. 'Glad you like it.'

As grand and luxurious as The Creel was, this was much more "them" – done out in yellow and blue, with soft, salt-scented cushions, bright crockery and pictures of Mediterranean scenes, worn wooden tables and scuffed floorboards. There was a jam jar of wild flowers on each table – blue meadow cranesbill, red wild poppies and yellow buttercups. The vibe was chilled, the music laid-back and jazzy, and, as she ate a delicious vegetable lasagne with spinach sauce, she relaxed. She might be on her first date with a darkly attractive man, but it was only Cal, her old friend, and they'd shared many meals, from school dinners right up to their recent night out at Carlyle Hall. By the time they were on the sticky toffee pudding, their conversation was as easy as it always had been, full of memories, laughter and recognition.

'This is scrumptious,' she remarked, scraping up the last spoonful. 'Wonder if they'd give me the recipe.'

'D'you remember the puddings at school?' Callum asked.

'Mmm. Pure stodge. They were the only thing that made it bearable.'

Back in the car, they sang along with the driving playlist, belting out *This is the Life, Dani California* and *Have a Nice Day*. But her heart began to beat faster as he drove through the hotel's gates, and parked just outside the door. It was getting dark, now, and his face was in shadow as he turned towards her. 'Night, Ames. Thanks for a lovely evening.' He seemed stiff and formal again.

'No, thank *you*,' Amy said. 'But I think you may have forgotten something.' She leaned across the seat and put her arms round him, kissing him gently – his top lip, then his bottom lip, but then ever more deeply.

'What do you think, Ames?' he asked, when they finally broke apart. 'Do you want to give it a try?'

'Yes,' Amy whispered, leaning in to kiss his cheek. 'I think I do.'

★

'When did you realise you'd fallen in love with me?' Amy asked, placing a bowl of homemade popcorn on the coffee table, and joining Callum on the sofa. A couple of weeks had passed and they were having a movie night, just the two of them. He would know – there was never anything about him that was vague. Everything was clear-cut.

'The Laird's ball,' he said, at once. The Laird's Hogmanay Ball was the social event of the year. Everyone in the village was invited and it went on all through the night until breakfast was served. It was always such a wonderful evening, the castle looking like something out of a fairy tale and all the villagers in tearing high spirits. Last year, Amy's party had comprised Duncan and Misty, Callum and Sheena and Brooke and James. She and Stuart had travelled up from Edinburgh for the occasion. Brooke hadn't long been seeing James at the time and they'd spent the evening gazing into each other's eyes as if frozen before sloping off to one of the many bedrooms upstairs – Amy assumed – as they'd returned much later flushed, tousled and radiant. Misty and Duncan had also been loved up and were engrossed in each other. Guiltily, Amy remembered that she and Callum had spent most of the evening chatting, laughing, catching up, pretty much leaving their partners to fend for themselves. Stuart and Sheena, however, had seemed to get on well, accomplished at social small talk. 'You'd just come off the dance floor and you looked beautiful. All glowing and sparkly – and I just knew.'

Amy smiled so hard there was a danger her face would split. She'd felt beautiful that night – Gregor had done her hair, setting it into soft waves which he'd studded with ruby red brilliants. She'd been wearing a dress in an eye-grabbing scarlet and Jen had lent her her killer red heels. She'd been Amy deluxe.

'You did, too,' she said.

'Thank you.'

'Why didn't you say anything?'

'I was with my girlfriend. You were with Stuart. Anyway, I was con-fused – we'd been best friends forever. I didn't want to risk that, but I've been trying to get up the courage to tell you ever since you moved back to the village, which is why I lost it about you and Lewis that night –'

Callum held her hands even more tightly. 'You are definitely over him, aren't you? You're not on the rebound?'

'You know I'm not. I think you've always been The One - it just took me a long time to realise it. I'm over him. I just had to get him out of my system.'

'Like a virus?' Callum asked hopefully.

Amy giggled.

'Sheena knew, too,' Callum said. 'That was one of the reasons we split up.'

'I thought it was because she'd taken that job in Glasgow.'

'Yeah, that's what we told everyone.'

'I love you,' Amy said, the words tumbling from her lips as naturally as the flow of a mountain stream.

Amy awoke to the sound of waves crashing against the seawall. She sat up in bed and stretched, enjoying the particular pleasure of being snug and warm while the weather raged outside. The door opened and Nutmeg padded in, jumped on the bed and curled up at the foot. Callum had trained her to do this so that she could double as a hot water bottle. He was just behind the dog, stark naked, carrying a tray, which he carefully deposited on the bedside table. He climbed back into bed beside her and handed her a mug of coffee and a piece of toast. This was another great pleasure: breakfast in bed which she hadn't had to make. They munched the toast in easy silence.

'Definitely a day for staying in bed,' she murmured.

'Definitely.'

It had been a huge leap from best friends to lovers, and Callum had waited until she felt ready. But she shouldn't have worried: he was the same in bed as he was in life – accomplished, confident, considerate, caring more about her pleasure than his own. Another man might have been intimidated by the intense physical connection, the chemistry, she'd shared with Lewis, but not Callum – he was too comfortable in himself and their mutual love. They began kissing and then slid under the duvet, their mouths still glued together.

Chapter 20
Unbreakable Bond

THREE MONTHS LATER

'Gorgeous,' said Callum, as Amy walked into the foyer, wearing the red dress she'd had on the night he'd fallen in love with her.

'Thank you, Mishter Bond,' said Amy. He looked extremely handsome in a dinner suit and black bow tie.

Just then, Brooke came slowly down the stairs, holding up the skirt of her long dress. She was ravishing in floor-length teal satin, nipped in to show off her tiny waist. Her hair, coloured a rich auburn, gleamed softly in the light of the chandelier which sparkled off her earrings. Amy knew she was totally over-shadowed, but it didn't matter. She still felt beautiful – completely confident, totally secure in her relationship – there was no fear that Callum harboured a secret desire for her pretty younger sister.

Amy now spent all her spare time with Callum, out on long walks with him and Nutmeg, sitting in their favourite alcove in the Claymore, or at his flat above the chandler's, watching Netflix, doing crosswords, having Scrabble tournaments with Misty and Duncan, lingering over breakfast and the Sunday papers. His kitchen now contained food – pasta and rice and oils and spices and sundried tomatoes and pots of herbs on the window sill. She often cooked for him and whenever she was in the kitchen it was debatable who had the more pleading brown eyes – him or Nutmeg. With Callum, she felt comfortable, relaxed and at peace, but looked forward to their future with excitement also. She'd never felt so free. Because she'd known him all her life, there were absolutely no skeletons in his cupboard. They hadn't yet discussed getting married, but she knew it would happen sometime soon. He also wanted children as much as she did. As the icing on the cake, Sheena had phoned a few days earlier, bubbling over with excitement, and talked at length about her new – doctor – boyfriend. Although he'd never said as much, Amy sensed that Callum had felt guilty about their break-up.

Behind Brooke was Emily. For once, she was wearing a colour: dusty pink, the perfect contrast to Brooke's dress.

'Wow, don't you look lovely?' Amy cried, in surprise. Emily had ditched the Wednesday Addams look this evening, her make-up light and natural, her various pieces of facial metalwork forsaken for once. She could easily pass for eighteen.

'Yeah, she's all grown up,' Brooke said proudly. She slipped her arm round the teenager's shoulders and kissed her on the cheek.

'Yuck. Get off,' Emily said, wriggling free. She rolled her eyes. '*Sooo* embarrassing.'

Jen tapped across the foyer, then, looking very smart in a long midnight-blue dress with a Flower of Scotland tartan sash. She and Patrick couldn't come to the Laird's New Year ball, as the hotel was hosting a traditionally Scottish Hogmanay party. They'd been planning it for months, having booked the Drystane Dykes, a groovy all-female counterpart of the Red Hot Chilli Pipers, folk band Accordion to Angus, a country dancing troupe, a young Highland dancing champion, and Matt Carver, a Glaswegian comedian with a sense of humour drier than sandpaper and blacker than a rock star's bank balance. A feast of Scottish fayre had been prepared, and Amy had baked black bun and rich, buttery shortbread which melted in the mouth. There was also a fine selection of aged malt whiskies. The hotel was fully booked. Jen didn't mind missing the Laird's ball this year; she was in her element directing and overseeing preparations, anticipating a huge profit.

There was the sound of slamming car doors outside – some more guests arriving.

'Haw, it's pure Baltic out there,' said a shrill voice from the doorway. 'I'm bursting. See if I don't get to pee soon, yous are gaunnae need a mop.'

'Hi, Tiara,' Jen said drily.

Holding hands with her husband, Tiara made her way across the foyer. She looked amazing, like something out of Doctor Zhivago, in a long white fake fur coat and matching hat teamed with high white boots. A few snowflakes nestled in her golden hair. 'Aura, hen,' she called. 'Could you bring in wur bags?'

Walking behind the couple were Chanel and, presumably, her boyfriend, also hand in hand. 'This place is the nuts, Nell,' Pascal said, gazing around him in wonderment.

'I know,' beamed Chanel, as if she were personally responsible. 'We're so going to have a top night. It's a shame Armani couldnae make it, but.'

Unlike the divine Jaden McGaughey, Pascal was by no means good looking, but he had a lovely, warm, goofy smile and it was obvious that, in Chanel's eyes at least, he was Richard Madden.

Bringing up the rear in a Primark leopard print coat and pushing the Rolls Royce of all prams, was Jaden's young sister Demi, now back to her ultra-petite figure. Her beautiful, coffee coloured baby lay in a deep sleep against a candy striped pillow. 'Cal,' she screeched suddenly. Racing out from behind the pram, she hurtled across the room, tripping in her six inch heels and catapulting into Callum's arms.

'Fell for you that time, didn't I no'?'

'Me and Jaden's took the honeymoon suite 'cause we're still on wur honeymoon, sure we are, babes?' Tiara was saying.

''Course we are, sweetheart.' Jaden put his arm round her and hugged her to his side. She nestled into his black wool coat.

'My mum and dad couldn't come,' she went on. 'They've went to Benidorm with my Auntie Bella and Uncle Tam for Christmas.'

'Oh, that's a shame,' said Jen, with a very convincing show of sincerity. Two McCrackens were quite enough to deal with.

When Amy's party was finally assembled, the friends headed out into the cold night. A few snowflakes swirled around as they made their way across the hard, glittery ground towards their cars. Callum was driving Amy, Misty and Duncan and, in tearing high spirits, they sang along with the radio all the way. James, looking like Antonio Banderas at an awards ceremony, was just behind them with Brooke and Emily. As always, Amy caught her breath as they approached the castle. The trees in the garden were all draped with coloured lights and it looked beautiful and magical.

Inside, they made their way down the black and white tiled hall, passing the suits of armour that dated back to the Battle of Bannockburn.

The ballroom was large and with a beautifully restored natural wood floor and wood panelling. A large fire burned in the grate and the air was heavy with the scent of applewood, myriad perfumes and mulled wine. At one end of the room, a wide staircase swept up to the first floor balcony and a massive stained glass window. The ceiling rose up and up, like that of an ancient church. A Christmas tree reached as high up as the balconies, which were swathed with holly, ivy and white fairy lights. Bunches of mistletoe hung from every chandelier.

An energetic eightsome reel was in progress, then the bagpipes screeched to a halt and they were swept into the Dashing White Sergeant by Gregor and Robbie, both brilliant dancers. Niamh, back for the party, had, for once, dropped her über-cool pose and was helpless with laughter as she tripped over her own feet. Even Emily, leaping around between Brooke and James, had unbent, her eyes sparkling, giggling uncontrollably. Robert Kingsley danced expertly by with Annalie clasped to his manly chest.

Across the floor, Amy spotted Maree, Lewis' mum, pretty in a coral coloured dress, her dark curls long and loose. She was dancing with Ian, a handsome widower – perhaps romance was in the air for the two of them. She was relieved that neither Lewis nor Evie Martin had come home for the festive season.

Lewis had sent her a brown padded envelope containing a CD of music they'd written together, including *Me Without You*, which she assumed was his way of apologising. She'd cried a little after hearing the poignant, familiar songs and his smoky, rich and husky voice filling the room, but it was a sweet sadness, a sense of closure, a letting go of the past. Maybe, right now, he was sitting in another messy room, hundreds of miles away, his fingers caressing his guitar strings, singing his songs to another mesmerised young girl with dewy skin and doe eyes and long shiny hair. Afterwards, he'd take her to bed – or, more likely, the sofa or the hearth rug, and make love to her as if he meant it. Perhaps he'd never find the fulfilment and happiness she now had.

She felt someone touch her arm and turned to see Maree standing there, looking a little sheepish. She'd never been able to see any trace of Maree in Lewis – he'd told her, in an intimate moment, that he looked like his father. 'Hello, Amy.'

'Hi, Maree. How are you?' This was so sad. Over the years she and Lewis had been together as teenagers, she'd come to see Maree as a second mother.

'Amy... I had to speak to you. I'm so, so angry with Lewis for... what he did. I've told him I'm ashamed of him. And I know he's ashamed of himself, too. And he's hurting at throwing away what he had with you. His dad leaving when he was so young was tough on him, but – '

'Thanks, Maree,' said Amy, so she didn't have to go on. Maree gave a brief smile, touched Amy's back, and disappeared into the crowd.

'I heard you'd split up with Lewis,' Emily said, later, as they ate their first course – a delicious seafood chowder, the fish all caught locally. Emily was pretty drunk by now – Amy had spotted her, with incredible sleight of hand, discreetly neck several glasses of wine.

'Mmm,' Amy said – nothing was secret in Kirklochy.

'Always knew he was well dodgy.'

'Sure you did, Em,' Brooke said, winking at Amy.

After the lovely meal, everyone sipped coffee, nibbled mints, mingled and chatted. Later, there would be more dancing, partying and carousing until breakfast was served.

★

Over at the hotel, Jen congratulated herself on a very successful evening, which would significantly reduce the hotel's overdraft. All the preparation had been exhausting, but then, she and Patrick thrived on hard work. She felt ready for anything. She'd only diverted from her five year plan in one respect – falling in love hadn't been on the agenda. But, then, Karren Brady had managed to combine a fabulously successful career with a happy marriage and motherhood, and if it was good enough for Karren, it was good enough for Jen.

It was a brilliant night. The Drystane Dykes had stormed their way through an exhilarating set, and Matt Carver had been so hilarious that a young man from Broughty Ferry had practically needed to be hospitalised. Brooke had recommended Matt after seeing him perform at the Queen Margaret Union, but Jen predicted that, in a couple of years' time, he'd be selling out the SECC.

It was definitely Tiara's evening. There was nothing like a blonde in red, Jen thought, and everyone else obviously agreed, as the women looked at her in envy and the men in desire.

'Nice dress, babes,' she'd said, patronisingly, to Chanel earlier. 'Is it coutour?'

'Yeah. Matt Allan,' Chanel had said, totally deadpan. Jen had stifled a giggle. She knew that Chanel had picked up her party dress for £6.99 on Matalan's sale rack.

'Don't think ah know him,' Tiara had answered, looking perplexed. 'Is he a Scottish designer?'

Now, she watched Chanel and Pascal come off the dance floor, his hand resting on the small of her back. Jen could feel his kindness, and sensed that this was the real deal. Chanel had found her Mr Right.

'We want to get married here,' she said, eyes shining, as she sought out Jen.

'Me, too,' Jen heard herself say, glancing over at Patrick, who was pouring champagne.

'Jenny! I thought you said marriage was... what was it? An archaic, patriarchal ritual.' 'It is,' Jen agreed. 'But I guess I could make an exception.'

*

Dong dong dong.

Callum pulled Amy into his arms for a passionate kiss – Brooke had been totally right about that. When they finally broke apart, she saw Brooke and James kissing on and on, as if they were alone in the room, while Emily pretended to retch behind them. But then Brooke stretched out an arm and pulled the teenager into a three-cornered embrace.

'Happy New Year, Cal,' Amy shouted, hugging him again.

She knew it would be.

THE END

Epilogue

Lewis Burns is living in a flatshare in Camden Town, just beside Chalk Farm tube station. He is still unsigned, despite having slept with A&R guru, Abi "Foxy" Fox.

Evie Martin is studying Modern Musicianship in Edinburgh. She is thoroughly enjoying the freedom of the city, partying 24/7, and is fronting an indie band. Two of her fellow students have so far sworn undying love. Her parents have disowned her.

Niamh Malahide's latest novel, *Stuck in Traffic*, has been short-listed for the Orange Prize. She is currently working on a TV script for a comedy drama set in the Highlands, which, it is expected, will be screened on Sunday evenings.

Bridie Walsh has joined a Scrabble group in her local café, and has taken up crochet and patchwork.

Glamour model Natalee has had a busy year. As well as celebrating her 30th birthday in a hip Ibiza club, she has: had her fifth boob job, starred in her own reality show, published part 3 of her auto-biography, launched her own line of lingerie and swimwear, divorced her third husband, been runner-up on *I'm a Celebrity,* fallen "literally head over heels in love" with a toy boy, and out-sold the entire Booker Prize list with her novel *Topaz.*

Emily Carlin has passed her National 5s with flying colours, but has found time to pen a new song, *Long to Die*. She has a new beau, a monosyllabic, sticky haired Emo called Taz.

Alan Govan's collection of gritty short stories has been published by Saltire Press, priced £9.99. This is available on Amazon and in all good bookshops.

Jason Gibson has gone south to Cornwall, the spiritual home of surfing dudes, in search of the perfect wave. He is currently selling ice cream on a beach in Newquay.

Euan Buchanan has been unmasked as Sarah Michelle Cox, Madame Zara and "Ask Annie" McAdam. He has yet to live this down.

Jaden McGaughey has transferred to Real Madrid, justifying his ludicrous transfer fee by scoring two goals in his first match. His total inability to speak any Spanish whatsoever has in no way affected his relationships with the local girls.

Tiara McGaughey is due to publish her auto-biography, *Up a Close and Personal* (ghosted by journalist Pearl White) in time to catch the Christmas market. It tells of her life with Jaden "the most talented and glamorous footballer since David Beckham" McGaughey. Her people are also in talks with the producers of *I'm a Celebrity*.

Lily McVey is working on a new novel so raunchy that it puts *Fifty Shades* in the shade. She and Ava Hunter have become firm friends, and have booked a holiday in Rome to visit the Trevi Fountain.

Chanel McCracken and Pascal Mulrooney have moved into their first home together, a council flat in Drumoyne. They are blissfully happy and intend to marry in Kirklochy, but Chanel doesn't want to consider starting a family until she has completed her accountancy degree, is established in her career and has achieved her ambition of a "boat hoose". She has opened an ISA to save up for the wedding.

Ciaran Walsh and Saoirse Lynch are living together on the Upper East Side in New York. Their careers have gone stratospheric. They plan to marry, but so far have been unable to find a window.

Dr Brooke Grant is totally engrossed in her new job as a lecturer in English Literature at Glasgow University. To her great relief, and everyone else's, she has given up waitressing.

Amy Grant and Callum Buchanan are deeply in love. Amy has found a security, peace and contentment that she never before believed possible.

Jennifer Grant and Patrick Walsh recently married in a secret ceremony in Ewensay Registry Office, with just the MacPherson-Forbeses, Gregor and Robbie, as witnesses. Jen has kept her name and they are both full of plans for further expansion, far too detailed and ambitious to mention here.

Glossary of West of Scotland Terms:

flitting	*moving house*
jakey	*an alcoholic vagrant*
ned	*a chav*
ginger	*a generic term for any fizzy drink e.g. Cola or Irn Bru*
The Barras	*a notorious Glasgow flea market*
polis	*the police*
bealin'	*very angry*
wean	*"wee one"; a young child*
scheme	*a council estate*
close	*the entrance and stairs to a tenement block of flats*
skooshy	*squirty (as in cream)*
hoor	*a prostitute*
Baltic	*extremely cold*
a boat hoose	*a house or flat purchased outright or on a mortgage*

Acknowledgements

I'd like to thank:

Tracy Patrick for her skilful editing, which really did make the best of this book.

Mairi Murphy for taking the time to read my book and make helpful suggestions.

The members of Johnstone Writers' Group for their advice and constructive criticism, not least the late, great Anne Green and Mary Strick, and Kathryn Metcalfe and The Nights at the Round Table for their encouragement and support.

My mum, Margaret and my brother, Duncan, for helping out with story ideas and funny lines.

Louise Farquhar Yates, hairdresser extraordinaire, for coming up with the name "Tiara".

My friends Lynn Holmes, Eileen McDonald and Sheila McLachlan for their unceasing support and inspiration.

John and Janet Stewart and everyone in Oakshaw Trinity who bought my previous book, and for their kind words and good wishes.

About the Author

Fiona Lindsay was born in Paisley. She studied English Literature at the University of Glasgow. She is an active member of Johnstone Writers' Group and the Romantic Novelists' Association. Do Not Disturb is the second novel in the Kirklochy Chronicles trilogy, following The Consolation Prize.